Jacqueline Wilson

Illustrated by Nick Sharratt

LOVE
frankie

DOUBLEDAY

DOUBLEDAY

UK | USA | Canada | Ireland | Australia
India | New Zealand | South Africa

Doubleday is part of the Penguin Random House group of companies
whose addresses can be found at global.penguinrandomhouse.com.

www.penguin.co.uk
www.puffin.co.uk
www.ladybird.co.uk

First published 2020

001

Text copyright © Jacqueline Wilson, 2020
Illustrations copyright © Nick Sharratt, 2020

The moral right of the author and illustrator has been asserted

Set in 11.75/16 pt New Century Schoolbook LT Pro
Typeset by Jouve (UK), Milton Keynes
Printed and bound in Great Britain by Clays Ltd, Elcograf S.p.A.

A CIP catalogue record for this book is available from the British Library

Hardback ISBN: 978–0–857–53589–4
International paperback ISBN: 978–0–857–53590–0

All correspondence to:
Doubleday
Penguin Random House Children's
One Embassy Gardens, New Union Square
5 Nine Elms Lane, London SW8 5DA

To Emma Middleton
with love and thanks

'I haven't got a clue what I'm going to give anyone for Christmas,' I said, sighing.

'Me neither,' said Sam.

I was lying on the bedroom rug with my dog, Bear. He was taking up more room than me because he's a gigantic long-haired German Shepherd. He was dozing and I was doing my maths homework. Well, Sam was the one actually doing it. I can barely add up accurately, whereas he's a total genius at maths. At more or less everything. He's even better than me at English, which is seriously annoying, seeing as I'm the one who's desperate to be a writer. I've started a novel in a special notebook with a skull pattern on the black cover. It's a dystopian novel written in the first person, present tense, and it's very dramatic and depressing. *I* like it but I'm not sure anyone else would. Girls like my sister Zara just want to read love stories. I definitely don't want to write anything remotely romantic. I don't think I'm ever going to fall in love.

Sam was sitting at Zara's dressing table, experimenting with hairstyles while dictating all my maths answers. His hair had grown quite a bit, so he was seeing if he could twist the top part into a man bun.

'What do you think, Frankie?' he asked, peering at it from all angles.

'I think you look ridiculous. Zara would go completely crackers if she knew you were using her hairbrush,' I said.

I wasn't just being snippy – I truly thought it a ridiculous hairstyle, but he still managed to look OK with it. Sam is effortlessly good-looking, no matter what. He's got blond hair and brown eyes and that peachy sort of skin that never gets spotty. All this, *and* he's really clever. But he's not the slightest bit vain or conceited. That's why I'm so glad that he's my best friend in all the world.

We've been best friends since we were four, when he moved into the Turret House next door to us. It's got three storeys, so it's much bigger than our house, and real turrets, and a wisteria climbing up the white walls that looks beautiful in spring. They have a very formal box garden – little hedges cut into an elaborate pattern of triangles. It's an enormous house for a family of three – just Sam and his parents, Michael and Lucy. Our house is called Rose Cottage. It's small, as the name implies, Victorian red brick, with two and a half bedrooms upstairs. Mum has one, Zara and I share another, and Rowena squeezes into the box room with her hundred and one Sylvanians. Mum's made the garden really pretty with red and pink and white rose bushes and beautiful big ferns, but they're all tangled up together because she can't garden much any more. I still think our garden looks much nicer than the Turret House one. Sam does too.

We started at primary school together, in the same class. We made sure we always sat next to each other and we played together at dinner time. We had a habit of walking down the school corridors hand in hand. Our teachers called us the Heavenly Twins, though we don't look at all alike. I'm a bit taller than Sam, and I'm skinny, with brown eyes and long brown hair that never stays tidy. I've always been a bit of a scruff. Even now I can't seem to help spilling stuff down my front, and my woolly tights wrinkle, my school shoes need heeling and my Docs new laces.

Sam and I were in the nativity play in Year One. He was the Angel Gabriel, and looked adorable in his long white dress and wings, though he said he felt silly. I was the ass.

I thought we'd spend all our school days together, but when we were seven Michael and Lucy sent Sam to a posh prep school instead of letting him stay on at Wickstead Road Juniors. It was so lonely without him. And of course we're at different secondary schools now. I'm at Barlow Community College. Sam's at Barlow Grammar School. They're both called Barlow but they are worlds apart.

Sam poked his tongue out at me now, a trio of Sams reflected in the three mirrors. He unknotted his hair and ran his fingers through it. It stuck out a bit at the side. He'd obviously slept on it the wrong way and hadn't bothered to wash it this morning.

'It keeps going weird. I'd better have it cut,' said Sam. His hand reached out for Zara's manicure set.

'Don't!' I said as he pulled out her nail scissors. 'You'll just make a terrible mess of it.'

I should have held my tongue. It was as if I'd dared him to do it. He held out the stray lock and gave an experimental snip.

'Are you completely nuts?' I said, scrambling to my feet. Bear moaned softly, not wanting to be disturbed. 'Oh, Sam, what have you done?'

He looked as if a giant sheep had come along and mistaken his hair for grass.

'It does look a bit weird, doesn't it?' he said. 'I'd better do the whole lot now to make it look even.'

'Stop sawing at it! You'll make it worse,' I said, snatching the scissors from him.

'You do it then,' he said.

'Me? Look what I did to Pearl!' I said ruefully.

I quite liked dolls when I was little. I didn't take off their clothes and put them to bed and wake them up and dress them all over again, the way Zara played with *her* dolls. I didn't see the point. I liked to turn our bedroom into Yosemite and make my dolls climb El Capitan (our wardrobe) and then get into mortal combat with my teddy bears. Sometimes they trekked to the hot springs in our bathroom, where they swam naked and fought the giant ducks with toothbrushes. They all looked the worse for wear after their adventures – but Pearl stayed pristine.

She'd been given to me by my godmother, Coral, Mum's best friend from way back. She lives in Hong Kong now. Pearl was a Chinese doll, with glossy black hair down to her shoulders. She wore a scarlet silk jacket and trousers with a tiny gold dragon pattern, and had a little scarlet cap to match.

I couldn't help taking the little red cap on and off though, and brushing her hair every day. (Strange when I could never be bothered to brush my own.) One day I scraped her hair back and plaited it. It suited her. She looked just like a boy. I decided she'd *like* to be a boy, so I tried giving her a haircut. It kept getting shorter and shorter as I tried to even it up – until she was practically bald.

Zara said I'd ruined my best doll. I said I *liked* her new haircut, but I didn't really. She looked all prickly and peculiar and her hat didn't fit her any more. I stopped playing with her after that, and passed her on to our little sister, Rowena, who has a whole orphanage of waifs and strays on her windowsill.

Sam remembered Pearl and put the scissors down. 'What am I going to do then?' he said, pulling a face. 'My mum won't be too thrilled. Do you think your mum could sort it out for me?'

I hesitated. 'She *would*, but she's in bed at the moment. She's not feeling very well,' I mumbled.

5

'Oh. Sorry,' Sam said. 'Well, maybe I'd better go and get a proper haircut in town then.'

'Have you got enough money?' I asked.

It was a daft question.

'I've got heaps,' said Sam. 'Dad gave me a handout this morning so that I could buy Christmas presents. Hey – you could come to Whitelands with me, Frankie. We'll buy our Christmas presents together.' He paused and added delicately, 'We can pool our money, if you like.'

'It's OK, I've got lots saved up,' I said.

This wasn't true, and Sam knew I was lying, but he also knew that I was too proud to take his money. I did have a *little* saved. I hadn't been able to get a babysitting job, but I ran various errands for an old lady down the road, who gave me a pound for my trouble each time. It was clear she thought this a small fortune, but it didn't add up to much. Eleven pound coins precisely.

Eleven pounds wasn't nearly enough for proper presents for seven people: Mum, Zara, Rowena, Sam, Granny, my godmother Coral, and Mr White at school. He's the school librarian and I adore him.

I'm not giving Dad a Christmas present this year. I don't see why I should. I utterly despise him now.

'Do they have a Poundland at Whitelands?' I asked.

'I don't know. Maybe. They've got all sorts of shops,' said Sam vaguely.

The girls in my class love going around Whitelands after school and at weekends. When I was much younger I liked going there too because they have these animatronic polar bears. In summer they dress them up in Hawaiian shirts and shorts, and they sit on a sandy beach making sandcastles to 'We're All Going on a Summer Holiday'. In the winter, slightly more logically, they give each polar bear a woolly hat and scarf, and they build a snowbear and jerk about to 'Walking in a Winter Wonderland'.

The bears were ready to be retired now, their white coats tinged with yellow. One day their mechanism failed so they froze mid-action, looking so creepy they made the little kids cry. They were soon working again, but they'd lost all attraction for me now. I didn't like the shops much either. I wasn't into clothes and make-up like Zara, or little toy animals like Rowena. But I was looking for presents for them, not me. I wasn't silly enough to think eleven pounds would be enough, but I could maybe get some ideas. And I was really sick of doing my maths homework, even with Sam's help.

'Come on, Sam. Let's get going. What do you want for Christmas? Shall we go to Claire's and buy you a hairband?' I said, getting up.

'Cheeky muppet,' said Sam, giving me a shove.

We had a mock wrestle, and Bear joined in and won.

'We can't take him to Whitelands,' said Sam, fondling his ears the way he likes best. 'No dogs allowed.'

'I'll ask Zara to look after him,' I said.

She was in the bathroom. Zara can stay in there for hours and hours. She'd been plucking her eyebrows into surprising shapes, and now she was sitting on the loo painting her fingernails. She was doing it very carefully, with tiny silver stars on top of navy polish. She jumped when I opened the door, and made a little splodge on the last nail.

'What did you have to come barging in like that for? Now look what you've made me do!' she wailed. 'My star's gone all blobby.'

'It can be a little moon instead of a star,' I suggested. 'Zara, could you possibly keep an eye on Bear for a bit? He'll need to go out for a quick wee in a while,' I said. 'Sam and I are just going to Whitelands.'

'I thought you hated Whitelands,' she said. 'Anyway, I can't, because *I'm* going to Whitelands.'

'How can you be so mean? You weren't even thinking of going there until I mentioned it!'

'Yes I was! I'm meeting Julie and Tamsin and Joy for lunch at McDonald's,' Zara insisted.

'Like you've got enough money to go to McDonald's,' I said.

'Julie always gives me half hers.'

'Sponger!'

'I am not! I'm doing her a favour. She says she's on a diet. So *anyway*, I can't have Bear.' Zara paused. 'Is Mum still in bed?'

'Yes, and I'm not disturbing her,' I said.

I left the bathroom and went towards Rowena's room.

'Are you asking Rowena? She's too little to take Bear for a walk by herself,' Zara called.

'She could just pop him out into the garden. He'd be fine with her. He loves her best, after me,' I said.

Rowena was kneeling on her bedroom floor, arranging her Sylvanians into neat family groups. I could see all the mummy bears and bunnies and pandas and badgers, and the little girls and little boys and babies, but there weren't any daddies.

'Hey, Rowena,' I said, squatting down beside her. She's only six and a half – perhaps it wasn't fair to ask her – but she's very good with Bear. He doesn't growl a bit when she brushes him. He's always extra gentle with her.

'Hey, Frankie,' she said, smiling.

'I have to go to Whitelands with Sammy,' I said. 'Do you think you could be an angel and look after Bear for me? Perhaps take him in the garden if he looks like he needs a wee?'

'All right,' she agreed.

'You're a star,' I said. 'You're totally my favourite sister.' I made all the little girl Sylvanians dance and sing 'We love Rowena!' in tiny voices. Rowena giggled.

'Where have all the daddies gone, eh?' I asked.

Rowena pointed to the windowsill. They were marooned up there, in a shoebox.

'Aha! Are you banishing the fathers because ours has cleared off?' I asked, flicking each little figure over onto his back. 'Are they in prison?'

'No, they're at *work*,' said Rowena.

'What about the mummies then? Why aren't they at work?'

'They're tired because they're a bit ill. They're having a nice rest at home.' She stroked their heads in turn.

'Poor mummies,' I said softly. 'So, Bear's lying on my rug at the moment.'

'He's like a great big rug himself,' said Rowena.

'Maybe you'd better not let him in your room in case he tries to eat your Sylvanians,' I said. 'Only joking!' I added quickly when she looked alarmed.

I thought I'd better peep in at Mum just to make sure she was all right. She'd insisted on getting up early and making us our favourite Saturday pancakes, but she'd looked particularly pale, and had purple shadows under her eyes. She said she was absolutely fine and started making a list of all the things she wanted to do today on the telephone pad.

Lesson plans! (Use Gingerbread Man as
    folk-tale example)
Make gingerbread men for class???
Tidy up!
Put on a wash. Several washes.
Emails.
Juggle bills.
Take in seams of baggy blue dress.
Lunch – soup?
Take Rowena to feed ducks? Then charity shops?
Discuss Zara's exam results!
Find new laces for Frankie's Doc Martens. Ribbons?

The list went on and on. We had cleared the breakfast dishes, and Mum had sat down with her school briefcase and started writing lesson plans, but five minutes later her head started nodding and she fell asleep, her pen still in her hand. Zara and I helped her upstairs and put her to bed.

I opened her door very cautiously now and crept inside. She was still lying on the bed in her pyjamas and the bedsocks with the penguin pattern.

Mum's eyes were shut, so I backed away towards the door – though perhaps not quietly enough.

'Hey, Frankie,' she murmured.

'Hey, Mum. Sorry to wake you. Go back to sleep,' I said, tucking the duvet over her.

'I've got so much to do,' she protested.

'Tomorrow. You need to rest now,' I said. 'Nurse Frankie says.'

'Oh, love. I feel so lazy, sleeping in on a Saturday morning.'

'You're not the slightest bit lazy, you're simply tired out, running around after all those little kids all week – and us lot too.'

'I'll just have ten minutes more, and then I'll be fighting fit and raring to go,' said Mum.

We both knew perfectly well that she never felt fighting fit and raring to go any more. We knew why. Mum had glossed over the details to us when she first got her diagnosis. One day her eyes had gone funny. Another day she could only see in black and white. Then she went completely blind, but only for a few terrible hours. The optician sent her to hospital and they did all kinds of tests. Her eyes got better, but they still said she had this awful illness. Mum insisted that it wasn't all doom and gloom. People with MS often went into remission and never got ill again. I think Rowena believed her, but Zara and I googled multiple sclerosis in private, and panicked.

We don't always get on – in fact, we *rarely* get on because we're so different – but that night I squeezed into Zara's bed and we hugged each other tight and cried, our heads under the duvet so that Mum wouldn't hear.

Mum hasn't got better. Now her legs are playing up and she's terribly tired all the time.

'You have your little nap, Mum,' I said. 'I'm just going to Whitelands with Sammy. OK?'

'Mmm, OK,' she murmured. Then her eyes opened properly. 'Hang on. *Not* OK. Zara's here, right?'

'Yes,' I said, but I had to add truthfully, 'Only she might be popping out too. But it's all right, Rowena's playing happily in her bedroom and she's going to look after Bear.'

Mum struggled up onto one elbow. '*I'm* the mum. *I* do the looking after,' she said.

'No, Mum! Please, it's all sorted. You need your rest,' I said, feeling dreadful.

'I've been sleeping for hours already,' said Mum, looking at her alarm clock. She sat up properly and made an attempt to swing her legs out of bed.

'Mum! Look, I won't go. I don't *need* to. You're making me feel so bad,' I wailed.

She slid out of bed and took hold of me by the shoulders.

'You mustn't feel bad. You're nearly fourteen. You have a perfect right to go out with your friends. It's not your job to stay home looking after your little sister,' she said, looking into my eyes.

'It's my job to look after my dog. I promised I would when I begged to have him,' I said guiltily.

'And you do look after him nearly all the time. And you do a great job looking after Rowena too. You're lovely with her.'

'I'm not lovely with Zara,' I pointed out.

'Well, nobody's perfect. Where's my dressing gown? If Sammy's around I don't want to scare him silly prancing around in my PJs,' said Mum.

They were very old pyjamas, with a faded pattern of blue roses. Mum always looked extra cuddly in them, even though she was so frail now.

'You look lovely in those pyjamas,' I told her, giving her a hug.

Mum hugged me back. It wasn't a very strong hug. She seemed so much weaker now. I worried that if Bear got overexcited and jumped up to give her face a lick, he might send her flying.

'I don't think I can be bothered to go to Whitelands actually,' I said quickly. 'It's boring. I was just going to keep Sammy company because he has to go to the barber's to sort out his hair. He tried to give himself a haircut but it went wrong. Still, it's his fault. He can sort it out himself.'

Mum gave me a long look. There was no fooling her. 'Frankie, perhaps I won't be able to look after you all properly in the future,' she said huskily, 'but I can manage now. So let me. Please.'

I swallowed and then nodded.

'Off you go then,' she said, sniffing. She gently pulled on a strand of my hair. It's nearly down to my waist now – it's a terrible bore trying to keep it washed and tidy, but I know it's my best feature. My *only* good one. 'Don't *you* try giving yourself a haircut, young lady.'

'I won't, promise,' I said, miming crossing my heart and hoping to die if I told a lie.

It was just a silly rhyme we'd said at nursery school, but nowadays anything about death made me shiver. You could die of MS. Mostly not for years and years. But it could happen.

'Don't frown like that, poppet,' Mum said, rubbing my forehead.

'I'm not frowning,' I said quickly, and gave her the biggest, cheeriest grin I could manage.

Mum went off to the bathroom wrapped up in her dressing gown and I went to collect Sam. I found him peering at my dystopian story in the skull notebook.

'Hey! Don't you dare look in that,' I said, snatching the book and swatting him with it.

'Hey! I was just having a little look, that's all,' said Sam, rubbing his head.

'What bit of *PRIVATE!* don't you understand?' I demanded.

'We're mates, aren't we? We don't have secrets.'

'Yes we do.' I stuffed the notebook in my half of the

chest of drawers under my tumble of T-shirts and socks and underwear.

'Is it a secret diary?' Sam asked eagerly. 'Oh, Frankie, *please* let us have a look. Have you written stuff about me?'

'I haven't written anything about you, silly, because it's a story,' I said.

'Oh, one of those.' He sounded disappointed.

I used to share all my stories with Sam. In fact, when we were little we'd make them up together. I'd do most of the writing and leave gaps for his illustrations. We once created a whole series of booklets about the Gruesome Twosome – twins who vied with each other to make up the grossest pranks. But we were past that stupid stage now. I wanted to write serious stories. Last year I'd poured my whole heart and soul into a dramatic story about an amazing warrior girl who led a tribe of savages. I read the first part to Sam – but he *laughed* at it.

We had a fight then and he said he was sorry, he thought I'd *meant* it to be funny, which made me even more upset. After that I vowed to keep my stories strictly to myself. I was particularly attached to the dystopian story, which was about a devastating plague affecting the whole Earth. My girl hero was one of the last people left alive, recording all her struggles. I'd written pages and pages, and planned to fill the entire big notebook, with the last entry petering out as the pen falls from her fingers and she dies too.

I'd been really excited by the idea, but as Sam and I walked into town I started to worry. He could only have glimpsed a paragraph or two, and he hadn't laughed this time – but somehow it felt as if he had. I went over the story in my head, dwelling on the best parts, though now they seemed weird and melodramatic. Maybe it wasn't any good after all. In fact, maybe it was complete rubbish.

I felt extremely irritated with Sam and bickered with him all the way to Whitelands. It was very crowded, with everyone rushing around doing their Christmas shopping. The polar bears were doing their slow-motion dance to 'Winter Wonderland' watched by dozens of toddlers. Sam started imitating their robotic movements, and a couple of girls our age started giggling at him, clearly impressed. He started showing off even more.

'Look at those girls staring!' he said, grinning.

'Oh, for goodness' sake, Sammy, they're just having a laugh at your hair,' I said meanly, and then felt bad.

He didn't seem to mind. 'You're just jealous because they fancy me,' he said infuriatingly.

'Kid yourself!' I said. 'Come on, let's get your hair cut.'

Whitelands didn't have a proper barber's. Sam went to a unisex place called Quick Cuts. I sat waiting with him, watching. There was a girl a bit older than me having a very short haircut. I couldn't understand it because her hair looked great – long and blonde – and just at first it started to look awful. I could see the girl staring at herself in the mirror, looking agonized. But then, gradually, the hairdresser styled it into the coolest cut, and by the time she finished blow-drying it the girl was looking incredible.

I nudged Sam. 'Do you like her hair?' I whispered.

'Yeah, it's OK. Though she looks a bit like a boy now,' he said.

'Yes, but it suits her, it really does.' I couldn't stop staring at her. 'Do you think a cut like that would suit me, Sam?'

'You'd look like a boy too,' he told me.

'So? It's cool to look kind of androgynous,' I said loftily, though I wasn't sure I was pronouncing the word correctly.

Sam stared at me. 'You're not serious, are you? You can't really want to have your hair chopped off! Are you crazy?'

'It's *my* hair. I can do what I like with it,' I said. 'Yes, I'm going to, right now.' I didn't *really* mean it, and I knew that eleven pounds probably wasn't enough for a radical haircut anyway, but Sam took me seriously.

'Please don't!' he said, looking horrified. 'You've got lovely hair.'

I was surprised. Sam and I were mates. We didn't usually compliment each other.

I shrugged, embarrassed. 'All right, I won't. Not just yet.'

I wouldn't have done it anyway, because it would have upset Mum so. I heard the girls at school going on about their mothers, moaning and complaining, or raising their eyebrows and shaking their heads, saying they were pathetic. Well, maybe they were. But *my* mum was the best ever. Maybe I'd forget everyone else and just spend my eleven pounds on a proper present for her.

The girl with the new cool haircut paid at the desk and then walked past us. She was patting her ears and neck anxiously now that they were suddenly exposed.

'Your hair looks great,' I said.

She glanced round at me, startled, and then gave me an uncertain smile.

'Why did she look at me like that?' I asked Sam.

'Maybe she thought you were coming on to her,' he suggested.

'Don't be so daft!' I said, but my cheeks were hot and I hoped I wasn't blushing. 'I was trying to reassure her.'

'I'm just joking,' said Sam.

'I know.'

'I hope you'll tell me *my* hair looks great afterwards.'

It *did* look great actually. The hairdresser didn't make it too short, just enough to disguise the missing locks, and she fluffed it up a bit so that Sam looked weirdly like a pop star.

He kept glancing in shop windows, very pleased with himself.

'Come on. Let's do some serious present shopping,' I said.

We trailed round and round the three different levels, dashing in and out of any likely shops. Sam bought his dad a key ring with a little toy rugby ball, which was clever, because his dad's very into rugby and often goes to Twickenham.

'You could get *your* dad one,' he said. 'Maybe with a football. Or a little mobile phone. Or whatever he's into.'

'I don't know what he's into nowadays. I couldn't care less. I'm not bothering to get him a present,' I said.

'Oh well.' Sam knew when it was better to drop a subject. 'So, mums next? I'm getting mine perfume, I think. Let's try Boots.'

I wondered about getting the tiniest doll-size bottle for Mum, but I was astonished by the prices. Sam spent ages choosing, making me spray my wrists with about six different kinds. They all smelled so powerful they made me feel sick, especially all together. It felt weird too, having him sniffing up and down my arm. Even he was a bit startled by the cost, not sure they were worth it.

'You could always get your mother eau de toilette instead. It's not as expensive and many ladies prefer it because it's not so intense,' said the shop assistant, a helpful, smiley lady, obviously taken with Sam.

'Eau de toilette?' he said. '*Toilet* water?'

He burst out laughing, in such an infectious way that the shop assistant laughed too, and even I got the giggles.

'Oh come on, Sammy, even I know about eau de toilette,' I said.

'It just sounds so funny,' he spluttered. 'OK, can I have a little toiletty bottle of this rosy-smelling sort, please?'

It was still nearly twenty pounds, which seemed ridiculous, but Sam paid for it happily.

'I'll get you one for your mother,' he said, trying to press a note into my hand.

'It's ever so kind of you, Sam, but she's not really the perfume sort,' I told him. 'She usually just smells of her coconut-milk shampoo.'

'Well, you could get her a big bottle of that if she really likes it.'

'Yes, I suppose, but it's a bit ordinary for a present, isn't it? And she's got about five in the bathroom cabinet because they were on special offer. There's no point in getting her any more,' I said, sighing.

Still, while we were in Boots I found a little bottle of silver nail varnish I thought Zara would like, and next door in Smiggle I bought a yellow pen shaped like a banana with a little brown furry monkey clutching the end, totally Rowena's cup of tea.

'There, that's my sisters taken care of. But I've only got just over three quid left!' I wailed as we walked past a chocolate shop giving out samples of their special Christmas selection.

'Hang about and look hungry,' said Sam. 'And stop fussing about your money, Frankie. We'll pool mine, like I said.'

'No, we absolutely won't. It's very sweet of you, but no. Definitely no,' I insisted.

'OK, OK.' Sam reached out, his hand hovering near the sample tray. 'May I?' he said hopefully.

'Of course, dear,' said the chocolate lady.

'One for me, one for her?'

I had a milk chocolate vanilla fudge, Sam a white chocolate truffle.

'There are benefits to going shopping with Mr Charm,' I said.

Sam bowed.

'Mmm, absolute bliss,' I said with my mouth full.

I knew it was stupid, but I looked at the price of the smallest box of chocolate fudge. Then I sighed.

'*I* know!' said Sam. 'I know a way you can give everyone little boxes of fudge.'

'I keep *telling* you—'

'I'm not offering you money, I'm offering you a great idea. We can *make* fudge. We'll google a recipe and I'll raid Mum's larder and we'll make it at yours because my mum hates it if I make a mess in the kitchen. Good plan?'

'But it'll still be using all your mum's ingredients – the butter and the sugar and whatever else we need,' I said.

'Look, my mum's kitchen has as much stock as a small branch of Waitrose. And she'll be thrilled if we use up all the sweet stuff now she's on her health kick. Don't be so proud and independent – it's getting irritating.'

'Sorry,' I said. 'And thank you, Sam. Actually home-made fudge is a great idea. All hail the maestro!'

I put my fingers to my mouth and blew him a theatrical kiss. The smell of perfume made me reel. 'Oh God, I smell disgusting with all these different smells. I'm going to have to find the Ladies and scrub my arms,' I said.

We went up the escalator and found the toilets on the top floor. There was a huge queue to get in, and when I walked past, women started moaning, thinking I was pushing in.

'I just want to wash my hands,' I gabbled, but they still stared at me suspiciously.

They didn't have any proper basins with taps and plugs and bars of soap. There was just a weird trough thing and automatic dispensers. I waved my arms around and got my cuffs soaking wet, so I took off my jacket altogether, clamped it between my knees so that no one would nick it, and had a proper scrub. I was up to both elbows in suds when I heard a voice say, 'Hey, look who it isn't!'

I turned round and saw Sally Macclesfield and her little gang, Marnie and Georgia and Scarlett. My deadly enemies.

I forced myself to stay soaping away in my ridiculous pose, trying to take no notice of them whatsoever. They couldn't say too much in a public lavatory with hordes of people surrounding us.

I looked in the mirror and saw Sally standing there, one hand on her hip, staring at me. She looked annoyingly cool, wearing a trilby hat at a jaunty angle on her fair curls, and a long red coat swinging open to show a tiny black miniskirt, her long legs in shiny black tights. She had black boots a bit like mine, but hers had red mouths painted on the leather. She had red lipstick too, making her teeth look very white. I could imagine her biting into my cheek as if it was an apple.

It was weird to think that I'd hardly been aware of her in Year Seven. I mean, I knew perfectly well who she was, and that at least half the girls were vying to be her friend, and that the teachers took more notice of her because she was bright and sassy and often argued, but in such a cute way she rarely got into trouble.

I didn't hang out with any of the girls then. I wasn't a Billy-no-mates – I just went around with the boys. I was used to boy jokes and boy banter. I was good at games too, and played footie with them. I was good old Frankie, counted as one of the lads, in spite of my long hair.

Year Eight was a bit of a nightmare because Dad left and then Mum's eyes started playing up and she eventually got the diagnosis of MS. Dad came back for a bit then, feeling guilty. Zara and Rowena hoped he'd come back for good. I don't know what Mum thought. I *knew* he'd clear off again – and he did.

So I wasn't in a larking-about-with-the-boys mood for most of last year. I didn't want to hang out with anyone, so every lunch hour I went to the library. That's how I got to know Mr White, the librarian. I talked to Ivneet too, a girl in my class who goes to the library a lot. She's not very popular because she's terribly clever and always comes top. Ivneet doesn't seem to care what people think.

'Ivneet is a Sikh name. It means Brave,' she told me. She grinned. 'It's a good name, eh? I like the idea that I'm brave.'

I looked up the meaning of the name Frankie. It just meant someone from France, though the Urban Dictionary said all Frankies were dead sarcastic.

I suppose I can be sometimes, especially with girly girls like my sister. When I started Year Nine I tried to get back in with my old boy gang, but they didn't seem to want me hanging around with them any more. They were suddenly interested in all the other girls, rating them in the most offensive way, saying stuff that sometimes made me laugh at them, sometimes made me rage at their stupidity. The girls had changed too, flirting and giggling, fussing with their hair and wearing make-up to school and hitching their skirts up.

But Sally Mac wasn't like that. She acted like she didn't give a stuff about any of the boys in our class – or Years Ten or Eleven, though most of the older guys really fancied her. I quite liked her for that. We weren't *friends*, but sometimes we came across each other on the stairs or in the corridors and nodded. We were in the same netball team and often passed the ball to each other and high-fived if either of us scored a goal.

But then, the week before half-term, Mum came to meet me from school a bit early. I had a boring dental appointment and she wanted to discuss the pros and cons of me having a brace. I very much hoped the cons would outweigh the pros. But we ended up missing the appointment altogether because, hurrying along with Rowena, Mum had a fall outside the school gate. Her leg just gave way and she toppled right over, banging her chin so badly she cut it open and it bled.

I saw it happening as I was crossing the playground, and I went charging over. Rowena was terrified, kneeling down beside Mum and sobbing. Poor Mum was trying hard not to cry too, struggling to get up, with a crowd gathering around her. Someone was trying to help her to her feet, someone else was shouting that she should stay put until an ambulance came.

'I'm so sorry! I'll be fine, honestly! Just give me a moment,' Mum kept saying, through gritted teeth.

'It's all right, Mum. I'm here. Let me help you,' I said, elbowing everyone out of the way. 'Rowena, it's OK, don't cry so. We'll help Mum into school, away from all these people.'

Mum had twisted her ankle and could hardly stand, but Rowena was too little and distraught to give her much support. Thank goodness Zara came running up, white-faced. She got hold of Mum on one side and I supported her on the other, and together we managed to stagger into school, Rowena running behind wringing her hands. Mum simply wanted to wash the blood away and sit down for ten minutes until she felt better, but there was a big flap inside too, until the head teacher, Mrs Hurst, came and helped Mum into her office.

I've never really liked Mrs Hurst, thinking her a right old bossy boots, but she was surprisingly nice to us. She gave Mum a wad of tissues to stop her chin bleeding and even examined her ankle, which was starting to swell.

'How did it happen, Mrs Bennet? Did you trip over something?' she asked, concerned.

Mum shook her head.

'Did you feel faint?'

'No, I just fell over,' Mum murmured.

'Well, I don't think you've done yourself any serious injury, but I'd better drive you to A and E so they can check you over. There could be some underlying reason why you fell.'

'There is,' said Mum. Then she suddenly started crying after all. 'I've been diagnosed with MS and I'm so scared this trouble with my leg is the start of another relapse.'

She'd made Zara and Rowena and me swear we wouldn't tell anyone. She was desperate to keep her teaching job as long as she could. But now here she was, blurting it all out to Mrs Hurst of all people.

'Mum!' said Zara sharply.

'Oh God, I shouldn't have said that,' Mum wept. 'I'm such a fool!'

'No you're not, Mum! You've had a nasty shock. And you won't tell anyone, will you, Mrs Hurst?' I begged.

'Of course not.' She was really kind and understanding. She made us cups of tea, and got out a packet of chocolate Hobnobs too. She said she thought Mum was being very brave. Then she insisted on driving us to the hospital, and we had to wait for hours until Mum could get four stitches in her chin and a tight bandage round her ankle.

'There we are. Mummy's all better now,' the nurse said to Rowena, who was still a bit tearful.

'Have you made her MS better too?' Rowena asked hopefully.

'Oh, love, I don't think anyone can make it completely better,' said Mum, putting her arm round her. 'But I'll just have to try harder not to be silly and fall over. Don't look so anxious, girls. I'm fine now.'

She wasn't fine. And I wasn't fine either. My life at school changed. The next day, when I was about to go into the classroom, I heard everyone sniggering about it.

'She just collapsed, like she'd been drinking!'

'Imagine, falling down drunk at three o'clock in the afternoon!'

'She had Frankie's little sister with her too.'

'I think it's disgusting, a mother getting so sloshed.'

'Yeah, my mum sometimes cracks open a bottle of wine in the evening, but she never drinks a drop in the afternoon.'

'And Mrs Bennet's a *teacher*. I wonder what all those little kids make of her, staggering about.'

'Little Year Ones going, "Look, Mrs Bennet's just been sick in the sand tray!"'

They were all chiming in, but it was Sally Mac singing when I burst through the door: *'Ten wine bottles, hanging on the wall, ten wine bottles, hanging on the wall, and if Frankie Bennet's mother should accidentally fall, then she's drunk all the bottles hanging on the wall.'*

They were all giggling away, but stopped when they saw me. I went straight up to Sally and slapped her hard across the face. There was a big gasp. Sally rocked on her heels in shock, one side of her face white and the other bright red.

'For Christ's sake, Frankie!' she said.

'Slap her back, Sally,' Marnie egged her on.

'Hey, there's going to be a cat fight!' said one of the boys.

'Fight, fight, fight!' they started chanting.

'Don't you dare slap me around!' said Sally. 'It's not *my* fault your mum's a drunk!'

'She is not a drunk! She couldn't help falling. She's ill!' I hissed.

'Oh yes, my dad always says he's ill when he's had a few,' said Marnie.

'My mother didn't have a drop to drink. Now shut your stupid faces or you'll all get slapped,' I said wildly.

'Frankie's gone berserk! Look at her eyes! Get out of her way or she'll go for you!'

'Maybe she's been drinking too!'

They all tittered nervously, acting like they were really scared of me. But Sally wasn't, though her cheek was still a bright burning red. She came right up to me, so we were nose to nose.

'Don't you *dare* slap me again, freak,' she said.

After that we were deadly enemies. Whenever they saw me, Sally and her gang mimed drunkenness. For several days the whole class joined in, except the geeks, Ivneet and Rangan and Ezra. But then it was half-term and the novelty wore off and they stopped the game – all except Sally and Marnie and Georgia and Scarlett.

Sally was particularly inventive, knowing just what to say and do to wind me up, especially when we were all in the playground out of sight of any teachers. I shut up about it at home, of course, but Zara saw what was going on. She wasn't getting teased herself – none of the Year Tens had seen Mum falling over – but she was angry on my behalf.

'Why don't you tell your form teacher? Or Mrs Hurst? She was so kind to us about it. Have a word with her, Frankie. She'll soon sort those little cows out,' she said.

'Seriously? Don't be daft, Zara, that'll only make it worse. Listen, I don't give a stuff about Sally and her gang,' I lied.

'But it's horrible. She's turned everyone against you,' said Zara indignantly. 'You haven't got any friends any more.'

'I've got Sammy,' I said. 'I don't want anyone else.'

'Have you told him what's going on?'

'No. And don't you dare tell him, Zara.' I didn't want him to know because it was so humiliating.

Yet here I was now, in the Ladies at Whitelands, with Sally and Marnie and Georgia and Scarlett – and Sam waiting outside.

'Hello, Frankie,' said Sally, and she came and perched on
the rim of the trough beside mine.

I nodded at her curtly. I knew she wasn't trying to be
friendly.

'Out shopping, are you?' she said.

'So?' I muttered.

'She certainly needs some new clothes,' said Marnie,
eyeing me up and down.

She was actually right. I didn't have many clothes at
all because I hated wearing Zara's hand-me-downs. She
always chose sickeningly girly things – pink with unicorn
and kitten and heart motifs. Even her *jeans* were pink.

But nowadays her choice is worse if anything. She likes tiny T-shirts and blouses that cling to her chest and show a glimpse of waist, and tiny skirts that barely cover her pants.

I was wearing an old pair of Zara's jeans now, but thank goodness they're black. I was also wearing an enormous T-shirt I found for two pounds in an Oxfam shop. It was advertising some heavy metal band I'd never heard of, but I liked the picture of a wild woman carrying an axe. She wore a leopard skin and big boots rather like my own Docs.

'Cool T-shirt though,' said Sally. It was clear she meant the opposite.

'Shame about the black skinnies. She looks like Minnie Mouse,' said Scarlett, and they all laughed.

'And those ugly old Docs are enormous! What size shoe do you take, Frankie? Size nine? Size ten?' said Georgia.

'Why are you washing all the way up to your elbows?' Sally asked.

'I know!' said Marnie, eyes glinting. 'Her mum's been sick and Frankie's had to clear it up.'

They all wrinkled their noses and shuddered, tittering.

My wet hands clenched into fists.

'Ooh, watch out, she'll be giving us all a slap in a minute,' said Scarlett.

'Poor Frankie,' said Sally silkily. 'It must be horrid for you having to cope with your mum.'

'Shut up, you cow,' I muttered.

'So where *is* your mum then, Frankie? Is she in the food hall stocking up on bottles of Pinot?' asked Scarlett.

'My mum doesn't drink – I keep telling you,' I said, shaking my hands. I hurried over to the dryer but they followed me.

'Is she having a little rest at home then?' Sally asked softly.

'Yes, she is. So what?' I said, dangling my hands in the hot air.

'So are you all on your own, Frankie? Because you haven't got any proper friends, have you?' she persisted. 'Perhaps you'd like to hang out with us.'

'No thanks,' I said. 'And I'm here with a friend, if you must know.'

'Oooh!' said Marnie. 'Well, there's a surprise! Who'd want to go round with Skanky Frankie? They must be pretty weird!'

'Does she go to our school, Frankie?' Sally asked, eyebrows raised quizzically.

'Mind your own business,' I snapped.

'Oh, don't be like that!' Sally took off her hat and plonked it on my head. 'Hey, it suits you!'

We both knew it didn't suit me in the slightest. It looked cute on Sally, but I could see in the mirror that it looked ridiculous on me. I flipped it off so that it fell on the floor.

'Naughty!' she said, retrieving it. 'And naughty girl for telling fibs too. Because you haven't got any friends, have you?'

'I have so.'

'Then where is she?' asked Marnie, peering around.

'It's not a she, it's a he. And he's waiting outside, obviously.'

'A boy!' said Sally. 'So you've got a boyfriend, Frankie?'

It wasn't a serious question. She was certain I didn't.

I'd had enough. 'Yes, it's my boyfriend,' I said, just to fool her.

'OMG, she's got a boyfriend!' cried Marnie.

'How come *she's* got a boyfriend?' said Georgia.

'She's telling stupid lies,' said Scarlett. 'As if a girl like Frankie would get herself a boyfriend.'

'*Are* you telling lies, Frankie?' Sally asked.

'No, I'm not. I don't tell lies,' I said. 'And he's been waiting ages, so I'm off now. Bye.'

'Well, we're coming too.' Sally jumped off the basin. 'We want to see what he's like, don't we?'

'Yeah, and I bet I can guess,' said Marnie, pulling a silly cross-eyed goofy face.

'Wait just a minute,' pleaded Georgia. 'I still need a wee!'

'You'll have to hold it in,' said Sally, actually linking her arm through mine. 'Frankie's about to introduce us to her boyfriend.'

'We don't know him already, do we?' asked Scarlett. 'Is he in our class?'

'I bet it's Rangan or Ezra, someone swotty and serious,' said Marnie.

'He doesn't go to our school. Let *go*, Sally. I'm not introducing you, not for anything.' I tried to shake her off.

She clung onto me as we emerged from the Ladies, with the others following, even Georgia, though she looked desperate.

'So, which one is the boyfriend?' said Sally.

There were several bored-looking father types waiting for their wives, and a couple of little boys messing about play-fighting. There was no sign of Sam.

'Well, who's the lucky guy?' Sally asked. 'So you've got an older man, Frankie! Is it the one who's going bald or the one in the golfing sweater or the one clutching all the carrier bags? Perhaps he's bought you lots of presents!'

'No, *I* think it's the little one in the Thomas the Tank Engine jumper!' exclaimed Marnie. 'Frankie's got a toy boy!'

They all spluttered again.

'Do you have to be so childish?' I said, trying to pull my arm free. Sally still hung on.

'You're the one who's being childish, telling such naughty fibs,' she said. 'Because you haven't really got a boyfriend, have you?'

'Yes I have!'

'Well, where is he then?' Marnie demanded.

'Perhaps he's an imaginary boyfriend. Frankie makes him up and he trots around with her and tells her she's wonderful and that they're soul mates,' Sally suggested. 'She's an imaginative girl, our Frankie. Fancies herself a writer. Perhaps she keeps a secret journal and writes about all the things they do together.'

She was talking nonsense – but how did she know I wanted to be a writer? And I *did* once keep a secret journal that I hid from everyone. I wrote down all my most private hopes and dreams – things that I would never, ever tell anyone.

'She's blushing!' said Marnie. 'Oh, Sally, you're so right! You're pathetic, Skanky Frankie.'

'Look, wait here, I'm going to rush back or I'll wet myself,' said Georgia.

'Yeah, why are we wasting our time on a loser with an alkie mother?' said Scarlett.

'Shut up! Don't you *dare* call my mother an alkie!' I said. *And was I really a loser?*

'Watch out, Scarlett, she's getting all het up,' said Sally, accurately enough. 'It's your turn to get your face slapped. Shock, horror, girl brawl in Whitelands shopping centre!'

'Hey, Frankie!'

I looked round – and there was Sam strolling out of the nearby Waterstones. He waved cheerily and then came strolling over. Sally, Marnie, Georgia and Scarlett stood still, staring.

'What's up?' said Sam, looking at me. 'Did you think I'd disappeared? I just nipped into Waterstones to look at their science fantasy stuff.'

He smiled at the other four girls. 'Hi,' he said, nodding at them. 'Are you Frankie's friends from school?'

'No, they're more like deadly enemies,' I said.

Sam thought I was joking, especially when Sally smiled back.

'Hi, I'm Sally. And this is Marnie and Georgia and Scarlett. We're all in Frankie's form. So you're . . . ?'

'I'm Sam. We're doing our Christmas shopping, aren't we, Frankie?'

'Trying to,' I said. 'We'd better get on with it. Coming?'

'Sure,' said Sam.

We walked off together. I felt as if my Docs were on springs and I was bouncing up to the domed ceiling. Sally's face! She really thought Sam was my boyfriend.

But then she ran after us. 'Hey, Sammy?'

He looked back.

'Are you really Frankie's boyfriend – not just a cousin or something?' she asked, head on one side so that her trilby tilted.

My heart started beating fast. 'Just push off, Sally,' I said. 'Come on, Sammy.'

'Cool hat,' he said to Sally. He tipped it gently, saving it from falling off. 'Yes, of course I'm Frankie's boyfriend.'

She was actually struck dumb.

'OK, Frankie?' said Sam, and he put his arm round me.

We walked off together. I couldn't believe it. Sam and I didn't even touch nowadays. As little kids we'd curl up together when we were tired. We pretended to be the parents of our dolls and teddies, and called each other Mummy and Daddy. We even had mock weddings, with me dressed up in one of Mum's white petticoats and Sam with a black bow tie and his dad's old dinner jacket, the sleeves trailing on the ground.

I can't quite remember when we became self-conscious about being so close. Maybe it was when we started secondary school. We didn't stop being friends or anything – in fact, we've never had a serious quarrel – but we were just more wary. Once we played some furious digging-for-treasure game and came home filthy dirty. Mum had run a bath for us, expecting us to hop in together, but we suddenly felt shy and awkward.

And now it felt so strange, Sam's arm round me, his hand cupped round my shoulder.

'It's OK, they've gone back into the Ladies,' I said. 'You can take your arm away. Oh, Sam, you saved my life! I can't stand those girls.'

'No, let's hang on a bit, just in case they come rushing out again,' said Sam. 'Why can't you stand them? Sally looks like she could be good fun.'

'She's the worst. They kind of gang up on me and she's the leader,' I said, all in a rush. I'd kept it a secret for so long, but now I couldn't stop talking. 'It started when they saw Mum . . .'

'When they saw your mother?'

'She came to pick me up from school, and when she got to the school gate she fell. Because she's ill. She's been ill for a while.'

Sam nodded. 'I know. My mum's been really worried about her, but your mother always insists she's fine.'

'Yes, I know. But she isn't fine. Look, I swore I wouldn't tell anyone, but she's got multiple sclerosis,' I whispered.

'Oh goodness. That's serious, isn't it?'

'Yes, it is.'

'Very? I mean, is she going to *die*?' Sam said, his grip tightening round my shoulder.

'Not yet. Maybe not till she's an old, old lady. She might not get any worse. Some people even get better. It depends on what sort you've got, and Mum hasn't said because she hates talking about it. You won't tell your mum and dad, will you, Sam? Or anyone else?' I asked anxiously.

'Not if you don't want me to. But maybe Mum could help a bit,' he offered.

'But that's just it. Mum doesn't *want* any help, even though she gets terribly tired. And she's desperate to keep working for as long as possible,' I said.

Sam had to let go of me then because we were going down the long escalator, all the way to the ground floor. The giant Christmas tree and the flashing fairy lights and all the sparkly decorations made my eyes ache. The polar-bear Christmas songs boomed inside my head, deafening me.

'Frankie? Are you all right?' Sam asked urgently.

'Sort of. I feel a bit funny. I suppose it's talking about Mum. Once I start thinking about her I can't stop worrying.'

What was going to happen when Mum couldn't work any more? What if she kept falling over all the time, or stopped being able to walk at all? Which part of her would go wrong next?

'Let's go and sit down somewhere, have a cup of coffee or something,' said Sam. 'McDonald's?'

'No, Zara might go there. And Sally and her gang.'

'OK, I know a place round the back of Whitelands. It's a bit like a greasy spoon, but I quite like it. Some of the boys from school hang out there at lunchtime. OK?'

It was a cosy little café. On a Saturday it was full of older people, chatting away about the price of everything and the political situation and kids nowadays, though they nearly all smiled at Sam and me, and I heard one old lady say we were a sweet little couple. We sat right at the back, where it was quieter and darker. We had a coffee each and shared a big iced bun. Sam paid, and for once I didn't argue.

'So, Sally and those other girls saw your mum fall down?' Sam prompted.

'Yes, and they all said awful stuff at school the next day. Someone started saying she'd fallen over because she was drunk, and then they all went on about it, like she's an alcoholic or something,' I said.

'*What?* Oh, for God's sake, your mum hardly ever drinks. They couldn't seriously think she was falling down because she was drunk.'

'They did. Or they said so, anyway. And they kept on about it. Sally was the worst so I slapped her face,' I said.

'Wow! Actually smacked her round the chops? Didn't you get into trouble? Any boy who starts a fist fight at my school is for it – double detention for a week, and a lecture about anger issues.'

'Well, none of the teachers saw.'

'And Sally didn't tell?'

'No, I suppose not,' I said, shrugging.

'That was quite decent of her,' said Sam.

I was so angry I nearly slapped *him*. 'How can you possibly say that? She was being absolutely vile and hateful about my *mum*. I wish I'd knocked her flying!' I said, biting savagely into my half of the iced bun.

'OK, OK, keep your hair on.' Sam reached across the Formica table and gave my hair a gentle tug.

'I thought you'd be on my side!'

'I am, I am. I'm always on your side.'

'Sticking up for Sally of all people! What's the matter with you? You don't *fancy* her, do you?' I asked, still angry.

'You're the only girl I fancy, seeing as I'm apparently your boyfriend,' said Sam.

'Oh, ha ha,' I said, but I reached out and gave his hand a squeeze. 'Thanks so much for saying that though. Her face was a picture!'

We both made a Sally shocked face simultaneously, and then laughed. The two old ladies at the next table smiled at us benignly.

'Love's young dream!' one whispered loudly to the other, which made us both giggle even more.

'But it's not really funny,' said Sam. 'It's terrible news about your mum. Why don't you just explain the situation to Sally and the others, and then they'll feel awful.'

'I told you, I can't tell anyone. And that means *you* mustn't tell anyone either,' I said urgently.

'But it also means they'll keep on being cruel to you,' said Sam.

'As if I care,' I said, acting tough. 'I can manage. They're just idiots.'

'Your poor mother, though, with this MS thing. It's so unfair when she's had so much to deal with already – your dad going off and everything.' Sam paused. 'It wasn't *why* he left, was it?'

'No, it hadn't started then.' Dad had fallen for horrible Helen, an executive at work. Zara and Rowena and I all hated her, though she tried to be so nicey-nicey to us when Dad took us out on Sundays. We still couldn't understand why Dad liked her better than our lovely mum.

'Does he know about your mum's illness?' Sam asked. I nodded.

'And he *still* won't come back?'

'No, because he's a selfish pig,' I said. When he *did* come back for a few weeks, he acted so martyred and proud of himself for being noble that Mum said he could push off again. She didn't want him back, she could manage fine without him, we all could. And it was true. Even though Mum's had another relapse.

However, when Sam and I got home, Mum really *did* seem fine. She was up and dressed with her hair all silky and fluffy, kneeling on the floor with Rowena, helping her create a plasticine picnic for the hundred and one Sylvanians. Bear was lolling on most of the sofa, watching them.

'Hi, you two,' Mum said brightly. 'I was just thinking about a late lunch, seeing as all the Sylvanians are fed. Zara's out at McDonald's. I thought we could have all have a Bennetburger – even better!'

She'd already made the mixture, and Rowena had helped peel the potatoes, so in fifteen minutes we were eating our own burgers and chips. They were much better than McDonald's too.

'This is extra yummy,' said Sam. 'I wish my mum made burgers. She's on a health kick, so Dad and I have to eat disgusting stuff like quinoa and kale and endless fiddly little pomegranate seeds.'

'Very good for you too,' said Mum. 'But when you need cheering up, it's nice to have something just because it tastes yummy.'

'Do you need cheering up then?' Sam asked.

I glared at him, but he went on smoothly, 'Have you got heaps of lesson plans to do?'

'Yes,' said Mum, sighing. 'But maybe I'll leave them till tomorrow when the girls are out with their father.'

'I'm not going,' I said. 'It's ridiculous making me. We always end up rowing.'

'I don't want to go either,' said Rowena. 'Dad gets cross if I play with my families. He says I'm too old for all that baby stuff.'

Mum sighed again. 'You both have to go. Stop your moaning. You'll probably have a great time. Your dad's always taking you out for treats. Now, who wants a coffee or a juice? And then you guys might like to help me make gingerbread men. Thirty of them!'

'Yes, of course – if Sammy and I can make something afterwards,' I said.

'And I'll bring all the ingredients,' said Sam.

'Don't be so daft, Sam. If it's in the cupboard it's yours,' said Mum. 'You're part of our family. The son I never had.'

'Well, you're like my second mum,' said Sam.

'Please! You're making me go all squirmy,' I said, but inside I was touched.

We had a lovely afternoon. Sam and I cleaned up the kitchen while Mum drank her coffee and Rowena bustled about getting out all the bowls and tins for the gingerbread men. Sam and I did the measuring, and we all took a turn at the rolling and the cutting out, half with two legs, half with a skirt shape.

They didn't take long to bake. When they were cooling we started on the fudge, while Mum sat down at the table with a packet of copy paper and drew thirty outlines of gingerbread people for her class to colour in.

'We haven't got enough brown crayons so I'll tell them they can be rainbow-coloured,' she said.

There wasn't any condensed milk for our fudge in the cupboard, but Sam charged down the road to the local shop and bought a tin.

Then Zara came home and exclaimed over all the sugar I was pouring into the mixing bowl, saying I'd end up with spots. This was a bit pointed, because I was starting to get one or two, especially on my nose. Zara does too, though she lathers ointment on at night and covers her whole face with concealer and foundation during the day so they don't really show.

Still, she was keen enough to help make the fudge, *and* scraped great dollops out of the pan with a spoon.

'Don't you dare have any more! It's not for us, it's for Christmas presents,' I said, shoving her out of the way.

'It's a bit lame giving home-made presents,' she said.

'Is it really?' asked Rowena anxiously. She had started to draw a picture, resting the paper on a tray on the floor. She was huddled over it to hide it, but I could read her writing upside down: *Merry Christmas, Mum.*

'I think they're the very best sort of presents,' I said firmly.

'They're the sort I like most of all,' Mum insisted, and Rowena relaxed.

I hoped Mum really meant it. But I couldn't just give her fudge, could I? It wouldn't even be a surprise because she'd seen us making it. I hoped I'd come up with another idea somehow.

We still had to find little boxes or packets to put the fudge in to make it look pretty. Mum didn't have anything, but Zara redeemed herself by taking the two new pairs of tights she'd just bought out of their cellophane packets and cutting these into little parcels. Rowena contributed some narrow velvet hair ribbons she used to wear on her plaits. When the fudge was completely cold I cut it into squares, which I wrapped in the parcels, and they looked quite pretty.

I kept a square of fudge from each parcel and gave one to Mum, one to Rowena and one to Sam.

'You've already had masses of the mixture, Zara,' I said, and popped the last one in my mouth before she could argue.

Then Sam and I took Bear all the way to the sports centre because he'd been so good all day. It was brightly lit so he could have a good run on the field off his lead. We ran too, racing each other to the old oak right in the corner. Sam is good at all sport, and is in all the teams at his school – but I'm a very speedy runner. We ended up jostling each other, red in the face, and threw ourselves at the oak simultaneously. I was so determined I grazed my hands on the bark.

'Dead heat!' I gasped, wringing my hands.

'Have you hurt yourself?' Sam asked breathlessly. He took hold of one of my hands. 'I bet it stings!'

'It's fine,' I said, just like Mum. I kept hanging onto Sam's hand and squeezed it. 'Thanks so much for being such a sport today, telling Sally you were my boyfriend and all that.'

He squeezed my hand back. 'Well, I am, aren't I?'

Then he leaned forward and kissed me on the lips. It was a quick kiss, over in a couple of seconds. It wasn't really romantic, because we were a bit sweaty from running, and both tasted of fudge. But it was a definite kiss, and Sam had his mouth slightly open, though I kept mine firmly shut.

It felt so weird, him kissing me like that. I didn't know what to say or do. I felt myself blushing and found it difficult to meet his eyes.

'That was a surprise,' I said stupidly.

'A pleasant one?' he asked.

I didn't know what to say. I hadn't really liked him kissing me, but I didn't want to say so in case I hurt his feelings. There was nothing wrong with the kiss itself. It just didn't feel right because it was Sam.

Luckily Bear started barking, hoping we'd start running again, and so we did. Then eventually I put him back on his lead and we walked home. I talked non-stop all the way, going on about Christmas, and how I didn't want to see Dad tomorrow, and how irritatingly superior Zara was nowadays – all kinds of trivial stuff because I was scared Sam might say something serious.

We paused outside my house. I was worried he'd try to kiss me again.

'Your mum's home,' I said quickly, seeing her car in the drive. 'You'd better go back, Sam. Thanks again.'

Then I opened our front door and rushed inside with Bear.

I waited until Zara and I were in bed late that evening.

'Have you ever been kissed, Zara?' I whispered.

'What?' she murmured, half asleep already.

'You know. Kissed by a boy,' I said.

Zara woke up properly. 'Well, of course I have,' she said. 'Heaps of times.'

Heaps? 'Truly?'

'Yes!'

'But you never said.'

'Oh, come on! What do you expect me to do – come barging in and announce it to everyone?' said Zara, yawning and stretching.

'You could have told *me*,' I said, a little hurt. Zara and I used to tell each other everything when we were younger.

'Yes, and you'd have gone *Yuck* and *Oh, Zara, you're such a tart*, and *What on earth do you see in him?*' she said.

I thought about it. 'Probably,' I admitted. 'So who exactly have you kissed?'

'Pete Smith. Toby Royal. Micky Andrews . . .' said Zara.

They were all boys in her class. She was right about my reaction. They were all horrible.

'*All* of them?' I said incredulously.

'At different times, you idiot!' said Zara, reaching out to my bed and giving me a thump. 'I don't kiss, like, *anyone*. Micky was actually my boyfriend, and dead keen on me, but he thought he could boss me around so we broke up.'

'Did you like kissing them?' I asked.

'Well, sort of. Yeah. But they're not really great kissers like Gary.'

'Who's Gary?'

'Gary Masters,' Zara said proudly. 'You know. He's in Year Twelve.'

'Which one?'

'Oh, for heaven's sake! Dark-haired boy with amazing blue eyes. Used to be a bit of a rebel, but clever. You *must* know Gary, Frankie. All the girls fancy him,' she said smugly.

'Is he your boyfriend now?'

'Well, not really. You didn't *ask* that. You said, who have you kissed?'

'So how did it happen? Did he just lunge at you in the school corridor or what?' I asked.

'Of course not! It was at Jude's party – you know, Julie's big sister. Jude's in Year Twelve too. And she had this huge party where she invited heaps of people, and Julie was allowed to ask me. Jude's parents weren't even there, and everyone drank too much and danced and smoked and some of them took drugs too, but I didn't,' said Zara. 'Julie overdid it a bit, but she was OK again after she'd been sick. Don't tell Mum though, will you, or she'll never let me go to another party ever again.'

'Well, promise you won't take any drugs. You're the only big sister I've got.'

'Don't worry about me – I can look after myself,' said Zara. 'And I don't usually get to go to parties like that, worst luck. *Anyway*, someone switched the lights off, and I somehow ended up on the sofa with Gary and it was just incredible. Like, it was just the most amazing experience in the whole world.'

'Zara, you didn't . . . ?'

'It was just kissing. Well, a little bit more. Oh, he's so fantastic, Frankie. I keep seeing him at school, and I'm desperate for him to ask me out, but I suppose he's worried that people will think it weird as he's older than me.'

'Maybe he doesn't even recognize you in daylight,' I said.

'Oh, trust you to be mean and try to spoil it!' said Zara. She plumped up her pillow. 'Shut up and let's go to sleep.'

'I didn't *mean* to be mean,' I said. 'Zara, please! Won't you tell me what it felt like, Gary kissing you? You said it

was incredible and amazing, but they're
everyone uses. Was it just the fact that it was (
you, the boy everyone else fancies?'

'Partly,' said Zara honestly. 'But mostly beca\
made me feel so tingly and helpless and just lovi _ .

'So it didn't just feel like lips touching your lips? It
was more?'

'It was much, much more. Oh, I get it! Someone's kissed
you!' she said.

'Yes. No. Maybe.'

'*Who?*'

'Don't say it like that, as if no one in the whole wide
world would ever want to kiss me,' I said, hurt.

'Yes, but you're young. Thirteen! I hadn't kissed anyone
at thirteen,' said Zara, reluctantly impressed.

'I'm very nearly fourteen, only one year younger than
you!' I snapped.

'You're the one who started asking my advice,' said Zara.

'No I didn't. I don't need your advice, thanks very
much. I just asked you what it felt like, that's all.'

'Why ask me, if you've already done it?' said Zara,
reasonably enough.

'Because it didn't feel like anything,' I said. 'It didn't
feel tingly and all the rest of it.'

'Well, it's not *literally* tingly, like an electric shock,'
said Zara. 'And it depends one hundred per cent on who's
doing the kissing. If one of those totally dumb boys in Year
Nine kissed you, then obviously it wouldn't be very
exciting. Nauseating, more like!'

'He's not dumb,' I insisted, unable to stop myself. I always came to Sam's defence no matter what. And Zara knew it.

'Oh my God, it's Sammy!' she said. 'How *weird*!'

'Why is it weird?' I demanded. 'Sam's the nicest boy I know. And he's very good-looking – everyone thinks so. Even horrible Sally Macclesfield acts like she fancies him. She saw him when we were at Whitelands and she went all flirty.'

'But I thought you and Sammy were just best mates,' said Zara.

'I thought we were too. But then he kissed me when we were in the park,' I said.

'Wasn't he just messing around?'

'I don't think so . . . He told Sally Mac he was my boyfriend. And now he's acting like he *is*.'

'Well, he's kind of a status boyfriend, isn't he? Not in the Gary Masters league, obviously, but heaps of girls would want to go out with someone like Sammy. If he was a couple of years older, *I'd* even consider it,' said Zara.

'So why did the kiss feel wrong?' I asked. It was so important my voice wobbled, as if I was about to start crying.

'Hey,' said Zara. She reached out and found my hand. 'Don't get upset. It just took you by surprise, that's all.'

'I suppose,' I said. 'But I wish he hadn't done it. I want us to stay just friends. *Best* friends – but no lovey-dovey stuff.'

'Well, you'll have to tell him that,' said Zara. 'But I'd still pretend to little Sally Show-Off that he's your boyfriend, just to make her jealous.'

'Good plan,' I said. 'Thanks, Zara.'

'Night then.'

'Night.'

We hadn't had a night-time sisterly chat for a long time, not since Mum told us about her illness. I lay awake thinking about it, and what a terrible shock it had been. I think Zara must have been thinking about it too.

'Are you still awake, Frankie?' she whispered. 'Was Mum OK when you and Sammy were out?'

'Yes, she was fine. I think that lie-in did her good. She helped make the gingerbread people and drew outlines for those little kids in her class. She was just like she used to be. Better, even,' I said.

'Do you think she *could* be getting better?' Zara asked. 'You know, in remission?'

'Maybe,' I said. 'It would be so wonderful if she was. And *some* people never get a recurrence. I know it's only a very few, but it could happen.'

'Then let's pray for a miracle,' said Zara.

I don't think she meant us to pray literally. We're not a religious family at all. But sometimes I pray privately inside my head. I went to sleep praying that Mum would get completely better. Then I prayed that Sam and I could go back to normal tomorrow and stay best friends but without any kissing. Then I prayed that Dad would cry off tomorrow for whatever reason so we could have a quiet cosy Sunday at home with Mum.

It didn't happen. Dad came knocking at our door at ten o'clock, with his jaunty rat-tat-tat-tat-tat-*tat-tat*.

Bear started barking loudly, charging for the door.

'Daddy!' Rowena cried, actually running into the hall.

'What's the big rush, Rowena? He comes every Sunday,' said Zara, but she was in a fluster too, checking her hair in the hall mirror and practising silly smiles as if she was posing for a selfie.

I stayed sitting at the kitchen table with Mum. She could have had a proper lie-in as she wasn't going anywhere, but she was up, showered, dressed in a big stripy shirt and good jeans, with full make-up on, though she rarely bothered with it even on school days. It wasn't because she wanted to impress Dad. It was because she needed to show him that she was coping just fine without him.

'Will you be OK, Mum?' I asked softly.

'Of course. Don't be daft,' she said.

'You won't be lonely?'

'I'll be glad to have a bit of peace,' she said, taking a sip of her coffee. 'Stop worrying about me, Frankie. *I'm* the mother. *I* do the worrying, not you. And actually, I *am* a bit worried. You were ever so quiet last night.'

'It's because I don't feel very well,' I said quickly. 'I've got stomach ache. And a headache. Maybe I'm starting my period at last.'

Zara had started hers when she was in Year Seven. She made quite a lot of fuss over it, needing hot-water bottles and paracetamol and goodness knows what. I was totally dreading having to go through all that performance – but I felt a bit weird being stuck in childhood.

Mum looked a bit concerned. 'Maybe you'd better stay at home then,' she started, but I grinned too quickly. 'Or maybe not! You monster fibber, don't you dare try to kid me! You're going and that's that. And you'll enjoy yourself too.'

'I absolutely won't,' I said.

'Hey, Frankie? Where are you?' Dad called from the hall.

'Go on,' said Mum.

'Frankie?' Dad repeated, and he put his head round the kitchen door. 'Hi, Jen,' he said awkwardly. 'How *are* you?'

He said it every time he saw Mum now, in that special concerned tone. He didn't really care in the slightest, I was sure.

'I'm fine, thank you, Richard,' said Mum briskly. 'Off you go, Frankie.'

I was too old to throw a tantrum. I gave Mum a quick kiss and stomped off with Dad.

'How's my best girl?' he said, giving my shoulders a squeeze.

I'm not his favourite. He says it to Zara and Rowena too, in a clumsy attempt to make us each feel special. I suppose I *was* his favourite once upon a time. Zara giggled at his jokes, and loved it when he made a fuss of her, but I was always the one who helped him wash the car and learned how to change the washer on the tap and sat watching football on the television. On Saturdays we sometimes used to go to the local match, wearing matching bobble hats and long scarves. Dad used to joke that I was his number-one son.

Dad bought me Bear when he was a puppy, and we trained him together and took him for really long walks when he was old enough. When Dad left home, Bear pined for ages. He stood up on the sofa, staring out of the window, looking and looking and looking for him.

Bear's still ecstatic when he sees Dad every Sunday. It just about breaks my heart. I absolutely *hate* seeing him. Well, perhaps there's just a very tiny part of me that wants to fling myself at him like Rowena does.

'Frankie?' Dad said softly. He says it in a wheedling way, as if he can get round me.

I wriggled my shoulders so he had to let go of me. I went to the coat hooks in the hall. I ignored my own jacket and reached for Mum's ancient black fun fur, the one she wears when she gardens in the winter. It's very shabby now, and so huge it makes you look like a yeti, but it smells of Mum's perfume.

'Oh, for God's sake, Frankie, you can't go out in *that*!' said Zara.

She was wearing the precious leather jacket she'd found in an Oxfam shop. It's a skimpy little thing that only comes down to her waist, and one of the buckles is missing so it doesn't even do up properly. She must be freezing cold in it, but she winds a very long fluffy scarf round and round her neck to compensate.

'At least I'll be warm,' I said.

Rowena was the only one of us dressed conventionally, in her padded green jacket with the fur trim round the hood. She always looks so cute when she puts that hood up, like a little goblin.

'Come on, girls. Helen's waiting in the car,' said Dad.

Helen? Dad nearly always took us out by himself. The Helen times were awful. We hated her.

We'd have disliked her even if she hadn't lured away our father. She's like a living Barbie doll, blonde and busty, with an eerily smooth Botoxed face. Some men go off with really young women, but Helen is three years older than Dad. How does that make any sense?

They work in the same big PR agency. She's actually senior to Dad, one of the executives. She was married too, but she got rid of her husband when she fell for Dad. She doesn't have any children. And she needn't think *we're* going to be her steps.

She greeted us with a big smile, showing off her whitened teeth. 'Hi, girls, great to see you!' she gushed. She was wearing an expensive-looking pale camel coat, not a good colour when a big eager dog is around. She made an attempt to pat Bear, dabbing at him clumsily. He growled softly to warn her off. Perhaps we should all growl when she dabs at us.

It was a struggle to get Bear in the back of the car with the three of us, but we managed it.

'Oh dear, you look ever so squashed in the back,' said Helen. 'Especially with the dog.'

'We're fine,' I said. 'Bear's like an enormous hot-water bottle. It's great when it's cold.'

'Where are we going, Dad?' Rowena asked.

'It's a surprise,' he said.

'What kind of a surprise?' asked Zara.

Helen gave a little chuckle. 'I think you're going to like it,' she said.

Zara and Rowena and I exchanged glances. It was so irritating. How did Helen know what we'd like? She didn't really know anything about us. We were never ourselves when we were forced to see her.

It was annoying to find that she *was* right. Dad took us to an enormous Christmas fair up in London. Thousands of other families were there too, so we had to queue for ages to park the car, and Bear got agitated, because the moment the car stops he wants to get out immediately, and he barks with excitement. We were queuing for over twenty minutes so it was very noisy in the car.

'Can't you get him to stop, Frankie?' Helen asked, her hands over her ears in an affected way.

'They don't make dogs with volume control, Helen. I can't mute him with the press of a button,' I said.

'Frankie! Less of the cheek!' said Dad.

'I wasn't being cheeky. I was simply stating a fact.'

'Look, that little dog in the car in front isn't barking his head off. Perhaps you could see a dog behaviourist who would help you train Bear,' Helen suggested.

'Bear is beautifully trained,' I said indignantly, which was clearly a preposterous lie. 'If you knew anything about dogs, you'd understand that it's simply in a German Shepherd's nature to bark to express himself.'

'I think we need a child behaviourist to train you to stop that lippiness, Frankie,' said Dad. He was kind of joking, but I could see he was getting annoyed.

'I think a child behaviourist would say rude behaviour is common in children from a broken home,' I said. 'Think about it, Dad.'

That shut him up. Zara widened her eyes to indicate I'd gone too far. I tried to act cool but my heart was thumping hard. Even *I* didn't like the way I was behaving. I sounded like a spoiled brat. I couldn't seem to help it when I was with Dad now. I was even worse when Helen was around too.

I kept thinking of Mum at home, all on her own. My eyes started stinging. I fought desperately hard not to cry. Rowena reached out and gave my hand a squeeze, and Zara wound a thread round and round one of the big buttons on Mum's coat to stop it falling off. It was comforting to be wedged between my sisters.

'Perhaps it would be more sensible if we left Bear at home when we went on an outing?' said Helen.

Even Dad seemed to think this a stupid suggestion. 'We can't leave him behind. The girls think of him as family,' he said.

'And you're not, Helen,' I muttered.

It looked like it was going to be a disastrous day, but when we'd parked at last we actually had a great time.

There were lots of Christmas stalls selling all kinds of things – even fudge in little bags tied with ribbon, though mine looked just as good, if not better.

Dad bought us all a little Christmas treat. Zara picked out a bright red lipstick called Hollyberry, and Rowena chose a hairband with reindeer antlers attached.

'We'll rub some of Zara's lipstick on the end of your nose and then we can call you Rudolph,' said Dad. 'And I'd better be Father Christmas!'

He bought himself a silly Santa hat, which made Zara and me cringe, though Rowena laughed and said it suited him. Then Helen said she wanted a Santa hat too.

'I can be Mrs Santa,' she said. This was beyond dreadful. She looked a perfect fool, though several men smiled at her appreciatively. Dad spotted me pulling a disgusted face. He gave my shoulder a little pat as if he were sorry for me. Did he think I was *jealous*?

'What shall we get you, Frankie? Would you like some lipstick too? You're allowed make-up now, aren't you?' he said.

'I don't like make-up, thanks,' I said. I'd tried wearing it but my hand always wobbled when I tried to do the line round my eyes and I forgot I was wearing it. I'd rub my eyes absent-mindedly and end up with black mascara marks all down my cheeks. I'd only tried lipstick once, but I hated the slimy feel and the taste of it.

'Well, what *would* you like?' Dad asked.

I shrugged. 'I don't really want anything, Dad. I'm fine,' I muttered.

Then I saw a stall of brightly painted wooden toys. There were nutcracker men with shiny black hats and those Russian dolls that fit inside each other. I stopped to look, though I was obviously too old for toys. At the back of the stall I spotted a little carved bear, about as big as my finger. He wasn't painted, he was his own dark wood colour. He wasn't jointed, so you couldn't walk him along or make him prowl on all fours. He was a totally pointless little ornament – but I wanted him passionately.

'What are you looking at, Frankie? The Russian dolls?' Dad asked.

'No. Nothing. Well, I do quite like that little bear,' I said.

My own Bear heard his name and looked up eagerly.

Dad laughed. 'OK. Our Bear approves too. We'll buy you the little wooden one.'

The little carved bear was surprisingly expensive, and I felt dreadful, but Dad bought him for me without hesitation.

'Thank you so much, Dad,' I said guiltily. I didn't want him to think I'd deliberately chosen something that cost a lot.

'Aren't you a lucky girl, Frankie!' said Helen pointedly.

The girl at the stall wrapped my bear up in red tissue paper secured with a narrow gold ribbon. I clutched him in my hand, feeling the shape of his head and torso and limbs through the thin paper. He was like a little talisman. I decided to call him Lucky.

He did seem to make the day lucky too. We had enormous hot dogs for lunch. I shared my sausage with

Bear, who wolfed it down joyfully. Then we went round the funfair part, and Dad had *fifteen* goes at the teddy stall until he won one for Rowena. It was nearly as big as her and she could barely see where she was going when she carried him, but she hung onto him happily, smiling from ear to ear.

'It's the day of the teddies, girls!' said Dad. 'Let's find you one too, Zara.'

We found a jewellery stall with tiny earrings: little hearts, birds, stars, butterflies – and silver teddy-bear heads. Dad bought Zara a pair, though he'd been furious last year when he discovered she'd had her ears pierced.

'What in the world was your mother thinking of?' he'd demanded angrily, which was so unfair.

Still, he was all smiles now, and suggested we go on the big wheel. We couldn't take Bear with us, but Helen said she'd wait with him.

'You're a star, sweetheart,' Dad murmured.

'Twinkle twinkle,' said Helen.

'I'll stay with her,' I said. I desperately wanted to go on the wheel. It was enormous, the biggest one I'd ever seen. It looked incredible. I'd love showing off about it to Sam. But I didn't trust Helen with Bear. She didn't understand dogs – she didn't even like them. If he got a bit grumpy she'd panic.

'No, I will!' said Rowena.

I thought she was just being incredibly noble, but it turned out she was scared of going on the wheel, especially when we were near enough to hear people screaming.

'That's just because they're having fun,' I said.

'I don't like that kind of fun,' Rowena said firmly.

She stayed with Helen and Bear, and I was free to enjoy the ride. Rowena might only be little, but she understood Bear and knew how to manage him.

Zara looked a bit pale when we got to the front of the queue. 'Maybe I won't go after all. I feel a bit sick actually,' she mumbled.

Even Dad didn't look too keen now. But the three of us climbed into the swaying seat and the fairground guy clicked our safety bar into place.

'It doesn't seem very safe to me,' said Dad. 'You girls could easily slip under that bar.' He put his arms firmly round both of us, holding us tight.

I hadn't been so close to Dad since he left us. I'd clung to him then, begging him not to go. And when he did I'd vowed never, ever to forgive him. But now his warm familiar smell of toast and clean shirt and lemony aftershave was overwhelming, and I felt like a little girl again, loving him painfully.

Our seat rose into the air and we all gasped. I put the little carved bear in my pocket in case I dropped him. But we weren't going fast at all, just edging gradually upwards, while people took their seats underneath us.

'It's not as bad as I thought it would be,' said Zara.

'You wait,' Dad told her.

When every seat was taken, the wheel suddenly started spinning, faster and faster, until the fair below us was just a kaleidoscope of colour. Zara screamed, I screamed, Dad screamed, as we whirled round and round. It seemed as if, any second, the whole thing might break free and cartwheel across the sky.

When we staggered off at last, we saw the photos taken automatically during the ride. We looked like zombies, our eyes squeezed shut and our mouths stretched wide.

'Shall we buy it as a memento of a happy day?' said Dad.

'No, *don't*, Dad! I look awful! Look at my hair! And I've smudged my lipstick!' Zara wailed.

'Maybe we don't look at our finest,' said Dad.

He found an actual photo stall instead, where families could have their picture taken with Santa Claus.

'We'll have a proper portrait,' said Dad.

The photographer arranged us carefully, Rowena sitting at Santa's feet clutching her teddy bear, Zara on one side, and Bear and me on the other.

'You go at the back, Mum and Dad,' he said.

We all froze. *Mum!* Even Helen looked embarrassed.

'I don't think you need us grown-ups in the photo. Let's just have the children,' she said quickly.

So Zara and Rowena and I smiled obediently, and when we came back from another circuit of the fair the photo was pinned up on the board waiting for us.

It was actually a good one. Well, the yeti coat did look a bit odd, and Zara's lipstick was very bright, and Rowena's face was half hidden behind her new teddy – but we were all smiling. It came in its own photo frame, with tiny silver sparkles to make it look frosty. It was perfect.

'My best girls,' said Dad, looking pleased.

He obviously wanted to keep it. But I needed it now. I waited until we got back to his new place. It's not a very big flat and Bear always takes up a lot of space. He wagged his tail just as Helen had made us all hot chocolate, and sent the plate of marshmallows flying. Dad went to get some more, and I went with him.

'Thanks for a lovely day, Dad,' I said.

'That's OK, darling,' he said, looking touched.

'I wish we'd had two photos taken. I'd love to have one too,' I said. 'To remember today being so special.'

'Well, look, you can have this photo if you really want it.'

'Really?' I said.

'Of course!' Dad said fondly.

I didn't want the photo for me. I knew it would make the perfect Christmas present for Mum.

On Monday Mum dropped Zara and me off at school really early so she could prepare for the gingerbread-man lesson. Zara rushed off to join her friends at breakfast club and catch up on all the gossip. I didn't feel inclined to hang around in my classroom. I didn't want to hear Sally Mac and Marnie saying stupid things about Sam.

I wandered down the corridor and up the stairs to the library, just in case it was open before school started. Mr White was at his desk, writing in a black Moleskine notebook, so absorbed that he jumped when I came up to him.

'Frankie! Hello, there. Bright and early this morning, I see,' he said, smiling at me. He had a lovely rosy face and a shortish haircut that made him look like a little boy, though he was probably fifty or so. I loved his clothes. They weren't at all school-teachery. Today he wore a bright blue checked shirt with a vivid green pullover, black cord trousers, and a pair of blue suede shoes.

He saw me staring down at them. 'I'm rocking my Elvis look today,' he said.

'I think you look very dashing, Mr White,' I said. 'Is it OK to be here? I don't want to disturb you.'

'You're very welcome. Whenever I'm here, consider the library open. Join my regular early birds,' he said, gesturing.

There were two smallish boys from Year Seven playing games on the computers. One had very large sticking-out ears and the other had ginger curls and glasses. They had deep frowns of concentration on their faces. There was a cluster of Year Elevens doing their homework at a round table, comparing notes and copying. And there was Ivneet sitting at a table by herself, colouring an intricate pink and red and blue design with her felt-tip pens. I was surprised to see an ultra clever girl like Ivneet doing something as childish as colouring.

I wandered across and peered over her shoulder. I was startled. She wasn't colouring a pretty pattern. She was shading in different parts of a dissected human body.

'Goodness!' I said.

'I suppose it does look a bit ghoulish,' she said, colouring a long line of blue vein.

'Well, I like ghoulish,' I said. 'I've been toying with the idea of dyeing my hair black and becoming a Goth.' I hadn't even thought of it before. I just wanted to make myself sound interesting.

Ivneet nodded, her teeth catching her lip in concentration.

'You should be one too. You've already got black hair,' I said.

'It would be a bit high-maintenance for me, seeing as Goth girls have chalk-white complexions,' she pointed out.

I felt stupid, but she smiled to show she was joking. Then she went on colouring, murmuring under her breath.

'Sorry?' I said.

'I'm just repeating all the medical words, trying to learn them by heart,' said Ivneet. 'I want to be a surgeon when I'm grown up.'

'Oh, I see.' I was impressed she was already preparing for her career when she was only in Year Nine like me.

'What do you want to do, Frankie, apart from becoming a Goth?' she asked.

'I want to write, but I'm not sure that's a proper career. When I was little I wanted to be a vet, but I didn't realize you had to be brilliant at exams, and I'm not,' I said.

'You generally come near the top in class,' said Ivneet.

'Yes, but I'm never first like you, not even in my best subjects.'

'I have an unfair advantage in that I've got a photographic memory.' Ivneet wasn't showing off, she was simply stating a fact.

'And clearly a very high IQ,' I said.

'Yes. How sickening of me,' said Ivneet.

I hadn't realized she could be so dry. I'd always dismissed her as the geeky girl who always knew the answers, but now I decided I rather liked her. I liked her colouring book too. If I had one like that, I wouldn't stick to the appropriate colours. I'd invent a new exotic race with green and purple organs and silver blood in their veins.

I felt a bit awkward hovering by her side, so I wandered off and peered at the books.

'If you're in a Gothic mood, why not give *Frankenstein* a go?' Mr White suggested.

'I didn't know it was a book – I thought it was just an old film,' I said.

'A very good book, written by a teenager,' said Mr White, finding it on the shelves.

'A teenager? Seriously?'

'Mary Shelley. She was nineteen and already married to Percy Bysshe and had a baby.'

She sounded interesting, but *Frankenstein* was a Penguin Classic and I thought it might be very hard work reading it. Still, I wanted to impress Mr White so I said it looked brilliant.

'I'll put it on my list of books to read,' I said.

'I like a student who takes on a reading challenge,' said Mr White, and he offered me a jelly baby from a crumpled paper bag in the top drawer of his desk. 'My wicked secret.' He patted his tummy ruefully. 'No wonder my trousers are getting too tight. You can have the last black jelly baby if you like, little Goth.'

I took it, smiling. I was so pleased he had a sweet tooth. He'd love a little packet of home-made fudge as a Christmas present.

He had a special box of ex-library books that had got a bit battered, selling for 50p each. I shuffled through them, wondering if there might be anything suitable for Sam – then I'd have all my Christmas presents settled. (Unless I weakened and gave Dad something after all.)

They were mostly too jokey or too girly, not Sam's taste at all, but then I came across a book called *The Chrysalids*. Some idiot had scribbled all over the cover but I could just about make out a picture of a footprint. It had six toes.

'Is this science fiction, Mr White?' I said.

'Yes, it is. It's very good. I've ordered a new copy as this one's been desecrated. Sharpies cause almost as much harm as knives, in my opinion,' he said, sighing. 'I think you'd enjoy it, maybe even more than *Frankenstein*.'

'It's not for me, actually, it's for a friend, but I suppose I could have a sneak peek first,' I said, scrabbling in my bag for my purse. I dropped 50p into a glass jar of silver coins. 'Is this your private jelly-baby fund?' I asked.

'I wish,' said Mr White.

Just then the ten-minute bell went.

'Come along, young people. Off to your various classrooms,' he called. He closed his black Moleskine notebook with a sigh. 'Work beckons for us all.'

'So is that your diary, Mr White?' I asked. I'd glimpsed the word *Monday* at the top of the page.

'It's a work of fiction, but in diary form. That's why I'm not typing it straight onto the computer. I'm trying for an authentic feel,' he explained.

'I didn't know you were a writer,' I said, interested.

'I'm not. Though I'd like to be. I thought I'd have a go at writing a children's book. What do you think, Frankie? Most kids like reading stuff in a diary format, don't they? Think of all those Wimpy Kid books,' he said.

'And Tom Gates,' I said.

'And then of course there's Adrian Mole. Hmm. Maybe the marketplace is a bit crowded,' said Mr White, sighing. 'Maybe I'll never make it as a writer.'

'I want to be a writer too,' I told him.

'Well, how about we start a school writing group?' he said. 'For all us library supporters.'

He looked at the two Year Seven boys jostling each other at the computer. 'Would you like to join a writing group, boys?' he asked.

'You mean like writing *stories*, Mr White?' they said in chorus.

'No need to look so disgusted, George and Peter. You could invent a whole new scenario for a computer game. That's writing, after all.'

'We don't have to, do we?' asked the ginger-haired one, George.

'No thanks, Mr White!' said Peter, the one who had the distinctive ears. 'We want to *play* games, not write them, don't we, Ginger?'

Mr White looked at the Year Elevens stuffing textbooks and files and paper back into their school bags. 'What about you guys?' he asked.

'Per-lease, Mr White! We don't have the time,' said one, answering for the group.

'Or doubtless the inclination,' he said, sighing.

'I'll join,' said Ivneet.

'That's very tactful of you, Ivneet,' said Mr White. 'But you always seem to be doing so much studying too.'

'My parents are nagging me to get some hobbies. They want me to grow up well rounded.' She paused. 'And they know it will look good on my UCAS form when I apply to university.'

'You're way too young to be thinking about university,' said the biggest boy in the Year Eleven group. 'You haven't even done your GCSEs yet!'

'Maybe I'm so brilliant I've done them already,' said Ivneet, deadpan.

They rolled their eyes derisively. She laughed when they shuffled out of the library clutching their bulging school bags.

'You haven't really done your GCSEs, have you?' I asked.

'Of course not!'

'You'd better get going, girls. The final bell is going to clang at any moment,' said Mr White.

I wished I could stay in the library all day long. I sighed as I said goodbye to Mr White and walked down the corridor, clutching *The Chrysalids*.

'Do you think he's serious about this writing group?' Ivneet asked.

'I hope so,' I said. 'It might be fun.'

The bell went. We were supposed to be in our classroom within a minute, but I dawdled down the stairs as slowly as I could. I thought Ivneet would hurry on ahead of me, but she stayed by my side.

As we approached the classroom she said softly, 'Just smile at them in a superior way if they start having a go at you.'

I was startled. I hadn't realized the whole class knew that Sally and her gang were being hateful to me. I didn't want Ivneet feeling sorry for me.

'As if I care about them,' I said. I flicked my hair over my shoulders and marched into the classroom, my head held high.

Miss Eliot was at her desk, looking irritated. 'You're late, girls. Hurry up! Ivneet, I'm surprised at you!'

I looked up, up, up as I went towards my desk – and then tripped over the strap of someone's school bag. There was a titter of laugher when I staggered.

'Try to stop clowning about, Francesca,' said Miss Eliot before starting to take registration.

Did she think I was doing it on purpose? I sat down hurriedly, trying not to look in Sally's direction. It was almost a relief that it was double maths, the most terrible start to the week. Miss Eliot took it herself, and she was very strict. Most teachers let us muck around a bit the last week of term, but Miss Eliot's only concession to the time of the year was to set us a complicated problem about the transportation of Christmas trees to a marketplace.

I felt even more woolly-headed than usual and didn't know where to begin, let alone how to proceed. As we struggled, Miss Eliot started marking our maths homework. I was pretty certain I'd got all those sums right because Sam was a genius at maths. Perhaps I should have made a few deliberate mistakes. Miss Eliot would sense something suspicious if I got ten out of ten for my homework.

Ivneet was sitting at a desk in front of me, her pen working steadily down the page of her maths notebook. She already had a long tail of answers, as neat and tidy as the plait down her back.

Halfway through the second lesson Miss Eliot started giving back the marked notebooks. I waited, heart thudding. She stood beside my desk, peering down at the incoherent workings on my page. I'd abandoned the first question, bodged the second and was stuck on the third.

'Mmm,' she said wryly. 'Struggling, are we?'

'Yes, Miss Eliot.'

'So it looks as if you had a little private tuition over the weekend . . .'

I nodded. There was no point pretending.

Miss Eliot shook her head.

'Now the Frankfurter's for it!' Marnie whispered to Sally. It was a very loud whisper.

Perhaps Miss Eliot saw me twitching. 'Oh well, you clearly need further tuition over the Christmas holidays,

Francesca, so you can shine in class too,' she said, and moved on.

I couldn't believe it. She'd never been so easy on anyone else. And when she handed back Marnie's homework, Miss Eliot was very tart with her, saying she really had to try harder.

I was dreading break time. I was dying to go to the loo but didn't like to go to the girls' toilets. I was pretty sure they'd be in there, waiting for me. Zara saw me sitting on the steps in the playground, writing in my school jotter, and left her friends to come over.

'You OK, Frankie?'

'Yes, of course,' I said.

'You look a bit fed up,' she said. 'Have Sally and those others been bullying you again?'

'I'm not being bullied,' I insisted. 'They say stupid stuff, but it doesn't bother me.'

'OK, OK. Keep your hair on. What are you doing anyway? Not homework?'

'I'm planning a new story. Mr White's started up a special writing group,' I said.

'Seriously? What, just for the geeky library lot?' asked Zara. 'You don't want to hang out with them, Frankie. They're so not cool. It'll only make the Sally Mac gang pick on you even more.'

'Did I ask for your advice? Just push off, Zara. I'm fine,' I said.

'OK. Suit yourself. Loser!' said Zara, and she flounced off back to her friends.

After that I *had* to face the toilets, because I was scared I was going to burst into tears. Thank goodness Sally and her gang weren't there after all. I hated being called a loser, especially by Zara. I knew she'd tried to be kind to me. I shouldn't have told her to push off. But she was only making me feel worse. Anyway, what was wrong with the library crowd? What was so dreadful about being a geek? Ivneet was very bright and hard-working, and it seemed certain she'd achieve her dream and be a surgeon one day. Zara wanted to be a famous YouTuber, like a million other girls. She practised demonstrating make-up and hairstyles, staring into the mirror on her dressing table. She wasn't very good at it. In fact, she sounded pretty dreadful – affected and self-conscious.

I looked down at the few sentences I'd scribbled in my jotter about the agonies of a transparent green boy in a world of purple people who sneered at him. He cried copious chartreuse tears. Wasn't *that* affected and self-conscious? I wasn't even sure chartreuse was a green drink.

I tore the page into tiny shreds and threw them down the loo. Then the bell went for the end of break. I thought of all the other bells clanging, until at last the bell at twenty to four signalled home time, with Mum and Rowena coming to pick us up in the car.

What if Mum's eyes went funny again or she had another stumble? How would we manage if she couldn't drive any more, couldn't work? I felt as if my brain was swelling like a balloon with all these worries. The rest of morning school seemed interminable.

I had the canteen ordeal to get through next. I wished Ivneet didn't sometimes go home for lunch. I selected a triangle of pizza and some salad, and then looked around for somewhere to sit. It was absolutely heaving. There was one space at a table of Year Nine boys. They'd been my mates once, when we'd played football together, but they didn't seem to like me any more.

'Get lost, Frankie,' they said – or words to that effect.

I kept hold of my tray and tried to spot another spare seat.

'Hey, Frankie. Come and sit with me! I'm all by myself.'

It was Sally Macclesfield! She was sitting with spare chairs around her.

It was a trick, of course. I was the last person in the world she'd want to sit with. And she wasn't all by herself. I could see Marnie and Georgia and Scarlett standing in the pudding queue, waiting for trifle, everyone's favourite.

'Come on,' said Sally, and she patted the chair beside her. The sun was shining right onto her through the canteen window, making her blonde hair glow like gold. She was the sort of girl who could look stylish even in school uniform. She had her sleeves rolled up, showing her slender white wrists. She'd inked a little bluebird on one, and on the other she had a scarlet thread bracelet with a tiny gold heart charm. Mock tattoos and jewellery were forbidden at school, of course, but Sally didn't care.

She smiled at me in a friendly way. I was certain she was playing games with me, but I found myself sitting down beside her.

'Hey there,' she said softly. She looked at my single slice of pizza and salad. 'That's not much.'

She had a large plate of chips with a pool of tomato sauce on the side. She dipped a chip in the sauce, nibbled it, and then pushed the plate in front of me. 'Go on, help yourself.'

'No thanks.' I stared at her flawless skin. 'How do you manage to stuff yourself with chips and never get spots?' I asked.

She grinned. 'Will power,' she said. 'How do *you* manage to get the hottest guy in town as a boyfriend?'

Ah! So this was all about Sam. OK, I could joke too.

'It's my fatal attraction,' I said, picking up my pizza slice and taking a bite.

Sally laughed. 'You never even said you had a boyfriend, let alone one like *him*.'

'What do you want me to do? Go round school with a megaphone announcing it?' I said.

'So where did you meet? At the Gold Star?'

The Gold Star was the nightclub in town. You had to be eighteen to get in, and they were very strict about it too, but on Fridays they lowered the age to fourteen. Zara was desperate to go, but Mum wouldn't let her, as it had a reputation for drug-taking and fights.

'Do you really think *I* could blag myself into the Gold Star?' I said to Sally.

'Maybe not,' she said. 'So, did you just bump into your Sammy somewhere?'

'It wasn't that difficult. He lives next door. We've been bumping into each other since we were toddlers,' I said.

'Oh, you lucky thing!'

Marnie and Georgia and Scarlett came over, each balancing a big portion of trifle. They looked at me in astonishment.

'Get out of my seat, Frankfurter!' said Marnie.

'Hey, don't be like that,' said Sally. 'Sit on my other side, Marnie. Frankie's just telling me about her boyfriend – you know, the one we saw at Whitelands. Though is he *really* your boyfriend, Frankie? Aren't you just boy-and-girl-next-door pals? I mean, there's no romance going on, is there? Kissing?'

I thought about Sam's kiss in the park and felt my cheeks going hot.

'You're blushing! So you *do* kiss?'

'What else do you do then?' Marnie said, sitting down. She made some crude suggestions and I blushed more.

'No! And mind your own business,' I said.

'Yes, shut up, Marnie. You're just jealous because you've never kissed a boy,' said Sally.

Marnie looked stunned. We all were. Sally was snubbing her best friend and sticking up for me!

'How old is he then, Frankie?' Scarlett asked. '*My* boyfriend's sixteen.'

'Sammy's our age,' I said.

'Boys our age are so immature,' she said.

'If you're talking about Mike, I don't think it's very mature to get drunk on six cans of lager and then spew up all over your mother's sofa,' said Sally. 'And he's not really your boyfriend anyway – he's your brother's best mate, that's all. None of you have a proper boyfriend.'

'*I* have,' said Georgia. 'Jake.'

'Jake!' exclaimed Sally. 'The lovely, adorable Jake who's sent you a couple of texts since you met on holiday. The romance of the century.'

'Why are you being so mean, Sally?' asked Scarlett.

'Because you all get on my nerves sometimes,' she said. She stood up. 'Come on then.'

'We haven't finished our trifle!' said Marnie.

'Well, you guys carry on guzzling. Come on, Frankie.'

I couldn't believe this was happening. Everything had changed so quickly. It was as if I'd entered another dimension. I knew that Sally was only interested in me because of Sam. She was acting nice to me now, but I still hated her, didn't I? Why was I standing up too? Why was I going off with her?

'Come with me,' said Sally.

We walked across the playground together, right to the fence at the end. The gate was locked and bolted, because it was strictly forbidden to go into the orchard behind. Sally vaulted right over the gate, and so I did too.

I'd been there once before, to rescue a football. The boys all dared me – so I did. It wasn't really a big deal. It wasn't as if it was a special secret garden with wonderful flowers. It was only an old orchard with small stunted trees, and all the apples were maggot-ridden and sour. In December there weren't even any apples, and the ground had so many rabbit holes you had to watch where you were going or you'd twist your ankle. But somehow it felt as if Sally and I were wandering in an enchanted wood.

She jumped up to grasp an overhanging branch and swung herself backwards and forwards, laughing. 'You're staring at me,' she said.

'Well, you're acting so weird,' I said. '*Why* were you so mean to Marnie and Georgia and Scarlett just then?'

'Because they get on my nerves sometimes. They'll get over it. What do you care anyway? They've all been mean to you.'

'Yes, and you've been the meanest of all, Sally Mac,' I said.

'You shouldn't have slapped my face like that, in front of everyone,' she told me, jumping back down.

'You shouldn't have been so hateful about my mum,' I said.

'I know,' said Sally meekly, taking me by surprise.

'She isn't a drunk. She's ill,' I said.

'Really?'

'*Yes.* Only I don't want anyone to know.'

'I don't want anyone to know about *my* mother. Because she *is* a drunk,' said Sally.

I thought maybe she was just saying it for effect. I probably looked suspicious, because she took hold of my elbow.

'She is,' said Sally. 'I don't just mean she gets a bit tiddly at parties. Before she even gets home she's had several glasses of wine with the people at work. And then she opens another bottle and carries on. She's all chatty at first, and she can be quite funny, I suppose, but she never stops at that stage. She starts getting sarcastic, picking holes in everything Dad says and does, and that's when my brother and I clear off to bed. You can still hear her ranting away though, even if you put a pillow over your head. And then sometimes she rushes upstairs sobbing and comes into my room and cries about her life being rubbish, all self-pitying and maudlin. Sometimes she just passes out on the sofa. If I go downstairs for a glass of milk, she's lying there, snoring away, with her mouth open, drooling.' Sally said it all in a rush, her face getting pinker and pinker. 'There. I haven't told anyone else that. Not even Marnie. She envies me my high-flying executive mother. If she only knew what she's really like!'

'So why on earth be so horrible about *my* mum?'

'I don't *know*. I just started saying it. I can't seem to help it. I turned myself into your worst enemy when I actually wanted to be your friend,' said Sally. 'There's something about you. You don't suck up to me all the time. You act like you don't care what people think of you. You've never even said a word about Sammy. If any of us had a boyfriend like that we'd be showing off like mad.'

'He's just *Sammy*. It's not like he's on YouTube with a million followers,' I said.

'Where does he go to school? The grammar?'

I nodded.

'I thought so! So he's a total brainbox as well as hot?'

'I suppose.'

'And you hang out together a lot?'

'Most of the time,' I said, shrugging.

'I bet your sister fancies him, even though she's older,' said Sally.

'No she doesn't!'

'But *you* fancy him?'

'Well, of course,' I said, after a little pause.

'You don't sound very enthusiastic!' said Sally. 'Like you take him totally for granted!'

'I've known him all my life, so it's different for us,' I explained.

'So what's going to happen, do you think? You'll stay childhood sweethearts and go to the same uni and set up home together?' Sally asked.

'Perhaps,' I said.

'You're not so keen on that idea?' Sally put her head on one side. She was looking at me intently.

I shrugged. 'Yes. No. *Maybe*. What about you?'

'Oh, I've got it all mapped out,' she said. 'I'm going to get Sammy to go out with me instead, and *we'll* be the childhood sweethearts and all the rest of it, blah blah blah, walking off into the sunset together hand in hand. Oh, your face, Frankie. I'm *joking*!'

'You'd better be!' I said.

I heard the distant ringing of the bell for afternoon school. Sally didn't seem to hear it. She was dancing round and round in the tufty grass, waving her arms in the air.

Then she tripped in a rabbit hole and nearly lost her footing. 'Whoops!'

'Are you OK?'

'Course I am,' said Sally, quickly rubbing her ankle and then starting to dance again.

'Anyway, the bell's gone,' I said.

'I know.' She jumped up to grab another branch and made her feet polka in the air. She was immensely good at it and made me laugh.

'Come on then!' I said.

'Not coming,' said Sally. 'Neither are you. We're going to stay here in this gnarly old orchard and have fun. Who wants to do . . . What the hell is it?'

'Biology. And then double PE.'

'Well, we'll do them here. We'll look at flowers and their petals and sepals and what have you—'

'It's December, idiot. No flowers,' I said.

'Then trees! And for PE we'll climb *trees* rather than boring ropes. And we'll run around in circles and dance,' said Sally.

'And fall down more rabbit holes.'

'And have a cup of tea with the Hatter and the March Hare and the Dormouse,' said Sally.

'When I was little, Mum made us fancy-dress costumes for some summer fete. Zara was the Hatter with a proper top hat and a checked coat, and I was the March Hare with long ears and whiskers, and my little sister Rowena looked adorable as a sleepy little Dormouse. We came second,' I said.

'You should have had me as Alice, then you'd have come first,' said Sally. 'What about Sammy?'

'He was going through a *Star Wars* phase and already had a Luke Skywalker costume,' I said. 'Sally, we're going to be ever so late. We have to go now,' I insisted.

'We don't *have* to do anything. We can just stay here and chill.'

'We'll get into so much trouble.'

'Oh dear, I'm so fwightened!' said Sally in a little girly voice.

'Look, I don't really care either, but if we play truant someone will ring my mum and I don't want her to get stressed. It's not good for her,' I said uncomfortably.

'Mine wouldn't notice if I stayed out for a week,' said Sally, but she jumped down from the tree and started walking back towards school. 'So what illness has she got?'

I took a deep breath. 'Promise not to tell. Not even Marnie?'

'I actually tell her very little,' said Sally. 'Go on. I totally promise.'

'Well, she has MS.' I tried to say it casually, but my voice went wobbly.

'MS? What, that illness where teenage girls can hardly get out of bed?'

'That's M*E*. Totally different. MS is a neurological disease. It affects your nerve fibres and your nerve cells. They gradually conk out,' I said.

'That's awful. So how long will it take your mum to get better?' Sally asked.

'She won't,' I said.

'What? Not ever?'

'Well, she's OK some of the time, but then suddenly something goes wrong and it can take weeks to get right again. Or it doesn't get right at all. And she's always so tired now. She has to go to bed right after tea sometimes,' I said. It felt so weird saying it all out loud. I felt a tear roll down my cheek and prayed Sally wouldn't notice.

'You're crying,' she said softly, and then she put her arm round me and kissed my cheek. 'No wonder you slapped me. Like I said, I'm so, so sorry. Come on then, let's hurry. I'll make something up so we won't get into trouble.'

She started running and I ran after her, in a daze. Sally Mac had just kissed my cheek! We weren't worst enemies any more. She was acting like we were best friends.

'I'm so sorry we're so late, Miss Eliot,' she said when we burst into our classroom to get our school bags for the afternoon. 'It's all my fault. I was messing about doing this silly dance and twisted my ankle. I could hardly walk at first, but Frankie was so kind and helpful, and massaged it until it was better.'

Miss Eliot stared at us. She was well aware that we were deadly enemies. It seemed so unlikely that she ignored Sally and looked at me.

'Frankie?' she said. 'Did Sally really twist her ankle?'

'Yes, she did, but I don't think it's a proper sprain. She can walk on it now, more or less,' I said.

'Well, she'd better hobble off to biology pronto,' said Miss Eliot. 'And you too, little Florence Nightingale.'

When we were out in the corridor Sally high-fived me. 'See! I told you we wouldn't get into trouble,' she said.

Well, we did actually, because Mr Peters, the biology teacher, gave us a pompous little lecture and set us extra homework – as if I cared. Sally kept catching my eye, and it was hard not to burst out laughing. Then Sally and I were on the same team in netball and I scored three goals and all my team patted me on the back and Sally gave me a hug in front of everyone. Marnie and Georgia and Scarlett huddled in a corner, whispering like the three witches in *Macbeth* trying to hex me.

I practically skipped out of school I was so happy. Mum and Rowena were waiting at the gate. They looked like they'd had a good day too. Rowena was holding a baby badger wearing a minute pink nappy knitted in embroidery thread.

'Look, I was playing Sylvanians with my friend Molly and we did swapsies and I've got Baby Betty Badger – isn't she sweet? Molly's nan knitted the nappy. I don't think it comes off, but isn't it adorable?' said Rowena. 'Such teeny weeny stitches. Could you make a little nappy like that, Mum?'

'No, I could never make a little pink nappy for a tiny badger, but actually it's not high on the list of things I agonize about,' said Mum cheerfully.

'Did your kids like the gingerbread-man lesson?' I asked.

'They loved it! Well, Danny Diddums got a bit whiny and spat his gingerbread man out because he said it tasted horrid – but he's always a pain,' she said.

I'd never set eyes on this Danny Diddums, and he obviously had a different surname, but we all loved Mum's tales about teaching him. Rowena sometimes asked for them instead of a bedtime story. She listened to *'The Day Danny Diddums stuck a Smartie up his nose'*; *'The Day Danny Diddums wet his trousers and insisted the boy next to him in class had made the puddle'*; *'The Day Danny Diddums stole a unicorn pencil from a little girl and denied all knowledge of it, even though the head was sticking out of his jumper'*.

We were all laughing about Danny as Sally and Marnie and Georgia and Scarlett came out of school together. They seemed to have made friends again. Sally was looking at Mum. She came right up to her.

My stomach churned. I tasted a little bit of sick in my mouth. Had she been playing a trick on me? Maybe she wasn't really a friend now, even though she'd said she was sorry and kissed me. And I'd told her that Mum had MS when I knew it was meant to be a strict secret.

Sally opened her mouth and I stood there, dying. But she simply said, 'Hi, Mrs Bennet. Frankie scored three goals at netball. She was ace!' and then she walked on, the other three following.

Mum raised her eyebrows. 'Isn't that Sally? I thought you'd gone off her?' she whispered.

'Well, we've kind of made friends again,' I said.

'Good Lord.'

'Oh, Mum!' said Rowena. 'That's what girls are like. Me and Molly are forever breaking friends and then making friends.'

'I know you are, darling,' said Mum. 'You're right. It's the same for me.' She said it light-heartedly, but it made me burn. Mum used to have a little bunch of women friends, and they'd play badminton on Monday nights, and often go for a Thai meal on Thursdays, and then set out for a long walk together along the river on Saturday afternoons. It was their girl time.

But then Dad cleared off and wasn't around to look after us, so Mum couldn't go out so much. Then she got ill and was too tired to play badminton or go for long walks any-way. Zara and I insisted we'd be fine looking after Rowena on Thursdays so she could still go for the Thai meal, but Mum said she'd sooner stay in with us, and every now and then we treated ourselves to a Thai takeaway.

Mum asked her friends round for drinks one evening, and everyone seemed to have a good time, but no one asked Mum round to their place in return. As they were fetching their coats I heard one of them say, 'Jen's not so much fun now, is she?' I wanted to slap her, and ask if *she'd* feel like being the life and soul of the party if she was dog tired and her legs were burning and she was scared of another relapse. But Mum still didn't want anyone to know so I had to keep quiet.

Mum had some teacher friends, but they never went out in the evenings. She was sort of friends with Lucy,

Sam's mum, but Lucy had been a bit odd when our dad left, sort of extra kind and concerned and yet acting wary too, as if marriage break-up might be catching.

If my lovely godmother, Coral, was still living here instead of thousands of miles away in Hong Kong, I'm sure she'd still be a wonderful friend. They'd always got on so well together. Mum wouldn't be able to keep her MS a secret from her – she'd just guess. I wished Mum would tell her during one of their FaceTime sessions.

'I don't want to worry her or start whining away when there's nothing she can do about it,' Mum said.

She was so determined to keep quiet about it now. She needed to keep her job for as long as possible, and she didn't want people feeling sorry for her. I did understand. I wished wished wished I hadn't blurted it out to Sally. I'd told Sam too, but I knew he'd never tell. I didn't know Sally properly at all. What was the matter with me? I still didn't really trust her. I'd been terrified that she'd blurt out something awful to Mum. It was as if she had some kind of weird power over me. Why was I so thrilled that she seemed to like me now?

Zara was astonished when she came hurrying out of school and Rowena told her.

'Frankie and Sally are friends now!' she said.

'Yeah, as if that's ever going to happen, silly girl,' said Zara.

'We are, actually.' I felt myself blushing crimson.

When we were in bed that night, Zara made me tell her the whole story. I didn't really want to talk about it.

It was special. Precious. I knew Zara would spoil it. And she did.

'Are you thick, Frankie? It's totally obvious why she's suddenly sucking up to you. She wants to take Sammy off you,' she said.

'She said that herself,' I told her.

'She said it *herself*?' Zara repeated.

'Yes, but she was only joking.'

'*You're* the joke, Frankie! How can you let her treat you like this? What's the *matter* with you?' she demanded.

I didn't *know*. I couldn't sleep for a long time, thinking about Sally, going over everything we'd said in the orchard. There was a constant murmur inside my head: *Sally, Sally, Sally, Sally, Sally . . .*

When I woke up in the morning I couldn't quite believe that it had happened. It was just like a dream, lovely but embarrassing. I kept blushing just thinking about Sally. I started to dread going to school. I tried to get out of it, telling Mum I had a bad headache.

'Oh, come off it, Frankie,' she said.

'Seriously. And I feel sick. I think I might *be* sick,' I lied.

Mum peered at me. 'You do look a bit pale,' she said, putting her hand on my forehead. 'I hope you're not going down with something.'

'She's fine,' Zara snapped. 'She's just gone off her head, that's all.'

'Shh, Zara, don't be mean,' said Mum. She put her arm round me and gave me a cuddle. 'Do you feel really dreadful, baby? I don't know what to do. I've really got to go into school.'

'It's OK, Mum. If I just go back to bed I'm sure I'll be OK,' I said, feeling guilty.

'I can't leave you on your own though,' said Mum.

'She needn't be on her own,' said Rowena. 'I could stay at home with her. I don't really want to go to school today either because Molly might want Baby Betty Badger back, even though we both said swapsy-no-backsy and shook hands as a solemn promise.'

'No, you're both going to school,' said Mum. 'But if you feel any worse, Frankie, then ask to go to the sickroom. If you feel desperately terrible, then get someone to phone me and I'll try to find someone to look after my class and come and get you.'

I nodded, and tried to smile to reassure Mum. It was horrible of me to worry her so. When we got out of the car, Zara made everything worse, telling me over and over again that Sally was playing games with me.

'She just wants to make a fool of you. You don't want to end up looking a total loser,' she said fiercely.

'Just shut up, will you? When I want your advice I'll ask for it,' I snapped.

'I just don't want you to get hurt.'

I didn't want me to get hurt either. I chickened out of going straight into the classroom. I went to the library instead. Mr White greeted me warmly, Ivneet smiled, and the computer kids and the Year Elevens ignored me. It felt safe and ordinary.

I browsed in the Myths and Magic section, wanting to look up the concept of 'enchantment'. It was depressing reading. I flipped through the pages of a fairy-tale book, beautifully illustrated with medieval princesses, golden hair in plaits, and sad, wizened little creatures crouched in corners, staring at them wistfully.

'Are you in a fairy-tale mood?' Mr White asked, standing beside me.

'I suppose it's a bit babyish,' I said sheepishly.

'Not at all! They're frequently bloodier, scarier, sexier than – I don't know, *Game of Thrones*, which I very much hope you haven't watched, because you're too young,' he said. 'They fascinate me, though when I was four years old I was scared silly by the picture of the wolf in *Little Red Riding Hood*. Howled the house down. To this very day I go a little quivery when I see a long-haired German Shepherd.'

'Seriously?' I said, because I was never sure whether Mr White was simply fooling around. It was one of the reasons I liked him so much. 'Then I'd better not invite you to my house because I've got an enormous hairy German Shepherd called Bear. He's an absolute softie and would never hurt a fly, but I suppose he can look a little scary.'

'Particularly if he's got big white teeth, all the better to eat me up,' said Mr White.

Ivneet looked up from her colouring. 'Actually, that's a fallacy. Healthy wild wolves rarely attack human beings. And domestic German Shepherds only attack when they have been treated savagely or trained to be guard dogs.' She paused. 'But actually I'm still a bit scared of them too.'

'No going round to Frankie's house for you either then,' said Mr White.

'That's a shame,' said Ivneet, which surprised me.

'I *liked* the wolf in *Little Red Riding Hood*,' I said. 'I *cried* when the huntsman chopped him up.'

'Perhaps you should rewrite the story from the wolf's point of view,' said Mr White. 'Ah! This could be the first task for our writing group. Over the Christmas holidays let's each choose a fairy story and write it from a different point of view. Do you fancy that, everyone?'

Ivneet and I nodded enthusiastically.

'What about you two, George and Peter?' Mr White asked.

'Write a *fairy* story?' said George, screwing up his face in disgust.

'What, like homework, when we haven't even done anything wrong?' said Peter.

Mr White sighed. 'It's an uphill battle with you two. How about working together on a scenario for a computer game based on a fairy story? Not the pretty princess type. Something with a dragon? An evil monster? A giant with an appetite for wriggly little boys?'

They looked more enthusiastic and conferred.

Mr White shook his head at them fondly.

'So which fairy tales will you choose, girls?' he asked Ivneet and me. 'Have a think about it today.'

Ivneet was clearly thinking about it already, staring into space, her eyes dreamy behind her little glasses. I tried too – but all I could think about was Sally.

My tummy went tight when the bell rang for morning school. It was a help walking to the classroom with Ivneet, who was counting all the fairy tales she could remember on her fingers. There was Sally, sitting on her desk, eating a rosy apple for her breakfast. Was she Snow White – or her wicked stepmother?

She smiled at me. Marnie and Georgia and Scarlett frowned. I gave her an airy little wave, trying to look ultra casual – and she waved back, calling, 'Hi, Frankie.'

Then Miss Eliot came into the classroom and we all scrambled to sit down properly. It was almost a relief. My mouth had gone so dry I didn't think I was capable of saying hi back.

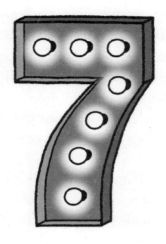

I kept wondering what would happen at morning break, but Miss Major, the PE teacher, asked me to stay in the gym to help her sort out the wretched games cupboard. It wasn't a punishment, it was because we'd become quite friendly and she wanted to discuss strategy for an inter-schools match in January. She gave me a little chocolate Santa for my trouble, which was sweet of her. I put it in my pocket for Rowena.

Mrs Legg the cook had made a special Christmas lunch: sliced turkey and roast potatoes and broccoli and carrots and peas, with mince pies and whippy cream for pudding. The canteen was crowded, as most of the packed-lunch pupils wanted the Christmas lunch too. Sally couldn't find four places for herself and Marnie, Georgia and Scarlett, let alone a fifth place for me.

I had to sit with the boys – my old football mates from Year Seven. They were messing about, flicking food at each other and telling stupid jokes. I took no notice, shovelling down my meal without tasting it. They were planning to go skating at the Christmas market's pop-up ice rink that evening.

'Are you coming, Frankie?' Josh Brown asked. He was one of the nicer boys, though not a patch on Sam. He wasn't very good-looking, but he had cute hair cut very short – not bristly like a crew cut, but fluffy like a duckling.

'I haven't got any skates,' I said.

'Don't be daft, you hire them. It's only three quid, plus the tenner entry fee,' he told me. 'Then you can stay on the rink as long as you like. Bargain!'

'Well, it might be a bargain to you, but I've spent all my money,' I said. 'I'm totally skint.'

'Get some from your mum then,' said Josh. 'No – tell you what, I'll treat you. I've been helping my uncle down the market and he's paying me. Go on, Frankie.'

All the other boys imitated him: 'Go on, go on, go on!'

'Do you fancy Frankie then? Yeah, you do! Asking her out on a date, eh?' said Josh's pal Richie.

'So what if I do?' said Josh, and there was a great outpouring of bawdy comments.

It was totally weird. All term he had taken no notice of me, and yet here he was asking me to go skating with him. I didn't know what to say. I was pleased he liked me enough to ask me out even though he knew all his mates would tease him. I did *like* him – but only as a friend. Did he want to be my boyfriend? What if he tried to kiss me?

I tried to imagine it. It might feel fine. I might even like it, and have the tingly sensation Zara kept going on about. It hadn't happened with Sam, but that was probably because he was just like a brother to me. Josh might be different.

I *wanted* him to be different. I wanted to be a perfectly ordinary girl who might have got her first boyfriend. I looked at him, this nice boy who was smiling at me but not quite meeting my eyes because he was actually very shy, though he tried to be a loudmouth in front of his mates.

I should have said yes. It was only going skating, for goodness' sake. I'd always wanted to go to that ice rink and see if I was any good. It looked great fun. But I knew I was kidding myself. I didn't want to go with Josh. I wanted to go with Sally.

'That would be great, Josh,' I said. 'I wish I could go, but I've got to stay home and do Christmas stuff with my family this evening.'

It was true. After school Mum was planning on buying a Christmas tree from the garden centre and we were all going to decorate it.

Josh looked disappointed, but shrugged his shoulders. 'That's OK,' he said. 'No probs. Perhaps some other time?'

'Yeah, perhaps,' I said. I saw Sally standing up and walking nonchalantly out of the canteen, though Marnie and Georgia and Scarlett were still stuffing themselves with mince pies. I hadn't even gone to fetch my pudding yet, but I didn't care.

'Got to go,' I said, and rushed off after her.

She was waiting for me outside. I tried not to smile, just in case she went back to being Old Sally and said something scornful. But she was smiling too.

'Come on!' she said. 'Sorry you got stuck with all those silly boys. They're so childish, aren't they?'

'Totally,' I said.

We didn't need to ask each other where we were going. We walked quickly and purposefully towards the fence that edged the orchard. Sally swung herself up and sat on top of the gate. I followed her. But before either of us could drop down into the scrubby grass a voice rang out:

'*Where on earth are you two going?*'

It was Miss Eliot, hurrying across the playground towards us.

'Oh help!' I said.

'Quick, let's run!' said Sally, grabbing my arm.

'Into the orchard?' I asked incredulously.

'Yes, and then out of it, and we'll keep on running, and we'll go round the town, and we won't go home, and we'll just have fun – come on, Frankie, jump down with me,' Sally gabbled.

'But she'll kill us!'

'She won't be able to find us. Quick!' said Sally. '*Jump!*'

I think I would have as well – but Miss Eliot was too fast for us.

'Sally Macclesfield! How dare you! And you, Francesca Bennet! Get back into the playground this instant!' she commanded.

Sally slid down gracefully and I struggled after her.

'We're so sorry, Miss Eliot,' Sally said. 'Don't be cross with Frankie. It was all my fault. I was messing about with her bar of chocolate, throwing it up in the air like a ball, and I threw it too far and it landed over the wall in all the ivy. And then I felt dreadful, so I was climbing over to see if I could find it, and Frankie hitched herself up onto the gate to help.'

I was amazed she could make up such an elaborate story on the spur of the moment, though Miss Eliot didn't look convinced.

'Well, you've lost your bar of chocolate now, if it ever existed,' she said crisply. 'And you can both stay in after school and do some extra maths.'

'Oh, Miss Eliot! It's the day before we break up!' said Sally.

'And I can't really stay after school because my mum's picking me up,' I said.

'So is mine. I have to help her with the Christmas shopping,' Sally added quickly.

'Then you'll have to text them and explain,' said Miss Eliot.

'I haven't got a phone,' I told her.

She raised her eyebrows. 'There's no girl your age anywhere who doesn't possess a mobile phone,' she said.

She was actually wrong. I truly didn't have one any more. Mine had died a few weeks ago. I suppose it was my fault because it fell out of my jeans pocket into a muddy puddle. Sam fiddled around with it for ages but couldn't get it going again.

Weirdly it was almost a relief. Whenever I used to post anything, I got all sorts of likes and comments, but this term no one had seemed interested in me. All the girls posted stuff on Instagram and practised pouty selfie faces, while the boys watched silly guys pranking each other or accessed hideous porn. I didn't seem to belong in either camp any more.

I knew that Mum couldn't afford to replace my phone. Zara told me to ask Dad for one.

'I'd sooner go without than ask him,' I said.

'Then that confirms it. You're completely, utterly, one hundred per cent crazy,' Zara said.

She thought I was even crazier when I had to find her in the playground and tell her that Sally and I had detention.

'Did you slap her again?' she asked.

'No! I told you, we're friends now. We were caught going into the orchard,' I told her, rather proudly.

'What? For God's sake, you can't go sneaking off like that with another girl! People will start talking about you!' she said.

'I don't care,' I said. 'Anyway, tell Mum I'll walk home by myself. I don't know how long old Eliot is going to keep us.'

'Mum will be ever so upset. We're supposed to be doing the Christmas tree,' said Zara. 'And it's for such a mad reason. Look at you, all thrilled because that devious Sally's being all nicey-nicey to you. She just wants to make a fool of you. How many times do I have to tell you?'

'Oh, shut your face,' I said. I was sick of her lecturing me. She didn't understand. All right, *I* didn't really understand either. Maybe she was right about Sally. But I couldn't help it. I wanted her as my friend, no matter what.

After school Sally and I waited in the classroom. Marnie hung about too, saying she'd wait with Sally, but Miss Eliot said she was being ridiculous and sent her out.

'I'll wait for you at the gate then, Sal,' Marnie said.

'Thanks, but I wouldn't bother if I were you. I might be stuck here ages,' said Sally.

'Sally is right,' said Miss Eliot dryly. 'Go home, Marnie.'

Marnie went, though she looked very reluctant. Miss Eliot gave Sally and me maths worksheets, printed on both sides.

'See how many of these sums you can do in an hour,' said Miss Eliot.

'I know how many I can do already,' I whispered. 'None!'

'Stop that whispering, Francesca! This is meant to be a punishment, not a gossip session. Now get on with your work.'

'And then we can go – in an hour?' Sally asked.

'I'm not saying that at all. I'm putting the finishing touches to my reports. I could be here half the evening.' Miss Eliot smiled at us maliciously.

Sally and I sighed in unison and attempted the first sum. It was a nightmare. I truly couldn't do it. And I was worried about Zara telling Mum I was in detention. I felt really bad about the Christmas tree. Yet somehow it still felt wonderful, sitting next to Sally. I kept stealing little glances at her. She was pursing her lips as she peered down the column of sums. Anyone else would look ugly doing that, but she just looked cute. I tried to work out whether she was wearing lipstick or not. Her lips were much pinker than mine, but they weren't shiny at all. She hadn't left a smudge when she kissed my cheek in the orchard.

She *had* kissed me, hadn't she? Already it seemed hazy, like a dream. Could I have imagined it? I stared at her, trying to imagine it now.

'You're not going to find the answers written on Sally's face, Francesca,' said Miss Eliot.

I blinked and blushed, staring down at my worksheet. I didn't dare look up for ages, but when I did Sally pulled a funny face at me. She wrote something in tiny letters on the corner of her worksheet, tore it off, and quickly passed it to me.

I can only do three so far!
Sally x

I wrote on my own worksheet, though it didn't seem a very bright way to pass messages. How were we going to explain the missing edge? Tell Miss Eliot a mouse had jumped onto our desks and nibbled the paper?

Count yourself lucky! I'm still stuck on number one!
Frankie x

Sally read it and then cautiously tipped her worksheet towards me, so I could just about see her answers. I smiled gratefully and copied them down quickly, then added some messy scribbled-out calculations to make Miss Eliot think I'd had a proper go at working it all out.

I somehow managed the fourth question by myself, and had a stab at the fifth too, though my answer didn't seem at all likely.

'Right, girls!' said Miss Eliot. 'Come and show me what you've done so far.'

We'd only been in the classroom fifteen minutes! Was she going to turn this into a tedious maths lesson? Would we have to do our workings on the board? Miss Eliot glanced at Sally's paper and wrote something. Then she looked at mine and wrote again, and then handed them both back. She'd written identical messages.

You can go home now, you bad girls.
Happy Christmas from Miss Eliot.

We both burst out laughing.

'You're a star, Miss Eliot!' said Sally.

'Thank you, Miss Eliot! Happy Christmas to you too,' I said. I suddenly liked her so much I wished I had a spare bag of fudge to give her tomorrow.

Sally and I went out into the corridor together.

'She's not a bad old stick after all,' I said.

'For a teacher,' Sally added.

'Hey, watch it. My mum's a teacher,' I said.

There was a little moment of awkwardness while we both remembered how we'd become deadly enemies.

'Can she still teach?' Sally asked softly.

'Yes. She says there's no reason why she can't go on teaching for years yet – but she does get ever so tired,' I said. 'Sally, you haven't told anyone about her MS, have you?'

'Of course not.'

'Not even Marnie?'

'Especially not Marnie,' said Sally. 'She's a right old blabbermouth. I don't ever tell her anything important.'

I stared at her in surprise as we walked out of the school entrance. 'But she's your best friend!'

'Yes, I suppose – but she's not like a *real* best friend. She just hangs around and agrees with me all the time. It's a bit boring, to be truthful. Don't look so shocked, Frankie,' she said.

'Well, you sound a bit callous,' I told her. 'She thinks the world of you.'

'I can't help it. I didn't try to make friends with her – she was the one who did all the running.'

'And what about Georgia and Scarlett? What do you think of them?'

'They're OK. Georgia's a bit wishy-washy but Scarlett can be fun at times. Though she can also be spiteful. But then, so can I!' Sally said. 'Hey, let's go down the town for a bit.'

'What?'

'Your sister's told your mum you've got a detention, right? So no one's expecting you home for ages. Come on, Frankie, let's have a bit of fun,' Sally urged. 'Shall we go to the ice rink?'

'I can't! I've got to help with the Christmas tree, and Josh Brown and all the other boys will be there,' I said.

'So? We don't have to talk to them,' said Sally.

'Yes, but I told Josh I couldn't go,' I said.

'He asked you?'

'Yes, at lunchtime.'

'Hey, what is it with you and boys? You've got Sammy, and now Josh Brown is after you, and he's the only halfway decent boy in the class.'

'He's just a mate, Sally. Same as my Sammy is,' I tried to explain.

'*My* Sammy?' she said, eyebrows raised.

'Anyway, I can't go skating because I haven't got any money.'

'Yes, but *I* have,' said Sally, fishing several twenty-pound notes out of her pocket.

'Oh my God! What did you do, rob a bank?' I gasped.

'Not a bank. I robbed my mother,' said Sally.

'What, you asked her for it and she just gave it you?' I asked incredulously.

'I stole it out of her handbag. I often do. I don't think she even notices,' Sally told me. '*I* know what we'll do if you won't go skating. There's a Christmas fair at Stanford Rec. We'll go on the big wheel!'

I wasn't even sure where Stanford Recreation Ground *was*, but I loved big wheels. It was a good half-hour trek, and then it wasn't a really *big* big wheel – only half the size of the one at the London Christmas market – but I didn't care. We went on it, scrunched up together, our fingers touching as we clutched the handrail, and as it gathered momentum we screamed in unison. Sally managed to stay pretty even with her mouth open. Her teeth were white and perfect, and the inside of her mouth was very pink.

My eyes started watering in the wind and she blurred into several Sallys, each with a halo of golden hair, all laughing triumphantly.

'It's great, eh?' she shouted.

'Fantastic!'

We stayed on for another ride, and then reeled off, dizzy, still laughing.

'Do you feel sick now, Frankie?' Sally asked.

'Not really.'

'Good, because I'm starving. What do you fancy – hot dogs, burgers, chips, candyfloss? *All* of them?'

We settled on hot dogs – giant ones, smothered in tomato sauce. I suppose they were only ordinary fairground hot dogs, but they tasted incredible. We bolted them down. Sally got a smudge of sauce on her cheek. I wiped it off for her.

'Another one?' she suggested.

'Then I *will* feel sick,' I said.

'Then chips. Go on. We'll share a portion.'

We wandered around the fair taking it in turns to pick out a chip. It was a very large portion and I soon felt stuffed, but I was happy to carry on sharing with Sally all night long. I wanted to stay at the fair with her for ever.

It was Sally who eventually looked at her watch. 'Hey, it's late. Better get back. My dad will be home by now. What time does yours get back?' she asked.

'He doesn't,' I said stiffly. 'He cleared off. He lives with this other woman now.'

'Oh, Frankie, I'm sorry.'

'Don't be. We get along fine without him.'

'When did he leave? Ages ago?'

'Round about the time my mum got ill.'

Sally looked appalled. 'That's awful,' she said.

'Yes, it is,' I agreed.

'It's making me feel even worse, being mean to you about your mum,' said Sally. She seemed to be almost in tears. 'Sorry, sorry, sorry, Frankie. How could I have been so horrible?'

'It's OK. You didn't know. We're friends now anyway.' I paused. 'Aren't we?'

'The best of friends,' she agreed.

I wondered if I dared kiss her cheek the way she'd kissed mine in the orchard. I wanted to so much. But I couldn't manage it, not here in the noisy, crowded fairground. And I was scared she'd push me away, even though she'd kissed me.

'The best of friends,' I echoed instead.

We paused at the gate of the rec.

'I go this way,' said Sally. 'I live in Compton Grove – do you know it? About three streets away.'

'I live in Lime Avenue. Near the library. *Hundreds* of streets away,' I said.

'Oh no! I didn't realize! It'll take you ages to get home. Have you got a bus pass?'

'It doesn't matter. I'll run. I'll be home in no time,' I said. 'Thanks so much for treating me at the fair, Sally. I'll probably get some money for Christmas, so maybe after that I can treat you one day. If you'd like to?'

'Sure,' said Sally. 'Bye then. See you at school. Last day!'

'Hurray,' I said, though I hated the thought of not seeing her till January.

But we were best friends now. Would we see each other in the holidays? How would I get hold of her? I didn't even know her phone number. If she didn't mention it tomorrow I'd have to ask her.

We made little waving motions with our hands, even though we were still standing close together, as if she was maybe reluctant to leave too. Then she turned and started walking, and I did too. After about twenty paces I craned round. She was looking round too. We waved properly – and then I started running.

I couldn't run all the way home, of course. I had to slow down every so often, leaning against walls and lampposts, trying to catch my breath. My heart was thudding, but it wasn't just because I'd been sprinting.

I could only manage to walk the last few streets, my school bag banging against my hip. We still had homework to do, even the night before we broke up, which was monstrous. It was only a short essay for history and analysing a poem for English, but it would take time. I wondered how I'd ever be able to concentrate. My head could only sing the Sally song.

I knew I'd be in trouble when I got home. In the lamplight I saw Mum standing out in the garden. Zara was holding her arm, while Rowena hovered about like a little Santa pixie in her hood.

'Frankie!' Mum called. Her voice was hoarse. Oh God, she'd been crying!

Mum hardly ever cried. Once when Dad left. Again when she got the diagnosis. They were the only times I could think of. She always tried so hard not to cry, but now she actually started sobbing.

'Oh, Mum! Don't cry! I'm all right, truly. I'm so, so sorry. I didn't mean to worry you so,' I said, running over and giving her a careful hug. She was so thin now, and sometimes a little unsteady on her feet. I was always terrified of knocking her over.

'Of *course* I've been worrying! What have you been *doing*, you dreadful girl?' Mum said, holding me tight.

'Come on, let's go indoors now. We're all freezing. I'll make us hot drinks,' said Zara, all bossy big sister, smug that *I* was the one in trouble, not her.

Bear charged towards me in the hall, butting his big soft head against me, licking me desperately, telling me he'd been worrying too. I felt worse than ever when I saw the Christmas tree behind him. It was set up on its stand, but it had no lights or decorations.

'Didn't you *tell* Mum I was in detention?' I asked Zara as I hugged Bear.

'Of course I did,' she said. 'But we're not daft. No detention lasts this long!'

'I tried phoning the school, but the secretary had gone home and there was just the stupid answer machine,' said Mum, sniffing. She grabbed some kitchen roll to mop her face, and then sat down heavily on a chair. I stood beside her and she rested her head against me. 'What possessed the teacher to keep you so long? We were all so worried. We drove down to the school but the gates were all locked. I couldn't even see any lights on. So I decided to phone the police—'

'*What?*' I said, appalled.

'But Zara said I should wait a bit longer,' Mum went on. 'She thought you might have gone off with a friend.'

Zara looked at me over Mum's head. '*With Sally?*' she mouthed as she started spooning hot chocolate powder into four mugs.

Mum was still sniffing. 'Frankie, you smell of fried onions,' she said, peering up at me.

'It's school dinners,' I told her.

'Do you think I'm stupid? It's fairground food! *That's* where you've been,' she said, suddenly furious. 'How dare you!'

'Look, I'm nearly fourteen, for goodness' sake, Mum. There's no need to make such a fuss. Heaps of people in Year Nine go out after school and nobody turns a hair,' I said.

'I know that! If you'd asked, I'd probably have said you could too. But you lied to me, saying you'd got detention – and you made Zara lie too!' said Mum.

'It wasn't a lie! I *did* have detention, but it was just a short one, so I decided to go to the fair, just for one ride. The big wheel. I told you how much I liked it when I went with Dad,' I gabbled.

'You went on this big wheel by yourself?'

'No! I was with someone,' I said. I could feel my cheeks getting hot.

'Did you meet up with Sammy then?' Mum asked.

'Mmm,' I said, not wanting to tell any more outright lies.

Mum wasn't having it. 'What does "Mmm" mean? You went off with some other boy? Someone in your class?'

'It was just one of the girls,' I said. *Just!* Sally was far more special than any of the boys – Josh Brown, even my

114

own Sam. I didn't want to tell Mum though. I didn't want to talk about Sally to anyone. I just wanted to go off somewhere private and think about her. But there was no chance of that.

'It was Sally!' said Zara, slamming my mug of hot chocolate down so hard it spilled. 'Oh God, Frankie, you are so incredibly stupid. What's the matter with you? How can you possibly want to be friends with her when she's been so hateful to you?'

'Why was Sally being hateful?' Mum asked.

I hadn't breathed a word to Mum about the bullying. I couldn't bear her to hear what they'd said about her.

'She was just teasing a bit, that's all. Her and her friends. Just stupid stuff,' I said. 'But now we've got to know each other properly and we actually have a lot in common. It's kind of like we're best friends now.'

'*Kind of like?*' said Mum. She hates it when we don't talk grammatically. She's cool in lots of ways, but she can also be very schoolmarmy. 'Well, I'm glad you've got a best friend now, Frankie, but if you decide to go off on a jaunt with her again, will you *please* let me know? We were waiting for you to come and help decorate the tree.'

'Well, I would have done, but I don't have a mobile phone now, do I?'

'Oh, for God's sake, you were the one who dropped it!' said Zara. 'Honestly, Frankie, can't you stop arguing and just say sorry? Poor Mum's been off her head worrying. Hasn't she got enough to deal with?'

'You keep out of it. Stop being so self-righteous,' I snapped. She was being so mean, reminding me of Mum's illness, making me feel worse than ever.

Rowena put her hands over her ears. She was very pale, though her nose was still bright red from the cold. She hates it when we quarrel.

'Come here, chickie,' said Mum, pulling her onto her lap. 'Let's warm you up. And drink your hot chocolate. Zara, there might be a few marshmallows left in the cupboard. Thank you, darling.'

I wanted to be the helpful big sister – to be called a darling. I wanted to be the little sister getting a cuddle. I hated being the bad girl upsetting Mum. Yet surely she was overreacting this time. Zara had often been late back when she went out with her pals.

Mum saw my face. 'Come on, cheer up, Frankie. I know you didn't mean to worry me. Just never be so spectacularly late again, please. I'd still get in a state, even without this new nonsense to fuss about.'

'What new nonsense?' I said, sitting beside her.

'It's Danny Diddums!' said Rowena, sprinkling marshmallows onto her hot chocolate.

'Would you believe the Diddums mum is on the warpath about the gingerbread-man lesson,' said Zara, licking a spoonful of creamy froth.

'She came to see me at home time. She was livid,' said Mum, sighing. 'And Danny whimpered and pretended to cry, clinging to her skirt like a two-year-old.'

'About the gingerbread-man story?' I asked incredulously.

'Apparently he was upset because the gingerbread man gets eaten at the end. Mrs Didsbury said I had no business telling such a scary story to five-year-olds. Though I seem to remember Danny happily biting the head off his own gingerbread man, *and* the head off the biscuit I'd given poor Daisy, who has to sit next to him,' said Mum, raising her eyebrows. 'When I couldn't take her complaints seriously, she said she was going to take it up with Mrs Seaton.'

'Well, she's clearly a nutcase,' I said. 'Your Head won't take any notice.'

'Actually, she's a *clever* nutcase. She says he's being bullied now, because he has ginger hair and some of the kids are calling *him* the gingerbread man and chasing him in the playground. I saw them and thought they were all just having fun. Danny didn't look at all upset at the time. But now he says they're all calling him Ginger,' said Mum. 'She's saying it's discrimination and it shouldn't be allowed.'

'*All* red-haired kids get called Ginger,' I said indignantly. 'It's no big deal. There's this boy called George who goes to the library every morning, and he doesn't give a stuff when he's called Ginger.'

'Well, it's traumatizing Danny, according to his mother. Unfortunately Mrs Seaton's just started up this stringent anti-bullying campaign, and all us teachers are meant to be extra vigilant. And I wasn't,' said Mum, sighing. 'And Mrs Seaton has sent me a text telling me to come and see her before school tomorrow.'

'I bet it's just so you can both have a laugh about the awfulness of Danny Diddums and his mum,' said Zara.

'Yes, you'll have a cup of tea together and chat about what you're doing over the Christmas holidays,' I said, trying to reassure Mum too.

'*I* used to get called names,' said Rowena. 'Remember when I was in Year One and some of the boys called me Roweewee?'

'Until I bashed their silly heads together,' I said.

'Yes, you did,' she said happily, looking up at me.

At least Rowena wasn't disappointed in me. And Mum seemed to have forgiven me. No one had had proper supper yet, and we were all tired out, so she phoned for a giant pizza, and then we all went to bed.

Zara started to nag about Sally again, but I pulled my duvet over my head.

'Can't hear a word!' I kept saying, and then I pretended to be asleep.

Zara gave up at last and fell asleep herself. I stayed wide awake, feeling bad about Mum. She'd looked so exhausted. It was incredibly mean to worry her when she was having to make such an effort to keep going every day. Yet I couldn't regret going off with Sally. I lay there, wondering if we'd try to go to the orchard again tomorrow.

On the last day of term we didn't have to wear uniform. I never usually gave this much thought – I just wore my usual jeans and any old sweater. But today I dithered getting dressed. My black Topshop jeans were OK, and my

Docs with their new red ribbons looked cool – but I couldn't decide on the right top. I had three sweatshirts: one was two years old and embarrassingly tight now – I didn't want the boys ogling my chest, such as it was. The second was a childish superhero affair, not really appropriate when I'd be fourteen in January. The third one was black with a dog motif, which would have been fine, but I discovered I'd somehow dribbled chocolate all down it. I tried spitting on a tissue to wipe it off, and just made it worse.

'Stop being disgusting!' said Zara. 'My sister, the Big Slob.'

She was wearing a very big blue jumper she'd knitted herself. The roll neck came up to her chin and the sleeves came down to her fingertips, but I could see it made her look cute. She wore it over the tiniest red skirt ever. If she hadn't been wearing black tights you could have seen her knickers.

'My sister, the Big Tart,' I said. 'Do you have to look so *obvious*, Zara?'

'I can't help the way I look,' she said, smiling at herself in the mirror – though she did try to pull her skirt down a fraction. 'Look, give up on the black sweatshirt, you'll never get that chocolate drool off. Wear the Superman thing – at least it's clean.'

'But it looks silly. It's the sort of thing I wore at primary school,' I said, trying it on.

'So why did you choose it, you daft thing?' said Zara. 'I agree, it looks totally stupid. Look, if you absolutely swear to keep it clean, you can borrow one of my tops.'

I was so desperate I had a good look in her wardrobe. Then I sighed. 'They all look so girly!' I wailed.

'Yep. Guess what. I *am* a girl. And so are you. Try the pink one – it might just look OK on you,' she said.

'I'm not wearing *pink*. Especially that fluffy one!' I protested.

'Well, wear your own stupid sweatshirt then. But don't just stand there topless!'

'I just want something decent to wear.'

'Like?'

I thought of a big dark checked shirt, hanging loose about my hips, the sort boys wear. And then I suddenly realized who had a shirt like that. I quickly pulled Superman on and rushed out of the bedroom.

'Back in a minute,' I yelled to Mum, who was making toast.

I ran next door, shivering without my coat, and rang the Turret House doorbell. Sam's father, Michael, answered the door – his mother would have left for London an hour or so ago.

'Hello, Frankie,' he said. 'Are you OK? Is your mum all right?'

'Yes, she's fine. Could I just see Sammy for a minute?'

'Yes, sure. Don't be too long though, we're already late,' he said, glancing at his watch.

Sam came running down the stairs. He always seemed so different in his posh blue and grey uniform – not at all the sort of boy who'd be my best mate. I almost expected him to talk in a sneery, snobby sort of way.

'Hey, Frankie!' he said, grinning at me, his usual friendly self.

'Sam, I know it's a bit of a cheek, but could I possibly borrow one of your shirts just for today?' I asked. 'It's a stupid mufti day and I can't find anything to wear.'

'Sure! Though I think your Superman top looks great,' said Sam. 'OK, come and choose.'

I hadn't been in his bedroom for a while. He usually hung out at our house because it was more relaxed and untidy and cosy. Sam's house was beautiful, the kind you'd see in a magazine, but it was all white and pale grey and sand, the sort of colours that stain easily. You couldn't sprawl on the snowy rugs or clunk your mug down hard on the glass coffee table. It was all incredibly tidy too, with no half-read books or forgotten toys on the floor. Every cushion was plumped up, every curtain hung just so. The mantelpieces displayed art deco ladies dancing or walking long, lean dogs, whereas ours held a jumble of old letters and stamps and torn-out recipes and scissors and Sellotape and half-tubes of sweets and little piles of change.

Even Sam's room was astonishingly tidy, with his childhood collection of small soldiers in regiment formation and his posters of footballers stuck on the inside of his pale wardrobe. He'd kept some of his old soft toys, but they were lying rigidly inside a trunk, like little corpses in a morgue.

Sam didn't have to search for his shirts. They were hanging in the wardrobe on identical padded hangers, all freshly laundered, in careful colour order like a paint chart. The winter checks had a section all to themselves. I seized a navy and red and green one, thick and soft.

'Could I borrow this? I'll bring it back properly washed and ironed, promise,' I said.

'Course you can borrow it. You can have it if you like, I don't often wear it,' said Sam.

'Really? Won't your mum mind?'

'Of course not. She won't know, anyway. Keep it, Frankie. It'll look good on you.'

'Oh, Sam, you're a star.' I gave him a hug without thinking – and then suddenly it stopped being ordinary and friendly. Sam was looking dreamy and different. I wondered if he was going to try to kiss me again.

'Sam?' It was his dad calling from downstairs. 'We have to go now or we'll both be late.'

'Come on then,' I said, wriggling out of the embrace. 'Thanks again. See you.'

'Tonight?' asked Sam.

'Probably. Whenever,' I said, and rushed out.

Mum and Zara and Rowena were all in their coats when I got back.

'Two secs,' I said, charging upstairs.

I tugged off the Superman sweatshirt, found a short-sleeved black T-shirt that wasn't too washed-out, and tried the checked shirt on top. It worked. Then I thumped downstairs again in my Docs, and grabbed Mum's black yeti from the coat hook.

'Really?' said Mum.

'It's a mufti day, we can wear anything,' I said.

I gave Bear a big hug. He looked at me mournfully, his eyes pleading. He hated it when we all went off to school, but he was never on his own for long. Mr Humphreys up the road was a retired policeman who had once been a dog-handler. He had a key to our house, and at ten every morning on school days he came calling for Bear and took him for a long hike in the woods.

'Mr Humphreys is coming soon, you know he is,' I told Bear.

Bear didn't look convinced, but I had to leave him.

'Holidays tomorrow!' I said – but for the first time ever I couldn't conjure up any excitement.

I wouldn't be seeing Sally.

I wanted to rush straight into the classroom to see what she was wearing, but first I had to go and give Mr White his present. He seemed genuinely touched.

'What a treat, Frankie! I absolutely adore fudge,' he said, rubbing his big tummy.

'I hope it's not too lumpy,' I said.

'I shall chew on it for inspiration while I'm writing my fairy story,' said Mr White. 'You'll write one over the holidays, won't you, Frankie?'

'Definitely,' I said.

'And you, Ivneet?' Mr White called over to her.

'I've started mine already,' she said.

We were the only three in the library. George and Peter hadn't bothered to come, and the Year Elevens had no homework to check.

'It looks like our writing club has been whittled down to an exclusive trio,' said Mr White.

'I'm afraid it'll have to be a duet – I've got to rush and see someone,' I told him.

'Oh dear,' he said. Ivneet looked disappointed too.

I felt a bit mean, but I couldn't help it. Mr White offered first me then Ivneet a piece of fudge. I left them munching away and ran down to our classroom.

It was all for nothing too, because Sally wasn't there. Neither was Marnie, though Georgia and Scarlett were sitting in a corner discussing some guy on YouTube. They glanced at me and then murmured something to each other. Sally might like me, but it was clear they still couldn't stand me.

Sally and Marnie didn't appear until ten minutes through the first lesson. Sally looked amazing in a white silk shirt, a black ribbon hanging loosely like a tie, and a tight black velvet skirt that fell demurely past her knees, yet clung to her flat stomach and slim hips. She was balancing in glorious blue boots, tightly laced Victorian style. Marnie looked cheap and childish beside her in a short skirt that was tight in the wrong kind of way. She'd pushed one sleeve of her sweater up to her elbow to show off a plaited friendship bracelet with a little bead heart.

I stared at it. It looked brand new. My heart started thumping. It was clear who had given it to Marnie.

Miss Eliot told them off for being spectacularly late, taking no notice of their plea that they hadn't been able to get on their usual bus because of Christmas shoppers.

'So strange that the rest of the class managed to board their buses without any problem,' said Miss Eliot. 'And it's a rather lacklustre excuse today, Sally, albeit a festive one. You're usually more inventive. Couldn't you at least suggest you're late because of a bolting reindeer or an elf running amok in Santa's grotto.'

'I promise I'll sharpen up my wits and embellish my imagination next time, but please don't be cross with me today, dear Miss Eliot,' said Sally. 'Not on the very last day of term.'

She was being outrageously cheeky, but somehow she could get away with it.

'Very well, you bad girls. Sit down at once and stop plaguing me with your nonsense,' said Miss Eliot.

Sally caught my eye as she sat down, and grinned. Marnie saw me smiling back at her and glared at me. Still, she had the friendship bracelet. I had nothing.

We didn't get a chance to talk at break either, because Year Seven did a ten-minute Christmas carol concert in the playground and we all had to watch. At lunchtime it looked as if Sally had saved a place for me at her table, but I got waylaid by Josh Brown. He was wearing a checked shirt very similar to mine.

'Hey, we look like twins,' he said delightedly. 'You should have come skating last night, Frankie. It was amazing. I bet you'd be a brilliant skater. Why don't you come some other time in the holidays?'

There was a predictable Greek chorus from the other boys: '*Oooh, he's asking her out! Will she, won't she, will she, won't she, will she cop off with our mate?*'

Josh did his best to ignore them, but he went very red. Even his ears were scarlet. I felt really sorry for him. I didn't want to make him look an idiot in front of the other boys.

'I'd love to go skating some time – but I'm not sure it'll be possible. I have to go and stay with my dad, you see,' I said. It wasn't a lie. We did have to stay with him during that long gap between Christmas and the New Year. I always hated it, especially having to say goodbye to Mum when Dad came to collect us. She always said she didn't mind a bit, she had heaps of things to prepare for school, and maybe she'd go to a gallery or the cinema or just have coffee with a girlfriend. This year she'd probably have extra long lie-ins, and stay in her dressing gown all day and have a proper rest. But I couldn't bear the thought of her being left alone with none of us to look after her and cheer her up.

I must have been looking sad because the boys shut up and Josh looked sympathetic.

'Sorry, Frankie. I didn't realize your mum and dad had split up,' he said.

'Yeah, well, it's not something you advertise, is it?'

'Well, look.' He fumbled in his pocket and found a biro. 'Oh rats, I haven't got anything to write on. Hey, give us your hand, Frankie.'

'What?'

He wrote rapidly on my wrist. It tickled rather. 'Here, it's my phone number. Get in touch if you can make it, OK?'

'Yes, sure,' I said. 'Well, I'd better go – my friends are saving me a place.'

I hurried away, but then I saw Sally. Some Year Twelve boys had paused as they were pushing their way through the crowd. One of them was Gary Masters, the boy who'd kissed Zara at the party. He was standing right beside Sally, clowning around, balancing his tray on one hand like a waiter. She was laughing. He said something and she replied. They seemed to be having a proper conversation now – Sally chatting away, dipping her head so that her blonde curls fell across her forehead. She tossed her head impatiently and smiled up at him, dimples in her cheeks. He put his tray down on the table and sat beside her.

I waited for her to explain that she was actually saving that seat. It was mine. But as he started eating she carried on chatting. She seemed to be commenting on his big pile of chips because he offered her one. She nibbled at it, looking straight into his eyes.

The whole canteen blurred, and the noise got louder, deafening me. I stood clutching my tray, swaying on my feet.

'Are you looking for somewhere to sit?' It was Ivneet, sitting with Rangan and Ezra and a few ultra geeky boys from higher up the school. She patted the empty place beside her, her head on one side.

I sat down gratefully. I'd been clutching my tray so hard that my palms were damp. I wiped them quickly on my jeans and tried to compose myself. I was so hot. I could feel my fringe sticking to my forehead. I prayed I didn't smell sweaty. I took a long drink of water, trying to think of something to say. Everyone was having a shouty conversation about some match. I couldn't work out what they were on about.

They were a pretty weird bunch. Ivneet was OK, but I couldn't stand Rangan and Ezra, who were both terrible show-offs, and the other boys looked even worse. It turned out they were all members of the Chess Club. Nothing is more boring than listening to people talking about a chess game when you don't even know the moves.

Ivneet shook her head sympathetically at me. 'Sorry. They do go on. Do you play chess?'

'Nope. But you do, obviously.'

'My father taught me when I was three,' she said. 'Please don't wince! My parents are crazy. They're determined I'm going to be an intellectual genius. It's a wonder they didn't try to teach me to read when I was still in the womb. Apparently they *did* play classical music to me when I was just a blob, can you imagine!'

I smiled at her. 'Are you an only child?'

'No, I've got an older brother, and they went through this whole rigmarole with him, but he's never been as biddable as me,' said Ivneet. 'He's clever, but he gets bored studying. He's desperate to go to art school. He's ultra cool and stylish, into fashion in a big way. My parents are very traditional, so you can imagine their despair. So now they've focused on me.'

'You want to be a surgeon though, don't you?'

'Well, I want to do medicine. I'm not sure about being a surgeon though. Last night my mum cut her finger badly and I practically fainted at the sight of all the blood. I don't think you can be a very competent surgeon if you're squeamish. I fancy studying to be a psychiatrist. I'm interested in what makes people tick.' Ivneet nudged her glasses down to the end of her nose and looked over them. 'Lie down on my couch, Miss Bennet, and tell me what's troubling you,' she said in a mock-German accent.

'No fear!' I said. I *did* like Ivneet. She was fun to talk to, even though she was a bit weird. She didn't just go on and on about hairstyles and make-up and clothes and boys. Today she was wearing her hair in its usual long fat plait, she hadn't bothered with any make-up, and her plain green dress would have made Zara raise her eyebrows and exclaim, 'Per-lease!'

I craned round, trying to see Sally. She seemed to be laughing her head off at something Gary Masters was saying. When I turned back to take another bite of pizza, Ivneet was looking at me curiously. Her dark eyes were slightly narrowed, as if she could really read my thoughts.

I put the slice of pizza back on my plate, feeling queasy.

'Are you OK?' Ivneet asked.

'Course I am. It's just a bit greasy, that's all,' I said.

'Are you looking forward to the holidays?'

'I suppose. I mean, yes, of course I am.' I looked at the scribbled number on my wrist. Ivneet looked too, raising her eyebrows. 'It's Josh Brown's number. He wants me to go skating with him some time.'

'And will you?' Ivneet asked.

'Probably not. I didn't like to say no outright, not in front of all his mates. Was that silly?'

'No, kind. But maybe he's got the wrong end of the stick now,' said Ivneet.

I sighed. 'I wish life wasn't so complicated.'

'Tell me about it!'

It was just an expression – Ivneet didn't really want me to tell her what was on my mind. And yet I wished I could blurt it all out.

'Would *you* go out with Josh?' I asked her.

'Well, it would depend. As a friend, maybe. In a crowd. Not otherwise. I wouldn't be allowed, anyway,' said Ivneet. 'My parents are very strict.'

'Are they religious?'

'Not particularly. They just want me to concentrate on my schoolwork.' Ivneet nudged a little closer to me. 'Though they've taken a shine to Rangan. We know his family, worst luck. Imagine, me and Rangan!' She pulled a funny face.

'You'd have the brainiest children ever,' I said. 'They'd be reading Shakespeare plays before their first birthdays and babbling about string theory, whatever that is. I bet *you* know.'

'Haven't a clue,' said Ivneet cheerfully. 'My parents want to enter me for that *Child Genius* programme. Have you ever seen it? Imagine how cringe making! I probably wouldn't be able to answer a single question – I'd bring shame on the family. Or I'd gabble my way through the answers and get everything right, but everyone watching would hate me because I'm such a geek. I'd like to meet Richard Osman though – he's so kind and funny.

I absolutely love him. I watch *Pointless* with my granny every afternoon after school. She wrote off to him for his autograph, and he sent a signed photo with a lovely message on the back. Dear, lovely Richard!'

I wondered if Ivneet was teasing, but her eyes were shining and her voice went all soft when she said his name.

'Oh, Ivneet!' I said fondly.

'I know I'm weird. I can't help it,' she said.

'So what's your story about, hmm? The one we're doing for Mr White?'

'Aha!'

'How many pages have you done?'

'About twenty.'

'Really? You're kidding me, aren't you?'

'No, I just got into it last night. I'm not even halfway through yet,' said Ivneet.

'It's supposed to be a story, not a novel!' I said.

'I know. And it's quality that counts, not quantity. Don't worry, yours will be heaps better than mine.'

'No it won't!'

'Come on! I remember that thing you wrote about the Second World War when we were in Year Seven – you had to read it out. It was absolutely incredible. It made you feel as if it was actually happening. That part about the children on the train – I was practically in tears.'

'I went a bit over the top,' I said, thrilled that she remembered it so vividly.

'I'm sure you'll be a writer when you grow up,' said Ivneet.

'Maybe,' I said. 'I'm not really serious about it.'

At home we sometimes fooled around about our futures. Zara wanted to be a YouTuber, I wanted to be a writer, and Rowena wanted to be an artist, so we'd decided I'd write a book, Rowena would illustrate it, and then Zara would promote it on her YouTube channel. It was just a game, but I couldn't help hoping it would come true.

I went off into a little daydream, wondering if I would ever get to write a proper book – and then my eyes focused on Sally, walking towards the exit with Gary Masters. They weren't on their own. Marnie and Georgia and Scarlett were with them, and a bunch of Year Twelve boys – but it was as if Sally and Gary Masters were lit up with neon. It was a wonder the whole canteen wasn't staring at them, dazzled.

My stomach turned over. 'Got to dash,' I said urgently to Ivneet, and ran for the toilets.

I only just made it in time. I hadn't eaten much pizza but I was still horribly sick. I couldn't help making a noise, and I heard some girls commenting outside. I hated the flimsy cubicles. I waited, hoping they'd leave, but they started experimenting with hairstyles in front of the mirror, so at last I gave the toilet one last flush and crept out to wash my hands.

They all stared at me. They weren't Year Nine girls, thank goodness, they were older, and some of them looked sympathetic.

'Are you all right now?' one asked. 'It sounded like you were very sick.'

'I was,' I said, scooping up cold water in my hands and

washing my mouth out. 'But I'm OK now. It must have been the pizza.'

She didn't look convinced. 'Are you sure you weren't making yourself throw up?'

'Of course I wasn't! Why would I want to do that?' I asked, leaning weakly against the washbasin.

'To lose weight? You're very thin,' she said.

'I'm naturally like a beanpole,' I said truthfully.

'You're not bulimic, are you?' said another girl. 'That's a truly crazy thing to do. You lose all the enamel on your teeth because of the stomach acid.'

'Stop it!' I said. 'I'm not bulimic – I've just got a stomach upset, that's all.'

As if I could ever explain to these girls *why* it was upset! I felt shivery, the way you do after being sick, so I just went into the cloakroom, huddling into Mum's black fur coat. The carved bear ornament was in the pocket and I stroked his little wooden snout and ears and paws. I couldn't wait to get home to see real Bear and enjoy his uncomplicated delight at the sight of me.

I wanted to run right out of school, but the teacher on playground duty was standing near the school gate. I stayed lurking by the toilets when the bell went, but she spotted me as she came in.

'Hey – Francesca? Didn't you hear the bell? Chop chop!'

So I trudged back to the classroom.

'Cheer up! Only one more afternoon and then you're on holiday!' she called.

I gave her a weak smile. It was art all afternoon. I

wasn't much good at it. Rowena could already draw better than me, but it was usually fun working with Mr Robinson. He wasn't really like a teacher. He chatted and joked and didn't mind that we all called him Rob.

We'd been working on a still-life drawing, with an impossibly difficult bowl of fruit and a cup and saucer arranged on a little table with a checked cloth. We had to concentrate on shading and perspective. I tried, but my crockery looked as if it was sliding off the table, the checks wavered wildly this way and that, and you couldn't distinguish my apples from my oranges. The still life remained set up at the front of the art room and we all sighed.

'OK, it's getting a bit boring, isn't it? Let's do some painting instead. Something Christmassy. You choose. Off you go then!' Rob said cheerfully.

I'd gone right to the other side of the room from Sally, careful not to look in her direction, but when I went to collect some paints she came up and gave me a little poke with her pencil.

'Where have you *been*?' she asked. 'I've been looking all over for you. Why didn't you come and sit with us at lunch? I saved you a place.'

'Yes, and Gary Masters sat in it,' I muttered.

'I only let him because I'd given up on you coming. I don't even like him,' said Sally. 'He tries to act so super cool.'

'For God's sake, you were flirting like anything – I saw you.'

'Yes, well, it's fun, isn't it, knowing how many pathetic girls fancy him.'

'Yes, pathetic girls like my sister,' I said angrily.

'Whoops! Sorry. I didn't know. Anyway, it wasn't serious. He thinks I'm just a silly little kid,' said Sally.

'You are,' I told her. 'You just like playing games with people, don't you?'

'Hey,' she said. 'Come on. We're friends now, right?'

She gave me her little winning smile, her head on one side. My heart turned over – but I glared at her.

'Wrong!' I said, and stalked back to my desk.

I kept my head down, working on my painting, though the others were messing around, not really bothering, and Rob didn't seem to mind. I didn't paint a nativity scene or a Santa or a happy family in pyjamas opening Christmas presents. I daubed white paint on grey sugar paper, doing blobby polar-bear figures plodding through a dance. I gave them knitted bobble caps and stripy scarves just like the ones at Whitelands. Their legs were different lengths and some of them seemed as if they were floating upwards, which made them look unintentionally eerie.

There were no crowds watching. They were all alone apart from one small figure leaning over the balcony peering at them. She was wearing a black coat and her face was blank.

'Interesting!' said Rob, peering over my shoulder. 'But a little bleak.'

'That's my life, Rob,' I said, sighing. I wanted to sound cool and mysterious, but it just sounded ridiculous, and I had to duck my head to hide my blush.

'Oh God, I remember being fourteen,' said Rob. 'Cheer up. It gets better, truly.'

I wasn't fourteen quite yet, but I nodded.

'It's a good painting though. Technically all over the place, but very imaginative,' Rob said, and moved on.

That was me in a nutshell. I wished I wasn't so imaginative. I kept making Sally up in my head and turning her into the friend I'd always longed for – *more* than a friend – though I knew perfectly well that Zara was right and Sally was just playing around with me. She'd made my life a misery for weeks, taunting me about Mum and getting the other girls to gang up on me, and now she was amusing herself making me believe we were friends.

Of course we weren't proper friends. Marnie was still her best friend. Sally had obviously given her that red friendship bracelet with the little heart so similar to the one she wore herself. Why did I wish so much that she'd given it to me? I didn't even like those silly bracelets. And why did I want Sally for a friend anyway? I knew all too well that she wasn't a kind and caring sort of girl. Sally was only kind when she wanted something, and she only cared about herself.

She wasn't even *that* pretty, was she? She looked too knowing, too deliberately cute, her curls too wild. She had that irritating habit of tossing them back from her face. Why didn't she simply have them cut? OK, she had a lovely slim figure, and her skin had that soft peachy quality, and her legs in her shiny black tights were slender yet shapely. I was slim too, but thin and angular, I was starting to get the odd spot, and my legs had a knobbly coltish quality that made me look awkward.

Why did I suddenly care so much about the way I looked? Until recently I'd barely bothered to look in a mirror. I'd never wasted time worrying about my hair or my face or my figure. I had fretted about clothes, but that was because I didn't want to wear Zara's girly stuff, especially as it smelled of her sickly perfume, no matter how many times it was washed.

I wanted to look like myself – yet I didn't know who I really was any more. I dug my nails into the palms of my hands, trying not to feel so sad and self-pitying. I was being stupid and self-indulgent. I had to stop mooning after Sally and be the old Frankie. Of course Christmas wasn't going to be bleak. Mum would do her best to make it fun for the three of us. We'd have a great time and we wouldn't miss Dad for one minute. We'd have to see him and Helen at Granny's for a few days, but they'd be over quickly. Then Sam and I would hang out together, taking Bear for long walks and chatting and laughing and mucking about the way we'd always done. We'd both forget all about that silly kiss.

I wouldn't give Sally a single thought over the Christmas holiday. When I went back to school I'd take no notice of her. I wouldn't even care whether she was friendly or not. I wouldn't *want* to be her friend. I'd find myself another friend – someone kind and interesting like Ivneet.

This seemed such a good idea that I rushed after her the moment the bell rang, and caught up with her in the cloakroom.

'Hey, Ivneet!'

She looked round, surprised. She was wearing a pale blue padded jacket and a red bobble hat with matching mittens – clothes that even I could see were hopelessly uncool, but they were warm and sensible. She smiled at me enquiringly.

I didn't really know what to say.

'Well, Happy Christmas,' I blurted out. Then I thought. 'Oh. Sorry. That was silly of me. You probably don't celebrate Christmas.'

'Oh yes we do!' she said. 'Any excuse to get together with family and friends and give presents and have a big feast! It goes on for days.'

'And there's me imagining you up in your bedroom swotting away and writing your story and colouring in all those muscles and veins and organs,' I said.

'Oh, I'll be doing a lot of that too,' said Ivneet, grinning. 'Anyway, you have a happy Christmas too, Frankie. See you in the library first day of term next year!'

'It's a date,' I said.

Ivneet waved and walked off while I was struggling with the hooks on Mum's furry coat.

I felt a light thump on my shoulder.

'There you are!' said Sally breathlessly. She'd obviously been running.

I didn't say anything.

'Oh God, you're not still feeling grumpy, are you?' she said. 'Hey, I've got you a Christmas present!'

'What?' I said.

'Here!' Sally fished a rectangular package out of her school bag. 'Sorry it's not wrapped. I only bought it this morning. Marnie and I did some early Christmas shopping at the station. Go on, open it now!'

'But it's not Christmas yet,' I said.

'Never mind. I want to see if you like it,' said Sally. 'Quick, before the others catch up. They're just in the toilets.'

I opened the paper bag warily, thinking it might be a stupid joke. I pulled out a beautiful scarlet-leather manuscript book with creamy-white blank pages.

'Do you like it? It's for your stories. I've seen you scribbling away in that old notebook. I thought you might like this one,' said Sally.

'It's . . . lovely.' I'd always longed for this kind of notebook, but the real leather sort were so expensive. I'd always thought I'd be able to write much more stylishly, like a real author.

'You *do* like it, don't you?' Sally's eyes were shining.

'How did you know I wanted one like this?' I asked.

'I just guessed,' she said. 'So we *are* friends again now?'

'Yes. But I haven't got you a Christmas present!' I wished now that I hadn't given Mr White the fudge.

'Never mind,' said Sally.

'But I want to give you something special,' I said, though I had no money left.

'Well, listen, in the holidays—' Sally began.

But just then Marnie and Georgia and Scarlett came barging into the cloakroom.

Sally looked at them. She looked at me. 'See you then, Frankie,' she said.

Was she simply saying goodbye? Or did she mean she'd actually see me during the holidays?

I suddenly felt around in the pocket of my coat and dropped something straight into Sally's pocket.

'It's yours,' I said, and then I ran out of the cloakroom.

I'd given her the little carved bear.

Mum and Rowena were waiting at the school gate. Zara was with them, fuming.

'Did you see the way Sally Mac was behaving in the canteen at lunchtime? She was practically flinging herself at Gary. It was unbelievable. You *can't* want to be friends with that little flirt, Frankie!'

'Don't talk about her like that, Zara. Even if she is,' said Mum. She looked grey with tiredness, but she was determinedly smiling.

'Oh shut up, Zara. You're just jealous because you fancy Gary and he doesn't even give you a second glance,' I said spitefully.

'You're just defending Sally because you've got a stupid crush on her,' said Zara. 'You're pathetic, Frankie.'

'Why are Zara and Frankie quarrelling, Mum?' Rowena asked.

'Because they're silly,' said Mum. 'Now pipe down, both of you. Let's get into the Christmassy spirit, please. It's officially holiday time, so let's be jolly and festive.'

Mum played a Christmas song CD in the car going home, and commanded Zara and me to sing along with Rowena. We sat sulkily silent for a minute or two but then joined in the ridiculous oldies, rocking around a Christmas tree, wondering if people knew it was Christmas, wishing everybody Merry Christmas and giving our heart last Christmas.

When we got in we helped Mum decorate the tree, and then Rowena showed Mum all the drawings in her school book, Zara messaged friends she'd said goodbye to only an hour before, and I sat stroking the scarlet leather of my new notebook. I wanted to start writing in it straight away. I could make a start on my fairy tale, but the notebook seemed far too beautiful to waste on a story for school.

Maybe it was time to write my first serious novel. The apocalypse story seemed silly and overblown now. I wrote a practice paragraph or two at the back of my rough book, but I didn't really feel like making up a story. I was too absorbed in real life. Perhaps I should keep a journal. It seemed a splendid idea. I selected my nicest pen and opened the notebook to the first creamy page. I knew exactly what I wanted to write. The words were in my head already.

I think I am in love with Sally.

But I didn't dare. I'd die if Zara found the notebook and read it. And even if I managed to hide it from her, I wasn't sure I was ready to commit it to paper. Then I'd have to admit it was true. I didn't really want it to be. It was too scary. I still didn't totally trust her. Sometimes I didn't even *like* her. But I just felt helplessly drawn towards her. I didn't just want her to be my friend. I wanted her to be my special girl, my one and only.

So what was I going to do? Keep it secret, even from Sally? If I told her, she might tell Marnie and Georgia and Scarlett. They'd mock and tease and make my life hell all over again. What if everyone knew? Josh Brown and all the boys? *Miss Eliot!* I'd die of embarrassment.

We'd had the inclusivity lessons, we had our celebrity icons, we all said it was totally cool to be gay – and yet I'd heard people being teased and called stupid names, especially the boys. I supposed it was admirable to dare to be different – but I mostly longed to be the same as everyone else.

What about my family? Zara would be appalled. Rowena would be baffled. Mum would be . . . What would she be? She'd tell me she understood and she loved me no matter what, and she'd maybe even say she was proud of me – but what would she *really* feel? Dad would be more straightforward. He'd insist I was simply going through a phase.

Could that be right? Or was I going to like girls for ever? Was that why it felt so weird when Sam kissed me?

I wanted to write it all down, try to find some answers, but the scarlet notebook was still blank when Mum called to say that supper was ready. It was a big veggie pasta tray-bake, golden cheese bubbling on top. It was one of my favourite suppers, but my stomach was churning and I just took a very small portion – but then it tasted so good I heaped my plate as usual and ate ravenously.

Zara and Rowena munched away too. Mum was the only one who toyed with her food, only eating an occasional mouthful. I watched her anxiously. She wasn't joining in the conversation much. She seemed absorbed in her own thoughts.

I wondered if anything worrying had happened at her school. Then I remembered.

'How did you get on with Mrs Seaton, Mum? Did you both have a good moan about Danny Diddums and his wretched mother?'

'Oh, she was fine about it,' Mum said, but her voice sounded strange. She put down her fork.

Zara and Rowena and I stared at her anxiously.

'Mum?' Zara said gently.

'Mum!' said Rowena, and she slid down from her chair and went to nestle up to her.

Mum pulled her onto her lap and held her close.

'Sorry, girls. Everything *is* fine school-wise. Mrs Seaton agrees that Danny and his mum are royal pains. Danny declared war on the whole class and shot them all with his water pistol. He soaked several kids to the skin before

144

I managed to confiscate it.' Mum acted it out, trying to make it funny, but we knew her too well.

'You said everything was fine, school-wise. So what *isn't* fine?' I asked.

'Please, Frankie. Just leave it, OK?' said Mum. 'I want us to have a lovely Christmas holiday. Now, who wants some pudding? Clementines or grapes?'

I couldn't bear it though. I had to ask. 'Mum, have you had another one of your turns?'

She took a deep breath. '*Stop* it!' she mouthed over Rowena's head. '*Not now!*' but Rowena looked up and saw.

'I'm part of the family too, Mum,' she said. 'Tell!'

'There's nothing much *to* tell. It was just a little slip-up, but it was unlucky it happened in Mrs Seaton's study.'

'Oh, Mum, did you fall over again?' said Zara.

'No. Worse. I dropped a cup of tea,' she told us.

'Well, that could happen to anybody,' I said. 'Heavens, I'm always dropping cups and mugs and all sorts, you know I am.'

'Yes, I know, darling, but that's because you're always in a bit of a rush and not looking properly. I was sitting in an armchair in Mrs Seaton's study holding one of her best china cups, and then my fingers lost their grip and it just fell, and tea splashed everywhere – my skirt, the armchair, her carpet. And I just sat there like a lemon, staring at my hand, and then – oh God, this is so embarrassing – I started crying like a baby,' said Mum, her voice wobbling as if she might start crying all over again.

We all three hugged her tight.

'Was Mrs Seaton cross with you?' Rowena asked.

'No, she was incredibly kind. She helped mop me up, and then she cancelled her next appointment and we sat and had a heart-to-heart. She guessed about the MS. It's just so depressing. This hand thing is something new. My hands have been feeling a bit odd and tingly for a while – I hoped it wasn't going to lead to anything. But now it seems to be affecting my grip. It's a new symptom. I so hoped I'd be one of the lucky ones and go into remission for a couple of years or more – but this seems like another relapse,' said Mum.

'How did Mrs Seaton know though, just from you spilling your tea?' I asked.

'Apparently her brother-in-law has MS. He's had it for quite a while now. He's more poorly than me, and needs a lot of day-to-day support, but he started off with similar symptoms. And she's noticed how tired I've been looking too – although all the staff are pretty exhausted by the end of term.'

'Is she going to let you stay working, Mum?' I asked. 'Because if you can't, you mustn't worry too much. Zara and I have looked it up on the internet and you should get proper sickness benefit, and if you can't we'll make Dad pay more money for us, and as soon as we're able we'll get Saturday jobs and we'll manage OK.'

'Oh, Frankie. Bless you, darling. But I'm OK for the moment,' said Mum. 'Mrs Seaton has been incredibly understanding. She's going to try to juggle the timetable so I don't have to take PE and she'll let me off playground duty so I can have a proper rest at lunchtime. She's going to do her best to keep me on for as long as possible. She's being so kind.'

'Well, you're obviously the best teacher in the whole school, so of course she wants to keep you,' I said.

'Will you need this day-to-day support, Mum?' Rowena asked.

Zara and I held our breath. Mum rubbed her cheek on the top of Rowena's head.

'Not yet, darling. Hopefully not for ages and ages – probably not till you're grown up. Maybe never.'

'It's so scary though,' whispered Rowena.

'I know. I find it scary too,' said Mum. 'Actually, Mrs Seaton said I should get in touch with my doctor again, as I've had another relapse. I'll wait until after Christmas and then phone for an appointment.'

'Phone tomorrow!' I insisted. 'Maybe he can give you some different pills or something.'

'He's probably off on his holidays already. Still, I'll phone, I promise – though he doesn't seem to think there's much more they can do at the moment, and it just makes me feel depressed,' said Mum. 'Now, let's forget about my boring old illness and have some fruit. Or maybe ice cream!'

Mum made a big effort all evening. There was nothing much on television so we watched an old DVD, all of us snuggled up on the sofa, Bear at our feet like a big rug. Zara and I knew most of *Frozen* by heart because we'd watched it so many times when we were little. Parts made us groan now, but Rowena still loved it, and all four of us sang along to every single song.

Mum let us stay up, as we could all have a lie-in the following morning. But at last I got to go to bed, though I didn't get any peace there. First Zara and I whispered about Mum.

'I wish Dad was here,' she said. 'It's awful being the eldest. I feel I should be looking after Mum now and yet I don't know how.'

'We'll both look after Mum. Dad was pretty useless anyway. He just kept telling her she'd get better, which is rubbish, because she's actually getting worse,' I said.

'What are we going to do if she gets much, much worse though?' Zara whispered. 'I mean, will we be able to leave home when we're old enough?'

'Don't be so selfish!' I hissed.

'You're the selfish one, making Mum so worried when you went to the fair with your precious Sally,' said Zara. 'Only she's not *yours*, she flings herself at everybody.'

I wanted to show Zara my wonderful scarlet notebook to prove that Sally thought I was special – but I wanted to keep it hidden away too. I wanted to tell Zara all the sweet things Sally had said to me over the past few days – but I wanted them to stay secret more. I simply put my pillow over my head and kept it there, blotting out Zara's voice until it faded away altogether, and I knew she was asleep.

Then I went to sleep too, and dreamed about Sally.

We all had a bit of a lie-in, and we were still in our pyjamas when Sam came round. We didn't worry as he's like family. Mum just made more tea and toast, and Sam pulled up a chair and had a second breakfast with us.

Then Zara went to get herself ready – she was meeting her friends at Whitelands again.

'Per-lease don't say you want to go to Whitelands too, Frankie,' said Sam.

'No, I thought I'd take Bear for a really long walk as he's been a bit cooped up recently,' I said.

'Great,' said Sam.

'Can I come too?' Rowena begged.

I hesitated. I knew it would be good to take her with us, so that Mum could rest with a book – but Rowena was a bit of a pain on a long walk. She always got stones in her shoes or thought she was getting a blister, and then her nose started running and she never had a hankie, and was always needing a wee – we had to stand guard while she went behind a bush. She wanted to play interminable Would-you-rather? games too, or tell us long rambling jokes, always forgetting the punch line.

'Not this time,' I said. 'I want to take Bear to Fenton Ponds and you'd be tired before we even get there.'

'Oh please, I love Fenton Ponds!' said Rowena.

'You and I could go to the library, chickie,' Mum offered sweetly.

'I like the library, but Fenton Ponds is much more fun.'

'Yes, and what happened last time? You went paddling and slipped and fell in up to your neck. That was OK in the summer, but if you do that now you'll freeze to death and turn into a snowman,' said Sam. 'Sorry, little pal, but this is just going to be a big kids and big dog expedition. And then, when we get back, I'll give you a ride on the front of my bike, OK?'

'Oh yes, Sammy!' said Rowena, her eyes shining.

'You've got such a winning way with everyone, Sam,' I said when we were walking to the ponds. 'You know how to make everyone love you.'

'Do I?' He said it evenly, but there was a little edge to his voice that made my tummy go tight.

'Yes, of course you do,' I said. 'You're Sammy the golden boy. Mum always says she wishes you were *her* son. And we all want you for a brother. You're *like* a brother.'

'Am I?'

'Yes! What's up with you? You're in a weird mood,' I said. It was cold and I pulled the collar of Mum's black fur up round my ears. I felt the soft checked shirt I'd pulled on without thinking. 'Oh God, I'm wearing your shirt again! I'm sorry. I'll shove it in the washing machine when we get back.'

'It's OK. Keep it. It looks better on you than it does on me,' said Sam.

'Really?' I looked at his woolly black hat and his cool leather boots with the buckles. 'Can I have your hat and your boots too?'

I tried to snatch his hat, but he ducked away from me.

'Leave off! It's bad enough to take the very shirt from my back,' he joked.

'Hey, remember when we swapped clothes once when we were very little, and I called myself Sammy and you were Frankie and we kept it up all day long?' I said.

'Yeah, and we drove everyone else mad. And remember when your mum was in the hospital having Rowena so you and Zara were staying at our place and we pretended we were twins and spoke in unison all the time and spooked everyone out?'

We carried on remembering all the fun times we'd had and it was suddenly OK again. We were Frankie-and-Sam the way we always were, and we sang daft songs and raced each other all the way to the ponds. We let Bear off the lead there, and he decided to have a swim, even though it was one of the coldest days of the year.

He shook himself vigorously when he came out, so we had to take giant leaps backwards to avoid being soaked. We ran to get Bear warmed up again, and then we went to the café, and Sam forked out for two cups of tea and three toasted bacon sandwiches – the third one was for Bear, who was very appreciative.

'Thanks! I was starving, even though I had a late-ish breakfast,' I said. 'Still, it was great to sleep in. Mum should really have stayed in bed even longer – she gets so tired, poor thing, and yesterday she had another relapse. Oh God! I was going to make her phone for a doctor's appointment today and I forgot – and Zara's off out and Rowena won't remember. Why did I drop my stupid phone?'

'You can use mine if you like,' said Sam, handing it over. 'So did your mum have another fall yesterday?'

'No, it was her hand that went numb this time. It's so scary. I think I'm going to actually call her, not just text. She might listen more that way,' I said.

I dialled the land line, because Mum has a habit of leaving her phone in her bag, where she can't hear it. She was a long time answering and I started to worry, but at last I heard her husky *'Hello?'*

'Mum, it's me, Frankie.'

'Are you all right? *You* haven't fallen in the pond, have you?'

'No, though Bear had a little swim. I'm just phoning to ask if you've made a doctor's appointment.'

'Oh, Frankie. Look, it's all a bit pointless. If he hasn't gone away, he'll be booked up—'

'*Mum!*'

'OK, OK,' she said. 'But it will have to be after Christmas now. Look, can you get home as soon as you can. One of your friends has come round to see you.'

'Who?' I lowered my voice. 'It's not Josh, is it?' He knew where I lived because his parents had once given me a lift back from football practice.

'It's Sally,' said Mum.

'What?' I said, though I'd heard her perfectly.

'Sally,' she repeated softly.

'Oh goodness!' I said, stunned. 'OK, well, tell her I'll be back in half an hour. Maybe less. OK?'

'Would you like to talk to her yourself?' Mum asked.

'No! Yes. No,' I said idiotically. I was suddenly ludicrously shy – and yet I longed to talk to her, just to check it was really her. What was the *matter* with me? Did I seriously think someone was impersonating Sally? 'Bye, Mum,' I said hastily, and rang off.

Sam was staring at me. 'Who's Josh?' he asked.

'Oh, he's just a boy in my class. But it's not him, it's Sally!'

'Sally?' said Sam. 'But she's your deadliest enemy, isn't she?'

It was so weird realizing that Sally and I had been friends for such a short time Sam didn't even know about it.

'Well, we were kind of enemies for a while, but now we're friends,' I said. 'I never thought she'd come round to see me! How did she even know where I live? Come on, Sammy. Hey, Bear! We're going back now. Home!'

'I thought we'd stay out a while longer. Maybe go to our lunch place.'

'We've just had bacon sandwiches!'

'But you liked it at the caff I took you to when we bumped into those girls at Whitelands. Is Sally the blonde one with the trilby hat?'

'Yes, that's Sally. She's kind of my best friend now.'

'You girls!' said Sam. 'You're so weird, forever making friends and breaking friends. It's all so intense. We boys have lots of mates and go round in a gang, and if we fall out we just have a bit of a fight and then we're mates again.'

'Well, it's different for girls,' I said. 'Can we go a bit faster? Poor Sally will be waiting for ages. I don't want her to give up and go home.'

'*We* don't want to go home yet, do we, Bear?' said Sam. 'We were having a great time here, weren't we, boy? Why is Frankie making such a big deal about this girl coming round? Give a bark if you think she's acting crazy.'

He put his hand in his jacket pocket where he sometimes kept dog treats. Bear immediately barked eagerly.

'There!' said Sam, giving him a little chew.

'Will you guys stop ganging up on me? Come on, for God's sake!' I was starting to get irritated by Sam's clowning.

It came out sharper than I'd meant. Sam stared at me and then quickened his pace, so I had to scurry to keep

154

up. We marched along for several minutes in silence, and inside my head I rehearsed how I was going to greet Sally.

I was determined not to sound pathetically grateful to her for coming round. I didn't want to turn into another Marnie. I'd act pleased but ultra casual. *Hello, Sally. Hi, Sally. Hey, Sally.*

My nose started running in the cold and I wiped it fiercely. It was probably bright red. And I had another spot, though hopefully it wouldn't show underneath my fringe. I looked OK otherwise, didn't I, in Sam's shirt? But maybe she'd think me totally gross for wearing it two days running. I hadn't got it sweaty or anything, I was wearing a clean T-shirt underneath. Maybe I could charge upstairs and change before she saw me, though that might look ridiculous. *I* was ridiculous, getting in such a state.

She probably wouldn't even notice what I was wearing. She'd be eyeing Sam up. Was *he* the reason she'd come round? I glanced at him, trying to see him objectively. I forgot he was so good-looking, especially nowadays. He'd suddenly grown quite tall and thin, though he never looked gawky like some boys. He had an effortless lithe grace, whatever he was doing. He had Sally's trick of tossing back his fair hair. In fact, he really did look rather like Sally. Why hadn't I realized that before?

'Why are you looking at me like that?' he asked.

'I was just thinking you look super cool.'

I thought he'd laugh but he actually blushed. 'Really?' He paused. 'Cooler than Josh?'

'Who?' I was astonished.

'This guy you thought had come round to see you,' said Sam. 'Maybe you fancy him.'

'Are you crazy? *Josh!* He's one of my football mates, that's all. He's OK, but I'd never fancy him in a million years,' I said.

'So he's not your boyfriend?' Sam persisted.

'Oh, Sam, don't be daft. I haven't *got* a boyfriend. *You're* the only boy I want to hang out with,' I said.

'Truly?'

I wondered whether I dared tell him how I felt about Sally. We'd always been so close and told each other everything. Patrick, one of his best friends at school, had been cheerfully telling everyone he was gay since he was eleven. It was quite brave to carry on saying it in Year Nine, because some of the boys at the grammar were totally pathetic and called each other gay as an insult. Some possibly thought Sam was gay too, but he didn't care, and happily stayed pals with Patrick.

Sam would stay best friends with me. He'd be totally supportive. Fascinated too. But I couldn't possibly blurt it out. It was still so private. And nothing had happened. I didn't think Sally would ever feel the same way about me. She might laugh. She might be appalled. I had to keep my feelings to myself and act in a light-hearted, casual way.

But I was totally dumb-struck when I went into the living room and saw Sally there, sitting cross-legged on the floor beside my little sister. Rowena had all her

Sylvanian families out, and Sally had lined them up in rows. Rowena was giggling so much she was actually snorting.

'Oh, Frankie, Sally's making all my Sylvanians do line dancing, it's so funny!' she said, barely able to get the words out. 'And Baby Betty Badger's useless and keeps going the wrong way and bumping into people!'

'I've still got my own Sylvanians stuffed in a cupboard somewhere. I'll show you sometime, Rowena,' said Sally, as if she was expecting us to pop round any old day.

Bear rushed through the door at the sound of this new voice, barking his head off. He was so big and sounded so fierce that most people got alarmed, especially if they were sitting on the floor, but Sally's face lit up.

'Hey, lovely boy!' she said, and stroked him enthusiastically, rubbing her face against his.

'Careful!' I blurted out, because Bear likes to take his time getting to know you.

But Bear seemed to have made up his mind instantaneously: he nuzzled up close, and then flopped down beside her. He rolled onto his back and waved his great legs in the air.

'Oh, Bear, you like Sally too!' said Rowena.

'Sally and the incredible dancing Bear,' said Sam. 'Hi, I'm Sammy. We met incredibly briefly at Whitelands, but I don't suppose you remember.'

'Of course I do! Hey there,' said Sally. Then she looked up at me and smiled. 'Hey there, Frankie. I hope you don't mind me coming round.'

'No, it's fine. Cool,' I said, trying not to sound flustered.

What should I do? Suggest I take Sally up to my room? But that might sound weird. My end of the bedroom was in such a mess and had such silly childish things in it: my old teddy, Mr Nighttime; the cowboy hat I'd worn every day when I was seven; the collection of trophies I'd won at primary school sports days; my badge collection; my papier-mâché witch suspended from the ceiling as if she were flying through the air on her broomstick.

Zara's half was a total contrast: neat and ultra girly, her perfume and make-up and brush and comb laid out in a pattern; her posters of pop singers properly framed; her dresses and tops suspended on padded hangers outside the wardrobe because she said the inside smelled musty.

Sally seemed happy enough to stay sitting in the living room, chatting. She paid particular attention to Mum, asking her all about her teaching, admiring the shelf of picture books she used for her Year Ones.

'*Where the Wild Things Are*! *The Tiger Who Came to Tea*! *The Gruffalo*! I had all those but they got chucked out ages ago! I wish *my* mother had kept them,' she said. 'Did you read them to Frankie and her sisters when they were little?'

'Mum still reads to me,' said Rowena. 'We're reading all the Narnia books now, aren't we, Mum?'

'You're so lucky!' said Sally.

I looked at her carefully. She didn't seem to be taking the mickey. I was worried Sally might say something about Mum's illness, but she chatted away naturally, and when Mum got up to show off her collection of Ladybird books, Sally didn't jump up to help her.

Mum seemed totally steady on her feet and her fingers were nimble as she turned the pages of the little books. I went to look too, wanting to remind myself about fairy tales.

'*The Sleeping Beauty*? *Cinderella*? *The Princess and the Pea*?' said Mum. 'When you were little you never had time for all those silly princesses, Frankie.'

'I belong to this writing club,' I said self-consciously. 'We've got to write our own version of a fairy story over Christmas.'

'A writing club!' said Mum. 'Are you in it too, Sally?'

'Not me!' she said. 'Frankie's the one who's good at writing.'

'I'm not,' I said stupidly.

'So Miss Allen has her own little writing club, does she? Teacher's pet!' said Sally, but fondly.

'No, I wouldn't want to join *her* writing club if she ever started one,' I said. Miss Allen was our English teacher and she was unbearably gushing. 'This is Mr White's idea.'

'Oh, the sweet library guy. I understand now,' said Sally. 'Lucky you.'

'Maybe you could join too, if you wanted.'

'Maybe not!' Sally looked at Rowena. 'I bet you're good at writing stories too! You make up lovely things about your Sylvanians.'

Rowena's face shone. 'I *like* making up their games. So do you think I should write them all down as stories?'

'Good idea. Though you'll need a notebook.' Sally looked at me. 'Maybe Frankie could find you one.'

'Or Mum,' I said. I was keeping the scarlet notebook for myself, no matter how much I loved Rowena.

Sally looked amused. Then she turned to Sam. 'Do you like writing too, Sammy?' she asked.

He pulled off his coat and bobble hat and sat on the arm of the sofa, smoothing his hair straight. 'I do, as a matter of fact. I write science fantasy,' he said.

'Oh, dragons and sexy ladies in brief costumes and endless battles?' said Sally.

'That's a very old-fashioned idea of science fantasy,' said Sam, in his poshest voice. But then he grinned. 'But I would say it's a fair summary of my work so far.'

'It's actually very good,' I said. Sam was always showing me his work – he had several novels' worth stored on his computer. I quite liked the people parts, but I skipped the battles because they were so tedious.

'Let's play that game where one of us starts a story and says a few sentences and then the next person has to carry on,' said Sam.

I was sure Sally would pull a face, but to my surprise she nodded eagerly. So *did* she want Sam for herself? She seemed keen to please him. It was exhausting trying to keep track of everything. I was also on tenterhooks waiting for Zara to come home. She hated Sally now. She wasn't good at keeping her feelings to herself. She'd likely say something scathing, and then Sally would take offence and leave, and be my enemy all over again.

I knew perfectly well that if Sally started tormenting me again simply because of something my sister said, then she wasn't worth having as a friend. I couldn't seem to think straight any more. I hated this new helpless feeling, this uncertainty, this awful anxiety – and yet at the same time I'd never felt happier.

I was in such a turmoil I wasn't concentrating on the story and could only mumble rubbish for my contribution. Rowena wasn't particularly inventive either, wanting everything to end happily ever after before the story had got properly started. Sam was suspiciously good, making me wonder if he was using ideas from some book he'd read – but Sally was outstanding, inventing all kinds of mythical beasts, some fierce and bloodthirsty, some bumbling and flatulent.

Rowena laughed so much she had to lie down on the carpet, hooting and hiccupping. 'You're so funny, Sally,' she snorted. 'I do love you!'

It was so easy when you were Rowena's age. You could tell someone you'd just met that you loved them, and nobody turned a hair. But if I said I loved Sally, they'd all stare at me, and then . . . How would they all react? What would Sally say? What if she told Marnie and Georgia and Scarlett? They might spread it around the class – the whole *school*.

Well, so what? Did it matter? Yes, it did! It was private. I didn't want people asking me stuff, commenting, wondering what it was like. I didn't know! I just knew what I felt. I suddenly understood Mum's secrecy. She wasn't keeping quiet about her MS just because she needed her job. She didn't want everyone discussing her, asking her how she was coping, wanting to know all about it.

She seemed happy now, lounging in her chair, sewing new teddy-bear buttons on a charity-shop cardigan for Rowena. She was half listening to us, half listening to some old rock tunes on her old iPod. Her toe was tapping to the beat.

She used to love dancing. Years and years ago, before Rowena was born, Mum and Dad used to prance about the kitchen sometimes, jiving away, lost in the music. Zara and I tried to copy them, but we were useless, and we soon got out of breath pushing and pulling each other. Mum and Dad seemed so light and bouncy compared to us, as if they were on springs.

Even on a good day, legs working properly, Mum couldn't possibly dance like that any more. It must be awful. I felt a sudden rush of love for her. I caught her eye, and mimed making a telephone call, raising my eyebrows enquiringly.

Mum raised her own eyebrows back at me, but nodded. I relaxed a little, and then I got absorbed in the storytelling game, and became me again, not this shy, awkward new Frankie who agonized over everything.

It was past lunchtime now, and Sally and Sam were showing no signs of going home. Mum didn't fuss. She simply made a huge amount of pasta with pesto.

Zara came in when we were halfway through. 'Yum, that smells good,' she said, shrugging off her coat and scarf. 'I hope you greedy pigs have left some for me.'

Then she saw the extra guest at the table.

'Hi, Zara!' said Sally, as if they were old friends.

Zara screwed up her face in a stupid way. 'What are you doing here, Sally?' she asked.

'Zara!' said Mum.

'What does it look like she's doing?' I said fiercely. 'She's having lunch with us.'

'We've been having such fun,' said Rowena.

'Well, good for you.' Zara turned on her heel, pulling on her coat again, rewinding her scarf around her neck.

'What are you doing, Zara?' Mum asked quietly.

'I'm going out again.'

'How about having some lunch first? There's plenty left.'

'No thanks.'

'OK,' said Mum. She reached for her shoulder bag and found her purse. She casually gave Zara a ten-pound note and patted her on the shoulder. 'Have some lunch out. See you later.'

Zara flounced off. For a second we all looked as if we'd been freeze-framed. Then Rowena said, 'Mum, what's the matter with Zara?'

'I'm not sure, pet,' she replied.

'I don't think she likes me,' said Sally. 'Perhaps I'm the one who should have gone.'

'Absolutely not,' I said. 'Take no notice of Zara. She's ever so moody, that's all.' I started gabbling some silly half-made-up story about Zara and her moods to try to ease the atmosphere. I felt deeply disloyal to poor Zara, but I couldn't help it. I couldn't bear the thought of Sally going and never coming back.

So she did stay, all afternoon. Mum went upstairs to have a rest after lunch. Sally drew some of her monsters for Rowena, giving them little speech bubbles so they could say funny things, while Sam and I washed up.

I'd rolled my sleeves up and suddenly saw that Sam was peering at my wrist.

'What's that?'

I hadn't scrubbed my arms properly in the shower and I still had faint biro marks scrawled on me.

'Oh, it's just a silly scribble,' I said, reaching for the nailbrush.

'No it's not, it's numbers,' said Sam. 'A telephone number?'

'Oh, that!' I said, scrubbing too hard. 'Ouch!'

'Don't you want to keep it?'

'Not particularly.'

'Whose telephone number?' said Sally, overhearing. 'It's not mine, is it?'

'Of course not,' I said. 'I don't even know your phone number.'

'Then come on, whose is it?' she said, coming into the kitchen, Rowena trotting after her.

'It's no one exciting. Look, it's Josh's number, if you must know,' I said.

'Josh?' said Sam. 'The one who asked you out?'

'Josh Brown asked you out!' Sally exclaimed.

'I didn't go. And it wasn't a *date*, it was just to go skating with him and his mates,' I said. 'And I didn't want to. End of story.'

'So how come he scribbled his number on your wrist?' asked Sam.

'In case I wanted to go another day. For goodness' sake, why are you making such a thing of it, both of you?'

'Don't you like skating?' Sally asked.

'I've never tried it, actually, but it looks fun. I just didn't want to go with Josh – though that sounds a bit mean, doesn't it?' I said.

'No, it sounds sensible. I mean, Josh Brown!' said Sally. 'So, come with me, tomorrow. You come too, Sammy.'

'Can't I come?' Rowena asked from the doorway.

'Yes, of course you can come,' said Sally, picking her up and scooting her round and round.

Rowena squealed excitedly. 'Promise?'

'Absolutely promise. We'll all go. I'll meet you there at . . . when? Elevenish? OK?'

'OK,' I said, trying to sound casual, though I wanted to squeal like Rowena.

'And we'll get some lunch there too. Just street food,' said Sally, seeing my hesitation.

'Well,' I said, wondering if I should just tell her outright that Rowena and I didn't have any money.

'My treat,' she said firmly. 'As I've just had lunch at yours. And I'll pay for the skating too – I've got heaps of money. Oh well, I suppose I should clear off home now.'

'Oh don't go yet!' Rowena begged. 'Play with me again, Sally, please!'

'Yes, play with us, Sally,' said Sam, in a silly Haribo voice.

'Idiot,' said Sally, splashing washing-up water at him.

'Let's play Trivial Pursuit!' cried Rowena.

Mum had bought some ancient board games at a boot fair, maybe hoping that the four of us would sit playing together like a family in the olden days. Zara would never join in, and I could only play for ten minutes or so before I got terminally bored – and even Mum started to yawn. Rowena was the only one with a passion for playing. She especially liked Trivial Pursuit, though she rarely knew any answers.

'OK, let's play,' said Sally, smiling at her.

'You'll regret it,' Sam told her.

'We don't *have* to play,' I said.

'I *want* to play! I love Trivial Pursuit,' said Sally.

She really seemed to enjoy it too. Actually, we all did. We spent the rest of the afternoon on Trivial Pursuit, and when Mum came downstairs again she teamed up with Rowena so that she could actually win.

'I really must go home now,' said Sally. 'Thank you so much for having me, Mrs Bennet.'

'It's been lovely,' said Rowena, and she reached up to give Sally a big hug.

'Yes, it's been fun,' I said, wishing I could do the same.

'Yep,' Sam agreed.

He was smiling at Sally. Maybe he wanted to hug her too.

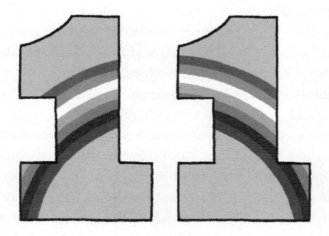

Mum had been phoning Zara again and again all afternoon, but she'd switched off her mobile. She didn't come
back till after suppertime, when Mum was going frantic.
Zara didn't even come into the living room. We heard
the front door slam and then her footsteps rushing upstairs.

'Thank God,' said Mum, and hauled herself out of her
armchair to follow her.

I got up too, but Mum shook her head.

'No, I need to talk to her,' she said. She swayed very
slightly.

'Mum!' I rushed to her side.

'No, I'm OK, truly. I just felt dizzy for a second, that's all. From relief!' Mum rubbed the back of her neck to ease the tension. Then she wiggled her shoulders and took a deep breath. 'Right!' she said, and headed up the stairs.

Rowena and I looked at each other.

'Zara's for it now!' said Rowena.

I hoped Zara wouldn't tell Mum why she hated Sally. I muted the television and tried to listen. I could only hear the faintest murmur in the bedroom above my head. At least they weren't shouting.

Mum was gone a long time. Rowena kept pestering me to draw some magic monsters like Sally's so I did my best. I could be inventive enough inside my head, but the right shapes wouldn't come out on paper.

'They look all weird and wobbly,' said Rowena.

'They're supposed to,' I pretended.

'But their legs don't match,' she said, pointing.

'I know. They're called the Leggonewrongs. They can't walk, so that's why they fly everywhere,' I said, quickly giving them rudimentary wings. 'And then when they land they have to sit like broody hens, though the little light ones sometimes manage to hop.'

'That's a bit silly,' said Rowena. 'You're just making it up. Do some proper animals like Sally's.'

'I can't draw like she can,' I said. 'You really like her, don't you, Ro?'

'She's absolutely lovely. She's my best friend.'

'What about Vivien?' I asked. She was a rosy-cheeked little girl who wore a plastic Alice band with Mickey Mouse ears. She sat next to Rowena in class and shared her little packet of raisins at break time.

'Vivien's my ordinary best friend and Sally's my *big* best friend,' said Rowena.

'She's my big best friend too,' I said. 'We'll have to share her.'

'Why doesn't Zara like her?'

'I don't know,' I lied.

'Zara's silly,' said Rowena. 'She still likes us, doesn't she?'

'Well, she likes you. She's maybe cross with me,' I said.

When Mum came downstairs at last, she looked shattered. Oh God, *had* Zara told her everything?

'Where's Zara?' Rowena asked.

'She's tired so she's gone to bed,' said Mum.

'She wasn't walking around by herself all this time, was she?' I asked, my voice wavering.

'No, no, she went to her friend Julie's house.'

'Sally's *our* friend, Mum,' said Rowena. 'Isn't she, Frankie?'

'*Is* Sally your friend, Frankie?' Mum asked, looking at me.

Zara had said something. I knew it.

'Yes, she is. Though actually we didn't use to be friends at all. More like enemies. Funny, that,' I said as casually as I could.

I think Mum might have said more, but Rowena was intent on showing her my silly Leggonewrongs. 'I think they're meant to be funny. But they're not as good as Sally's, are they?'

'That's not very tactful,' Mum told her.

'Frankie doesn't mind,' said Rowena. 'She thinks so too.'

'You both sound like paid-up members of the Sally fan club,' said Mum. 'Shall *I* have a go at drawing you some magical creatures, Rowena?'

'Yes, please!'

Mum sat down between us on the sofa and flexed her fingers several times. Perhaps she was seeing if they were working properly. But then she started sketching confidently on a blank page of Rowena's drawing book. She drew a whole herd of unicorns galloping along a beach, baby unicorns with fluffy coats and tiny horns prancing beside their mothers.

'Oh, Mum, they're wonderful! The best ever!' said Rowena.

I knew Mum was good at drawing but I was still astonished by her unicorns. 'They look so *real*,' I said. 'And horses are ever so difficult. I can never make their legs go the right way.'

'I've had plenty of practice. There was a time when almost every child in my class came to school clutching a toy unicorn,' said Mum. 'On Friday afternoons I used to draw them on the whiteboard as a treat.'

She sighed. I wondered if she was worrying about a time when she might not be able to draw unicorns or gingerbread men, or plait Rowena's hair or tighten the nut on my roller skates or show Zara how to use eyeliner so it didn't smudge.

I leaned against her, and she put her arm round me. I was so thankful that she didn't seem cross with me. I nestled close, wishing I was as young as Rowena and didn't know enough to worry about anything.

I don't think Zara was asleep when I went up to bed, but she lay very still, keeping her breathing slow and steady. I quickly got into my pyjamas and then bent down beside her.

'Zara?'

She didn't answer.

'Zara, what did you say to Mum? You didn't tell her why Sally and I started being enemies, did you?'

Nothing.

'Sally feels awful about it now. You've got her all wrong, you know. She can be mean sometimes, but she can be so lovely when you get to know her properly,' I whispered.

Zara gave a contemptuous snort and turned her back on me.

'Zara, don't be horrible. I sometimes don't like your friends, but I don't act all funny about them. And, look, so what if she likes Sammy? Everyone likes him. She doesn't try to flirt with him. And I know she was acting a bit daft with Gary Masters at lunchtime yesterday, but that was just showing off in front of Marnie and the others. Zara! Are you listening?' I said desperately.

'I can't help listening to you going on and on about your dear, precious, saintly Sally,' Zara hissed. 'Will you just shut up about her? I'm sick of the sound of her name.

I never took you for a fool, Frankie – but you're being so stupid now I'm sick of you too.'

She pulled the duvet over her head and wouldn't say any more. I got into my own bed, feeling all jangled up inside. I hated it when Zara and I quarrelled, but I wasn't going to break friends with Sally just to please her. Sally meant everything to me now.

I woke up early the next morning, excited about the skating date. I didn't know what to wear. I couldn't wear Sam's shirt *again*. In the end I went up into the attic and rummaged through a big bag of Mum's clothes from ages ago. I found an old jumper, grey with rainbow stripes. It looked OK when I tried it on. One of the cuffs was coming a bit unravelled, but I turned it over a few times and hoped it wouldn't unravel all the way up to my armpit.

I still had traces of Josh's biro on my wrist so I gave it another fierce scrub in the shower. Then I went downstairs and laid the table for breakfast and boiled the kettle.

'Thanks, darling,' said Mum, coming into the kitchen in her dressing gown.

'Shall I get started on the toast, Mum?'

'I think you'd better have porridge – something warm to keep you going while you're skating,' she said.

'You don't mind me going, do you?' I asked. 'It won't cost anything. Sally says she's paying for Rowena and me.'

'No, I'll give you money from the housekeeping purse. I took out extra for the holidays. Of course I don't mind you going skating. But you'll look after Rowena, won't you? Keep hold of her so she doesn't fall over.'

'*I* might fall over,' I said, hoping I wouldn't make too much of a fool of myself.

'You'll pick it up in no time – you're an ace roller skater. You'll love ice skating. I used to go when I was your age,' said Mum.

She sounded so wistful that I said, 'Well, maybe you could still go now if your legs don't feel too wobbly.'

'I think that might be tempting fate. One little slip and I could end up breaking a leg, and then where would I be?'

'It must be so frustrating, having to be so careful all the time.'

'Sometimes, yes,' said Mum, smiling weakly. 'You're being very grown up and sensitive, sweetheart.'

'I'm fourteen next month,' I reminded her.

'True,' said Mum.

'I *feel* grown up. Almost.'

'I remember what nearly fourteen feels like.' Mum stopped measuring porridge oats into the saucepan and gave me a sudden hug. 'My girl,' she said.

'Mum, you like Sally, don't you?' I blurted out.

I felt Mum tensing slightly. 'Yes, I do, but . . .'

'But?' I echoed.

'But nothing,' said Mum. 'I just don't want you to get hurt, that's all.'

She gave me a kiss on the top of my head. 'There now. I'd better get on with the porridge. Can you give the others a shout?'

Rowena came scampering downstairs straight away. She looked extra cute in my old Spider-Man pyjamas and a pair of woolly red socks.

'Look, I can skate already,' she said, zigzagging her way across the kitchen floor.

'Very graceful, chickie, but you'll wear holes in your socks if you're not careful,' said Mum.

I called Zara again. She didn't answer. Eventually Mum yelled up the stairs that the porridge was on the table and Zara's would be stone cold if she didn't come down right now.

So she came down in her flowery blue dressing gown, her hair unbrushed and her face pink with sleep. She looked so much younger without any make-up.

'Oh, Zara, let's be friends,' I said, rushing over to her.

She stiffened at first, but then hugged me back. 'OK, loopy girl. Friends. Now get off me,' she said, wriggling away.

'Will you come skating with us too?' I asked.

'With Sally? You have to be joking.'

'But it feels so mean, us going out and leaving you behind.'

'I'm not a Billy-no-mates. I'm going out too, with my friends,' she told us. 'And, Mum, can I go to the Gold Star tonight? Julie and heaps of the other girls are going. It's the special Christmas party teen night.'

'I don't much like the sound of the Gold Star,' said Mum. 'It's got a bit of a reputation. Some of the kids take drugs there.'

'No they don't! Not us lot. We just want to dance,' Zara insisted.

'And kiss the boys,' said Rowena, grinning. 'I can't wait till I'm old enough to go to the Gold Star!'

'I'm not sure *you're* old enough, Zara,' said Mum. 'I'd really rather you didn't go.'

'But that's not fair! Half the girls in my class will be going! Oh please! I won't take any drugs, I'm not stupid. I won't even drink. I'll just dance and have fun.'

'How are you going to get home then? I don't want you taking the bus late at night. The deal is, I come and fetch you in the car at . . . eleven?'

'Eleven! But it'll only just have started livening up at eleven. Julie always stays till one, sometimes even later.'

'Twelve then. On the dot, Cinderella. Otherwise you don't go,' said Mum firmly.

'OK,' said Zara. 'Mum, you know you said you'd taken out lots of money for Christmas? Well, there's this sparkly top in Primark – it's specially reduced – do you think there's any way you could just lend me the money, and then Dad's bound to give us some cash for Christmas so I can pay you back—'

'Stop nagging Mum,' I said. 'You're always trying to get her to buy you new stuff.'

'Well, it's OK for you, Frankie, you don't care what you wear. Like that ridiculous jumper you've got on over your pyjamas!'

'It's a great jumper. I love it. And it's really cosy for skating.'

'You can't wear it *out*! And it's got a *rainbow* on it!'

'I like rainbows,' said Rowena.

'Yes, what's the matter with rainbows?' I asked.

'Well, it's sometimes a sign that you're gay,' said Zara.

I willed myself to stay cool, but I felt the blood rushing to my face. 'So?'

'Well, you're not gay, are you? So don't go round dressing as if you are.'

'Mum wore this jumper once. And she's not gay.'

'True,' said Mum. 'But isn't there something wrong with the sleeve?'

'It doesn't show,' I said, tucking it up.

'Honestly!' said Zara. 'Why can't you take pride in what you wear?'

'Honestly!' I echoed. 'Why can't you stop obsessing about all the tat *you* wear?'

'Girls!' said Mum. 'Stop bickering.'

'I've got little rainbows on my lunch box,' said Rowena. 'Does that mean *I'm* gay?'

'No, darling, it just means you've got a pretty lunch box,' Mum told her. 'Eat your porridge.'

'Could I possibly have golden syrup on mine?' Rowena asked. 'It's starting to taste a bit boring.'

I wondered whether to wear the jumper or not. I didn't want Sally to think I was making some sort of statement. Surely Zara was being ridiculous. I'd seen hundreds of people wearing rainbow motifs – they couldn't all be gay, could they? I didn't want Zara to win the argument, so I decided I'd jolly well wear it. I'd keep my coat on because it was probably freezing at the ice rink, so it wouldn't show anyway.

I was ready far too soon. Zara had only just gone into the bathroom and I knew she'd be there ages and ages. I risked taking out the scarlet notebook and found my best rollerball, ready to make a start on my fairy story. I wanted to write about a fair princess. Was she languishing in a tower, stoking the cinders, fast asleep in a four-poster, waiting for her handsome prince to rescue her? I could write the story from the prince's point of view. Or maybe my story didn't need a handsome prince. It could be about two girls, a golden-haired proud princess and a serving maid, dark and bold and gallant. *She* could rescue the fair princess.

I daydreamed for twenty minutes, but in the end shoved the notebook back in my drawer, the pages still blank. Zara came back from the bathroom. I watched her getting dressed.

'Stop staring at me!' she snapped.

'What do you want me to do, wear a blindfold? I can't help staring at you when we share a bedroom, you idiot,' I said.

I kept watching as she started carefully applying make-up at her dressing table.

'That cream stuff you're rubbing on your face – does it cover up spots?' I asked.

'Foundation. Well, it helps. If you put concealer on first,' said Zara.

I'd never even heard of concealer. It sounded a comforting concept. I'd like to rub concealer all over my face so that it became a smooth mask, hiding the real me. Zara handed me the little stick and I started rubbing it on liberally.

'Not like that! Here, I'll show you.' She smoothed it on carefully and then applied foundation on top.

I peered in her mirror. It seemed to work.

'How about I put a bit of make-up on you? You've got lovely eyes, actually. If we put a bit of shadow and eyeliner and mascara on them, they'd look incredible,' she said.

'Would they?' I asked hopefully.

I let her apply it all, though she kept telling me off for blinking at the wrong moment. I didn't like the feel of all that goo on my eyes, and wanted to give them a good rub, though I knew I mustn't smudge them. I looked so different with make-up. I wasn't sure if I liked it or not.

'You need a bit of lipstick to balance it,' said Zara, getting into the swing of things now.

'I hate lipstick,' I protested.

'Not bright red. Pale. Lip coloured,' said Zara.

'Then what's the point?' I asked.

'You'll see. Keep still and stretch out your lips.'

I did this reluctantly and Zara applied the lipstick.

'Let me see, then,' I said as she peered at me.

'Wait a minute. You still look so pale. You need a little bit of blusher.'

'Oh God, no, I'll look like a painted doll,' I protested, but Zara was already dabbing it along my cheekbones.

'That's better. It gives your face more definition too. Oh, Frankie, you look almost pretty!' said Zara.

'Almost?'

'Really!' she said. 'Maybe I'll demonstrate on you when I start my YouTube channel.'

I looked in the mirror at this new highlighted version of me. I didn't look pretty, sadly, but maybe I looked cooler? Older? More knowing?

'I could try to put your hair up too,' Zara offered.

I experimented with scraping my hair up to see what it looked like. 'No, it makes my ears look sticky outy. But the make-up looks all right, doesn't it?'

'Yes, it does. You'll have to learn to do it yourself now. And why not dress up in something *nice*?' said Zara. 'That jumper really is awful, Frankie. Why not wear a skirt for once? Your legs aren't too bad, though they're a bit skinny. Go for it!'

'Zara, I'm going skating, not prancing down a catwalk,' I said. 'But thanks for doing the make-up.'

I felt a bit self-conscious showing it off to Mum and Rowena. Mum raised her eyebrows when she saw me.

'Oh dear, do I look like a clown? It was all Zara's idea,' I said hurriedly.

'No, it looks great. You just look different, that's all. But in a good way.'

'I think it looks amazing!' said Rowena. She went dashing upstairs. 'Zara, will you put make-up on me too, *please*!'

'Just a tiny dab of lipstick,' said Mum. 'Two grown-up girls is quite enough. I need one baby still.'

'What are you going to do while we're all out, Mum?' I asked.

'Have a read. Put all the groceries away when they come. Maybe make some mince pies.' Mum yawned. 'Or maybe go back to bed and have a little nap. Lovely!'

It didn't sound very lovely to me. It sounded a bit sad and lonely. I suddenly burned with hatred for Dad all over again. I remembered the Christmassy things they used to do together. I wished Mum had more friends now. She'd had fun with Coral before she went to work in Hong Kong.

'Why don't you FaceTime Coral?' I suggested.

'Yes, maybe I will.'

'And you could text one of the teachers from work, see if they want to meet up for a coffee or something. Maybe that Chris someone – the one who takes Year Five. Didn't he ask you out for a meal once?'

'Ages ago. He's living with his girlfriend now. Frankie, I'm fine. Dear Lord, you'll be suggesting I go on Tinder next.'

'Well, you could, you know. Or maybe Match.com?'

'I don't want a match. Which is just as well, because who wants a faded old forty-something, in debt, with three girls, plus an incurable illness,' said Mum.

'It isn't always going to be incurable, not when they've found the right drug to use. And some people go into remission and it never, ever comes back,' I pointed out.

'Yes, and other people have two relapses in one year,' said Mum. 'Don't let's put a downer on the day, Frankie. I'll have a lovely potter at home, and then we can stay up late and watch a DVD this evening, OK?'

'If you absolutely promise it won't be *Frozen* all over again,' I said, trying to lighten the mood, but feeling so sad for Mum that I was almost crying.

I took Bear out to the park and threw his ball for him again and again to try to wear him out. 'You look after Mum while we're gone, promise?' I whispered into his gorgeous ears.

Yet when Sam came round and we set off for the skating rink with Rowena, I'm ashamed to say I forgot all about Mum. My mind was so full of Sally that I could barely make conversation with the other two.

'Are you OK, Frankie?' Sam asked.

'Of course,' I said.

'Are you *crying*?'

'No, silly!' I wasn't crying, not even about Mum. The wind was simply making my eyes water – but I couldn't dab them with a tissue because they might smudge. I hoped I didn't have little black trails running down my cheeks.

Sam was still peering at me.

'What?' I said, slightly irritated.

'Why have you got all that make-up stuff on?' he asked.

He hadn't mentioned it when he first saw me, so I'd assumed he hadn't noticed.

'I often wear make-up,' I said stupidly. I hadn't worn it since I was Rowena's age, and then only playing.

'No you don't,' he said. 'It looks weird on you.'

'Well, thanks very much for the compliment!' I almost *was* crying now. Why did he have to be so horrible? Did I really look weird? Should I rush home and scrub it all off before Sally saw me like this?

'I think Frankie looks beautiful,' Rowena insisted. 'And I've got make-up on too! Just a little lipstick, but it feels lovely.' She smacked her lips at him.

'Yes, she does,' said Sam. 'You *both* look lovely. I really didn't mean *you* looked weird, Frankie, though I suppose it sounded like that. It's just I never thought you could be bothered with make-up and stuff like that.'

'Well, I've started bothering now,' I said. 'Nearly all the girls my age wear make-up. Even *boys* bother with make-up nowadays.'

'Count me out,' said Sam. Then he suddenly gave me a hug. 'Sorry. I didn't mean to upset you. You really do look great in make-up – just different. Grown up.'

'That's a good thing, isn't it?' I asked.

'Yes, only I wish you weren't wearing an old teddy bear for a coat – I've got a mouthful of fur now,' said Sam.

'All the better to give you a bear hug back,' I said, and we started mock wrestling.

'Honestly, you two, you're like little children!' Rowena said prissily. She started zigzagging along the pavement. 'See, I can skate already, Sammy. I bet I'll be able to do that whirly round-and-round thing too.'

'I should practise keeping upright first,' he said. 'It's a bit harder than it looks. I'll be all right though, seeing I'm an ace roller skater.'

'*I'm* the ace roller skater!' I said indignantly, and then I realized he was teasing.

'I bet Sally's the best skater though,' said Rowena.

She was right. Sally was on the rink before us, wearing a thick cream Aran sweater, woolly red hat and mittens, black jeans and snowy-white boots. She was skating around the rink in graceful strides, but whenever she found a space she did a spin.

'There's Sally! And look, look, she's doing the whirly thing!' Rowena shouted eagerly, hanging over the wooden barrier. 'Hey, Sally, will you show me?'

Sally stopped spinning and came flying over to us. She looked incredible, eyes sparkling, cheeks flushed pink.

'Hey there!' she said. 'I've already got your tickets. Here you are – and tokens if you need to hire boots.' She fished them all out of her jeans pocket. 'I'm so glad you came!'

I had a quick peer around the crowded rink. I couldn't see Marnie or Georgia or Scarlett anywhere. It was a huge relief. I felt my heart banging in my chest. I just hoped I'd be able to skate without making too much of a fool of myself.

Sally joined us after we'd gone through the entrance and collected our boots. Rowena was disappointed she couldn't hire white boots like Sally's.

'They've only got these ugly brown ones,' she said.

'Yes, but they match your brown eyes,' said Sally. 'Here, shall I show you how to lace them up?'

'Why are yours white?'

'Because they're mine. I go skating quite a lot, so I need my own boots.'

'I bet you've got ballet shoes too,' said Sam. 'And tap. And riding boots. And flippers for scuba diving.'

'And great big hairy yeti boots for stamping on cheeky boys,' said Sally.

I wasn't sure if this was flirting or not. It was the sort of silly conversation Sam and I had, always teasing each other. I couldn't be sure about Sam and Sally though. I wished I could get inside their heads to see what they were thinking. Yet I'd have died if anyone could see the turmoil inside *my* head.

I laced my ugly hired boots and stood up gingerly. So far, so good. I took a step and stopped dead. I hadn't realized it would feel so precarious. I was used to clumping around on roller skates without even thinking. It was so much harder balancing on a thin blade. But skates made everyone look clumsy on the ground. Even Sally looked odd. Once I was on the ice I was sure I'd be able to glide. I knew exactly what to do.

'Hold hands with me, Rowena,' I said. 'Come on, let's step onto the ice.'

'Can we hold onto the side?' she asked, hopping anxiously from one skate to the other.

'That's for babies,' said Sam, and stepped boldly forward himself.

'Can he skate?' Sally asked me.

'Roller skate,' I said.

'Hmm,' she said, raising her eyebrows.

Sam lurched forward, waving his arms to keep his balance. He wobbled alarmingly and tried speeding up. He staggered along till he was at breakneck speed, weaving in and out of the other skaters, his legs wobbling.

'Slow down, Sammy!' I yelled.

'How?' he shouted back, turning towards me.

This threw him further off balance, and he teetered on one leg, his arms waving like windmills. There was no way he could stop himself. He fell down hard on his bottom, practically bouncing with the impact.

'I think he needs a bit of help,' said Sally, dashing onto the ice.

She reached Sam before he could manage to haul himself up. She held out a hand and got him to his feet, then tucked her arm round his waist.

'She's cuddling him!' exclaimed Rowena.

'Of course she isn't,' I said. 'She's just supporting him so he doesn't fall down again.'

She was talking to him, her face very close to his, but then I suppose she had to make herself heard on the noisy rink. Then they both took a step forward, gliding slowly, then another, and another, and at last Sam's legs got into the right sort of rhythm.

'He's skating!' said Rowena. 'Oh, Sally, come over here, help me skate too!'

'I don't think she can hear you. But don't worry, Ro, I'll help you skate. You can clutch on to the rail with one hand and I'll hold the other. We'll glide just like Sally.'

'Promise we won't fall over,' said Rowena.

'I promise,' I said, crossing my fingers.

At first it seemed almost easy. Very odd, a bit scary, but we both stepped to the right, stepped to the left, nearly gliding. I knew I was poking my head forward to keep an eye on our feet – my bottom must have been sticking out comically – but at least we were moving and upright.

Then we came to a little cluster of people bunched up beside the rail, unwilling to let go even for a moment.

'No problem, we'll just skate round them,' I said. 'Come on – one, two, one, two, one—'

I don't know which of us wobbled first. It could have been Rowena, it could have been me. It didn't really matter. We both lost our footing and couldn't save ourselves. We slipped and fell down with a bump.

'Oh, that hurt! And it's all wet and cold! You promised you weren't going to let us fall over!' said Rowena, half laughing, half crying.

'I didn't mean us to,' I said, trying to get up but failing.

'Here.' Sally was skating over to us.

'Sally! *Please* will you skate with me and show me how to do the whirly thing!' Rowena begged, staggering to her feet.

'OK, OK,' she said. 'If that's all right?' she asked, looking at me.

'Sure,' I said.

So Sally skated off with Rowena and Sam made his way over to me. He faltered every now and then, but seemed mostly to have got into his stride.

'You didn't hurt yourself, did you, Frankie?' he asked.

'Of course not,' I said, though it had been surprisingly painful landing with such a bump.

'Here, take my hand. We'll go around together. I seem to have got into the swing of it now. Sally's a great skater, isn't she?' he said.

'Yes, she is.'

Sam clasped my hand and we crept slowly forward, out of step.

'No, left foot first. Here, we need to be closer. Sally did it like this.' He tried to put his arm round my waist. 'It's a bit difficult when you're wearing your hairy bear coat. Why don't you take it off?'

I clung onto it. I didn't want to risk anyone nicking it, though common sense told me no one would really want a matted fur coat that was twenty years old. And I didn't want to show the rainbow jumper in case Sally thought it was weird. So Sam and I staggered around uncomfortably. I kept looking at Sally and Rowena. Sally was wonderful with her, holding her upright and steering her carefully. Rowena's skinny legs kept buckling, but Sally made sure she didn't trip or fall, and when they'd been round the rink a few times she clasped her round the waist and spun her round and round.

'Did you see?' Rowena cried breathlessly when Sally brought her back to us. 'I did the whirly thing! I really did it! It was the most amazing feeling. Skating is the best thing ever!'

'Thanks, Sally,' I said.

'Come back and help *me* do the whirly thing,' Sam joked.

'You've had your turn. It's Frankie's go now,' said Sally.

'No, it's OK. I'm wearing this silly coat anyway, so I can't really skate properly,' I stammered.

'Don't be daft,' said Sally, and she took my hand.

It was just the simplest little gesture, one hand touching another, and we were both wearing woolly mittens, but my arm tingled right up past my elbow.

'You can do it, Frankie,' Sally murmured.

And I could, I really could! I held her hand, I felt the rhythm of her steps, I followed her lead, and all by themselves my feet glided forward in turn. I'd got my balance at last. We were skating, skating, skating . . .

Afterwards we had Thai food and spiced apple juice at one of the stalls. Sally insisted on treating us, not even letting Sam pay his share, but she did it in such a casual, easy way that it wasn't embarrassing. Rowena usually declared she hated any kind of Asian food, but she ate her tempura prawns with gusto and then licked her lips.

'Thank you so much for everything, Sally,' I said. 'Well, I suppose we'd better be getting home now.'

'Can't Sally come back with us? We could all play board games,' Rowena begged.

'Is that a threat or a promise?' Sam laughed. 'Still, do come, Sally.'

'Yes, come,' I said, my throat dry.

Sally considered, swinging her white boots by the laces. 'Tell you what,' she said. 'You lot come to me instead.'

'Oh *yes*!' said Rowena. 'I'm dying to see your bedroom!'

It was what all her friends did first when they went to tea with each other, though their bedrooms were all pretty similar, decorated in pink and pale purple, with cuddly toys all over the bed and princess costumes hanging outside the wardrobe. But of course it sounded so funny that Sally, Sam and I burst out laughing.

'Of course you can see my bedroom,' said Sally, grinning. 'Come on, then.'

I hesitated for a second. Mum would be expecting us back in half an hour or so. If we went to Sally's, I knew we'd probably be gone the whole afternoon. More than likely Zara would be out too. It wasn't fair to leave Mum all on her own when she'd be expecting to do family things with us. She was trying so hard to start new Christmas traditions just for the four of us – well, five counting Sam. And then, from Boxing Day onwards, we'd be with Dad and Helen. Mum wouldn't feel she had a family at all.

But I so wanted to see Sally's house, to spend the afternoon with her, to get to know her properly. I wanted it even more badly than Rowena, who was squeaking *'Please please please'* like a little mouse.

'Yes, though we'd better not stay too long,' I said quickly. 'And, Sam, could you text Mum to let her know we've gone back to Sally's?'

'You can ring her if you like,' he offered, handing me his phone.

'No, just text,' I said, knowing that hearing Mum's voice would make me feel guilty.

Yet *why* should I feel guilty? I reasoned to myself on the way to Sally's house. Zara was the eldest, so why didn't *she* feel responsible for Mum? She'd always gone out and done whatever she wanted, taking it for granted that I'd be around for Mum. Surely it was her turn? Every other girl my age saw their friends as a matter of course, I thought. Some of their parents had split up too, but that didn't stop them going out. And probably some of their mothers were also ill. It wasn't as if Mum couldn't cope without us. She acted fine most of the time. She was just a bit tired – and if that was the case, surely she'd welcome a bit of peace and quiet at home?

No, I knew I was kidding myself. And it wasn't as if Mum ever played the emotional blackmail card. She hardly ever complained or tried to make me feel sorry for her. If I spoke to her on Sam's phone now, she'd say it was a great idea to go to Sally's, forcing herself to sound enthusiastic. That somehow made it worse.

I wondered about stopping in my tracks and saying we'd better go home after all. But Rowena would make such a fuss and moan all the way back. And what if Sam let us go home without him? What if *he* went to Sally's without us?

I walked on resolutely.

'Are you OK, Frankie?' Sally asked.

'Yes, of course.'

'You do want to come, don't you?' she said softly, leaning towards me.

'You know I do,' I muttered.

'Good!' she said, and she linked arms with me.

'Me too!' said Rowena, reaching for her other arm.

'And me!' said Sam, tucking his hand through *my* other arm.

We marched along like Dorothy and her friends on the Yellow Brick Road. I started singing the song, and they all joined in. By the time we turned into Sally's road all thoughts of Mum had disappeared.

It wasn't actually a road, it was an avenue, with the space and the old trees and the big front gardens that the name implied. The houses were all Victorian, some of them huge, though they didn't seem to be divided into flats. Sally nodded at a pleasant, grey-brick, double-fronted house.

'That's where Marnie lives,' she said casually.

'Oh!' I didn't know what else to say. Was she going to suggest we call for Marnie and invite her along too?

'Yes. Ten doors along from me. We've been friends for ever,' said Sally.

'But she's not your best friend, is she?' Rowena asked, tugging at her arm.

'She wants to be. But she's not really. Not any more.'

I breathed out.

'I know just what it's like,' said Rowena. 'I used to be friends with this girl called Katy and we did everything together, but then one day I played with Vivien and she was *much* nicer so I wanted to be her friend, but it was so difficult because I didn't want to hurt Katy's feelings. But then I got fed up and simply told her I didn't want to be her friend any more.'

'That's my situation exactly,' said Sally.

'But you'll be seeing her over Christmas, won't you?' I asked.

She shrugged. 'Maybe. She's at their grandmother's cottage at the moment. She wanted me to come and stay, but I didn't fancy it this year. She got really upset with me, so I had to take her shopping before school and buy her a special present to make it up to her.'

'The friendship bracelet,' I said.

'But you don't want her to be your friend now,' Rowena pointed out.

'Yes, I know. It was silly,' said Sally.

'You girls,' said Sam.

'Boys can be equally silly at times.' I gave him a little dig with my elbow.

'I know they can,' he said.

Rowena was busy counting along the houses. 'Is yours the white one with the blue door, Sally? It's lovely! Oh, I'd have guessed it was yours, because it's the nicest,' she said.

It actually *was* the nicest, especially now, because there was a holly bush tied with scarlet ribbon on either side of the front door, which was decorated with an elaborate wreath. Even the trees in the garden were lit with silver fairy lights. The decorations were all very tasteful – not a flashing Santa in sight.

'Did you help your mum put the lights up?' asked Rowena. 'We helped our mum put the fairy lights on our Christmas tree. And most of the decorations.'

'We don't actually have a Christmas tree. Mum thinks they're a bit naff,' said Sally.

Naff? A Christmas tree? Rowena and I exchanged looks. How could anyone possibly object to a Christmas tree? Everyone had them. We only had a small one nowadays, but we smothered it in decorations. They were a glorious mixture of bright baubles; little woolly robins and Santas our grandma used to make before she died; foil stars we all made together; little bluebirds; and beautiful glass angels that Coral had sent from Hong Kong.

Sally let us in the front door. I made Rowena take her boots off before she stepped on the pale carpet. I took mine off too, and gestured to Sam to do the same. The hall and the huge living room were different shades of white and grey – no stains or scuff marks anywhere. There were black leather sofas with chrome arms and geometric rugs and white shutters at the windows. On the wall hung a big painting of a grey city with an orange setting sun. The exact shade of orange was echoed by one of the cushions on a sofa. It looked like an upmarket furniture shop, not a real home at all. I could see why Sally's mother didn't want a Christmas tree. They didn't make them in shades of grey, and she'd struggle to find an orange bauble. It was utterly silent in the house.

'Where's your mum?' Rowena asked.

'She's at work. And my dad,' said Sally.

'But it's Christmas!' Rowena was used to Mum being off work at the same time as us.

'They'll be off tomorrow, but it's a Saturday anyway,' Sally told her.

'And where are your sisters?'

'I don't have any. I've got a brother, but he's not coming back from uni till late tonight.'

'So you're on your own all day long! Don't you get lonely?' Rowena persisted.

'I like it. I'm free to do what I want.'

Rowena went around the room on tiptoe, and then gingerly sat on a black leather sofa. It made a funny farty sound as she wriggled backwards and she giggled nervously.

'Don't let's sit in here. It's not very comfortable,' said Sally. 'Come with me.'

'She *is* going to show us her bedroom,' Rowena whispered happily.

But Sally took us downstairs to the basement, which seemed strange. We didn't even *have* a basement. Sam had a cellar that was used for storage. It was fun to look through plastic crates containing his old picture books and his little plastic farm animals and his sets of junior Lego – they were part of my childhood as well as his. But it wasn't a proper room, more like a gigantic cupboard, with cobwebby pipes overhead and the boiler chuntering away in the corner.

Sally's basement was nothing like a cellar. It had rooms. The first was a proper gym with a rowing machine, a cross-trainer, a running machine, and several big balls and exercise mats. The walls were mirrored all round so you could see yourself from every angle.

'Wow!' said Sam. 'Can we go on the machines?'

'Take your pick,' said Sally.

He shrugged off his jacket and sweater and jumped onto the running machine. He set it at the fastest speed, showing off.

'Whoa, slow down, Tiger,' said Sally. 'You have to build up to that speed.'

'But hurry up too, because I want a go!' I said, wanting to show Sally how fast I could run, though she'd seen me in PE lessons for the last two years.

While I was waiting I tried the cross-trainer. I obviously couldn't do it in my coat, yet I felt terribly exposed in my sweater, as if the woollen rainbow stripes were a suggestive slogan. But Sally was busy giving me instructions on how to use the machine, and didn't even seem to notice what I had on. And then, after a ten-minute session, I was so boiling hot I had to pull the sweater off anyway. I went on the rowing machine in just my T-shirt.

Rowena clamoured to have a go on the machines, but we all agreed she was too young. Sally showed her how to use one of the balls and she bounced around on another herself, turning it into a game. She was so *good* with Rowena.

I liked all the equipment, but when I finally got a go on the running machine I decided it was by far the best. I started sensibly at a fast walk, and then gradually increased the speed and gradient, racing along and yet managing to keep my breath slow and steady. I felt my heart rate increasing and I wondered how fast I could make it beat. It was thumping hard, but not just with the exercise. Here I was, in a magical basement, with my oldest mate, my favourite sister – and my girlfriend.

I knew Sally wasn't my actual girlfriend, she was simply a girl who'd recently become my friend, but I kept saying the word in my head because it sounded so glamorous and grown up. I felt myself blushing, but it didn't matter, because it just looked as if I was getting hot with the exercise.

I was worried I was getting sweaty, so when I went to the nearby bathroom I had a quick wash under my arms and used the deodorant in the cupboard. I had a tiny dab of Italian pomegranate perfume too. It was Sally's smell.

My make-up had rubbed off a bit, but it didn't look too bad. The spot hardly showed. My hair was flying all over the place though. I combed it with my fingers without much success. I tried tying it up in a top knot instead.

'Frankie? Are you all right?' Sally called, just outside the door.

I let my hair loose again and quickly came out.

'Mm, pomegranate!' she said.

'You don't mind, do you?' I asked anxiously.

'Of course not.' She sniffed my wrist. 'It smells good on you. Hey, what have you been doing to your hair, it's all tangly.'

'I was just experimenting with putting it up,' I said.

'I think it looks great just hanging down your back,' she told me. 'Come here.'

She took a hairbrush from the bathroom shelf and ran it through my hair, from the roots all the way down to my shoulder blades. 'You've got lovely hair,' she said.

'No I haven't!' I said quickly, secretly thrilled.

Rowena appeared in the doorway. 'Are you playing hairdressers? Can I play too?' she begged.

Sally brushed her hair too. I wondered if she'd suggest brushing Sam's, but she didn't go that far.

'Shall we have a drink?' she suggested.

She led us into a room like a cinema, with a huge screen on one wall, and large soft sofas in front of it. There was a cocktail bar on one side, with a row of spirits and fancy glasses, and a giant fridge containing white wine and bottles of beer and tonic water and fruit juice and fancy lemonades and cans of Coke. There were snacks too – nuts and crisps and dried fruit bars and chocolates.

'What would you like?' Sally asked.

'I'll have a beer,' said Sam.

'Sammy!' I said.

'He can have a beer if he wants,' said Sally, taking the cap off for him. 'I'm going to have a vodka and tonic. You have one too, Frankie.'

'She's not allowed to drink stuff like vodka!' exclaimed Rowena.

'Neither am I, officially. See if I care.' Sally poured herself a drink and looked at me enquiringly.

'Well, just a very weak one then,' I said.

I'd had a few sips of champagne at Coral's farewell party before she flew to Hong Kong, and I'd tried drinking a tot of my dad's whisky, though that had made me choke because it tasted so fiery and vile. I was pretty certain I wouldn't like vodka either, but I didn't want Sally to think I was a baby.

'Me too,' said Rowena, but thank goodness Sally just laughed at her and poured her a rose lemonade.

'Let's watch a film,' she said.

There were so many to choose from it was almost impossible. There was an entire Disney collection that had Rowena cooing in delight, all Sam's favourite space fantasy classics, and any number of feature films that looked interesting. One was called *Two Girls*. It had a photo of the two girls on the cover, embracing. I badly wanted to see what the film was like, but I couldn't possibly watch it in front of Rowena or Sam. I'd have been too shy to ask even if it was just Sally and me.

In the end we watched *Little Women* because Mum had started reading it to Rowena. Sally and Sam and I all groaned, but we let her have her way. It was actually quite a good film. We slouched on the biggest sofa with our drinks and snacks. I sipped my vodka and tonic. It didn't really taste of anything but tonic, which was a relief.

There was one uncomfortable moment in the film when the boy next door, Laurie, falls in love with Jo, and she pushes him away. I didn't dare glance at Sam. But then later Laurie falls for the youngest sister, Amy, instead. Jo seemed very happy for them both. I decided I wouldn't mind a bit if Sam and Rowena started going out together in ten years' time, though it seemed unlikely. But then Jo falls in love with an old professor, and I was certain that would never happen to me. The only older man I liked was Mr White, but I definitely didn't want to *marry* him.

Rowena was sitting very still, absorbed in the film, sucking her thumb, but when at last the girls' father came back from the war, she suddenly started crying. I pulled her closer and cuddled her.

'I wish our dad would come back,' she whispered.

I hadn't realized she missed him so much.

'We've only just seen him. And we'll be staying with him after Christmas,' I whispered back.

'I know, but I want him to be with us all the time,' she said, sniffling.

'Well, that's not going to happen,' I said gently. 'Shh now. Just watch the film.'

She quietened down, and soon seemed to have cheered up again. I was the one who started howling when Jo's other little sister, Beth, got ill and died. There was an image of Beth's old dolls lying on their backs, and they reminded me unbearably of Rowena's tattered toys. I held onto Rowena tightly, wishing there was some magic way I could keep her safe for ever.

When the film finished and Sally switched on the lights, I wiped my eyes quickly, but Sam saw. I thought he might mock me, but he gave my hand a squeeze. Sally turned and noticed the gesture. I think she misinterpreted it because she gave a tight little smile.

'Do you want another beer, Sammy?' she asked.

Sam hesitated, looking at me. 'What do you think, Frankie? Should we be getting back?' he asked.

'She's not your mother, Sammy, she's your girlfriend,' said Sally.

'No I'm not!' I said quickly. 'Let's stay a bit longer.' Then I looked at my watch. 'Oh God, I hadn't realized how late it was. Sorry, we really had better get going.'

'Do we have to?' Rowena sighed. 'We haven't even seen Sally's bedroom yet.'

'OK, come and see my bedroom then,' said Sally.

'Fan-*tas*-tic!' Rowena started pulling at Sam and me. 'Come on then!'

'I think I'll just stay here and have a browse through the DVDs,' said Sam.

'I'll come,' I said.

Sally's bedroom was painted a dusty rose, with deep red velvet curtains. She had a red glass chandelier that made sparkles on the white ceiling when she switched the light on.

'It's beautiful!' said Rowena. 'But haven't you got any toys?'

'They're hiding,' said Sally, and she opened a big white cupboard. She had her own Sylvanian family house on the floor, and a bus and a hotel and a treehouse. Dozens of little animals were gambolling on all the equipment.

'Oh!' Rowena exclaimed.

'You can get them out if you want,' said Sally.

'This is absolute bliss!' she said, examining everything.

Sally raised her eyebrows at me. She had elaborate white bunk beds, and climbed up the ladder onto the top bunk, sitting there swinging her legs.

'I always wanted bunk beds,' I said. 'But Zara and I would have argued about who was sleeping in the top bunk.'

'That's the advantage of not having any sisters,' said Sally. 'I *always* get the top bunk. But if you ever come and have a sleepover with me, I might just let *you* have the top bunk for a treat. Guest's privilege.'

I swallowed. She was joking, wasn't she?

'Does Marnie ever come on sleepovers?' I asked, as casually as I could.

'Sometimes,' said Sally. 'Not so much now. Like I said, we're sort of growing out of each other.'

'Meaning you're getting fed up with her,' I said.

'Meaning exactly that.'

'Poor Marnie.'

Sally shrugged. 'You don't really think that,' she said.

'No, I don't.'

'Come up and join me,' said Sally.

'Is there room?'

'Cheek! Are you implying I'm fat?' she said, blowing out her cheeks.

I climbed the ladder. 'Budge up then,' I said, squeezing in beside her at the pillow end. I was sitting on something small and hard.

'What's . . . ?' I fumbled around and found it. My little wooden bear lay in my hand. 'Oh!'

'I keep him under my pillow,' Sally said softly. 'I hope you don't want him back.'

'No, I gave him to you. He's yours for ever,' I said, and I pressed the little bear into her hand.

We stayed holding hands for a few seconds, but then Rowena squealed, 'Look, I've fitted all the baby squirrels and rabbits and raccoons into the treehouse!'

We jumped down to admire her arrangement.

'Sammy will be wondering where we've got to. We'd better go down now,' said Sally. 'Tell you what, Rowena. You can have the treehouse. I'm way too old to play with it now.'

'Oh wow, how wonderful!' Rowena exclaimed.

'Hadn't you better wait and ask your mother first?' I asked Sally.

'I don't ask her anything,' she said. 'She's never here, is she?'

'What time does she get home from work?'

'It depends. She'll have finished early today, but then they'll all have gone for a Christmas drink. Or two or three or more. She won't be back for ages yet.'

'What about your dad?'

'He'll just stay working half the evening. He's a forensic anthropologist. He finds a pile of old bones much more interesting than real people,' said Sally.

I stared at her. It sounded so bleak.

Rowena clutched the treehouse to her chest, blinking at Sally. 'Who gets you your supper then?' she asked.

'Well, usually it's Morag. She used to be my nanny, and now she's the housekeeper. But she's flown up to Scotland to be with her family over Christmas,' said Sally.

'You poor thing,' said Rowena. She thought about it. 'So who will cook your Christmas dinner? If you're not getting one, I'm sure our mum will let you come to us.'

Sally smiled at her. 'That would be lovely – but we're actually going skiing in Switzerland tomorrow and having our Christmas there. Thank you very much for the offer though.'

'Will you be away skiing for the rest of the holidays?' I asked anxiously.

'We're back for New Year's Eve. My parents always give a big party,' she said.

'Can we come?' Rowena asked.

'Rowena!' I said.

'Well, it's really a grown-up party. I think you'd find it ever so boring, Rowena. But you can come if you want,' said Sally. She looked at me. 'You too, Frankie.'

'It'll seem like ages before we see each other again,' I said. 'Could I have your phone number?'

'I thought you didn't have a phone any more,' said Sally.

'I'm hoping my dad will give me a new one,' I said.

'OK then.' Sally took a pen out of a drawer. 'Shall I ink it on you like Josh?'

'A bit of paper?'

'Sure.' She took a sheet of notepaper and wrote rapidly on it, then folded it up into a tiny square. 'Here you are.'

I tucked it into the back pocket of my jeans, pushing it right down so I couldn't possibly lose it. Then we rejoined Sam down in the basement. He was still happily browsing.

'Borrow anything you fancy,' said Sally.

'Is the treehouse a borrow?' Rowena asked.

'No, that's definitely a gift,' she said.

'Are you sure? Thanks!' said Sam, selecting a couple. He smiled at Sally. 'I'm so glad you and Frankie are friends now!'

'So am I,' she said.

'We're *all* friends,' said Rowena.

'You bet.'

'I still wish you were coming to ours for Christmas,' said Rowena when we were on the doorstep. 'Can I have a hug?'

'Of course.' Sally bent down and put her arms tight round Rowena, plus the treehouse.

Sally and Sam embraced briefly.

Then Sally and I looked at each other. We opened our arms simultaneously. Then I was hugging her and she was hugging me, and although my big yeti coat muffled the experience, it was still amazing. I don't know how long it lasted. Probably only two or three seconds. It seemed to go on for ever but also somehow to be over in a flash.

'See you on New Year's Eve then?' I asked.

Sally nodded. We set off down the path, and right along

the pavement. Then the three of us turned back. Sally looked very small silhouetted in the bright doorway, the rest of the house completely dark.

'Hold my treehouse so I can wave,' said Rowena.

We all waved, and Sally gave a jaunty little wave back with a jazz hand, and then went inside.

'She's got a lovely house but I wouldn't want to be there all by myself,' said Rowena. 'I'd get so lonely. No wonder she wanted us to come and play with her.'

'She's just a poor little rich girl,' said Sam.

'Don't you like her?' Rowena asked, surprised at his tone. 'I think she's lovely.'

'She's not as lovely as you – or Frankie.'

'Oh, come off it, you can't mean that,' I said. 'Sally's got everything – looks, personality, style. She's so funny and generous and . . . Well, she's just *Sally*.'

'You sound as if you're in love with her,' said Sam.

I was pretty sure he was just making a flippant comment, but I felt myself going hot all over in spite of the chilly evening. I thanked God it was too dark for him to see me blushing.

'Wouldn't you fall in love with her, just a little bit?' I asked.

'Well, I'd sort of *fancy* her,' he said.

Rowena giggled.

'But I wouldn't love her,' Sam continued. 'It's like she's acting all the time. You don't know where you are with her.'

'I don't know what you mean!' I protested, though I knew exactly. 'She's been incredibly nice to us all day.'

'Yes, one minute she's all nicey-nicey, acting like a little Lady of the Manor, and then she turns into Little Girl Lost to make you feel sorry for her,' said Sam.

'She does not!'

We bickered for a while, taking it in turns to lug the treehouse for Rowena. It was getting surprisingly heavy and we were all tired. We tried waiting for a bus, but it drove straight past, full of people going into town for late-night Christmas shopping.

In the end we trudged all the way home, Sam giving Rowena a piggyback for the last couple of streets.

'I'd better not come in with you girls,' he said. 'Mum and Dad are having some people round for drinks and nibbles and stuff. I think Mum asked your mum, but she said she couldn't come.'

'She gets so tired now,' I explained. 'And you stand up most of the time at parties.'

'She could sit down. We've got heaps of chairs.'

'Yes, but she doesn't want to be the only one sitting. And she's worried she'd be the only one without a partner.'

'But that doesn't matter.'

'Maybe it matters to her,' I said. 'You have to make a bit more of an effort if you're on your own. And that's hard when you're tired out.'

'I suppose,' said Sam. 'I do wish you'd let me tell my

mum about her MS though. Then she'd be more understanding.'

'She doesn't want people to have to be understanding,'
I said.

'We're not allowed to talk about Mum's illness,' said
Rowena, sliding down off Sam. 'You shouldn't have told
him, Frankie.'

'Sammy's family,' I said firmly.

'Yes, I'm more your family than my own,' said Sam.
'Can I come round tomorrow and do all the Christmas
Eve things with you?'

'Of course,' I said.

'Can I have a hug?' said Sam, imitating Rowena.

'Yes, you fool,' I told him.

For a moment he tried to draw me really close – but
then he started clowning around, pretending he was being
hugged to death by a big black bear. It was a great relief.

Mum must have been worried about us staying out such a long time, but she was determinedly bright and breezy. She seemed happy we'd enjoyed the skating, she asked questions about Sally, but not *too* many, she smiled at the film choice, and she marvelled at the treehouse.

'You are a lucky girl, Rowena,' she said.

'I know!' she agreed. 'It's been a wonderful day. In fact, I actually think it's been the happiest day of my life.'

I felt exactly the same, but I knew we weren't being tactful to Mum.

'Did *you* have a good day?' I asked.

'Yes, lovely,' she said.

'What did you do?'

'Oh, nothing very much. Just a lovely, idle, pottering day. Bliss!'

Mum was sounding *too* cheerful now. I sometimes wished she would moan and weep and swear because she was stuck with a horrible illness that would probably get worse and worse. It was almost irritating to see her making such a superhuman effort.

At least I knew where I was with Bear. He bounded up and licked my face lavishly, telling me how much he'd missed me and how pleased he was that I'd come back at last. Apparently Zara had taken him for a walk before she went over to her friend's, but it would have been a very short one because she always wore silly high-heeled shoes and took tiny mincing steps.

My own feet were aching after the long trek home, but I took him out for a proper walk now, pounding the pavements because the park was shut after dark, and I didn't want to trail all the way to the sports centre by myself. Whenever we had room we broke into a run. Bear's soft paws were silent, but my Docs landed with a thud. They beat out a rhythm again: *Sal-ly, Sal-ly, Sal-ly*.

I wished I hadn't been so careless with my wretched phone. I longed to talk to Sally now, when we could be private. I spoke to her in my head instead, my thoughts so intense I almost felt they could reach her. I remembered the passage in *Jane Eyre* where Rochester desperately calls out to Jane, and she hears him, even though she's hundreds of miles away. I'd thought it was a bit silly when we first read it in class, but now I understood.

It was as if all the great love stories suddenly made sense. I looked up at the sky, and it seemed wonderfully significant that there was a full moon, a perfectly round pearly-white sphere. I could see a few stars too, though I couldn't name them because their shapes never seemed to make sense – though the Pole Star was unmistakable. The wishing star.

I stood still, puzzling Bear. He strained on his lead, wanting to hurry onwards.

'Hang on just a second, Bear.' I stared up at the star, my head flung back until my neck ached.

I thought of all the wishes I'd made on a star throughout my life: *I wish I could be a spacegirl*; *I wish I had a dog and a pony and an alpaca and a whole family of lemurs*; *I wish I had a trampoline*; *I wish Mum and Dad would stop quarrelling*; *I wish I could play rugby like Sammy*; *I wish Mum wasn't ill*; *I wish everyone at school liked me again*.

I had wished each one so hard I felt I was swelling up and bursting, but only one star wish had ever come true. I had a dog. But he was the loveliest dog in the world and I was the luckiest girl in the world to have him. Maybe, just maybe, I could get lucky again.

I wish Sally would be my proper girlfriend and love me the way I love her.

There! I'd said it. Perhaps she was looking out of the window in that great dark, silent house and wishing on the same star about me.

I went back home with my eyes full of stars and my head full of wishes, wanting to be by myself and think about Sally in peace. But the house was the exact opposite of peaceful, because Mum and Zara were having a huge row. Zara had been on her way out to meet up with her friends at the Gold Star – or more likely one of the nearby pubs. She was wearing her old coat, one that came right down to her calves, and that made Mum suspicious. She'd demanded to see what Zara was wearing underneath.

It turned out she was wearing hardly anything – just the tiniest little crop top and a strip of skirt that nearly showed her knickers. Her friend Julie had lent them to her. Zara clearly thought she looked great.

'You look ridiculous!' Mum said.

'What a thing to say to your daughter!' said Zara.

'What a way for my daughter to look! You're not going out like that. Go upstairs and change into something decent!'

'Like what? A Sunday school outfit? You don't go to clubs wearing something *decent*,' Zara shouted. 'You go to look good and get all the boys looking at you.'

'Yes, and I know exactly what they'll be thinking, seeing you showing off all that bare flesh. What is it, some kind of meat market? Why can't you wear a proper dress, for God's sake?'

'Oh, Mum, do you want me to look like a complete loser? No one ever wears *dresses*,' Zara wailed.

'Then you can set a trend,' said Mum. 'You're not going out at all if you insist on wearing that tacky little outfit.'

'Yes I am – and you can't stop me.' Zara wrapped her coat around herself and stalked out of the room in her high heels.

I thought she was bluffing, but then we heard the door slam.

'She hasn't really gone, has she?' said Rowena, shocked.

Mum heaved herself out of her armchair and hurried to the door, but by the time she got there Zara was halfway down the road, running in spite of her heels. We followed her into the driveway.

'Do you want me to go after her, Mum?' I asked.

'I don't think you'd be able to stop her either.' Mum leaned against the doorframe, shaking.

'Mum, are you OK?'

'I'm not feeling ill, I'm feeling furious,' she said. 'And so horribly helpless. Zara's right. I *can't* stop her.'

'I wish Dad was here,' Rowena whispered.

Mum made a strange noise. I thought she was just snorting in contempt – but then I saw that her eyes were brimming with tears.

'Oh, Mum, don't! It wouldn't make any difference whatsoever if Dad was here. You shut up, Rowena. You're just making Mum more upset,' I said fiercely.

'I didn't mean to!' Rowena was starting to cry herself.

'Oh, don't you cry too, kitten. It's not your fault. I know just how much you miss your dad,' Mum said, wiping her eyes with the back of her hand.

'Well, *I* don't miss him in the slightest. Good riddance, that's what I say,' I declared. 'I can't stand him. And

I don't see why we have to waste practically a whole week staying with him and his horrible girlfriend straight after Christmas. In fact, I'm not going!'

'Don't you start, Frankie. Come indoors, girls. We're all making a spectacle of ourselves,' said Mum. 'Let's have supper. Macaroni cheese?'

'Yes, let's. It's Zara's favourite too. Serves her right that she's missing out,' said Rowena. 'She's so bad, isn't she, Mum?'

'She's not really bad. She's fifteen, that's all. I just can't help worrying about her though, going to the Gold Star dressed like that,' said Mum, giving me the cheese to grate while she put the pan on to boil for the pasta.

'Did you see, her tummy was showing,' said Rowena. 'You could see her belly button! Mum, why is Zara's tummy so flat when mine's so roundy?'

'Because you're just a little girl,' said Mum. 'And you stay a little girl for a long, long time. I'd go bananas if you started flouncing off to the Gold Star in a weeny little skirt and not much else.'

'I won't be ready to do that for ages,' said Rowena, nibbling a bit of cheese. 'It'll be Frankie's turn before me.' She started giggling. 'Imagine Frankie in clothes like that!'

'Never going to happen,' I said firmly.

'Does Sally go to the Gold Star?' asked Rowena.

'Of course not,' I told her.

'Oh, Mum, Sally's so lovely.' Rowena started telling Mum about Sally and the time we spent with her, giving a blow-by-blow account.

It was fun in a way because it was all I really wanted to think about too, but I wished it could stay private in my head. After we'd had our macaroni-cheese supper I wanted to go up to the bedroom, but I felt I should keep Mum company and help amuse Rowena.

Mum made a determined effort to be jolly, but after Rowena was in bed I saw how anxious she was.

'I seem to spend my life worrying about you girls staying out late,' Mum said, thumping the sofa despairingly.

'Relax, Mum. Zara will be fine,' I said.

'Look, she acts so grown up now, but she's still a little kid inside. She can be so silly sometimes. And you get such horrible guys hanging around the Gold Star.'

'It's a teen night. It's just stupid young boys. And Zara's not daft, it's not like she'll go off with anyone and – you know – get into trouble,' I said awkwardly.

'I know Zara's desperate to get a proper boyfriend. If someone chats her up and turns her head, she might be idiotic enough to get herself in a bad situation. Maybe I ought to drive straight round and drag her out before she comes to any harm. You'd be all right looking after Rowena, wouldn't you, Frankie?'

'Yes, but you can't do that! Zara would feel such a fool in front of her friends. She'd be furious with you,' I said.

'Well, then we'd be quits, because *I'm* furious with *her*,' said Mum.

She didn't go, but she paced around restlessly, forever getting up and looking out of the window, or going outside and peering down the street.

Every now and then we heard little drunken gangs of people going past, laughing, singing, larking around.

Mum kept looking at her watch. 'When do the pubs close? I think I'd better drive over to the Gold Star now and wait outside. I won't go in, but I want to be there, just in case she comes out at eleven after all. Are you sure you'll be all right looking after Rowena?' Mum asked. 'You won't answer the door to anyone, will you?'

'I'll be fine,' I said. 'Go on then, Mum.'

I was getting pretty anxious myself. Maybe Zara thought that Mum wasn't coming to fetch her any more. I imagined her wobbling along in her high heels, her coat swinging open. I thought of all the drunken louts wolf-whistling, making crude comments, calling her names. Zara would stalk on, calling them creeps, but maybe they'd catch hold of her.

I tried not to think of all the awful things they might do to her.

'Frankie? Why don't you go up to bed? Squeeze in beside Rowena. You look so tired, darling. I should have sent you upstairs ages ago,' said Mum.

'I'm too wired to sleep,' I said.

'Well, I hope I won't be long. I'll just drive straight to the Gold Star and bring Zara back, OK?'

I started to panic the moment Mum had gone. What if she had an accident? Perhaps her hands or legs would suddenly stop working properly. What if her eyesight failed again?

I thought of Mum, I thought of Zara – and then went upstairs to check that at least Rowena was all right. She was lying on her back, spread out like a little starfish, her duvet slipping off. I tucked her up and she murmured something, but then went straight back to sleep. I gave her a kiss on the top of her head, breathing in her warm talcum little-girl smell, and then went to our bedroom.

I sat on Zara's bed and clutched her pillow, hugging it to me. 'Come home safe, you idiot,' I said.

To distract myself I started looking at all the Christmas presents I'd got, wondering if I should start wrapping them. I picked up the science fiction book for Sam and started reading the first few pages. It was one of those dystopian books about some terrifying future. It was weirdly distracting and I had finished the first chapter and started another before I checked the time.

It was getting on for midnight now. It shouldn't be too long before Mum and Zara were back. I forced myself to read another chapter, and then I snapped the book shut and started my own pacing around the room, down the stairs, around the living room and kitchen.

Please let Mum and Zara be all right, please let Mum and Zara be all right, please let Mum and Zara be all right!

What if Mum had found Zara and they'd had a furious argument and Mum was distracted and crashed the car. What if they ended up in hospital? What if they ended up *dead*? Rowena and I would have to live with Dad, and that would be awful. Well, maybe Rowena wouldn't mind so much, but I'd hate it. As soon as I was old enough, maybe sixteen or so, I'd come back to our house with Rowena and look after her, trying to be a good mother figure, though of course I could never, ever replace Mum.

I was so caught up in this fantasy that I didn't hear the car draw up outside. It was only when the doors slammed that I ran to the window and saw Mum and Zara coming down the path, alive and well, though when our security light switched on I saw that they both looked very cross.

'Oh, Zara, are you OK? We were so worried!' I cried as they came into the hall.

'Of course I'm OK, you idiot,' she snapped.

'Which is more than I can say for Julie,' said Mum grimly.

'She's fine now, Mum. And she wasn't *drunk*, it was just something she ate, that's all. She couldn't help it.'

'Well, you're going to help me scrub out that car tomorrow morning, do you hear me? It'll be ages before the smell wears off.'

'*OK!* Though it's not *my* fault,' said Zara. 'And all Julie needed was a bit of fresh air. If you hadn't come barging along, insisting we get in the car, then she wouldn't even have *been* sick.' Her voice rose. '*Why* did you have to come collecting me like I was a silly little kid at nursery school?'

'Will you please keep your voice down! You'll wake your little sister,' said Mum coldly. 'Rowena's OK, isn't she, Frankie?'

'Yes, she stirred when I tucked her up, but she didn't wake up,' I said.

'Thanks for looking after her, love,' said Mum. 'Now, let's all go up to bed. I don't know about you two but I'm exhausted. Night, Frankie. Night, Zara.'

Zara didn't even say goodnight back, just flounced upstairs, stumbling a little in her heels.

'Are you drunk too?' I asked, following her.

'No, I'm not!' she said. 'For God's sake, some boys in the pub next door just bought us a Jägerbomb, that's all. And we had a couple of mulled ciders to warm up because it's freezing out.'

'You were freezing because you're hardly wearing anything,' I said as she shrugged off her coat and stood there in her minuscule skirt. It was badly creased, making it tinier than ever. 'God, what do you look like, Zara!'

'You shut up, you smug little cow,' said Zara, quickly getting into her pyjamas. 'Mummy's little darling! The good little girly-wirly. And it's so not fair, because you keep staying out for hours and hours with your precious new friend Sally, and Mum never nags you in the slightest.'

'Yes, well, she knows I'm out skating or hanging out at Sally's house – not letting strangers buy me drinks and prancing about at a nightclub,' I said. 'I don't know why on earth you'd *want* to anyway.'

'Well, guess what, Miss Sunday School Teacher. Your little friend Sally seems to like going to nightclubs,' said Zara, getting into bed.

'Aren't you even going to wash all that mucky make-up off your face?' I said in disgust, not properly taking in what she'd just said. Then I stared at her. 'What do you mean about Sally?'

'She was there at the Gold Star tonight, whooping it up,' said Zara.

'Don't be pathetic – as if I'd believe that,' I said. 'Look, I was with her practically all day today.'

'So? You weren't with her tonight. She was at the Gold Star. And if you think *I* look tarty, you should have seen *her*!' said Zara. 'She was wearing this tiny dress with a great big zip at the front. All the boys were egging each other on, threatening to pull it down.'

'Sally never wears things like that!' I snapped. 'Which boys? Sally was there with some boys?'

'Well, she came with those friends of hers, but she was soon flirting with a whole load of boys from school,' said Zara.

'I know you're lying now, because Marnie's not even here, she's gone to stay with her grandmother.'

'Is Marnie the creepy one who fawns all over her? Not that one, the other two. Georgia and Scarlett.'

'But she would have told me if she was going!' I said, agonized.

'No she wouldn't. She's not really your friend, I keep telling you. She does all sorts behind your back. And she was making a right fool of herself tonight, flirting with Gary Masters,' said Zara.

'So *that's* why you're carrying on like this! You're just jealous because he likes Sally,' I said. 'I bet he didn't even give you a second glance.'

'Yes he did! As if I cared anyway. He isn't interested in having a proper relationship with a girl, he just wants to show off his pulling powers to all his friends. He's pathetic,' said Zara. 'Now shut up and go to sleep.'

'Look, I'd have been asleep hours and hours ago if you hadn't kept us up worrying. You're so mean and selfish. Didn't you see the state Mum was in? Didn't you read all that stuff on the internet about MS and stress?' I hissed.

'*You're* the one Mum's been stressed about, drifting about in her old clothes and going all moony-faced over a *girl*,' Zara said, and then pulled the duvet over her head.

I lay in the dark, quivering. It was awful when we fought. We understood each other so well we knew exactly how to hurt the most. I was so tired I had a thumping headache, and yet at the same time I felt wide awake. I couldn't get my head round the fact that Sally had gone to the Gold Star. Why hadn't she told me she was going? Why hadn't she asked *me* to go with her? And what did Zara mean by flirting? Was she just smiling at Gary Masters, chatting to him, acting friendly? Did she dance with him? Did they kiss? Did they go off together?

I wanted to pull the duvet off Zara and interrogate her – and yet I didn't want to show her how much I cared. Did she really know I loved Sally? Did Mum know too? Were they having anxious secret conversations about me? Was I really causing Mum even more stress?

I started shivering, unable to get warm. I got up, put on my dressing gown, along with a pair of socks for my freezing feet, grabbed my pillow and *The Chrysalids* and crept out of the room. I went down to the kitchen. Bear was stretched out on his bed, paws hanging off the side. I lay down beside him and he stirred lazily, licked my face twice, and then went back to sleep.

I cuddled close to him, breathing in his warm doggy smell, burrowing my face into his thick fur. I used to sleep with him in my arms when he was a puppy. Now he was big enough to support me, and one of his massive paws moved gently against me, as if he was stroking me. I wished loving people was as simple and uncomplicated as loving a dog. I loved Bear and he loved me. Neither of us was in any doubt about it.

I held onto him tightly, but there was hardly room for Bear on the bed, let alone me, and I was getting a crick in my neck and cramp in my legs. I struggled up again, put on the kettle and made myself a cup of tea. Then I settled myself on the sofa in the living room, propped my pillow behind me, sipped my tea and read some more of Sam's book. And then some more and some more.

I'd hoped I'd feel sleepy after a few pages, but I was still wide awake halfway through the book. I tried switching off the light and lying down properly, but thoughts of Sally flooded my head and I couldn't bear the anxiety. I switched the light on again and read some more, until at last I'd finished the whole book.

I still didn't feel I could ever sleep, but obviously I must have done, because the next thing I knew Rowena was jumping onto the sofa beside me.

'Wakey-wakey! It's nearly breakfast time. I went to see if Zara was back safely and she's upstairs in her bed, but I couldn't find you! I peeped in at Mum, I looked in the bathroom, everywhere. What are you doing here? You've not been here all night, have you? What's the matter? Have you got a tummy ache? You look all weird!' Rowena gabbled, her clear, high-pitched voice hurting my head.

'I'm tired!' I mumbled.

I wanted to crawl upstairs and go back to bed, but Rowena had a plan to make everyone a cup of tea to be helpful. She didn't have the steadiest hand and the full kettle was quite heavy for a small girl, so I did the pouring for her. Rowena used the best china, the red cups with the polka dots. Mum had bought one of those packets of iced gingerbread biscuits as a Christmas treat, and Rowena insisted on putting one on each of her four doll's saucers.

'But it's not Christmas yet, it's only Christmas Eve,' I said.

'Yes, I know, so it'll be a lovely surprise,' she said happily.

Mum did her best to act as if she was thrilled to be woken early with a fancy biscuit and a cup of tea. She propped herself up on her pillows, her hair tumbling over her shoulders. If you hadn't seen her face you'd have mistaken her for a little girl herself. She was as pale as her pillow, with dark circles like bruises under her eyes.

'Goodness, you're up early, girls,' she said, looking at her alarm clock.

'Frankie was up even earlier than me,' said Rowena. 'She was on the sofa reading her book with the funny name.'

'It's *The Chrysalids*. I'm giving it to Sammy for Christmas,' I said.

'He'll like that. I read it when I was about your age. Very stirring,' said Mum. 'Coral read it too, and we used to try to send thoughts to each other. I do miss her so.'

'We haven't had her Christmas presents yet,' I said. Coral always sent marvellous presents. Last year she'd sent me *The Diary of Anne Frank*, a jade bangle and a pair of embroidered green slippers.

'She said she's sending a surprise this year, but it might arrive a bit late,' said Mum.

'Oh no, I'll be at Dad's. Don't unwrap my present then, will you, Mum?'

'As if,' said Mum, giving me a poke.

'Will Coral send me another Chinese dolly?' Rowena asked hopefully.

'We'll have to wait and see,' said Mum. She looked at me. 'Is Zara awake?'

Rowena giggled. 'No, she's absolutely fast asleep. Snoring!'

It seemed incredibly unfair that she should be sleeping when Mum and I had had hardly any sleep because we'd been so worried about her.

'Let's give Zara her cup of tea and special biscuit,' I said to Rowena.

We took them in to her. Rowena had to put her head on Zara's pillow and shout right into her ear before she stirred.

'For God's sake!' she protested, disappearing under the duvet.

'Look, Rowena's made you a special cup of tea and a Christmas Eve treat,' I said, shaking her. 'Don't be mean and spoil things for her.'

'I don't want anything. I feel like death,' Zara mumbled. 'My head's splitting and I feel sick.'

'Serves you right.' I stared at her curiously. 'So have you got a hangover then? You said you didn't drink much last night – just a Jägerbomb, which is quite little, isn't it? And some cider?'

'Oh, shut up,' Zara said, and then she suddenly shot out of bed and ran for the bathroom.

'What's the matter with her?' Rowena asked.

'I think she's being sick,' I said. 'Serves her right.'

Zara crawled back into bed and stayed there till the afternoon.

'She's missing all the best bits,' said Rowena as we wrapped Christmas presents in bright tissue paper and tied them with ribbon.

Then we finished decorating our tree and switched on the lights and put the presents in little piles, ready for tomorrow. Sam came round with his presents for us, and his father, Michael, came too, carrying a huge great food hamper. It wasn't wrapped so we could see what we were getting: a Stilton cheese, a fruit cake, a box of marrons glacés, a couple of jams with brandy and cognac, gentleman's relish, pâté, and two bottles of posh wine, one white, one red. They usually only gave us a box of chocolate truffles.

'Happy Christmas,' he said, kissing Mum on the cheek.

'How lovely! Thank you so much!' she said, sounding as if she really meant it, though it wasn't our sort of food at all, and I didn't even know what a couple of the things were.

'Here's our present to you,' said Mum. She looked a little flustered. It was wrapped in purple tissue paper with red ribbon, but there was no way we could disguise the shape. It was a single bottle of wine – a Prosecco that was on special offer at Morrisons.

'That's so sweet of you,' said Michael. 'Sooo. How *are* you, Jenny?'

'I'm fine,' said Mum a little warily, and tried to change the subject by asking if he'd like a coffee.

We were all hoping he'd say no, but he stayed, sitting down at the kitchen table so we couldn't really get on with our wrapping. Sam looked irritated, but there was nothing he could do about it. His dad kept on asking Mum how she was coping. She insisted she was fine all over again.

'You will tell us if there's anything we can do, anything at all?' he said.

'It's very kind of you,' said Mum. 'But we're managing – really we are.'

'I heard you go out in the car very late last night.'

'*Dad!*' Sam said.

'I'm sorry if I woke you up,' said Mum stiffly.

227

'No, no, I was wide awake. It was just that I couldn't help being a bit worried. It wasn't an emergency, was it?' he persisted.

'No, I was simply picking Zara up from the Gold Star,' she said.

'Oh! Good Lord, the *Gold Star*?'

'It was a special teen night, apparently. But I agree, it's not the most salubrious of places.'

'Well, I suppose Sam will be clamouring to go there soon enough,' said Michael. 'Did Zara have a good time?' He looked around, as if she was somehow hiding in a corner of the kitchen.

'I'm not sure. She's not been very communicative,' Mum said.

'Well, listen, Jenny, if Zara needs picking up from anywhere at night, you tell me and I'll go and fetch her. I truly don't go to sleep till well after midnight, and I'd be more than happy to pop out. I don't like the idea of you going out late, especially if it's anywhere rowdy.' He said it so earnestly that it was hard for Mum to take offence.

'That's so kind of you, Michael. Let's hope Zara won't make a habit of it,' said Mum, her voice clipped. 'But please don't feel you have to keep trying to help us out.'

'I want to,' he said, and he touched the back of her hand.

It was the lightest of touches, but I suddenly realized that he wasn't just being kind or pitying – he really *did* want to. He cared about Mum. Maybe he wished he had a wife like her instead of bossy, brittle Lucy.

'Hadn't you better be getting back, Dad?' Sam said pointedly. 'Aren't you and Mum supposed to be going out?'

'Yes, yes – and make sure you don't overstay *your* welcome, Sam. You're forever hanging around here. Chuck him out if he becomes a nuisance, Jenny,' said Michael. Then he looked at me. 'Still, I know these two are inseparable.'

Sam and I took Bear for a walk while Mum and Rowena made dough angels.

'Sorry my dad acted like an idiot just now,' said Sam.

'He was just being nice, that's all,' I said.

'So, did Zara get drunk? Did she get off with anyone at the Gold Star?'

'Well, she said she hadn't drunk much, but I think she was fibbing because she was sick this morning and she's still in bed now. I don't think she can have got off with anyone – she'd be crowing about it if she had.'

'Do *you* ever want to go to the Gold Star, Frankie?'

'No!'

'Because I'd take you if you really wanted to.'

'It's not my sort of thing at all, you know that.' I thought about Sally. Was it really *her* thing?

'What about Sally?' said Sam.

'That's weird! I was just thinking about her. You're like the people in the book I'm giving you for Christmas. Which I've just read – I hope you don't mind. *Anyway*, they can read each other's minds, talk inside their heads – it's so cool.'

'I can do that with you. I've always known what you're thinking. Well, until recently.'

'What do you mean?' I said defensively.

'You don't always want to share everything with me any more,' said Sam.

'Yes I do! I've even shared your own Christmas present with you! Sorry about that, but I didn't tear any of the pages or break the spine. And it was second-hand anyway,' I said. 'A bit of a rubbish present, though it's a great story. You know I'd spend heaps on you if I had any money going spare. It's so embarrassing, your family having so much more money than ours. Look at that incredible food hamper!'

'Don't tell, but the hamper's second-hand too. This firm's trying to head-hunt my mother to work for them, so they sent her the hamper. She's not really into food – you know, she's always on some boring old diet – so she said she'd give it to you lot,' said Sam.

'Oh well. It's still very kind of her,' I said.

'You don't think that at all! It's not really the sort of food anyone likes, it just costs a lot. It means far more to me that you've carefully chosen a special book for me. I love books as presents, and I actually prefer it if they're second-hand.'

'I agree! I love to think about the person who owned the book before – whether they rushed through it at a single sitting, or read a chapter a night, with a cup of cocoa. You can often tell their favourite passages because the book opens naturally at them.'

'I've actually got you a brand-new book – it's still got its cellophane wrapper, but I'll dash home and have a quick read so you get more pleasure out of it.'

'Idiot! What's it about?'

'Wait and see! No, hang on. Sit on that bench! Let's see if you can read my mind and work it out.'

Sam pulled me down on the bench with him. Bear stopped too, looking pained.

'It's OK, Bear, we'll get going again in a minute,' he said.

Bear gave a tiny growl to show his displeasure, but settled down beside us like a furry foot-warmer.

'Right! Look into my eyes.' Sam put his head close to mine.

'No! I feel silly!' I protested. 'Turn round. We'll sit back to back. If we look at each other like this we'll just get the giggles.'

So we turned away from each other, straddling the bench. I could just feel the back of Sam's head against mine. I tried to concentrate on his mind under his mop of fair hair. I thought of a book. If it was wrapped in cellophane it must be a big gift book. An art book? Or photographs? What would Sam choose for me?

Bear started fidgeting, and I heard Sam chuckle. I suddenly thought of a book I'd seen reviewed in the *Pets at Home* freebie magazine – a beautiful book about German Shepherds.

'I'm getting a picture of . . . a dog!'

I felt Sam quiver.

'Yes, a dog like Bear. I'm right, aren't I?' I said triumphantly.

'Yes!' said Sam. 'Hey, this is amazing. We really *can* read each other's thoughts. Now, let's see if I can read yours.'

'OK. But hurry up! It's not fair keeping Bear hanging about and I'm freezing.'

'Shh! Just think of something and concentrate hard.'

I tried thinking of Mum, of Rowena, of Zara, of Dad, of Sam's dad, of Sam himself, of Sally . . . I thought of Sally sitting next to me in her cinema room, Sally playing Sylvanians, Sally putting her arm round me in the orchard, Sally skating, Sally in her trilby hat, Sally laughing with Marnie and Georgia and Scarlett, Sally at the Gold Star in a zippered dress, Sally smiling, whispering, flirting, kissing . . .

'You're thinking about Sally!' said Sam.

'No I'm not!' I said, flushing.

'You are so!' he crowed. 'See, I *can* read your mind.'

Of course he couldn't. We'd only just been talking about Sally. Yet it was still a bit creepy, as if Sam's brown eyes could look right through my skin and skull and the strange coils of my brain to see the thoughts inside me. I shivered.

'Hey, let's get walking again,' said Sam.

We reached the park and found there was ice on the pond. One duck struggled over the slippery surface, stepping gingerly on his wide orange feet, but the rest huddled in the small corner of water, quacking together worriedly.

'Remember when your dad used to take us to feed the ducks every Sunday?' said Sam.

I nodded. By the time Sam and I were old enough to be trusted to stand on the edge of the pond and hurl crusts, Zara had grown bored of it. She'd do a little dance, showing off her new shoes, or practise a handstand against a tree, or commandeer some other child's trike and ride round and round the pond triumphantly. Rowena wasn't yet born, and Dad was my hero then, the man I loved most in the world. When he took us for walks I hung onto his hand long after I needed to, just because I wanted to feel attached to him.

'Every single Sunday,' said Sam. 'My dad never took us out even once. On Sunday mornings he just wanted a lie-in.'

'Yeah, my big-deal dad,' I said sourly. 'Mum was at home cooking Sunday lunch and catching up with the housework and doing all her lesson plans, and yet Dad was the hero because he pottered down to the park and read the paper while we played.'

'Lighten up, Frankie. Look, half the dads in the world probably have affairs,' said Sam.

'Your dad doesn't,' I said.

'How do we know? I'm pretty sure my mum's having an affair with someone, actually. She stays out so late.'

'She's just working, that's all.'

'I think she's getting together with someone *at* work. And sometimes at the weekends I go into her room and catch her murmuring to someone on her phone, and when she sees me she always looks guilty and makes some pathetic excuse.'

'Oh God, Sammy. Do you mind?' I asked.

'Well yes, obviously.'

'Have you said anything to her?'

'No. I suppose her affair *is* her affair,' said Sam. 'I wouldn't want her poking her nose into *my* affairs.'

'Yeah, but you're not having any,' I said.

'Chance would be a fine thing. I haven't even kissed a girl properly, have I?'

'Oh shut up, Sam. Don't look like that, all reproachful. You don't really want to kiss *me*. You just want to experiment, that's all, and I'm the only girl handy,' I said, walking quickly, staring straight ahead.

'If you can read my mind, then you know that's not true,' said Sam.

'I don't know why you're so obsessed with kissing anyway,' I said. 'If you put me in a darkened room with ten other girls and you were told to kiss us all, you wouldn't have a clue which one was me.'

'Yes I would!' said Sam.

Maybe he would. If I was blindfolded and all the girls in my class lined up and I was told to kiss them, I'd be able to pick Sally out straight away. I started blushing again at the weirdness of this fantasy.

'What?' said Sam.

'Nothing. Anyway, I bet you'd want to kiss Sally,' I said, before I could stop myself.

'No I wouldn't.'

'But you said you found her attractive.'

'Yes, in an obvious sort of way. She's very lively and funny, and I suppose she's quite pretty.'

'Quite! She's only the prettiest girl in our entire school!'

'That's the point. She knows it. Like I said before, she's too full of herself.'

'No she's not,' I said, though once again I knew he was right.

'Still, I can see why you've made friends with her. She's good fun,' said Sam. 'I just hope you don't want to hang out with her all holiday.'

'Well, I can't, can I? You know we go to stay with our dad. And weren't you listening? Sally's going skiing. She'll probably be at the airport already. Or up in the air. Or wearing a posh ski suit, swinging her legs in one of those chair lifts.' I paused, thinking. 'Hey, Sammy, can I borrow your phone and send her a text?'

'Do you know her number?'

I didn't need to consult the little piece of paper she'd written it on, I already knew it by heart. Sam gave me his phone and I tapped in the number and then sent a text:

Happy Xmas Eve, Snowgirl. Have fun. Frankie xxx

I didn't quite dare put love, not even a jokey *luv*, but I thought three kisses were OK. Then I added:

PS Hey, u were spotted at the Gold Star last night!

Then I sent it quickly and handed the phone back to Sam.

'Of course she probably won't bother to reply,' I said. 'If she's still flying, or perched on a mountain top, it won't reach her.'

But almost immediately there was a ping back. I snatched the phone out of Sam's pocket.

'Hey, whose phone is it?' he protested.

'But it's my message!' I stared at the little box, my heart thudding. My eyes were watering in the cold and I had to blink hard to stop them blurring.

Wish u were here. Come skiing with me some time. Far more fun than Gold Star. G and S talked me into going. It was gross! Love Sally xxx

She wished I was with her! She'd put *love*. And three kisses back. And she hadn't liked it at the Gold Star. And she'd asked me to go skiing with her!

'What's she saying?' asked Sam.

'Oh, nothing much,' I said.

'Let's see.' Sam snatched the phone back before I could delete her message. He glanced at it and gave a little grunt, as if it was an ordinary, everyday text without any meaning at all.

Perhaps that was all it was. She was probably saying *Wish u were here* ironically, because that was such a classic thing to say it was almost a joke. And loads of people put *love* without it meaning anything. And she hadn't really said anything about the Gold Star and whether she'd got off with anyone there. And yes, she'd said *Come skiing with me some time*, but of course she hadn't really meant it. For a start I couldn't afford to go, and I couldn't expect Sally's parents to pay for me. I didn't have any skis, or a ski suit either. She hadn't typed *next* time. *Some time* wasn't specific, it was just a vague invitation that clearly wasn't meant to be taken seriously.

I wanted to stare at the text all the way home, analysing it as if it were a passage of Shakespeare, but I had to do it in my head because I didn't want Sam to think me a fool. I *was* a fool.

When we got back, I handed over his well-read paperback, wrapped in tissue – and he gave me my huge, heavy book, beautifully gift-wrapped in marbled paper with a purple satin ribbon.

'I love the way it's wrapped,' I said.

'Yes, well, Mum did it for me, as you've clearly sussed. I'd just stick it in a paper bag if it was left to me. Anyway. I hope you like it,' said Sam.

He'd bought books for Zara and Rowena and Mum too, all elaborately wrapped in different coloured papers and ribbons. His mother might have done the wrapping, but Sam would have chosen each book carefully.

'Mine looks the most splendid,' I said.

'Like you,' he said.

'Oh, Sammy.' I threw my arms round him the way I'd always done, and it was fine, just a big hug between best friends.

I wouldn't see him for ages now: he was going to see relations with his parents this afternoon, we were spending Christmas Day separately with our families, and then on Boxing Day Dad was coming for us.

'Have a happy Christmas! I shall miss you, Sam,' I said.

'I'll miss you too,' he said.

We were still hugging when Rowena darted into the hall.

'Hey, look at the lovebirds!' she said, relishing the expression. 'Can I come in the hug too?'

'And me,' said Mum, following her. 'Have a very happy Christmas, Sammy.'

Zara was the only one who didn't join in, but she smiled wanly and waved her hand from the stairs.

I wondered if she'd want to see Julie and the others again, but she seemed happy to stay in with Rowena and Mum and me. We three girls tried making a trifle for our Christmas Day supper. It was reasonably successful, with a very neat pattern of cherries and almonds on top of the whipped cream, though the jelly was a bit runny because Rowena had secretly eaten a square before we added water.

Then we watched *The Snowman* on television for what seemed like the hundredth time, and some silly Christmas special, and then Mum prepared everything for Santa with Rowena, pouring him a small glass of sherry and laying out cookies on our prettiest plate. There was even a scrubbed carrot on a saucer for Rudolph.

When I was Rowena's age Dad had dressed up as Santa, sticking a pillow up his jumper to give himself a big tummy, and wearing a false white beard. Of course I knew he wasn't the real Santa, he was just my dad, but he seemed magical all the same.

We went to bed early, but though I was exhausted after staying up half the night before, I couldn't drop off. I thought Zara was fast asleep because she was lying so still, but when I peered at her closely I saw her eyes were wide open.

'Are you awake?' I asked pointlessly.

'Mm. You can have the light on to read if you like,' she said.

'I've finished Sammy's book. It was so good I don't feel like reading another one just yet. I've read all mine dozens of times anyway.'

'You can read one of mine if you like.'

I wrinkled my nose. 'They're all a bit too romantic for me, even the vampire ones,' I said.

'I suppose,' said Zara, sighing. 'I wish people fell in love like the characters in books.'

'You want to fall in love with a *vampire*?'

'No, idiot! But at least vampires have a certain finesse. They generally make seductive small talk before biting your neck. Not like boys. They just go straight ahead. Oh God! Wait a minute! Screw your eyes shut, I have to put the light on,' Zara said urgently.

She ran over to her dressing table, scrunched up her hair and peered closely at her neck.

'You're looking for *bite* marks?' I asked, horrified.

'Not exactly. This guy – he was all over me – well, just kissing at first, and lots of other people were doing that, but then he started kind of nuzzling into my neck, sort of sucking it, and I think he was trying to give me a love bite,' said Zara. 'But thank God he hasn't left any marks.'

'Is that what people do then? Is it like a real bite? Why on earth would you *want* someone to do that?' I asked.

'Shh! Keep your voice down! I think I heard Mum go to the bathroom just now! Anyway he hasn't. I don't think so at least. You can't see any purple marks on my neck, can you?' Zara came to sit on the edge of my bed.

'No, none.'

'Phew!' She snapped the light off again and lay down beside me. 'Oh, Frankie.' She nudged up to me, and I put my arm round her.

'So who was this guy? It wasn't Gary Masters, was it?' I asked.

'No. I told you, he was with your friend Sally half the time. She makes it so obvious she's after him.'

'No she doesn't! And as a matter of fact she didn't even want to be at the Gold Star. Georgia and Scarlett made her go.'

'Oh yeah, sure!' said Zara sarcastically. 'As if! That Sally's the sort of girl who only does what *she* wants.'

'Why are you being so mean and saying hateful things about my friend, when I was being nice and sympathetic to you?' I said crossly.

'OK, OK. Sorry.' Zara sighed. 'Why do we keep squabbling nowadays? We never used to, did we? Well, sometimes, I suppose. But now we seem to row all the time. Why has it all changed?'

'*You've* changed. You're always fussing about the way you look – and you're boy mad,' I said resentfully.

'Well, you used to be the one who hung out with all the boys, not me.'

'Just as mates. Not as boyfriends. I'd never let them mess me around like that.'

'Well, I don't either. This guy, the slurpy kissing one, he seemed to think I'd go outside with him and it was perfectly obvious what he wanted. I couldn't believe it. He didn't even know my proper name. He kept calling me Sara instead of Zara.'

'So you didn't . . . you know?'

'Of course not!'

'Would you if it had been Gary Masters?'

'Well, not right away! I'd want to go out with him, get to know him properly, have him say lovely things to me – you know, like in books.' Zara sighed again. 'You're so lucky, Frankie.'

'Why?' I said anxiously.

'Because you've known Sammy all your life, and though he's irritating at times he's a really sweet guy and he obviously thinks you're wonderful. It's easy-peasy for both of you. When you're a bit older you'll start going out together properly—'

'No we won't,' I interrupted her. 'I keep telling you, I don't feel that way about Sammy. And it's not because I'm too young. If you must know, I'm in love with someone else.'

I clamped my hand over my mouth, wondering how I could possibly have said those words aloud. They seemed to echo around the room.

'Seriously?' said Zara.

'Yep,' I whispered.

'But we've been through all this before. You said you don't fancy any of the boys in your class,' she said.

'That's true.'

Zara turned towards me, leaning on one elbow. 'It's not a *girl*, is it?'

I swallowed. 'So what if it is?'

'Who *is* it?' Zara demanded.

'Well, who do you think?'

'Not *Sally*?'

'Of course it's Sally.' There! I'd told her!

'I know you *like* her . . .' said Zara.

'It's more than that,' I said.

'Does she *know*?'

'I think she does. And she feels the same way, I'm sure of it.'

'But she's into boys in a big way.'

'No she's not. She just likes flirting. And anyway, why can't she like both?'

'Well, she can, but – are you *sure* she feels that way about you? Have you actually kissed?' Zara asked.

'She's kissed me on the cheek,' I said. 'But not properly, on the lips.'

'But you want to?'

'Yes!'

'Oh God, this is so weird!' said Zara, lying back down again. 'You're my little sister! You're not ready to kiss anyone, especially not a girl. And especially not one like Sally. She was so mean to you before. Oh, Frankie, I don't want to see you hurt. You never seem to get how horrible people can be.'

'But she's not horrible now. She's lovely to me.'

'You're sure she's not just being Little Miss Lovely to you so she can get to know Sammy?' Zara asked.

'She *does* know him. And she likes him. But that's all. I'm absolutely certain,' I said.

'And you're absolutely certain this isn't just a crush?' said Zara. 'I remember thinking Miss Major was so cool when I was in Year Seven. I even tried to get my hair to go like hers, with those little flicky bits. And remember those amazing red boots she wore that winter? I'd have died for boots like that.'

'Sally's got blue boots and I think *they're* cool, but I wouldn't care if she slopped about in Dr Scholl's. It's her I love, not her footwear,' I said loftily.

'Why do you always have to make out I'm shallow? It's not a crime to care about your appearance! So, OK, you love her and you think she might love you back. What are you going to do when we go back to school? You're not going to tell everyone, are you?' Zara demanded.

'Why not?' I said, though my heart started thumping as I imagined it.

243

'Aren't you scared you might get teased? You know what people can be like, even though it's cool to be gay. Paul Benson got an awful lot of flak when he came out in Year Nine. Us girls were all thrilled. We've always adored Paul, but some of the boys were vile. They're kind of OK now, though some still go on about it – just banter, I suppose, but it can get quite nasty at times. I don't want your class saying stuff about you, Frankie.'

'They won't,' I said. *Will they?*

'Well, if they do, tell them your big sister and all her mates will come and beat them up,' said Zara.

'Thanks,' I said, giving her shoulder a pat.

'I still can't get over it. But, hey, I'm kind of proud of you, Frankie,' she told me.

There was a tap at our bedroom door.

'Are you two girls still awake?' Mum whispered. 'Santa won't come if you don't go to sleep!'

We giggled.

'Ah, are you cuddled up together? Glad to hear you chatting away, darlings.'

My throat went dry. 'Did you hear what we were saying, Mum?'

'Just the last bit, when Zara said she was proud of you. That was lovely. So what have you done to make her proud, Frankie?'

There was a sudden silence. I wondered if I could say it. I generally told Mum everything. I'd just been showing off to Zara when I said I was ready to tell everyone. Maybe telling Mum was a step too far for the moment.

'Oh, I was just asking her for advice about clothes,' I said.

I heard Zara breathe a sigh of relief.

I decided I wasn't being cowardly. I'd simply done enough confessing for one night.

Early on Christmas morning Zara and Rowena and I crowded into Mum's bed to open our presents from Santa. My stocking was filled with love-heart sweets, a little knitted mouse, a bar of chocolate, an elephant purse, a bag of balloons and a green pen. Even Bear had a stocking full of dog treats and chews and his very own rolled-up socks to stop him stealing ours. My present from Mum was a black sweatshirt embroidered with a pearly-white moon and silver stars. It was exactly the sort of top Sally would wear and I loved it.

'It's the best present ever,' I said, hugging Mum hard.

'No, mine is,' she said, because she'd just opened my framed photograph of us three girls and clearly loved it. She was thrilled with Zara's hairbrush and Rowena's special drawing too, and said we were her three favourite girls in all the world.

I got black nail varnish from Zara. I usually hated nail varnish, but black was kind of cool, and I liked the Goth look. She liked her silver nail varnish too, and was impressed that I'd chosen it for her.

Rowena gave me a bead bracelet in red and yellow – not really my sort of thing at all, but I said I loved it because I knew she'd made it herself. She loved her banana monkey pen.

My dog book from Sam was lavishly illustrated, full of facts and true-life stories. I showed Bear a photo of a long-haired German Shepherd the spitting image of him, but he was too busy chewing his Christmas socks to pay much attention. Sam had given Mum a new Anne Tyler paperback, Zara a fantasy novel called *Zara, Queen of Snake Planet*, and Rowena *The Worst Witch* – all excellent choices.

'Bless him,' said Mum. 'He's such a lovely boy.'

'I know he is,' I said. 'I love him to bits.' And I did too – but it wasn't *that* kind of love.

Mum made banana pancakes with maple syrup for breakfast, and then we lazed around in our dressing gowns for most of the morning. We didn't have to prepare a huge Christmas dinner. We just had chicken and roast potatoes and sprouts and peas. It would have been silly to roast a big turkey: Mum would have been stuck eating leftovers while we were away with Dad. We didn't bother with Christmas pudding, which none of us really liked. Instead we ate clementines and little marzipan sweets in the shape of fruit. After Mum had had a rest, we had fun blowing up all the balloons in my stocking and playing a hilarious game of Pass-the-balloon, twenty-five of them bobbing crazily about the room, with Bear leaping up at them, wild with excitement. For supper we had chicken sandwiches and the trifle, and then later that evening we roasted chestnuts.

I ate all my love hearts until I only had one left. It was a pink one with *I love you* written on it. I kept it at the bottom of the packet and put it beside my scarlet notebook.

I wondered about starting a diary, but I couldn't think of the right words to express all my feelings about Sally. *I love Sally, I love Sally, I love Sally* all the way down the page was a waste of paper, and there didn't seem much point in writing a prosaic account of our family Christmas, enjoyable though it was.

But then it was Boxing Day and we had to go to Dad's. Not to his flat, as it only had one bedroom and that was full of Dad and Helen. We went to Granny's house in the country. It had been great fun when Dad and Mum were still together. It was a rather dark, gloomy house, and Granny was very particular and didn't let us paint or bake or do anything that might make a mess – though she didn't mind if we played up in her attic, which was full of trunks of clothes and old books and a dressmaker's dummy we pretended was real.

We spent most of our time outdoors, even though it was always cold and often wet and windy too. We visited a farm where we were allowed to feed their two donkeys and collect eggs, and we went for long walks through the forest or up Paradise Hill. We could see for miles from the top.

I remembered Mum striding along, climbing a tree for a dare, often giving Rowena a piggyback. Now she was often exhausted just walking down to the corner shop and back.

Last year Helen had brought a special set of country clothes, a waxed jacket and green wellies, but she wasn't a proper walker and wouldn't go anywhere muddy, even in her new boots. We didn't want to go to our special places with her anyway. I'd spent most of last Christmas holiday up in the attic, reading, and planned to do the same this year.

Mum came to supervise our packing. 'Aren't you taking your new sweatshirt, Frankie?' she asked.

'No, I like it too much. I'm saving it for best.' I was wearing Mum's rainbow jumper again, and I had the black yeti coat on my bed, ready.

'Really?' said Mum. 'You'll look a bit of a scruffbag. Granny will turn her nose up at you.'

'Good. I can't stick Granny,' I said.

It was clear that I was her least favourite grandchild. She approved of Zara because she was neat and girly, and she was very fond of Rowena, but she found me exasperating because I was untidy and fidgety unless I was reading. I seemed to be clumsier than usual at her house: I once made the china crinolined ladies on her windowsill do a little dance and accidentally chipped part of a stiff lace petticoat. It was barely noticeable, but Granny was furious. And of course we always had huge arguments about Bear.

He came with us, but very much on sufferance. We all took our boots off on the doorstep, but Bear could hardly remove his paws, so he couldn't help making muddy marks on Granny's carpet. She seemed to think he should be kept in her horrible freezing garage, all on his own! At least Dad took my side and said that Bear was part of the family, but Granny complained that his hairs got everywhere and he had an awful doggy smell. What else did she expect him to smell of?

She made me put his bed in a miserable little utility room with damp washing hanging on a rack above him. He didn't like it there one bit and barked in protest, setting Granny off on a rant about *that damned dog!* I took to creeping downstairs when everyone else was asleep and curling up beside him.

'If only *your* mum hadn't died, Mum,' I said.

'Yes, if only,' she said, and her voice suddenly went wobbly. She sat down abruptly on my bed and shut her eyes.

'*Mum?*' Zara and I cried in unison. 'Are you having another relapse?'

'No, no. I'm fine,' she said, though her eyes were wet when she opened them, and she couldn't stop tears rolling down her cheeks.

'You're not fine, Mum,' I said, sitting down too and putting my arm round her.

'I am. I just missed my mum for a minute.'

Zara and I looked at each other. Mum's mum had died ages ago, before we'd even started school. I barely remembered her – just that she was soft and kind. I loved to nestle against her because she had a special smell. I smelled of it too if I sat on her lap.

'What did she smell of?' I asked.

'Frankie!' said Zara.

'She always smelled of lilac cologne,' said Mum, smiling now. 'It was lovely, wasn't it? I used to wear it for a while after she died, but somehow it didn't smell right on me.'

She still looked very sad, even though she was smiling. I thought about this long-ago grandma. I knew Mum's dad had died of a heart attack, but I never knew what her mother had died of. I suddenly went cold.

'Mum, did your mum die of MS?' I asked.

'What? No!' She saw my expression. 'I don't think MS is hereditary – you mustn't worry that you'll get it too. My mum died of pneumonia. There was a horrible flu outbreak and she couldn't seem to fight it off. She was always very thin and frail.'

'*You're* getting thinner and frailer, Mum!' I said anxiously. 'Promise you'll eat properly while we're away . . .'

'I promise,' she said, patting my hand.

'Yes, but seriously, it's so awful leaving you all alone. You look after us girls brilliantly, but you're not very good at looking after yourself. I think I'd better stay here. In fact, I'm absolutely one hundred per cent staying here,' I said firmly.

'No you're not,' said Mum.

'Look, I absolutely hate the idea of going off with Dad,' I said. 'I hate *him*.'

'No you don't,' she said. 'Now, is that you packed?'

'Yes!' I said, shutting the lid of my case with great difficulty.

'She hasn't packed sensibly at all,' said Zara. 'She's crammed about a hundred and one books in there, but I bet she's forgotten clean underwear and pyjamas and washing things.'

It was a total exaggeration, but with an element of truth. Zara sighed heavily and went off to the linen cupboard and bathroom to find my stuff.

'I shall miss you so, Mum,' I said. 'You've no idea how much.'

'I do have some idea. I was missing *my* mum just then.' Mum paused and then said softly, 'I know it's silly, but sometimes I want to be a little girl again and climb onto her lap so she can make everything better.'

'Oh, Mum!'

'Now don't you start crying too. Sorry, sorry, sorry. I didn't mean to get all maudlin. Look, I'd better go and supervise Rowena. Heaven knows what she's packing.

Probably every single Sylvanian *and* all their equipment. We'd better get a move on. Your dad will be here soon.'

Mum was still in her dressing gown, her face very pale, dark rings under her eyes. I wanted Dad to see her like that and realize just how ill she was – but by the time he turned up she was showered and dressed in a thick jumper that didn't show how much weight she'd lost, and she'd made up her face carefully.

'You look ever so pretty, Mum,' said Rowena. 'I bet Dad will wish he'd never, ever left you. In fact, maybe he'll come back again.'

'Oh, darling, that's never, ever going to happen – and I don't want it to,' said Mum. 'Anyway, Dad's got Helen now.'

'Then couldn't you find someone else, Mum, so you won't be lonely?'

'I don't want anyone apart from you girls. And I'm never lonely,' Mum said as cheerfully as she could.

She smiled resolutely when Dad arrived. They greeted each other awkwardly, both of them giving a little nod, not close enough to kiss any more, but not formal enough to shake hands.

Rowena hurtled forward and clutched Dad round the waist, butting her head into his stomach, squeaking, 'Dad! Dad! Dad!' as if she hadn't seen him for a year or more instead of a week. Zara said, 'Hi, Dad,' and gave him a little wave of her hand, not actually joining in the big Rowena hug. I said nothing at all and stood pointedly beside Mum.

'Hey, my three girls,' he said.

When he lived with us we were his *four* girls, Mum included. It sounded so brutal now, but Mum didn't flinch.

'They're all packed and ready,' she said pleasantly.

'One of us isn't ready. One of us isn't going,' I said.

'Frankie. Stop this, please,' said Mum.

'Come on, Frankie. It's Christmas time. Let's call a truce, eh?' said Dad.

He shuffled over to me, hampered by Rowena, who was still clinging to him like a limpet, and trod on Mum's foot. She gave a little scream and staggered backwards.

'Mum?' I said, trying to hold her up.

'Jen? I'm sorry I stood on your foot – it didn't *really* hurt, did it?' asked Dad.

Mum shook her head, but she was practically doubled up with pain. I sat her down on a kitchen chair and hovered over her anxiously.

'Let me see your foot, Mum,' said Zara, but she shook her head again, still bent over.

'Mummy!' said Rowena, unpeeling herself from Dad and running to her side too.

'It's all right, Rowena, I'm sure Mum's fine.' Dad bent down and took off Mum's slipper, though she tried to resist, crying now.

'There's no mark or anything,' he said. He tried bending Mum's toes and she pushed him away.

'They're all perfectly straight. They can't be broken. I'm sure it hurt, but I really think you're making a bit of a fuss. There's no need to make such a meal of it. It'll stop hurting in a minute or two,' said Dad.

'No it won't,' Mum said through gritted teeth.

'Look, you're being a bit over the top, aren't you?' Dad sounded impatient now.

'What the hell do you mean by that?' Mum muttered.

'Well, I know it upsets you when the girls come to spend time with me. I've tried to be understanding, but it was all agreed when we split up. I get the girls for five days at Christmas, at Easter and during the summer holidays. Surely you must see that's fair, when you have them all the rest of the year, bar the odd Sunday. There's no need for histrionics.'

Mum sat up straight and stared at him, eyes blazing. 'Do you think I'm acting? Have you forgotten I've got MS?'

'Of course I haven't, and I'm very sorry for you, but it's not as if it's painful. It isn't as if it's cancer,' said Dad.

'How dare you!' she said. 'It *is* painful, especially now my legs are affected. It's as if they're filled with concrete – I can hardly move them, and it feels as if I'm walking on hot coals. I can't bear the slightest touch, so you standing on me with your great clodhoppers is agonizing.'

We all stared at her. She'd never once mentioned that she was in pain – and yet I realized she sometimes flinched when Rowena jumped on her.

'All right, all right, if you say so,' Dad said uncomfortably. 'I'm sorry. How many more times can I say it? But there's no need to go on like this, especially in front of the girls.' He gestured at Rowena, who had started to cry.

'Oh God,' said Mum. 'Come here, darling. Don't worry, I was just having a little moan. It's nearly all better now, I promise. There, look, I'm smiley Mummy again.'

I realized what an enormous effort it must be for Mum to stay smiling nearly all the time. I hadn't known her legs hurt so. I'd thought I was so sensitive about her illness but I didn't have a clue. It made me even more determined to stay at home and look after her.

'There! See how ill Mum is! She won't be able to manage if she's all by herself,' I declared.

'I *can* manage.' Mum took hold of my wrist and pulled me nearer. 'Please don't argue, Frankie. *Please!*'

'Can't Bear at least stay with you?' I suggested, though I knew I'd miss him terribly. 'Then, if you have another fall or something, he could go and fetch someone.'

'That might be a good idea,' said Dad. I think he was saying it because Granny found Bear such a trial.

'I can't take him for walks – and he'd pine for you,' said Mum. 'Now, go, darling. All of you. I'm fine. I'm sorry I made such a spectacle of myself.'

So we went, and she went on smiling bravely all the time she was waving on the doorstep. I kept imagining her retreating into the hall and weeping. I had to screw up my face to stop bursting into tears myself.

Dad looked at me in the driving mirror. 'There's no need to look so sulky, Frankie,' he said sharply.

I *hated* him. To my surprise Zara reached out and held my hand tight, and Rowena nudged up close to me. They made me feel just a little bit better.

Dad turned on the radio, flicking from station to station to find music we could all sing to, though it was the last thing we wanted to do. Then he suggested we play I-Spy, which I've always thought was the lamest game in the world. But Rowena loved playing, and cheered up a bit, so I joined in for her sake.

After a while we stopped at a motorway café. They wouldn't allow Bear inside, so after I'd walked him for five minutes Dad insisted he go back in the car. I wanted to stay with him of course, but Dad told me I was being ridiculous.

'We'll leave the windows open a crack so he's got some fresh air, and I've got a treat for him – look.' He'd brought Bear his favourite rawhide chews as a bribe. Bear seemed disloyally appreciative, and stretched out on the back seat, looking perfectly happy.

Dad had a big fried breakfast, determinedly eating everything until his plate was clear. Helen fusses about his pot belly – she's always encouraging him to eat healthily. He tried to make us eat something too, but we weren't really hungry. He insisted on buying us huge Danish pastries all the same. I didn't touch mine, and Zara only nibbled the edge of hers. Rowena ate hers valiantly, though she picked out every single currant because she always worries they might be flies.

There was a little amusement arcade attached to the café. It had one of those glass booths stuffed with luridly coloured fluffy animals.

'Aren't they *sweet*,' said Rowena. 'I especially love the blue rabbit in the pink dress.'

Dad did his best to manipulate the crane to win the rabbit for her, but it was wedged in too tightly. He eventually snared a lime-green teddy in an orange T-shirt. 'Will he do instead?' he asked.

'He's not *quite* as sweet as the blue rabbit,' said Rowena. 'But Frankie likes bears. Can we give him to her? Remember you bought her a little wooden bear at the Christmas fair? She carries him around in her pocket everywhere.'

'No I don't,' I said.

'Yes you *do!*' Rowena tutted at me in a motherly way. Before I could stop her she delved into my coat pockets, first one, then the other. 'Oh, he's not there!' she said, disappointed.

'Told you,' I said.

'Well, you can squash the little green bear into your pocket instead,' said Rowena.

'I don't *want* the little green bear. I think he's hideous,' I said.

I was speaking truthfully, but I knew I was being childish. I said it to hurt Dad, but it was Rowena who got upset.

'Don't! You'll make the poor little bear so upset! I'll have him then, please, Dad. There there, little chap.' She cradled the bear in her arms, patting his back.

Zara looked up from her phone and raised her eyebrows. Dad was looking fondly at Rowena. As we walked back to the car and poor incarcerated Bear, he took me to one side.

'Are you going to be like this the entire time we're at the cottage, Frankie?' he asked in an undertone.

'I don't know what you mean,' I said.

'Sulking and surly. Behaving like a spoiled brat. Being mean to Rowena. I don't mind you being appallingly rude to me, it's water off a duck's back, but I won't have you upsetting your little sister,' Dad hissed.

I was outraged because I nearly always indulged Rowena, playing all her little games and making a fuss of her . . . Though I wasn't as good at it as Sally, I thought. It seemed so awful that I wouldn't be seeing her till New Year's Eve.

'There now,' said Dad, misinterpreting the expression on my face. 'Can't we call it a truce? This time's so precious to me, seeing you three girls. I look forward to it so much. Don't spoil it for me, Frankie.'

'You're the one who spoiled it,' I said. 'If you hadn't walked out on us you'd be seeing us all the time.'

'Don't you think I know that? I feel so bad about it, you've no idea,' he told me.

'Then why *did* you walk out?' I asked.

'I couldn't help it. You're too young to understand, but I just fell in love so deeply that I simply *had* to be with Helen,' said Dad.

I thought of Sally. Had Dad felt like that about awful Helen – saying her name again and again, lying awake at night thinking about her and then dreaming about her when he eventually fell asleep?

'Maybe I do understand, just a little bit,' I said. 'But it doesn't make it right.'

'I know it doesn't. Oh, Frankie. You and I used to be so close. I can't stand it – you act like you hate me now. You're still my little girl inside, aren't you?'

'I'm not a little girl any more, Dad. I'm nearly fourteen. And don't assume I can't understand about falling in love. I know all about it.'

'Of course you do.' Dad spoke solemnly enough, but I saw his mouth quiver and his eyes were bright. Oh God, he was trying not to laugh!

'You make me sick,' I said furiously. 'Now let's get back to poor Bear. Don't you know how cruel it is to leave a dog in a car?'

Bear seemed totally relaxed, but he started barking excitedly when he saw us.

'There, he's probably been barking his head off all the time we've been in that stupid café,' I said, and made a huge fuss of him as I climbed into the car.

He didn't really want to scrunch up small enough to let Rowena in too, and he thought the green bear was a special present for him and kept trying to snatch it from her. He was only playing, and Rowena found it funny, but Dad got uptight about it.

'That dog's getting totally out of control,' he said.

There were no more sing-alongs and games for the rest of the journey. Dad drove in silence. Rowena murmured to the green bear. Zara flicked through all her messages, and tapped away on her phone. I wondered about asking her if she'd let me send a message, but I knew she'd baulk at the idea of me contacting Sally.

At last we got to Haven Cottage – such a lovely name, conjuring up a thatched roof and a garden full of old-fashioned flowers running wild, when actually it was a gloomy, dark-brick house with severely clipped rose bushes. There was Granny at the door, Helen standing behind her.

'My girlies!' Granny cried.

We had to be hugged in turn. Granny seemed to get smaller each time I saw her. I was bigger than her now, and could look down on her grey head. Her hair was sparse so that I could see glimpses of her pink scalp. It made her look vulnerable, and I hugged her back carefully, suddenly loving her – but then she started tutting at poor Bear, who was gambolling around us in his usual guileless way, convinced everyone adored him.

'That dratted dog!' Granny fussed. 'I see he's still not properly trained.'

'He's saying hello, Granny,' I said.

'But he's so boisterous!'

'You just want to be friends, don't you, Bear?' I bent down and gave him a hug too in case his feelings were hurt. He licked my face enthusiastically.

'Ugh, don't let him lick your face like that!' Granny said, grimacing. 'Think of the germs!'

'He's clean as clean,' I protested.

'He's a lovely dog,' said Helen, patting him cautiously. She smiled at me, her lips very red and glossy, her teeth gleaming. Perhaps she'd had that special tooth-whitening treatment. In contrast to Granny, Helen's hair looked bigger than usual, fluffed all round her face. The rest of her seemed bigger too. She always wore very tight clothes to show off her figure, but now she looked a little bulky. Perhaps Dad would go off her if she got really fat.

She didn't try to kiss any of us, which was a relief. We didn't want red smears all over our cheeks. Bear was circling around everyone, getting a bit fidgety now. He'd been cooped up in the car for such a long time.

While the others went into the house I took him down the lane, and stayed out long after he'd had a good wee. There was a wintry sun and the countryside had a stark beauty that made me feel glad to be there in spite of myself. I remembered all the times I'd walked down the lane with Mum. We didn't just walk, we often ran along racing each other. I couldn't imagine Mum running now. I was scared she'd need to use a wheelchair soon.

'We'll look after her, won't we, Bear?' I said, and I imagined Mum sitting in a sledge while Bear pulled her along like a husky.

When we got back to Haven Cottage, the smell of roast turkey made my mouth start watering. Dad and Helen and Zara and Rowena were in the living room, sitting around a crackling log fire. Helen had made mulled wine. Dad was knocking it back, and I saw she'd given Zara a glass too. Rowena had warm Ribena. Granny was sipping her wine as if it was medicine.

262

'Can you wipe the dog's paws first if you're going to bring him in here, Francesca?' she asked. 'There's a clean J-cloth out ready, and a bowl of soapy water.'

I suppose it was a reasonable enough request because the lane was muddy, but it didn't sound very hospitable. Still, when Bear and I returned from the kitchen Helen had poured me a small mulled wine too.

It didn't taste very nice actually, like red jam that had started to go mouldy, but I drank it down eagerly, hoping it might make me drunk. It didn't seem to work at all. I felt exactly the same even when I'd drained my glass.

'Come and help me dish up, dear,' Granny said to Dad.

Helen followed them into the kitchen, not wanting to be left with us. We all breathed out. Bear made himself comfortable in front of the fire, and Zara and Rowena and I pulled faces at each other.

'Did you see Helen's dress?' Zara mouthed. 'She could barely squeeze herself into it! She hasn't half put on weight! You don't think she could be having a baby, do you?'

'No! Gross!' I said, trying to get the image of Dad and Helen making love out of my head.

'A baby!' Rowena looked delighted. She only had the sketchiest idea about how a baby got to be in its mother's tummy.

'Shh! No, she can't be. She wouldn't want to give up work. She's the least maternal woman I can think of,' I hissed.

'Maybe Granny will babysit,' Zara suggested.

'She'd wipe it with a J-cloth every five minutes and swab it with disinfectant into the bargain,' I said.

We all got the giggles, and Dad grinned when he came back into the room.

'Ah, good to see you've all cheered up,' he said. 'Come into the dining room then, girls. Helen's brought her own home-made cranberry sauce. Wait till you taste it! And Granny's produced her usual wonderful spread.'

'Helen's producing a wonderful spread herself,' I murmured into Zara's ear.

I stared at her all through the meal. *Could* she be pregnant? She was totally the wrong sort of woman, so immaculate, so carefully made up, so artificial looking. There were no soft places for a baby to nestle. It would be like cuddling a robot.

I wondered for the fiftieth time why Dad had fallen in love with her. He was gazing at her so fondly it made my stomach churn. He seemed a bit drunk, quaffing back the Chablis when he'd already had two glasses of mulled wine. Helen was primly drinking sparkling mineral water – did she have any mulled wine earlier? I wondered. Oh God, perhaps she really *was* pregnant.

Zara was right. After we'd eaten our turkey and the home-made cranberry sauce and crispy roast potatoes and little chipolatas and sprouts with chestnuts and cauliflower cheese and parsnips and peas, followed by a fruit and cream roulade and tiny mince pies and Helen's own bottled peaches, Dad passed round a box of posh chocolates and then cleared his throat.

'Helen and I have something very special to tell you,' he said. He was very flushed, but it seemed to be with pride as well as drink. 'We thought we'd wait until our special Boxing Day celebration, all of us together. We're going to have a baby.'

There was a little pause. We'd guessed, but it was still a shock to hear him say it out loud. We all stared at Helen and her stomach. She blushed, not quite meeting our eyes.

'Well, what do you think?' Dad asked.

'It's lovely,' said Rowena. 'I won't be the little sister any more! Can I help look after her?'

'Of course you can,' he said happily.

'And when she's a bit bigger she can play with all my Sylvanians!'

'The baby might be a little brother,' Helen said.

'Boys can play with Sylvanians too.' Rowena picked up the lime-green teddy that was sitting on her lap. 'Here, he can have my teddy. It's brand new.'

'That's so sweet of you, Rowena,' said Dad.

'Yes, thank you, darling,' said Helen, though she didn't look very pleased. Naff little arcade teddies wouldn't fit in with her nursery decor.

'Zara? Frankie?' said Dad.

'Congratulations,' said Zara in an offhand manner.

'Yeah,' I added.

'Of course we'll have to think about moving now,' said Helen.

We stared at her.

'Moving?' said Rowena.

'Well, it's such a tiny flat, and the second bedroom's so small, not much more than a cupboard,' Helen said determinedly.

'Surely it'll be fine for one small baby?' I said.

'Not when he gets a bit older,' said Dad. 'But there's no real rush for the moment.'

'Ideally we'd like a proper house, wouldn't we, Richard?' Helen persisted. 'Though London houses are going for such ridiculous prices now.'

'Move out to the country,' said Granny. 'Houses are much cheaper here. In fact, you could always move in with me for a while.'

'I'm not sure that would really work,' Helen said quickly.

'*I* know what would work!' Rowena said, her whole face lighting up. 'You could move in with us! The baby could have my room – it's a lovely room. I can share with Zara and Frankie, us three girls together – it'd be fun. And Mum's got ever such a big bedroom, so Dad and Helen could squash in with her! We could see Dad all the time then, it would be magic!'

We stared at her in stunned silence, and then Granny started tutting, and Zara and I giggled feebly.

'What?' Rowena said, looking hurt and puzzled.

'That wouldn't work, little chum,' Dad told her gently.

'But why? It would be so lovely, all of us together,' she said earnestly.

'Daddy couldn't live with your auntie Helen *and* Mummy,' said Granny. 'Now, I think it's time for the boxes.'

This was a new tradition. As we saw Dad on Boxing Day instead of Christmas Day, he gave us our presents in boxes, and Granny did too. Helen didn't give us presents, she was just *and Helen* on Dad's gift tags. Rowena adored the box ceremony, but she refused to be distracted now.

'It *would* be lovely,' she insisted.

'Now now. You're just being silly,' said Granny.

'I think *you're* all silly,' said Rowena, near tears. 'I know Mum and Helen don't like each other, but they could always make friends again, like Frankie and Sally. And Sammy is friends with Frankie *and* Sally and it all works perfectly.'

'That's right,' I said, pulling her onto my lap. I bent over her head to hide my red cheeks. I couldn't help blushing whenever Sally was mentioned. 'But it would be different with grown-ups. Dad and Mum used to be married but now they're divorced.'

'Is Dad going to marry Helen now, then?' Rowena asked.

'*Auntie* Helen,' Granny corrected. 'And it's none of our business, dear. Richard, for heaven's sake get the boxes!'

Dad was looking at Helen. She shrugged her shoulders and nodded.

'We *are* planning a wedding, Rowena. Just a very quiet affair,' he said. 'But perhaps you'd like to be a bridesmaid.'

Rowena cheered up instantly, but I went cold with horror.

'Zara and I aren't expected to be bridesmaids too, are we?' I asked.

'No, as your father said, it's going to be a very small wedding,' said Helen. 'Perhaps my little niece will be a bridesmaid – she's a couple of years younger than Rowena, but I think they'll get along – and of course they'll be cousins soon.'

That was another weird thought. I didn't want to be related to Helen and her family in any way.

'What colour bridesmaid's dress will it be?' Rowena asked. 'Could it be pink?'

'Not for a winter wedding,' said Helen. 'I was wondering about cherry-red velvet dresses, with little white lace collars and frilly white petticoats.'

'Oh *yes!*' said Rowena.

Zara and I cleared the table while Helen and Granny put the pans to soak and Dad went to get the boxes, Rowena trotting after him like a little puppy.

'Told you so!' Zara muttered to me. 'And a wedding too!'

'Thank God *we* don't have to be bridesmaids,' I said. 'You wouldn't have wanted to, would you?'

'In cherry red with white frills? Are you joking?' said Zara. 'But I expect we'll have to be on the sidelines, throwing confetti.'

'Throwing stones more like,' I murmured as Helen came bustling back into the room. Her tummy seemed more pronounced now, quite unmistakable. I imagined the little tadpole creature curled up inside her. My little half-sister or brother. I wondered if I'd hate it too. It would be more of an effort to dislike a tiny baby.

268

Helen saw me staring. 'I hope you don't mind too much,' she said.

'No, we don't mind at all, do we, Zara?' I said. 'I mean, like Granny said, it's none of our business.' It was meant to be neutral, but it sounded more forceful than I intended.

Helen's whole face went red, even her neck. 'Do you always have to be so hostile, Frankie?'

'I wasn't meaning to be,' I said. 'I didn't mean to upset you.'

She put her hand to her cheeks. 'It's my hormones. I can't help flushing. I'm not the one who's upset, as a matter of fact. It's your poor father. You're breaking his heart, do you realize that?'

'I rather think it was the other way round. He broke my mother's heart. He broke *her*,' I said furiously.

'That's so unfair. You can't possibly blame Richard for your mother's illness.'

'So you're the world's expert on MS, are you?' I said. 'Don't you realize that stress plays a part in triggering many illnesses, including MS?'

'Frankie!' said Zara.

I realized I'd gone too far. I didn't know anything of the sort. It probably wasn't true at all. But somehow it *felt* as if it was all Helen's fault.

'Don't you dare say that to your father,' she said. 'He feels bad enough as it is. He went straight back when your mother got her diagnosis. He was prepared to stay for ever.'

'Oh, wonderful martyred Saint Richard!' I said. 'And how long did he stay? A fortnight? Three weeks at the most! And then he cleared off again, making it worse for everyone, especially Rowena.'

'It wasn't working. Your mother didn't *want* him back.'

'Well, no wonder. And we don't want him either, do we, Zara?'

'No, we don't,' said Zara, though she sounded a little uncertain. 'But shut up now, Frankie. You'll spoil the box bit, and you know how Rowena loves it.'

I didn't want to shut up. I was still churning with rage, but I knew Zara was right. I managed to clamp my mouth shut and join in the box ceremony as if I still found it fun. We sat round in a circle in Granny's living room, with the boxes in the middle. Zara went to fetch her contribution – festive candles in their own boxes – and I got my two packets of home-made fudge, which I'd put in a couple of old chocolate boxes (I'd relented about giving Dad a present). Rowena had an extra big jigsaw-puzzle box for Dad. She'd filled it with drawings and stories, all marked *Espeshally for Dad.*

When he opened it, Dad looked as if he might burst into tears.

'Don't you like them, Dad?' Rowena asked anxiously. 'I tried really hard, but some of my people are a bit blobby.'

'They're wonderful, darling. I shall treasure them all and read a different story every night,' he said, in a choked voice.

'And I love my fudge,' said Granny, though she winced when she bit into a corner. 'It's very sweet. But delicious.'

She had bought special rectangular boxes for us girls, each containing a DVD. She didn't realize we could stream films now. She'd chosen *Grease* for Zara, an animated film about dogs for me, and a Disney princess film for Rowena. For Dad and Helen there was a bigger box containing several series of *Modern Family*.

'It's a box set. Do you get it? A box set in a box on Boxing Day!' Granny said, pleased with herself.

Dad gave Granny a small jewellery box containing an elaborate agate-and-silver brooch. Zara got a jewellery box too, with a pair of moon-shaped earrings set with tiny diamonds. Rowena got an enormous box which took her ages to undo. It was a huge holiday hotel for her Sylvanians.

My box was the biggest of all. It was a box inside a box inside a box inside a box inside a box. Perhaps I was going to end up with a matchbox with a spider inside and everyone would laugh. But it wasn't a joke present. The last slim box held a smartphone, the very latest model.

I was stunned by the smartphone. So was Zara, who stared at it enviously. Even Rowena was aware of its magnificence. They both exclaimed loudly.

I was utterly silent, incapable of speech. I didn't know what to do. I knew I should be rushing over to Dad, flinging my arms round his neck, thanking him again and again. And yet, if I did that, it would seem so hypocritical. It would make me look so shallow, as if my affections could simply be bought with an expensive gift. I wasn't daft, I knew just *how* expensive it was, and it was definitely brand new, in all its wrappings.

The amount Dad had spent on our Boxing Day presents was practically obscene, and he'd probably provided all the fancy food for our meal too. Yet he didn't give Mum much money for our keep. She was always having to scrimp and save. She had to provide all the boring things: school blouses, underwear, bus money, haircuts and trainers; all the bread and biscuits and baked beans and milk and apples and oranges; all the soap and shampoo and toothpaste and loo rolls; all the paracetamol and cough drops and plasters and ChapSticks.

Dad could just turn up and take us to the Christmas fair and shower us with diamond earrings and elaborate toys and smartphones.

'My goodness, Francesca! What do you say to your father?' Granny prompted.

There was a part of me that wanted to tell Dad to stuff his smartphone up his Christmas jumper. He couldn't buy my love back even if he bought me *all* the electronic goodies in the Apple store. Yet that would be grotesque. And what if he took the phone away? I badly needed one now.

'Thank you very much indeed, Dad,' I said. 'You shouldn't have – but I'm very glad you did.'

He held out his arms. 'Come and give me a hug and a kiss then.'

I took a deep breath. Zara and Rowena were staring at me, willing me not to spoil everything.

I made myself get up and walk over to him. I gave him a limp hug and brushed my lips quickly against his cheek.

273

'Oh, Frankie,' said Dad, pulling me closer. 'I'm so happy – so, so, so glad we're friends again.'

I looked over his shoulder and saw Helen watching us, her hands crossed over her rounded stomach. I couldn't quite read her expression. Was *she* happy Dad thought we were friends? Did she think I was a spoiled brat? Did she resent all the money Dad was spending on us girls, when he should be saving for the new baby, the new house, their new life?

'Who are you going to message first?' Zara asked. 'What a shame you haven't got your old SIM card – you won't know your contacts any more.'

'I know the ones I need,' I said.

I sent Mum a text first, in proper sentences because she hates text abbreviations.

Dearest Mum, this is my new phone! Missing you so much. Hope you're OK and not too lonely. Lots of love Frankie xxx

She replied immediately:

Fantastic! Missing you so much too, all of you, but not lonely, promise! Had a lovely surprise! Much love, Mum xxxxx

Then I texted Sam:

Hi, new phone! Happy Boxing Day! Luv Frankie x

He replied immediately too:

Gr8! Luv Sam x

and added several smiley faces.

Then I sent my third text, my fingers shaking so I kept having to delete mistakes.

Hey Snowgirl, having fun? Frankie xxx

I waited. Seconds, minutes, an hour.

I didn't get a reply until halfway through the evening, when I'd almost given up hope.

Yeah, having fun. Love S xxxxx

We texted every day after that. First thing in the morning, last thing at night, and many times in between. I moved through each endless day like a zombie, going for long walks, climbing hills, visiting the local shops, fetching eggs from the farm, eating interminable meals and playing pointless games of Monopoly and Ludo and Trivial Pursuit every evening, just living for the little ping of a text arriving on my phone. I checked it constantly, clutching it in my hand.

Granny quickly grew annoyed with me, especially when I laid it down beside me on the dining table.

'Do put that wretched phone away, Frankie! It's such bad manners, peering at it all the time,' she complained.

'Stop nagging her, Mother. Why can't you simply let her enjoy her present?' Dad said happily.

'It's ridiculous, giving a girl Frankie's age such an expensive present. She'll only break it again, like she did last time. If she must have a phone, why not give her one like mine? It's perfectly adequate.'

Granny had an ancient flip phone which she hardly ever switched on. She said it was just for emergencies, but if an emergency ever happened, she'd find she had no battery whatsoever.

I texted this to Zara and she giggled. It was a useful way of communicating with her right in front of the others. But Granny wasn't daft, even though she was so old-fashioned.

'It's even more bad-mannered to send each other those silly texts, especially when you're sitting next to each other,' she snapped. 'For the life of me I can't understand why you girls don't make proper phone calls instead of tapping away all the time.'

That night we watched a black-and-white film which showed several phone calls from those old telephone boxes. Granny was explaining how to use button A and button B – as if we cared – when another text pinged into my phone. I fumbled for it in my pocket.

'Francesca! For goodness' sake, surely you can wait till the end of the film!' said Granny.

'But – but it might be Mum,' I said.

I knew it wasn't likely. Mum only texted at bedtime to wish me goodnight.

'I have to check, just in case she's not well,' I said wickedly.

'Is she going through a bad spell?' Helen asked.

'Well, it's always a bad spell now,' I said, laying it on thick. 'Her legs are hurting her, and she's always exhausted.'

'Oh dear,' she said inadequately. She gave a little yawn and rubbed her back to show that she felt exhausted too – as if being pregnant was somehow the equivalent of MS.

'You're missing a really important part of the plot!' Granny complained, turning up the volume.

I took no notice and looked at my phone.

Can't w8 4 New Year's Eve! Miss u like crazy. Love from ur Snowgirl xxxxx

I gave a little gasp.

'What is it?' asked Granny. 'Oh dear, is it your mother? What's happened?'

They were all staring at me. I went hot all over.

'No, no, it's not Mum. Just a friend,' I said quickly. 'Sorry.'

'Well, something's the matter. You've gone bright red!' said Granny.

'Oh my goodness! Is it a boyfriend, Frankie?' said Helen, with a smirk.

'She's never got a boyfriend at her age!' Granny sounded shocked. 'Even Zara hasn't had a boyfriend yet.'

'Yes I have!' Zara lied indignantly.

'It's just Sammy,' said Dad. 'The boy next door. No surprises there. I'm right, aren't I, Frankie?'

I should have simply nodded. But they were all getting on my nerves, being crass, treating me like a comedy turn.

'No, you're wrong, actually,' I said.

'So who is it?' Dad asked.

'It's private.'

'Go on, let's see,' he said, reaching for my phone.

He was probably only pretending he'd look, but I switched it off quickly all the same.

'Stop it, Dad,' I said, shoving the phone in my jeans pocket.

'I think you must be right, Helen,' he said. 'I'm pretty sure Frankie's in love!' He pronounced it 'lurve', and pulled a ridiculous face, fluttering his eyelashes and pouting.

'Yes, I am,' I said, holding my head high.

'For heaven's sake, Richard, stop teasing her and let's watch the film in peace. We're missing half the plot, aren't we, Rowena?' said Granny – but no one was watching the film now, even Granny herself.

'So what's this boy's name?' Dad said.

Zara looked at me sharply. She shook her head. But I couldn't stop myself.

'It's not a boy,' I told him.

'It's not a man, is it?' he asked, not joking any more.

'It's a girl,' I said.

'You're in love with a girl?' he repeated stupidly.

'Yes,' I said steadily, though my heart was thumping like crazy.

'Seriously?'

'Don't be silly, Richard, of course she's not serious. She's obviously just got a crush on one of the older girls at school. It's a stage all girls go through. When I was Frankie's age I had a crush on our netball captain,' said Granny. 'Such nonsense, but perfectly natural.'

I don't know who was annoying me more, Dad or Granny. So I decided to show them both.

'It's not a schoolgirl crush,' I said. 'I'm in love with a girl in my class. And she's in love with me. We're girlfriends.'

Zara raised her eyebrows, giving up on me.

Granny looked startled and stood up. 'I think you'd better go to bed, Rowena,' she said quickly.

'But you said I could stay up till the end of the film, Granny,' she protested.

'Yes, well, no one's watching it now. And this conversation isn't suitable for little girls.'

'Yes it is!' said Rowena. 'I know all about it anyway. You're talking about Sally, aren't you, Frankie? I love her too!'

'Don't be so silly, Rowena,' said Granny. 'Now come upstairs with me. I'll read you a bedtime story if you like.'

She steered Rowena out of the room, even though Rowena kept protesting. Bear growled softly, sensing the sudden change of atmosphere.

'I'd better take him out in the garden,' I said.

'Leave him for the moment,' said Dad. 'Now tell me what on earth's going on. Does your mother know about you and this girl?'

'Sort of,' I said. I didn't want him to think I was hiding anything from Mum.

'Well, why on earth didn't she tell me? I'm still your father. I need to know these things,' Dad blustered.

'Your dad's only concerned about you, Frankie,' said Helen.

'I don't see why.' I looked Dad straight in the eye. 'Are you implying it's wrong for me to be in love with a girl?'

'I think you're a little young to be in love with anyone. Of course I don't think it's *wrong* as such. I just think your granny might actually be right. This is probably just a little crush – in a year or two you'll suddenly fall for a boy and—'

'Get married and have his children and then get my heart broken when he leaves me?' I said.

I wanted to hurt Dad, but he was suddenly *smiling*.

'I get it now! This is just a reaction to my leaving your mother. I know it's hit you really hard, Frankie. You've been furious with me. I can understand that too. You're off men in a big way – so you're kidding yourself you're into girls instead.' He sat back, shaking his head at me fondly.

'I'm not "into girls",' I said, hating the expression. 'It's just Sally. I love her.'

'It's not real love, Frankie, not at your age, though I know it feels like it.'

'How do you know what I feel? It *is* love. Please shut up about it. You're spoiling it all.' I was suddenly horribly near tears.

'Give her a break, Dad,' said Zara.

'So she's confided in you, has she?' Dad asked. 'Why didn't *you* tell me?'

'Look, I'm not going to spy on my sister and then report back to you!' said Zara. 'It's nothing to do with me anyway. It's up to Frankie.'

'Yes, but you don't want her getting teased at school if she goes around mooning after this girl, do you?'

I knew that this was exactly what Zara was worried about, but she was wonderful.

'Oh, Dad, get a grip. Being gay isn't a big deal nowadays. Honestly! Come on, Frankie, we'll both take Bear out for his wee,' she said, taking my hand and pulling me out of the room, Bear bounding after us eagerly.

I'd put on the black fur and wound my scarf twice round my neck, but I still shivered as we took Bear down the lane. My eyes stung and the tears started sliding down my face. We only had a little torch and it didn't throw out much light, but Zara knew I was crying. She put her arm round me and gave me a big hug.

'Oh, Zara, you're such a pal,' I said, snuffling. 'And I know you don't even like Sally.'

'I'm not having Dad sitting there so smugly, patronizing you, with Helen looking earnest like she's a psychiatrist and patting her stomach all the time,' she said. 'How dare they!'

'My loving Sally is nothing to do with Dad leaving Mum,' I said furiously.

'I know. Dad's got such a giant ego. He thinks he's the most important person in everyone's lives. Imagine expecting me to rush to him, telling tales about your personal life!'

'I hated the way he talked about it – as if I was pathetic,' I said. 'I'd sooner he was shocked and disapproving.'

'I think he is underneath, actually,' said Zara. 'He just wants to make out he's cool about it. *He's* the pathetic one. He thinks we're all influenced by him. I'm sure if I'd had a quick bunk-up at the back of the Gold Star and got myself pregnant, he'd say it was just me wanting affection because I was missing him so much.'

'I get your point,' I said, wiping my eyes with my woolly mittens. 'If Rowena started cheeking the teachers and hitting her little friends, Dad would say she was acting up because she didn't have her daddy with her.' I stopped. 'Poor little Ro, wanting us all to live together.'

'I know. Imagine Dad and Helen and Mum all squashed up in the same bed!' said Zara.

'Ugh! Please! And if Bear suddenly ran amok and started biting people, Dad would say it's because he needs a man in the house, although Bear doesn't even like men, do you, Bear?'

Bear gave a little bark at the sound of his name and bounded off into the darkness, delighted by all the new country smells and excited by the rustlings in the long grass.

'Let's give him a proper walk,' I said. 'I'm worried he's not getting enough exercise. I hate him being cooped up in the house, and every time he wags his tail Granny fusses he'll knock over some stupid teacup or ornament.'

We should have phoned Dad to let him know, but we couldn't be bothered. Perhaps we just wanted to worry him a little. After ten minutes both our phones pinged, but we decided to ignore the messages. We went for a marvellous long tramp, and Zara let me go on and on about Sally, and then I let her talk about Gary Masters and whether I thought she'd ever have a chance with him.

I still couldn't see what she saw in him. He seemed such a showoff, in love with his own looks, but Zara had been so good and loyal to me that I tried to be understanding. I assured her that the kiss at the party had meant as much to him as it did to Zara, and that sooner or later they'd get together again.

We were like two Agony Aunts, tactfully advising each other, so engrossed in our conversation that it was a while before we realized we'd somehow got lost. We'd thought we were walking down a long stony track, our usual route, but when we shone the dim torch at our feet we saw we'd somehow strayed onto a grassy path.

'Well, we simply have to turn and go back the way we came,' I said, spinning round. 'Bear, take us back to Granny's house. Come on, Bear. Good Bear. Show us the way!'

Bear darted this way and that, seemingly purposeful, but it soon became clear he didn't have a clue where we were either. My phone started ringing. Dad again.

'If we answer, he'll come and find us,' said Zara.

'Yes, and won't he crow! He'll be furious too.'

'He'll be furious anyway. He'll be so worried.'

'Who cares?'

'Do you really *hate* him now?' Zara asked.

'Yes,' I said.

'But why? I mean, he shouldn't have had an affair and left Mum, but heaps and heaps of men do that. And I know he can be beyond irritating at times – but he's still *Dad*,' said Zara.

'I don't want him to be my dad any more.'

'Well, he is, whether you like it or not. And I'm going to answer him.'

'No! Please don't!' I said. 'We can't be too far away. We just have to keep following this path, and then somewhere it'll cross the stony track and then we'll be back in ten minutes tops. Let's show him we really don't need him, Zara.'

'Well. Let's see if we can find this wretched track – but if we can't, we're phoning. Promise?'

'Promise,' I said, linking little fingers with her the way we'd done when we were kids.

We did find it too, though it took much longer than I expected. As soon as we were on the stony track we saw torchlight far away, and then heard Dad's voice calling and calling, sounding desperate.

My tummy clenched then, and I realized just how mean and irresponsible I'd been. I grasped Bear's lead and ran helter-skelter towards Dad, ready to throw my arms around his neck and beg him to forgive me – but he wasn't alone. Helen was there, puffing along, calling too, though surely she'd have been happy if we'd got lost in the woods for ever.

I slowed down. Zara reached Dad first, and sobbed all over him. Dad hugged her tight, not even scolding her, just saying, *'Thank God, thank God, thank God,'* like a fervent vicar. Then he tried to hug me too, and I didn't veer away – but I didn't hug him back either, and I didn't say sorry.

Granny thanked God as well when we walked back into the house. She didn't insist I wipe Bear's big paws as he bounded indoors. She made us all a hot chocolate. But then she got started, telling us how wicked and thoughtless we were, and how they'd all been worried sick.

'What were you thinking of?' she demanded. She looked at me. 'It was your idea to frighten us, wasn't it, Frankie?'

I shrugged. 'Think that if you like, Granny,' I said.

'Hark at your tone! You need a good slap to put you in your place, my girl,' she said.

'Hey, hey, Mum. It's all right, we've got in a tizz about nothing,' said Dad. 'Why don't you go up and check on Rowena, and then go to bed yourself. I'll deal with the girls.'

Granny mercifully did as he suggested. I wanted Helen to go to bed too, but she stayed put, her hands clasped over her stomach as if she was protecting the baby.

'What was all this about, Zara and Frankie?' Dad asked.

'It wasn't about anything, Dad,' Zara said quickly. 'We just took Bear for a walk, that's all.'

'I don't know what all the fuss is about. I always take Bear out before I go to bed,' I said.

'For five minutes. You've been gone well over an hour.' Dad looked at his watch. 'An hour and a half!'

'We just got a bit lost in the dark,' said Zara. 'Sorry if you got worried.'

'Your father was frantic. We all were. We thought something terrible had happened to you,' said Helen. 'Why wouldn't you answer your phones? Your dad tried and tried to get in contact with you.'

'Goodness, did he?' I said. I got out my phone. 'Oh yes, missed calls. There can't have been a signal out in the woods.'

Zara gave me an admiring glance. 'Yes, I've got missed calls too. So sorry, Dad,' she said.

But Dad saw the glance and narrowed his eyes. 'Stop trying to act the innocent. You were clearly up to something. You weren't trying to run away, were you?'

'Oh, Dad! Why would we run away?' asked Zara.

'Like children in an Enid Blyton story! Did you think we were going to find a hollow tree and set up home?' I said.

'Your granny was right about you, Frankie,' said Helen. 'You do deserve a good slapping. You think you're so smart and clever with all your wisecracks. You've no idea how much you worry your poor dad. He can't do anything right in your eyes. He spent a fortune on a new phone for you and yet you barely said thank you.'

'I didn't *ask* him to spend a fortune on me,' I said angrily. I bitterly resented her chiming in with her two pennyworth. 'Look, take your wretched phone back.' I held it out to him.

He just shook his head wearily. 'I can see there's no point talking to you when you're in this kind of mood,' he said. 'You'd better both go to bed.'

'We really are sorry we worried you, Dad,' said Zara, kissing him. 'Night, Dad. Night, Helen.'

I ignored them and settled Bear down on his bed in the utility room. Then we went upstairs. Rowena was reading her Worst Witch book by torchlight.

'Everyone was so worried about you two,' she said earnestly. 'I was too. I thought you might have both tripped in the dark and broken all your legs so you were just lying there in agony and no one would find you and then you'd die and I wouldn't have any sisters any more.'

'Oh, Ro,' we said. She scrabbled out of bed and sat between us while we both hugged her.

'Bear would have come running back home to fetch help for us if we'd broken *all* our legs,' I said. 'That sounds so weird, like we've got four legs each.'

'Don't tease, Frankie. I was so scared I started crying,' said Rowena.

'Oh, darling,' said Zara, rocking her.

We made a huge fuss of her, and as soon as she was tucked up again she fell straight to sleep.

'I feel awful, worrying her so,' I whispered.

'I think she was exaggerating for effect,' said Zara.

'It's kind of a relief, feeling sorry,' I said. 'I seem to have become a whole new person. I almost enjoy being horrid to Dad and Helen and Granny.'

'You're channelling your inner Sally,' Zara told me.

That brought me up short. 'Really?'

'You've even started tossing your head the way she does, and doing that smile of hers.'

'I haven't!' I said, but I wondered if she might be right.

I texted Sally, telling her we'd had a bit of a family drama and I was missing her heaps. I ended it with three *loves* too, and a whole row of kisses. I had a text back almost straight away, but it was just Mum to say goodnight. I lay awake for ages, waiting and wondering.

I didn't hear a word from her the next day either. I sent her a text just in case she'd accidentally wiped all my messages and forgotten to tap my number into her contacts. I sent her several texts actually, trying to sound as casual as I could. And then, when she still didn't reply, I started on variations of R u alrite? I tried to make them funny so I wouldn't sound too needy.

R u upside down in a snowdrift?
R u sliding down down down a glacier?
R u dangling from a ski lift screaming help?

But then I began to take my stupid suggestions seriously. What if she really was hurt? People had skiing accidents all the time. Perhaps she'd broken both her wrists and couldn't use her fingers for texting. Perhaps she'd had a serious fall and was lying in a hospital bed, unconscious. Her parents probably didn't even know I existed, so they couldn't let me know.

I asked Zara to text me just in case my phone had somehow stopped working. She did as I asked, but shook her head at me. The message pinged onto my screen immediately.

I gave a great sigh.

'Oh, Frankie,' said Zara. 'Don't get in such a state.'

'But I can't understand it. *Why* isn't she texting me? I think she's had an accident!' My voice rose, and Granny heard me from the kitchen.

'Maybe this is God's punishment for refusing to answer your phone last night,' she called.

She couldn't see me so I pulled a hideous face at her.

'I'm positive Sally's had an accident,' I whispered to Zara.

'Then phone her and find out.'

'But if she's in plaster or whatever, she won't be able to answer, will she?'

'But she'll have someone with her, and they'll answer, won't they? Go on, try. Put yourself out of your misery,' Zara argued.

'Won't it be very expensive phoning Switzerland?' I said feebly.

I didn't care about the expense – although I knew Dad would be cross when the bill arrived. I was desperate to find out about Sally, but scared of actually talking to her. But after another hour of agonizing I pressed her number and then the CALL option.

I waited, my heart beating fast, all my nerves jumping.

'Hi, sorry, can't come to the phone right now. Please leave a message. Cheers!'

It was Sally's recorded voice, so matter-of-fact and cheery. My throat was so dry I could barely speak after the tone.

'Hi, Sally, it's Frankie. Just wondering if you're OK as I haven't heard for a bit. Anyway, see you soon. Is it still OK to come to the party? Bye then.'

It sounded such a feeble message and my voice was a bit wobbly. 'Oh God, she'll think me such a fool,' I said to Zara.

'You sounded OK. Ish,' she said.

'I sounded pathetic. I *am* pathetic. I'm just so worried that something's happened to her.' I lowered my voice to the tiniest whisper. 'Or maybe – maybe she's gone off me already and is deliberately blanking me.'

'I hate to keep saying this, but maybe she's just playing games with you,' said Zara. 'I've seen her acting like that with the mousy friend, laughing with her one minute and then putting her down the next.'

I thought about Sally and Marnie. 'I suppose,' I said reluctantly. 'But I'm not like Marnie!'

'No, you're not. You're my sister, Frankie, and you've got too much spirit to let someone turn you into a jelly. The next time she texts you, don't reply for ages. Play her at her own game,' said Zara.

'I don't think there'll *be* a next time,' I said miserably.
But there was. Sally texted at twenty past midnight,
waking me up. I found the message, my hands trembling.

Soz, Snowgirl's been partying! But back soon and love love
love uuuuuu, Sally xxx

I managed to behave beautifully all our last day at Haven Cottage. It was easy enough with Zara and Rowena. It was a struggle with Granny but I persevered. I didn't just do the washing-up after breakfast, I swept the kitchen floor too. I showed her yet again how to google things on her old iPad and stayed patient when she kept forgetting. I watched one of those incredibly boring programmes about antiques and guessed the prices with her.

I didn't talk about Sally, but to my surprise Granny mentioned her.

'This girl you were talking about – Sarah?'

'Sally, Granny.'

'What sort of girl is she?'

'Well, she's very pretty and lively and clever,' I said lamely.

'So are you, dear,' Granny said surprisingly. 'What sort of family does she come from?'

'I don't really know. Her dad travels a lot on business. Her mother is some kind of executive. I haven't actually met them,' I said.

'So they're professional people?'

'I suppose.'

'Well, she sounds a nice enough girl,' said Granny. 'But I still think this is just a phase you're going through, Francesca.'

I didn't even rise to that. 'I know you do, Granny,' I said, giving her arm a little squeeze. 'We'll both just have to wait and see, won't we?'

Granny had already started knitting for the new baby – a white bonnet and cardigan and mittens and little booties from a pattern that looked as if it had been published in the 1950s. Helen murmured that they were lovely, and it was very kind of Granny, but she looked appalled.

'Never mind, your baby won't actually have to wear them – well, only when you visit Granny,' I whispered. 'Mum's got a whole carrier bag full of woolly bonnets and booties Granny knitted for the three of us and they're hardly worn. They're even more hideous, all pale pink.'

Helen gave me a wary smile, not quite sure if I was really being friendly.

'Do you know if you're going to have a little girl too? I bet Dad's hoping for a boy,' I continued.

'Well, I'm having a scan soon, so we could find out then, but we're not sure we want to. We'll be happy either way.' Helen hesitated and then said softly, 'It's such a wonderful surprise. I thought I might have difficulty conceiving.'

'You won't mind staying off work for a bit?'

'I can't wait! I suppose I'll have to go back eventually, as money will be pretty tight, but we'll manage.'

'So long as my dad doesn't keep giving us mega expensive presents?' I said.

'He loves to spoil you. He misses you all so much,' said Helen. 'He still feels so guilty. Do you think you'll ever be able to forgive him, Frankie?'

I shifted uncomfortably and shrugged. 'These things happen,' I mumbled, though inside I was screaming, *Never, never, never, because he made Mum so unhappy.*

However, I managed to be nice to Dad that last day. He came out with me when I took Bear for his night-time wee.

'It's all right, Dad, I'm not going to get lost again, or run away,' I said.

'I know. I just felt like a breath of fresh air. And to have a little chat.'

I sighed. 'Oh, Dad, please, do we have to?'

'Don't worry, I'm not going to say any more about you and this girl.'

'Sally.'

'Yes. Forget what I said about it before. I can see that was crass. And I'm happy if *you're* happy, if you see what

294

I mean. Though I do think you're a bit young to fall in love with anyone, girl or boy. And I've always had such a soft spot for Sammy next door. You two have been inseparable.'

'We still are. We'll always be best friends. Just not boyfriend and girlfriend.'

'Ah well. Just take it a little bit easy, OK? I don't want my girl getting hurt,' said Dad.

I wasn't his girl any more, but I let it go. And when we were nearly back at the house I managed to blurt out: 'Sorry for some of the stuff I said, Dad.'

'Oh, Frankie,' he said, giving me a hug.

'And thank you very much for the phone. It's an incredible present,' I added.

'So we're really friends again?' he asked.

'Of course,' I said, though I wasn't sure we could ever be proper friends any more.

When we left Haven Cottage the next morning, I kissed Granny's wrinkly cheek and she kissed me back. I even gave Helen a quick hug. Her tummy bumped against me and it gave me the weirdest feeling, as if my new little half-sister or brother was hugging me too.

I joined in the sing-songs in the car, acting as if I was the old uncomplicated Frankie, though inside I was starting to get anxious. I'd been so churned up about Sally all the time I'd been away I hadn't really given Mum much thought. I'd texted every day, just the once – variations on the same quick little message:

Hi Mum, hope you're OK, miss you, love you lots, Frankie xxx

I remembered not to use text abbreviations, but I didn't put much effort into my messages.

Mum had texted back with funny little anecdotes, and messages for Rowena. She texted Zara too, careful not to repeat herself, always so upbeat. In fact, she sounded so busy and happy – but maybe she was just being brave to reassure us.

When we drew up outside our house, I was out like a shot and running up the path, scared that Mum would look white and washed out, maybe even struggling with yet another terrifying symptom – but when she opened the door she looked marvellous. Her hair was in a new style, she had colour in her cheeks, and she was wearing her best red dress. It was too big for her now, but she still looked good in it. It was a similar style to the one Helen had worn, and it looked so much better without the bulge.

'Hello, Jen! You're looking good,' said Dad. Then he added quickly, 'Of course, I know you're not *feeling* good, just putting on a brave face.'

'Actually I'm feeling fine at the moment,' said Mum. 'I hear you've been incredibly generous with the girls' presents. Thanks so much, Richard. I'm sure they've had a lovely time.'

It was odd hearing them talk like polite strangers, but much better than them rowing. Dad looked extremely relieved. I wondered if he ever wished that he hadn't gone off with Helen, and was now starting a new family with her. Perhaps he sometimes wanted to be back with his old family?

'What do you think about this Sally, Jen?' Dad asked.

'Well, she seems very sweet,' said Mum, not understanding.

'Oh well. That's OK then,' said Dad.

I gave him a proper hug, and then we all waved goodbye to him and Helen from the doorstep, Mum, Zara, Rowena and me, though Bear squirmed in through the front door and charged around the house, barking in delight as he reclaimed his old territory.

'Come in, chickies,' said Mum. 'There's a big surprise waiting for you in the living room!'

'More presents?' Rowena asked.

'Yes, special presents. And the person giving you the presents is there too!'

'*Santa Claus?*' Rowena shrieked, and ran inside.

It was better than Santa! It was Coral, my lovely godmother! Dear Coral, with her glossy short black hair and her pink cheeks and red Cupid's-bow lips, like a glamorous painted Dutch doll – but there was nothing wooden about her big warm hugs.

'My girls!' she said. 'My goodness, you're all so grown up! Zara, you're bigger than me! Frankie, you look amazing, even in the yeti coat! Good Lord, I remember your mum wearing it years and years ago! And Rowena, you're practically a teenager! You've got the best girls in the whole world – do you know that, Jen?'

'I do know it,' said Mum. 'And I know I've got the best friend too,' she added softly.

'It's so great to see you, Coral!' I said. 'How much holiday have you got left? I do hope you don't have to go back to Hong Kong straight away!'

Coral was the head teacher at an international school in Hong Kong. She'd come to England the summer before last, when Mum and Dad split up, and stayed for weeks, looking after us all when we were so sad, but she had to go back for the start of the new term. I wasn't sure how long her school had for the Christmas holidays, but surely it wasn't more than a couple of weeks.

'I'm not going back!' said Coral.

We stared at her.

'I gave in my notice at the beginning of term. Hong Kong's changing – I'm not as happy there any more. A lot of my friends have left and my current guy's gone to Dubai.'

Coral had never married, but she usually had a boyfriend on the scene. They were business people who worked for international firms and moved around every few years.

'Are you going to Dubai too?' I asked.

'No, I've got a bit bored of being an ex-pat. Time I came home! Plenty of jobs in schools here, though I wish the salaries were as good. Still, I've got loads of savings. Time I started spending!'

'On us?' Rowena asked hopefully.

'Rowena!' said Mum. 'That sounds awful!'

'Sounds good to me,' said Coral. 'You four are like family to me. I'll be staying with you guys for a while, if that's OK?'

'It's more than OK, it'll be fantastic!' I said happily. 'And it will be lovely for Mum – she's always so tired these days.' Then I clapped my hand over my mouth, because Mum's illness was a secret and she said we must never tell Coral.

'She came and looked after us before and it was such a wonderful help,' Mum had said. 'If I told her about my MS, she'd probably want to come again, and I'd feel so dreadful, always being the helpless, needy one. I'm absolutely *not* telling Coral.'

'It's all right, Frankie,' Mum said now. 'Coral knows.'

'Your mum told me,' she said.

'Mum! You said—'

'I know what I said. But Coral FaceTimed me one night when I was feeling a bit rubbish and I must have looked pretty dreadful too. She knew there was something wrong and kept badgering me, and in the end I just burst into tears and told her.'

'About time too! Imagine keeping such a thing from her oldest friend! I was furious with her,' said Coral.

'No you weren't, you were absolutely lovely, and such a comfort – but I never dreamed you were planning to come here!' Mum gave Coral's hand a squeeze. 'I still can't believe it! You're the best medicine in the world. I feel so much better already!'

'Have you really made Mum better, Coral?' said Rowena, wide-eyed, taking the words literally.

'I wish I could, Rowena. But I'm going to do my best to make her feel as well as she can,' said Coral earnestly, pulling Rowena onto her lap.

'Coral's made me an appointment on the third with one of the leading MS specialists,' said Mum. 'She didn't ask me, she just went ahead and fixed it up.'

'Well, it doesn't sound as if the doctor you see is being much help. I got in touch with one of my old boyfriends whose brother is some kind of senior consultant over here, and he knows this MS specialist who's doing pioneering treatment with infusions,' said Coral. 'She can't cure MS as such, but she's trying to stop her patients having further relapses. I'm going to get you onto her programme if it's the last thing I do.'

I was so happy and hopeful for Mum, though I wished *I* had been able to find out about this specialist and get her an appointment.

'You're an absolute angel, Coral,' I said.

'No I'm not. I've always been considered a bad girl,' she said. (She'd never said anything to us, but Zara and I suspected that some of her boyfriends were married.) 'I just love your mum, that's all.'

'Like Frankie loves Sally,' said Rowena, nodding.

'Have you got a new best friend, Frankie?' Coral asked with interest.

'Well, she's not exactly a best friend,' I said, feeling ridiculously embarrassed now. I took a deep breath. I'd told Dad. I'd told Helen. I'd even told *Granny*. Why did it feel so impossible to tell Coral and Mum?

They were looking at me eagerly, smiling. I was still wearing the black fur coat and felt as if I was in a furnace. I wriggled out of it quickly and breathed deeply, trying to psych myself up. I had to speak up and sound proud, and above all I mustn't blush.

'Sally's my girlfriend,' I mumbled, feeling my face flood scarlet.

They didn't seem to understand.

'Yes,' said Mum. 'I know. You've made friends.'

'Yes, but she's not a girl who's my friend. She's my actual *girlfriend*. You know. As opposed to boyfriend,' I said huskily. Oh God, why did this feel so awkward? Why wasn't it all easy and matter-of-fact, the way it was supposed to be?

'Well, good for you,' said Coral. 'That's marvellous, isn't it, Jen? Though I thought you and Sammy next door were sweethearts. Still, as long as Sally's a lovely girl, then that's absolutely fine, darling.'

'She *is* lovely,' I said, instantly feeling so much better. But Mum was looking shell-shocked.

'Mum?' I said. 'You don't mind, do you?'

'Oh, Frankie, of course I don't mind,' she said. 'It's just – well, you're a bit young, aren't you, to be thinking about girlfriends, or boyfriends for that matter. You're only thirteen.'

'Nearly fourteen. And anyway, you can fall in love with someone at any age, can't you?' I said. 'Think of Shakespeare's Juliet. And what was the name of the girl Dante fell in love with? Beatrice!'

'Well done! A daughter to be proud of on all counts, especially her literary knowledge,' said Coral.

'I know.' Mum reached out to give me a hug. 'I'm proud of you in every way, Frankie – but just slow down a bit, will you?'

'Are you in love too, Zara?' Coral asked.

Zara sighed. 'Not really. The boys my age are so immature. And the older ones can be so gross. I wish I could go back to when you and Mum were my age and boys were more romantic.' She paused. 'Like the men in Jane Austen's books,' she added, not to be outdone by my literary references.

'I've always looked for men like that, but I'm not sure they actually exist,' said Coral.

'I'd like a man who'd give me magic sweets like Moonface in the Faraway Tree stories,' said Rowena.

While they were all chattering about men in books, Mum murmured in my ear, 'Does Sally think she's in love too?'

'Yes, she does!' I said.

'Well, that's good, but I'd still play it a little bit cool. Maybe keep quiet about all this at school. I'm not sure how the kids in your class will react. Or your teachers for that matter,' Mum whispered.

'It's nothing to be ashamed of!' I said.

'I know, I know. I'd say the same if you were in love with a boy. Well, I always thought you *were*. Poor old Sammy. I think *he* loves *you*.'

'No he doesn't!' I said, but I blushed again, remembering the kiss.

I imagined kissing Sally.

'Don't get too carried away with Sally,' Mum said, as if she could read my mind. 'You know what I mean.'

'Yes!' I said, desperately embarrassed now.

'And you'd better not tell your granny – she'd be very shocked.'

'She knows. And she *was* shocked, but she's sort of come to terms with it.'

'So your dad knows too?' said Mum. 'Oh, I see, *that* was why he was asking me about Sally!'

'I blurted it out because he was teasing me about stuff, and being so annoying. You know what he's like,' I said.

'And was he quite cool about it when you told him?'

'Well. Sort of. Though he thinks it's all because of him,' I said, sighing.

'Really?' said Mum.

'Yeah!'

'Yes, not yeah. Why does he think that, for goodness' sake?' Mum asked.

'He thinks I've been having issues with men since he left us,' I said.

'Give me strength!' said Mum.

Rowena had got bored of the discussion about literary males and had wandered over to the Christmas tree.

'Oh look!' she said, squatting down beside a new pile of presents: a set of large soft crimson parcels tied with gold ribbons, and another set of small slim packages in orange wrapping paper fastened with silver ribbons. We each had a big present and a little one, marked with our names and a Chinese message.

'It says *Happy Holidays*,' said Coral. 'At least I hope it does. I've never quite mastered Mandarin.'

The big present was an embroidered silk Chinese outfit. Rowena had red pyjamas with a tiny toy rabbit in the pocket wearing a diminutive matching pair; Zara had a blue dressing gown with pink blossom trees; and Mum had another dressing gown, navy silk with white swans. I had a Chinese jacket in forest green with little pale brown hares running around the hem and cuffs. It fitted me perfectly and I totally adored it.

I'd been worrying what to wear for Sally's New Year's Eve party. I couldn't wear Sam's shirt yet again, and it wasn't fancy enough for a party anyway. I didn't have any suitable dresses and I'd look ridiculous in Zara's clothes. But here was the perfect answer. I'd wear my new black moon and stars sweatshirt and jeans and Docs with my beautiful jacket. It was the sort of outfit Sally might wear herself.

The little packets were jewellery. Rowena had a Princess Elsa watch with a blue strap. Zara's was a silver link bracelet with a heart charm. Mum's was a pearl ring. Mine was a silver locket that opened. I decided to take a photo of Sally with my phone and get it printed so that she'd fit inside the locket.

'Dearest Coral! These are the most perfect presents in the whole world,' I said, hugging her.

The others joined in the hug, nearly knocking Coral over.

'Make the most of them, darlings. I'll never earn as much over here,' she said. 'Still, it feels marvellous to be back.'

'What about your boyfriend, Coral? Won't you miss him?' Zara asked.

'Oh, our relationship had started to fizzle out. We were both relieved to say goodbye while we were still on speaking terms. I'll have a little sabbatical, and then see if I can find a lovely hunky substitute. Maybe I'll find one for you too, Jen,' said Coral.

'Count me out!' said Mum.

'Count me in!' said Zara.

Mum cooked savoury pancakes for lunch.

'And I'm making supper,' said Coral. 'Chicken chow mein the way it's supposed to taste! You wait, girls, you're in for a treat. I should have brought back some Chinese lanterns. We'll have a proper New Year's Eve party. Won't that be fun? And when midnight strikes we'll all have a hug and make a wish!'

'Can I stay up and wish too?' Rowena asked. 'I've never, ever stayed up till midnight before. It'll be magic.'

'Of course you can stay up, darling – and if by any chance you're having a little nap on the sofa, we'll wake you up for the big countdown,' said Mum. 'We'll celebrate in style, all five of us. Six, counting Bear – right, Frankie?'

Had Mum *forgotten*?

'Well yes, but I won't actually be here, will I? I'm going to the New Year's Eve party at Sally's house,' I said.

Mum looked at me in astonishment. 'What?'

'Don't look like that, Mum! I *told* you.'

'You mentioned something vaguely, but surely you want to stay in now that Coral's here.'

'Well, of course I *want* to,' I said, trying to be tactful. 'But I did promise I'd go.'

'Just phone her and explain your godmother's on a surprise visit from Hong Kong. She'll understand,' said Mum.

'No, you don't have to cancel, Frankie. Go to your party, darling,' said Coral. 'That's absolutely fine. For goodness' sake, if she's your girlfriend now, then of *course* you'll want to be with her.'

'But she lives miles away. I suppose I could take you, but how on earth are you going to get home?' said Mum. 'Are you expecting me to stay up, go without a celebratory drink, and then come and collect you at one in the morning?'

'No, of course not,' I said, though I suppose that was exactly what I *had* been expecting. I thought wildly. 'Maybe I could get a taxi. Sam's coming too, and I know he'll have money, and I can always pay him back later.'

'Sammy's been invited too?' Mum sounded a little more relaxed.

I texted him, just in case he'd forgotten. He got back to me to say of course he was still coming, and his mother was going to be our taxi service because she was in the midst of a clean eating phase, and that meant healthy drinking too – bright green veggie smoothies and no alcohol whatsoever. I texted him back telling him about the baby – and he just texted back: !!!

Next I texted Sally to ask when we should come, my tummy tense in case it was one of those inexplicable times when she didn't text back, but within a minute she messaged to say: Anytime luv S xxx. It was an answer at least, but not a very satisfactory one. I'd so hoped she'd send a really caring message to say how much she'd missed me and she couldn't wait to see me, and ending with *love* spelled properly.

I wished I'd been more casual now. I didn't want to sound so needy – though I *was*. And I still didn't have a clue what time to arrive. I'd been to parties when I was a little girl, when you got purple lips from drinking Ribena and blew out the candles on the birthday cake, but nothing since then except Coral's farewell one.

I had no idea what you *did* at New Year's Eve parties. People drank, obviously, though that was a bit worrying.

What else did you do? You made conversation. I wasn't too sure about that either. I was fine talking one to one, but I wasn't sure I could hold my own among a cluster of people, everyone trying to score points. Perhaps the drink would help me chat a bit, though I seriously doubted it.

Then there was dancing. I could jog about a bit, but I wasn't a great dancer – I couldn't wriggle around in a sexy way like Zara. I even felt self-conscious practising in front of the bedroom mirror, so what would I be like at a posh adult party with a lot of strangers? And the only person I wanted to dance with was Sally. Would that be possible? And would she mind that I wasn't great at it?

I started to wish that I *wasn't* going after all. There was still time to cancel. Sam texted to say that his mum would take us at eight thirty. I thought that was way too late – we wouldn't get there much before nine – but Coral said that was a good time to arrive at a New Year's Eve party.

'Better late than early anyway. You don't want to be one of the first to arrive,' she told me.

'I'm not sure I even want to be one of the last,' I said. 'Maybe I won't go. I really would rather stay in with you, Coral.'

'Well, this way you can party with us first and *then* go on to Sally's party, so you get two parties on one night, lucky girl.' She looked at me. 'Don't be so worried, Frankie.'

'I am kind of nervous about it,' I confided, lowering my voice.

'Everyone gets nervous before a party,' said Coral.

'I bet you don't.'

Coral seemed the most sophisticated, sure-of-herself person I'd ever met, but she nodded emphatically. 'Yes I do. Especially if there's someone I really want to see there. I might be good at pretending to be cool, but inside I'm all dithery, trust me. And you won't have to walk in by yourself. You'll have Sammy with you for moral support, bless him. Is he still devastatingly good-looking? He was always such a handsome boy.'

'I suppose,' I said.

'Don't cross him off your romantic list for ever,' said Coral. 'But if you really don't want him, why not be kind to your sisters? Zara, you don't fancy a toy boy, do you? Or Rowena, how about a much older man?'

'I've got my own boyfriends,' said Rowena loftily. 'Chris Walker and Richard Peters *both* want me to be their girlfriend. They always want to sit next to me at lunchtime. It's a good job I've got two sides.'

As we were setting off so late, I almost did have two parties. I helped Coral prepare her chicken chow mein and then ate a portion, because I couldn't just sit there with my tummy rumbling, watching all the others tuck in. It was hot and spicy and delicious. I had some salted caramel ice cream too, and that was very sweet and cooling on the tongue.

'I'm making an awful pig of myself,' I said.

'It's good to line the stomach if you're going to be drinking,' said Coral.

'But she's *not* going to be drinking! Thirteen's way too young,' insisted Mum. 'Promise me you'll be sensible, Frankie.'

'I keep saying, I'm nearly fourteen. But I will be sensible. Don't look at me like that, Mum. I *promise*,' I said.

'Like you keep those kinds of promises when you're nearly fourteen!' said Coral.

'Stop it, Coral! You're practically encouraging her. I've had one daughter coming home drunk just recently, and that was shock enough,' said Mum.

'Rowena, you naughty little minx!' said Coral. 'How many Ribena and rums did you guzzle?'

Rowena snorted with laughter. 'Ten!' she said, and mimed being drunk, staggering all over the carpet.

'And *I* wasn't drunk, not in the slightest,' said Zara. 'You don't half exaggerate, Mum!'

'And that outfit you were wearing is seared on my eyeballs for ever!' Mum told her. 'You're not going to terrify me wearing a skirt up to here, are you, Frankie?'

'As if! I'm wearing my jeans.'

'You can't wear jeans to a party!' said Zara.

'Watch me,' I said.

At eight o'clock I went upstairs to get ready. Poor Bear thought I was fetching my coat to take him for a walk and barked excitedly.

'Oh, Bear, another walk? Well, all right, just a quick one,' I said.

'No! I'll take him!' said Zara. 'You haven't got time!'

I didn't really need much time. I had a wash, cleaned my teeth, and got dressed in clean underwear, best jeans, new sweatshirt – and my beautiful new green Chinese jacket. I wished I had a beautiful new face to put on too. I was glad that Zara had given Bear the shortest walk ever, because I got her to put a little make-up on me again.

'Though Sam thinks I look stupid in make-up,' I said.

'I'll do it very naturally. And anyway, this isn't for Sam's benefit, is it?'

'Don't tease me about it! I wish I hadn't told anyone about Sally now. I feel such an idiot,' I said. 'Hey, Zara, not that bright lipstick! I don't want any lipstick. Just make my face look a bit less blobby, that's all.'

'OK, no lipstick. Are you going to kiss her at midnight then?'

'Zara! No! Not in front of everyone! I'd just about die.'

'But maybe afterwards? In private?'

'I don't know!' I said. 'Maybe she won't want to. *I* wouldn't want to kiss me.'

'I think she's lucky to have you,' said Zara, and she gave me a hug, though cautiously, so she didn't smudge the make-up she'd applied.

'You're the best big sister ever,' I told her.

She brushed my hair, playing with the idea of putting it up in a knot, but in the end decided it looked best loose, straight and shining round my shoulders.

'There! You'll do. In fact, you'll more than do. You look great, Frankie. That green really suits you,' she said.

'I'm still not pretty though, am I?'

'Yeah, but pretty's kind of ordinary. You look different. Interesting. You watch yourself at this party. I bet Sally won't be the only one who's interested in you. Look after yourself, OK, Ms Frankfurter?'

'I will. Sammy will be looking after me too,' I said.

When he called for me he was looking ultra cool in new jeans and a new plaid shirt over a bright white T-shirt.

'Hey, Sam. Like the shirt! I'm going to want to borrow that one sometime!' I said.

'I like your . . .' Sam waved his hand round and round in the air, indicating all of me.

'It's the new jacket. Coral gave it to me. She's staying at ours for a while. Come and say hello to her,' I said.

Coral raised her eyebrows when she saw Sam. 'Oh my, you can't possibly be funny little Sammy-next-door. You look like the cutest one in a boy band! And, Frankie, look at you! The jacket looks marvellous. I feel very smug. Have a lovely party, darlings.'

'I wish I was old enough to go to New Year's Eve parties,' said Rowena.

'I'm kind of glad I'm too old for them,' said Mum.

'You're not. We're going out on the razzle-dazzle ourselves while I'm here, you wait and see,' said Coral.

Mum smiled. 'Anyway, have a lovely time, you two. And is your mum being kind enough to pick you both up from the party too, Sammy?'

'Yes, she thought about half twelve, quarter to one, some time like that,' he said.

Mum nodded and then took hold of my hand. 'Gosh, you're icy cold,' she said, rubbing it. 'Are you OK?'

'I'm fine, Mum, honest.'

'Honest*ly*.'

'I know. I was just winding you up.'

'You're a bad girl. But be a *good* girl at the party,' said Mum. 'Off you go then. Don't keep Lucy waiting.'

As we went into the hall I heard Coral say, 'Ah, don't they look sweet together!'

'*Us?*' Sam mouthed, and grinned.

His mum already had the car waiting at the kerbside.

'This is very kind of you, Lucy,' I said politely.

'No problem, Frankie. My, you do look grown up! You've really dressed up for once!'

'Mum!' said Sam.

'Did you have a good time at your father's?'

'Not really,' I said.

'Frankie's going to be a stepsister,' said Sam.

'Really! How do you feel about that, Frankie?' Lucy asked.

'OK,' I said, shrugging.

I always seemed to become monosyllabic with Sam's mum. I'd known her for most of my life but I'd never really felt comfortable with her. I got the feeling she didn't really like me and was baffled that Sam and I had been friends for so long. I expect she hoped he'd go out with one of the posh high-school girls.

She seemed interested in Sally, and wanted to know all about her. I said she was a friend of mine from school.

'So how does she know Sammy then?' she asked.

'We've met a couple of times when I was with Frankie,' said Sam. 'Do quit fussing, Mum.'

Lucy seemed reassured when we drew up outside Sally's. 'It's a lovely house,' she said. 'And the party seems to be going with a swing already.'

The lights were on all over the house, and we could see people bobbing about, laughing, dancing, throwing their arms around each other in a pantomime of merriment.

'Oh God,' I muttered.

Sam gave my hand a quick squeeze. His own hand was damp. He was nervous too, though he was trying to be reassuring.

'Well, party time, you two,' said Lucy. She was hesitating too. 'I wonder, do you think I should come in with you? Just to meet this Sally's parents and make sure everything's OK?'

'Mum! We're not five years old,' said Sam. 'Of course everything's OK. Come on, Frankie.'

'Well, you've both got phones on you, haven't you? If you need to come home early, just give me a ring. Otherwise I'll be here around half twelve. Bye then! Have a good time,' she said, falsely bright and cheery. Then, as we got out of the car, she called, 'Stick together, won't you?'

Sam sighed. 'We're not entering enemy territory, Mum!'

It felt as if we were. We'd been to the house before, spent the whole afternoon there, and yet it didn't seem at all familiar now. I looked through the nearest window, hoping to spot Sally, but I couldn't see her. The partying people seemed even more daunting now that there was just a pane of glass between us. They looked so grown up and glamorous.

'This *is* the right house, isn't it?' asked Sam.

'Yes, of course it is,' I said, though I was wondering the same thing myself. I took a deep breath. 'Well, here goes.'

I knocked on the door, careful not to scratch myself on the elaborate Christmas wreath. Then we waited. And waited and waited.

'Knock again. Louder!' said Sam. 'They're making such a row they can't hear us.'

The door wobbled slightly as I rapped. 'Oh my God, have I broken it?' I whispered.

'No, we're such fools! Look, it's been left on the latch. We're supposed to go straight in.'

But at that moment the door opened and there was Sally, looking incredible in a low-cut black dress with scarlet high heels. Her cheeks were flushed, almost as red as her shoes, and her eyes sparkled. She wore her own tiny version of a Christmas wreath on her curly hair – ivy and holly berries and mistletoe.

'Hey, Frankie!' she said, and she gave me a huge hug, kissing me on either cheek.

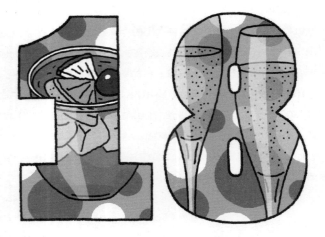

I was so happy I wanted the moment to last for ever. She seemed thrilled to see me. She was giving me a hug, kissing me twice! She really *did* love me the way I loved her!

But then she dodged round me. 'Hey, Sammy!' she said, in exactly the same tone of voice, and he got a hug too, and a kiss – two kisses. 'I'm so glad you came! Were you knocking long? We left the door open for people.'

Behind us, two older boys – certainly not schoolboys – came in, but Sally greeted them both with the hug, the double kiss, the dazzling smile. She was like one of the animatronic polar bears at the shopping centre, going through the same little routine again and again.

'Go party!' she said, gesturing to Sam and me. 'With you in a minute!'

I walked uncertainly towards the open door on the left.

'No, that's the boring old adult party! We're all down in the den,' Sally called.

Sam and I opened the door to the basement, and another blare of music rose up and deafened us. We went down together. There were couples in dark corners in the corridor, a rowdy cluster of boys in the kitchen cracking open some beers, and a dense throng in the big cinema room. The deep sofas were pushed back against the walls: on one, more couples curled up together, while on the other two, girls sitting with drinks made animated conversation. I knew three of them: Marnie, Georgia and Scarlett.

I hadn't realized they'd be here too. I'd thought Sam and I would be the only other young people. I realized now how stupid that assumption was. Sally was very popular and revelled in having heaps of friends. Of course she'd have her own big party. I couldn't see anyone else from our class – but Gary Masters was here with some of his mates. He was chatting up a girl I'd never seen before, who was gazing at him adoringly. I felt a pang for Zara.

Most of the boys were at least four or five years older – and then I worked out why. A tall good-looking guy was larking around acting as DJ, a familiar trilby hat on his wild fair curls.

'He must be Sally's brother,' I shouted into Sam's ear.

'Do you know anyone else?' he shouted back.

'Only those girls on the sofa – they're in my class,' I said. 'The ones you met at Whitelands.'

'Let's go and talk to them then,' said Sam.

'No!'

'We can't just stand here like dummies. Unless you want to dance . . .'

'Definitely not,' I said. Sam wasn't any better at dancing than me – he did too much leaping about.

'Well, you sit with your friends while I go and find us both a drink,' he said, steering me towards them, though I tried to resist. He smiled at Marnie and Georgia and Scarlett.

'Hi, girls. I'm Sammy, Frankie's friend,' he said.

They'd been staring at me sullenly, but they couldn't help smiling back at him.

'I'm getting us a drink. Can I fetch you girls a top-up?'

They quickly drained their tall glasses and held them out.

'Could we have more punch, please?' asked Scarlett.

'Coming right up,' said Sam. 'I'll get you one too, OK, Frankie?'

Zara had told me never, ever to drink the punch at any party. It might look like a pretty liquid fruit salad, it might even taste like lemonade, but usually someone would have spiked it. Even one glass could be lethal. Marnie and Georgia and Scarlett still looked stone-cold sober, but it seemed a serious risk all the same. I'd been planning to stick to a soft drink, a Coke or a juice, but I didn't want to seem pathetic in front of them, so I just nodded at Sam.

'Budge up a bit,' I said to Marnie, and squashed in beside her.

'What are you doing here then?' she asked.

'What do you think? Sally invited me,' I said.

'Do you think you're *friends* with her then?' Marnie asked spitefully, fingering her red bracelet.

'Yes, I do actually,' I said. 'We've spent lots of time together during the holidays. It's been great.'

I wanted to hurt her – but I suddenly felt bad when her whole face crumpled and her eyes filled with tears.

'You cow,' she said, and heaved herself up off the sofa. She blundered her way through the crowd to get out of the room.

'Oh God,' I said. 'I didn't mean to upset her, not like that. Do you think I should go after her?'

'Haven't you hurt her enough?' snapped Scarlett.

But Georgia was surprisingly sympathetic. 'She was in a bit of a state already,' she said. 'I think it's better to let her go off by herself for a bit. So, you're with your boyfriend?'

'Sort of,' I said.

'He's only our age, isn't he?' said Scarlett. 'Still a bit immature, like the boys in our class.'

'I think he looks incredible all the same,' said Georgia. 'I love the way he does his hair.'

'Well, he tried to chop a bit off and it was a disaster so he had to go and have it cut properly,' I explained.

'Isn't it about time *you* had your hair cut?' said Scarlett, smoothing her own sharp asymmetric bob. 'You look like a little kid with it hanging down your back. All you need is an Alice band.'

'I think Frankie's got lovely hair. And I think that jacket's fantastic too, by the way. It really suits you,' said Georgia.

'Jesus, stop smarming all over her. You'll be kissing her next!' said Scarlett.

Georgia blushed. I felt so sorry for her. And angry too. She'd only been trying to be kind.

'Why do you have to be so mean all the time, Scarlett?' I said. The words came out my mouth before I could stop them.

'Oh, diddums, have I hurt your feelings?' she said in a stupid voice.

'No, you haven't hurt mine. You've hurt Georgia's. Does it feel good to put people down all the time?' I asked.

'Yeah, it feels great, if they're stupid.' Scarlett got a pack of cigarettes out of her pocket and lit one ostentatiously. She inhaled deeply and then choked, which spoiled the effect.

Georgia and I exchanged glances and smirked. I nudged up towards her, away from Scarlett. I didn't want my beautiful jacket to smell of cigarette smoke, and she was waving her arm about theatrically. It would be awful if she burned it.

'Oh, cosying up together now, like a pair of lezzies,' said Scarlett. 'Yuck!'

Georgia blushed again. This was ludicrous. I didn't remotely fancy Georgia, and I was pretty sure she felt the same way about me. If Scarlett was so abusive about a non-existent situation, what would she be like when she found out about Sally and me?

'Do grow up, Scarlett,' I said, but to my fury I'd started trembling.

It was a great relief when Sam came back with a tray of drinks. I took a long glug of my punch, in spite of Zara's warning. It tasted OK – sweet but with a musty sort of undertone. Was that the alcohol? I didn't really care.

'I thought there were three of you,' Sam said affably to Scarlett.

'Oh, Marnie's pushed off somewhere else,' she said, suddenly all sweet smiles.

'And where's Sally?'

Scarlett shrugged. 'Who knows?' She offered Sam a cigarette.

'Thanks,' he said.

I'd never seen him smoke before, but he did it gracefully. He sat on the arm of the sofa, chatting to us. We couldn't hear half of what he was saying because the music was so loud, but Scarlett and Georgia acted like Little Noddys.

Then the DJ shifted to long-ago hits, playing that old Pharrell Williams song, 'Happy'. Sam and I used to bounce around to it when we were little kids, yelling out the words.

'Come on, Frankie, it's our song,' said Sam, stubbing out his cigarette, though it was only a quarter smoked.

I took another gulp of punch. 'OK,' I said, though I knew Scarlett would criticize my dancing. I decided

I didn't care. I quite liked Georgia now, I disliked Marnie, although I felt sorry for her too, but I absolutely hated Scarlett.

Sam and I started jogging and jumping the way we used to, but it didn't matter: there were lots of people playing the fool now, dancing wildly, even sideways like ancient Egyptians. I saw some of the girls glancing at Sam. It was so great to be with him. I really did feel happy, though I couldn't help peering around for Sally.

Then the music changed to a slow number.

'Shall we sit down?' I suggested.

'No, let's keep dancing,' said Sam, and he put his arms round me.

I stiffened up a little, but slowly shifted from foot to foot, still dancing with him. Then he put his cheek against mine. I didn't like that much, but it would have been so awkward if I'd pulled away from him. Everyone else was dancing cheek to cheek. It didn't really mean anything, did it?

Then he turned his head and kissed me, just lightly, barely touching my lips, but my own head jerked backwards of its own accord.

'What?' said Sam. 'Oh God, I suppose I taste of tobacco.'

'Yes, you do,' I said, glad of the excuse.

'I hate cigarettes. I only took one to look cool,' he said. 'That Scarlett girl fancies herself, doesn't she? The other one's OK though. But they're not a patch on Sally, are they?'

'No, they're not,' I agreed.

Where *was* she? And then I spotted her, right at the other end of the room, in the middle of a ring of her brother's friends, her head back, laughing at some joke.

'Let's dance over there, it's too crowded here,' I said, steering Sam towards her.

I kept my back to Sally, trying not to look too obvious. Sam didn't notice her until we were practically in front of her.

'There she is!' he said suddenly. 'Hey, Sally!'

There was a little pause, and then I heard her say 'Hey' back.

Sam gave me a dig. 'Give Sally a wave!'

I turned and gave the feeblest wave, but she just nodded vaguely in my direction.

'I don't think she can see you,' said Sam. 'Let's go over.'

'No! She's with all her friends,' I said.

'*We're* her friends. We don't want her to think we're ignoring her.'

This seemed such a crazily upside-down idea that I shook my head. But when we drew near to her, she smiled at us both.

'Hey, you two. Having fun? These guys are all at uni with my brother Nick,' said Sally. She reeled off five names, all of which I instantly forgot. 'And these are my friends Sammy and Frankie.'

They were talking about some dance they'd all been to – one of them had been so crazily drunk he'd put a traffic cone on his head and then got it stuck fast. I wasn't listening properly, so I jumped when one of the guys turned to me and said, 'So, are you really a Frances?'

'No, I'm Francesca. But nobody calls me that except my grandmother,' I said.

'Fancy a dance then, Frankie?'

I was amazed. I didn't fancy a dance with him at all. He was very red in the face and sweaty looking, with a crooked smile. I didn't feel I could just shake my head and say no thanks – that would sound so insulting, and it wasn't his fault he looked so unappealing. I glanced at Sam instead.

'Well, sorry, I'm with Sam,' I mumbled.

'That's OK, Sammy can dance with me,' said Sally.

So there I was, slow-dancing with the guy whose name I'd forgotten, his cheek stuck uncomfortably against mine, while Sally and Sam danced away out of my sight. Oh God, Zara had been right all along. Sally wasn't really interested in me at all. She was just after Sam.

I burned with the humiliation, getting almost as hot as my dancing partner. The hand I was having to hold was unpleasantly damp. His other hand was in the small of my back. I prayed he wasn't leaving a mark on my new jacket.

'So are you and Sam an item?' he asked.

'Yes,' I said firmly.

It didn't seem to deter him. He kept trying to clasp me nearer. I prayed for the track to come to an end, but there was no pause, and he kept a firm hold, still shuffling around.

324

We came close to Sam and Sally. They weren't dancing cheek to cheek, but they looked as if they were enjoying each other's company. Sam seemed to be telling her some joke. She waited expectantly, and then burst out laughing.

She was always laughing, laughing, laughing while she broke people's hearts. Marnie had crept back into the room and was resolutely drinking a pint glass of punch. She was looking mournfully at Sally too. I hated feeling that we were both in Sally's sad little fan club.

When the track changed again, Sweaty Guy still seemed determined to hang onto me.

'I think I'd like to sit down now,' I said desperately.

'OK! Good plan!' he said, holding my hand tightly. He nodded at a chair in the corner. 'Let's go over there.'

He thought I meant sit down *with him* – and I knew what that would involve.

'No! I mean I don't feel very well. I – I have to go to the bathroom,' I said.

'Too much to drink already?'

I let him think that, and dodged between the swaying couples towards the door. There were many more couples in the corridor and kitchen, and someone was in the loo. I waited outside. I could hear giggles behind the door. I really did need to use it now, and knocked. More giggling, but the door stayed locked.

I went up the stairs to the hallway, and then up more stairs to a big bathroom, which was mercifully empty. When I'd used the loo, I washed my hands and then splashed my face carefully with cold water. I looked weird in the mirror, very flushed, and my eyes were glassy.

Was I really drunk? I didn't think so. I could walk in a straight line, and when I spoke out loud – 'Sally, Sally, Sally' – my voice wasn't slurred. I felt foolish gabbling her name, and pulled a face at myself in the mirror. I wondered if Sally and Sam were still dancing together. Maybe *they'd* go and sit in that armchair in the corner. And I'd have to wait for hours until twelve struck, dodging Sweaty Guy until I could get home.

Why on earth had I come? I could be home enjoying Coral's company, the five of us together. It wasn't the New Year yet, but I could still make a resolution.

I resolve to stop being such a fool about Sally. I am NOT going to turn into a Marnie. I don't think I even love her any more, not now I see she was just playing a game with me. She's just a spoiled brat, desperate for attention. And now she's trying to get Sammy to fall for her, just as Zara predicted. Well, what do I care? I don't need either of them. I'm fine by myself. I'm fine, I'm fine, I'm fine.

The girl in the mirror didn't look fine. She seemed to be crying.

I pressed my hot face against the cold tiles, wondering if I should simply leave now. I didn't have any money on me so I couldn't get a bus. I'd have to walk, but it wasn't *that* far. I could do it in less than an hour. It was dark outside and there were raucous people milling about, but no one would take any notice of me. I wasn't a fool, I'd stick to the main streets, not cut down any alleyways.

When I was home safe, I'd text Sam's mum and tell her she didn't need to pick me up. I could text Sam too, though he might be having such a good time with Sally he'd probably not even notice I was gone.

I came out of the bathroom and went along the corridor, past Sally's room. The door was open and I heard someone inside. Was it Sally herself? I peered round the door. The light was off but the hall light showed a couple in there, embracing. I saw bright blonde hair, and for a moment I thought it *was* Sally, but then I saw that her face was hard and overly made up, her body sharply thin in her clinging dress. She was old enough to be Sally's mother. Maybe she *was* her mother. But from the closeness of their embrace, I was pretty sure the man wasn't Sally's father.

'Have you got lost, sweetie?' she said, quite unabashed. 'The children's party's in the basement.'

She spoke precisely, not slurring her words, but I think she was drunk. So was the man with her.

'This is our *private* party,' he said, and they both laughed.

I went out and shut the door on them, feeling disgusted. Somehow it was so much worse seeing *them* making out than the young people down in the den. And in Sally's room of all places!

I went hurtling down the stairs – and saw Sam in the hall.

'There you are!' he said. 'I was looking all over for you! What are you doing up here?'

'I needed to find a bathroom,' I said awkwardly.

'Oh, right! What a relief. I was beginning to think you'd cleared off!'

'Well, I was thinking about it, actually,' I mumbled. 'It's so noisy down in that den – and so hot. I'd give anything for a breath of fresh air.'

'OK, we'll sit on the doorstep and clear our heads a bit, eh?' Sam suggested.

'No, you go back to the party, Sam. Sally will be wondering where you've got to.'

'No she won't! She's surrounded by heaps of people. She's a real party girl, isn't she?'

'Yes, she is,' I said, sighing.

'What's up, Frankie?'

'Nothing! Nothing at all.' I opened the door and sat down on the step. The cold air was like a bucket of water over me.

'Wow! It suddenly hits you, doesn't it?' said Sam, sitting down beside me. 'It's like we're little kids again! I was telling Sally how you and I go *way* back. I think she was dead envious actually. I asked if she was close to her brother, but she said he didn't bother to hang out with her much. I feel quite sorry for her.'

'You really like her, don't you?' I asked.

'Well, yes,' said Sam.

'It's OK with me, you know,' I said, making a huge effort. 'I mean, if you and Sally want to hang out together. Be boyfriend and girlfriend.' The words were like broken glass in my mouth.

'What?' said Sam. 'It's not like that. I *like* her, but mostly because she's your friend. *You're* the only one for me, you know that.' He put his arm round me.

'Oh, Sam.' I wished wished wished I felt the same way. It would all be so simple then. I felt so fond of him I actually turned my head and gave him a kiss – but it was a quick friendly one, not the sort he wanted.

He didn't persist this time. He just held me close and I laid my head on his shoulder. We didn't say anything for a while. Then he gave me a little squeeze.

'Come on, you're shivering. Let's go inside and get warm,' he said.

He pulled me up and I followed him inside.

'Sammy, I'm sorry,' I muttered.

'It's OK,' he said. 'But I'm going to be the first person you kiss at midnight, all right?'

'It's a deal,' I agreed.

We went back to the party, and somehow it wasn't so bad after that. We had another dance together, and then there were a lot of raucous old rock songs that were fun to bounce around to, and practically everyone in the room joined in, wild synchronized dancing in a huge group.

Sally bounced the most, whirling about, making her way around the room. She stopped in front of Sam and me for a bit, and we danced, grinning at each other, and then she spiralled off to another group, and another and another. She danced with Marnie and Georgia and Scarlett. She made Marnie bounce too, and then took hold of her and whipped her round and round, both of them stumbling a little and laughing. Marnie was happy again.

I had to turn away, but when I looked back, Sally was right at the end of the room dancing with her brother's mates.

'She's a right little whirling dervish, isn't she?' said Sam. 'I'm getting out of breath just watching her. And thirsty. Shall I get us another drink?'

'Yes, but not that punch though, it's a bit sickly,' I said. 'Can I have something ordinary, like a Coke?'

'I'll have one too,' he said.

It was such a relief not to have to pretend to be cool. There was heaps of food laid out in the kitchen, and I realized I was quite hungry, in spite of tucking into Coral's chicken chow mein. I experimented with all the dips and crispy things, ate a slice of vegetable tart with my fingers, and then cut myself an enormous piece of cheesecake. I was worried about spilling it on my jacket, but didn't want to take it off in case I lost it. Sam tucked a tea towel under my chin, shaking his head at me.

He ate a lot too, and then, fortified, we went back to the cinema room. They were playing clips of old movies in a series of categories: dance routines; murders; chases; and then, inevitably, sex scenes. There were raucous commentaries on the action. The one that drew the most comments and whistles was a scene with two girls.

I watched, my heart beating fast. It was an art movie, not just crude porn, and the girls were gentle and loving –

but the boys' cat-calling spoiled it, made it horrible. It was a relief when the music started up again.

Scarlett and Georgia were dancing right in front of us, and Scarlett had the nerve to take hold of Sam and pull him up to dance with them. He protested, but eventually gave up to be polite. I was amazed to see Scarlett dancing so suggestively. Georgia looked uncomfortable, just doing a little jig here and a little jig there, and eventually drifted away to sit with Marnie, who was clutching yet another pint of punch.

Sam beckoned for me to come and dance, but I'd have sooner cut off my legs than dance with Scarlett. I looked around the room for Sally but she seemed to have disappeared again. Gary Masters saw me staring and gave a little wave of acknowledgement. I was startled and gave a stiff wave back, the kind royalty give from the back of a car.

Gary ambled over to me, holding a bottle of some trendy beer. He was wearing a tight navy polo shirt that showed off his six-pack, and cream jeans, even tighter. He looked a total poser, but I could see that some girls might find him attractive. He ran his hand casually through his dark hair. I wondered if he practised the gesture in a mirror.

'Hi there. I know you from somewhere, don't I?' he said, sitting down beside me.

'From school,' I said.

'Ah, you're one of Sally's friends,' he said.

'And Zara's sister.'

He looked blank.

'You got off with her at another party.'

'Did I? Does she have dark hair like you?'

'No, she's fair. And very pretty,' I said.

'So are you,' he said, raising his bottle to me.

It was such a cheesy gesture! Clearly he didn't even remember his encounter with Zara, when it had meant all the world to her. What did she *see* in him? What did Sally, for that matter?

'Don't look so sad,' he said, reaching out to tilt my chin.

'I feel sad,' I snapped.

Then he leaned towards me and kissed me full on the lips. Out of the corner of my eye I saw his bottle of beer tilting and pushed him away violently.

'Hey! What was that about? It was only a little kiss!' he protested.

'You nearly spilled your beer all over my jacket.'

'Oh dear, now that would have been a catastrophe,' he said sarcastically.

'Yes, it would! God, you don't half fancy yourself. You probably think girls would throw an entire bucket of beer over themselves for a chance to snog you,' I snapped.

'Temper, temper,' he said, getting up. 'I was only doing you a favour to cheer you up, you silly little girl.'

He sauntered off through the crowd. Sally had reappeared, and he put his arm round her. I watched, my eyes prickling. I knew exactly what he was going to do. In less than two minutes he was kissing her, and *she* didn't make any attempt to push him away.

It made me feel sick watching her. I dreaded midnight, when everybody kissed. I was starting to hate the idea of kissing anyone. Perhaps there was something the matter with me. Maybe I wasn't gay after all, maybe I was simply a prude. The boys at school had a horrible name for girls who wouldn't kiss. Yet they also had a horrible name for girls who did. It was all very well for women to stand up to men and refuse to be treated like objects, but it didn't seem to work like that when you were my age.

I was relieved when, at ten to midnight, Sally's mother came into the den, switching on all the lights. There was a lot of hasty sitting up and rearranging of clothes. I was pretty certain she *was* the woman I'd seen upstairs, but she seemed perfectly composed now, her hair and make-up immaculate, her tight dress unruffled.

'Hey, everyone, upstairs! We're going to count the New Year in together. Come, my darlings!' Her voice still wasn't slurred, but she said every word ultra distinctly, like a satnav voice.

There were a few groans and protests.

'We're fine as we are. Why can't we see the New Year in down here, Mummy?' said Sally. She said the last word ironically, drawling it.

'Don't be difficult, sweetie. I want you and Nick to usher all your guests upstairs now. Pronto!' she said, clapping her hands. She seemed slightly uncoordinated now, so that they flapped instead of clapped.

Sally's face was burning. 'Right. Got the message! Everyone upstairs, quick march!' she said. 'Prod the lazy ones, Nick. Mummy's given her orders.'

There were a few uneasy sniggers. Sally's mother's smile went tighter, her lips almost disappearing.

'OK, Mum,' said Nick. 'We're all coming.'

He cupped Sally's elbow and steered her towards the stairs, and everyone followed.

Sam and I exchanged glances.

'That was a bit awkward,' he whispered, pulling a face. 'Do you think you should try and calm Sally down a bit? You're her friend, Frankie.'

'I think I'd only make her worse,' I said. 'Besides . . .' I let my voice trail away. *Besides, I don't think I'm her friend any more.*

The stylish long living room looked different now, packed with all the adults in their party clothes. Some of the men were wearing smart suits, and some were deliberately casual, in open-necked shirts, even jeans. One wore a tight polo shirt like Gary's, but he had a little paunch so it wasn't a good look. Nearly all the women wore dresses, mostly short and low-cut. One of them rushed up to me and said, 'Oh, darling, what a fantastic jacket! Where did you get it?'

I saw Marnie glaring at her.

'Are you one of Marnie's friends?' the woman asked me.

'Not really,' I said uncomfortably.

There wasn't really time for any more conversation. We were all served with glasses of champagne, and then Sally's parents stood in the middle of the room, consulting their watches. Her father had his arm round her mother, but it seemed a stiff embrace. He started the countdown, and everyone joined in, glasses raised in anticipation.

Then he called out, 'Midnight! Happy New Year, everyone!' and gave his wife the briefest peck on the lips.

'Happy New Year, Frankie,' said Sam, and he kissed me.

I tried much harder to respond this time – and it was OK. Quite sweet really. A lovely gentle kiss with my dearest friend. But no tingling at all.

Then there were all the other kisses, a mad mass ritual. I saw two men kissing, and that looked momentarily strange but then perfectly normal, and I wondered, just wondered, if I dared go over to Sally and give her a kiss. She was surrounded by admirers, inevitably, but then she came purposefully in our direction.

She kissed Sam. She gave my hand a squeeze and said, 'Happy New Year,' but she didn't give me a kiss. I didn't try to kiss her. I was too scared she'd push me away in front of everyone. Then she wandered off, smiling, kissing, squeezing many more hands.

So that was it. I couldn't wait for Sam's mother to come and collect us. I finished my glass of champagne and accepted a refill just so that I had something to do. I liked champagne much more than punch. It was so easy to drink. I drained my glass again almost in one go.

'Hey,' said Sam. 'You're suddenly thirsty!'

'I know. It's great, isn't it.'

'Yes, but you shouldn't gulp it down so quickly. You'll get drunk.'

'I don't care. I think I want to get drunk.'

'OK. But don't throw up in my mum's car on the way home or she'll be furious,' said Sam, laughing at me.

Most of Sally and Nick's friends were going back down to the den. I had just one more refill, but when I got up and started walking I suddenly felt a bit wobbly.

'God, you *are* drunk,' said Sam.

'No, I'm not,' I insisted. 'I'm fine. I just have to nip to the bathroom though.'

'I'd better come with you,' he said.

'Don't be daft. I'm not a little kid. You go down to the den and I'll catch you up in a minute.'

I was starting to wonder if I *might* be sick and I didn't want Sam standing outside, hearing me. I walked up the stairs, trying to put one foot in front of the other and to hold my head high, but I seemed to have forgotten how to walk properly. I *couldn't* be drunk. I'd had the punch ages ago, and then just a couple of glasses of champagne. How pathetic of me.

I felt a little better when I was in the bathroom. I locked the door and sat on the edge of the bath, breathing deeply. No, it was all right, I wasn't going to be sick. I simply felt giddy, as if I'd been on a roller coaster.

'Giddy, giddy, giddy,' said the girl in the mirror, sounding like a fool.

It wasn't just the champagne. It was Sally making me giddy, never knowing where I was with her. She'd hated me, she'd liked me, she'd loved me, she'd singled me out, she'd ignored me. I had to stop caring about her. I couldn't stand the constant uncertainty.

I reached out to the mirror and high-fived my own hand. Then I walked purposefully to the bathroom door and opened it. Sally was standing there, looking at me.

'Hey there,' she said.

'Hey there,' I echoed. I moved aside for her.

'No, I don't want to go to the bathroom. I was following you. Come with me,' she said, taking my hand.

I let her lead me along the landing towards her bedroom. 'What?' I muttered.

'You know what.'

Sally pulled me inside. There was no one else there, no sign that anyone else had been there. It was just Sally's room, smelling faintly of her pomegranate perfume.

'Come here, Frankie,' she whispered. 'Happy New Year.'

Then she slipped her hand under my hair so she was touching the back of my neck and kissed me. It was all I had ever dreamed of.

I don't know how long we were together. It could have been minutes, it could have been half an hour or longer. We were in a world of our own until we heard footsteps, and then a tentative knock at the door.

'Maybe it's Sammy,' I whispered.

'Let's just keep quiet and then he'll go away,' Sally whispered back.

'Sally?' It was a girl's voice. 'I know you're in there.'

'Oh God,' said Sally. She raised her voice. 'I'll be down soon, Marnie.'

'Why can't I come in?' she said. 'What are you doing?'

'Just buzz off, will you?'

But Marnie took no notice. She came bursting in and snapped on the light. She gasped when she saw us.

'You're with Frankie!' she said, sounding agonized.

'Oh for goodness' sake, don't get all hysterical,' Sally snapped.

'I can't believe it!'

'Look, we were just *kissing*.'

'You're disgusting,' said Marnie, looking at me. 'You *know* Sally's my best friend for ever.'

'Stop being so childish,' said Sally. 'You're a little bit drunk, Marnie. I think we all are. Let's just shut up and go down to the den and get even more drunk together, OK?'

Marnie shook her head, and then suddenly put her hand over her mouth.

'Oh God, you're going to be sick. Run to the bathroom, quick!' said Sally.

Marnie ran, making horrible heaving sounds.

'Oh God, oh God, oh God,' said Sally. 'Why does she have to get in such a state? I'd better go and see she's all right. OK?'

'Yes, OK. But Sally . . . just now. It did mean something to you, didn't it?' I said.

'It meant so much to me,' said Sally. '*You* mean so much to me, Frankie – don't you know that?'

She kissed me again quickly and then hurried after Marnie. I stayed in her bedroom, hoping she'd come back soon, but after ten minutes there was still no sign of her. I went along to the bathroom but there was no one there.

339

Maybe Marnie had gone home and Sally had gone down to the den, hoping to find me there.

I went downstairs. Sam was in the hall.

'There you are! You keep disappearing! My mum's just texted. She's outside,' he said. 'Actually, she's been there some time. I must have missed her first two texts. Come on, Frankie, she's getting a bit fussed.'

'Just let me find Sally to say goodbye,' I said.

'Sally's even worse than you for disappearing. Please, Frankie. We don't want my mum banging at the door, now do we?'

So we left together. Lucy was cross at first, but then she calmed down a bit and asked if we'd had a good time.

'Sort of,' said Sam. 'We're not really party people, are we, Frankie?'

'True,' I agreed.

'Well, you both seem in reasonable shape. I was starting to worry you were both drunk or drugged and totally out of it,' said Lucy.

I *felt* drunk and drugged, but it was with happiness – though Marnie had taken the edge off the most beautiful moment of my life. I shut my eyes to relive it.

'Sleepyhead,' said Sam, and put his arm round me so I could lean on his shoulder.

'Ah!' said his mother, looking at us in her rear-view mirror. 'Two little baby lovebirds.' She sounded as if she was mocking us.

'*Mum!*' said Sam, but he didn't sound as if he minded too much.

I patted his chest guiltily, but then closed my eyes and fell properly asleep. It was hard to wake up when we got home. I gave Sam a quick hug, thanked his mother for fetching me and then stumbled up my own garden path.

Coral opened the door for me. 'In you come, sweetheart,' she said. 'I heard the car drawing up. Happy New Year!'

'Where's Mum?'

'I insisted she went to bed straight after midnight because she was looking so exhausted, but I expect she's still awake. Give her a quick kiss before going to bed yourself. You look shattered too. But happy?'

'Very happy,' I said.

'The Sally situation good?'

'Very, very good. And loads of people liked my jacket!'

'Great. Tell me all about the party tomorrow, darling. Night-night now. Sweet dreams.'

I could barely keep my eyes open when I crawled into bed, but I texted Sally.

Had to go, soz. This is my happiest New Year ever! All the love in the world Frankie xxxxxxx

I wasn't sure she'd hear my text with the hubbub of the party all around her, and she wasn't always prompt with her replies. But this time she texted back immediately.

All love to you too, your own Sally xxxxxxx

I did as Coral told me and had the sweetest dreams ever. When I woke early in the morning, the whole party *seemed* like a dream, and I started to wonder if it had really happened, though I had the thudding headache and raging thirst to prove that I'd been *somewhere*.

I crept downstairs to get myself a glass of water. I'd thought no one else was up, but Coral was in the kitchen, sipping a cup of coffee.

'Good morning, Frankie!' she said. 'I thought you'd be lying in till lunchtime! Oh dear, you look a bit pale. Too much to drink last night!' she said, shaking her head at me.

'No, not at all! I mostly drank Coke. I had one glass of punch when I first got there and didn't like it,' I protested, pouring myself a glass of water.

'You drank the New Year in on Coke?' said Coral, raising an eyebrow.

'Oh! I forgot. I did have a glass of champagne then. Or two,' I admitted.

'Dear goodness, a hangover and you're not yet fourteen!' said Coral sternly, but I could tell she was teasing me. 'I'll make you a coffee – and you'd better take a couple of paracetamol with that water.'

I swallowed the pills she gave me and gulped down the glass of water. I was ashamed but I couldn't help feeling a twinge of pride too. A hangover sounded so grown up! I was kind of equal with Zara now.

'You won't tell Mum, will you, Coral?' I said.

'No, she'd only worry. In a little while I'm going to make her breakfast in bed. She gets so tired out, poor love. She never complains, does she, and yet I can see how exhausted she is,' said Coral.

'I make her breakfast too. Sometimes,' I said guiltily. 'Oh, Coral, do you think this new treatment will make her feel a bit better?'

'I very much hope so, darling. I can't bear to think that she didn't tell me how ill she was – and I was so wrapped up in myself I didn't see how drawn she looked when we FaceTimed each other. How can I have been so blind when I love her so much?' said Coral. 'She means all the world to me.'

I picked up my coffee and took a sip, suddenly wondering.

'Coral . . .'

'Mm?'

'Coral, you and Mum . . . You're not *in* love with each other, are you?'

'What?' Coral blinked at me. 'Oh, sweetheart, what a lovely idea! Wouldn't it be neat if we were? We do love each other to bits, and we'll always be the bestest of friends, but no, we're both too hung up on men, more's the pity!'

'Sorry. It was a daft thing to think,' I said.

'It was very sweet, darling. And actually I'll give you a bit of advice, though I've always sworn not to come over all Auntie Coral and lecture you. I've fallen in love several times – many times – and it's wonderful, but it doesn't always last. Whereas really good friends generally stay friends, no matter what. Oh God, that sounds like the sort of banal tripe you read in birthday cards – but I do mean it.'

'Sammy's my best friend for ever,' I said.

'Though it's obvious to everyone that he'd like to be more than that,' said Coral. She paused. 'Maybe one day . . . ?'

'No. Though it would all be so much simpler. But I could never feel about him the way I feel about Sally.' Even saying her name out loud made me blush a little.

Coral sighed wistfully. 'I wish *I* was nearly fourteen and in love for the first time,' she said. 'There's nothing to beat it.'

'Who was your first love then, Coral?'

'Oh, it was the boy who did our newspaper round. He was a year or so older than me, and I thought he was quite wonderful. I'd get up an hour early and lurk in the hall until I heard the creak of our garden gate, and then I'd open the door and take the paper from him, just to have the opportunity of saying thank you! I was incredibly thrilled when he asked me to go to the pictures with him. I didn't have contacts in those days and I thought I looked a fright in my glasses, so I sat in the back row with him, the screen a total blur, but I didn't care a jot. I was with him and we were kissing and I didn't care about anything else.' Coral shook her head at herself.

'And?'

'And what?'

'You went out with him again?'

'Yes, for months. Practically every night. But then it sort of fizzled out,' she said.

'What was his name?'

'Mm, David something.'

344

'You were in love with him and you can't even remember his last name?' I asked incredulously.

'Well, it was a long time ago. And I've had a few boyfriends since!'

'So you and David aren't in touch any more?'

'No, I haven't got a clue what happened to him,' said Coral. 'I'd actually forgotten all about him till you asked.'

'Truly?'

'Well, maybe I get a little frisson in WHSmith when I see a pile of newspapers,' said Coral, but I think she was teasing me.

Maybe she was just spinning me a tale to warn me that first love doesn't last. I'd make sure I proved her entirely wrong. I was certain I was going to be in love with Sally for ever. I imagined us as two old ladies, when Sally's golden hair had turned silver, and I wore my long grey locks up in a bun. She'd be someone special and famous, maybe an actress – and I'd be a writer. Perhaps I could even write plays for Sally to star in. We'd have our own house and Bear's great-grandchild would be devoted to us.

It was just like a fairy tale. I remembered I was supposed to write a proper fairy tale for Mr White. I was sure Ivneet would have written hers by now. Dear Ivneet. I promised myself I'd get started that very day. I *did* write – page after page in my beautiful scarlet leather manuscript book – but it was the start of a diary, and I just wrote endlessly about Sally.

I texted her too, and she texted back asking if I was free the next day, because she wanted to go up to London and spend her Christmas money.

Just us? I texted, because I was shy of Sally's mother, and I definitely couldn't stand the thought of going in a girly gang along with Marnie, Georgia and Scarlett.

Of course just us!

I was thrilled, but had to tell a little white lie when I asked Mum if I could go.

'Would it be OK if I went shopping with Sally tomorrow?' I asked.

'Yes, of course, darling,' she said. She was in such a good mood now that Coral was here. She still looked tired, but her eyes were bright and she smiled a lot. In fact, Mum and Coral often acted like schoolgirls, getting the giggles and teasing each other.

I knew Mum assumed I meant shopping at Whitelands. I wasn't totally sure she'd let me go all the way to London just with Sally, so I didn't mention it.

I told Zara though, and she was really envious.

'I'd give anything to go shopping in London,' she said. 'But how will you get the money for your train fare?'

I'd already figured that out. I waited until the evening, when I was helping Coral make the supper while Mum put her feet up on the sofa.

'I feel awful asking this, Coral, but I don't suppose you'd lend me some money. Just enough for a return train fare and a very cheap lunch? I swear I'll save every penny of my pocket money and pay you back,' I said.

'Train fare?'

'I want to go to London with Sally,' I whispered.

'And your mum's said yes?'

'Sort of,' I said uncomfortably.

Coral looked at me long and hard, clearly not believing me.

'Well, I don't think I mentioned the London part. I didn't want to worry her, and you know how she fusses,' I said.

'You're a wicked devious girl, Francesca Bennet,' said Coral – but she slipped me the money all the same! 'Though for God's sake be careful and look after yourself!' she warned me.

I met Sally at the station at ten the next morning. I thought she might be late. In fact, I was terrified she might not turn up at all. I kept checking my phone to see if she'd cancelled – but there she was, waiting for me, in her red coat and black boots, with her trilby hat tilted cutely to one side.

I felt ludicrously nervous all of a sudden, my mouth drying so much I could hardly croak out 'Hello' – but then she grinned and said I was such a star for coming, and I felt I might burst with happiness.

'You truly don't mind going round all the clothes shops?' she asked.

'I'd love to,' I said, though I'd always moaned like anything when Mum and Zara dragged me on a clothes-shopping trip.

I'd never bothered about what I wore before, but today I'd abandoned the black yeti coat and was wearing my green Chinese jacket again, though I had a T-shirt underneath my new sweatshirt to keep me warm. It was very cold, even though the sun was out. My fingers were freezing – even wearing mittens – and I was sure my nose was bright red, but I was with Sally, and that was enough to keep me warm.

She insisted on paying my train fare, though I showed her I had enough money to pay my own way.

'Never mind, you pay for lunch then,' she said.

This unnerved me, because I wasn't sure my money would stretch to lunch for two. It would be fine if we stuck to McDonald's, but perhaps Sally would want to go somewhere posh.

'Where do you usually eat when you go to London?' I asked.

'It depends. When I go with my mother she likes places like The Wolseley or The Ivy,' said Sally.

That unnerved me totally. I'd vaguely heard of them and was certain I couldn't afford either. When Mum took Zara and Rowena and me up to London, we went to a Pret or ate home-made sandwiches on the train. When Dad took us, we went to a pub and had cheesy chips.

'But I think I like Maison Bertaux best. You'll like it too, I'm sure,' Sally continued.

I wasn't sure at all. It was obviously French and that probably meant it was expensive.

'Don't look so worried,' said Sally. 'I was only joking about you paying for lunch, Frankie.'

'You're a mind reader,' I said. 'For Christmas I gave Sammy this book called *The Chrysalids* – goodness knows what that means – but it's about these children who can read each other's minds.'

'Did Sammy mind you not spending the day with him? I know you guys usually hang out together. You could have brought him, you know,' said Sally.

I wished I could read *her* mind. Had she wanted me to bring him?

'I don't think Sammy would go a bundle on clothes shopping,' I said.

'True,' she agreed.

'And I thought this was an outing just for us,' I said, trying to sound as if I didn't really care one way or the other.

'It is!' said Sally. 'And first of all I'm planning to go somewhere specially for you, Frankie, because I know clothes shopping isn't really your thing either.'

Maybe she really *could* read minds.

The train was crowded with families going to the sales or to see the sights, and the tube was so jam-packed Sally and I had to cling to each other, our noses practically touching. We couldn't help getting the giggles, and a woman rolled her eyes and sighed at us, which made us giggle even more. I couldn't wait to see where Sally was taking me.

It turned out it was the National Portrait Gallery, which was a bit of a surprise. Mum had taken us there when Zara and I were still at primary school, so we could start at the Tudors and then walk through all the galleries and get a proper idea of history through the centuries. It had been fun at first, and I'd liked Elizabeth I, the Virgin Queen, with the body of a woman and the heart of a lion, and her big brainy forehead and enormous dresses that were stiff with jewels. However, to be honest, I got a bit bored after a while.

But Sally wasn't taking me on a whirlwind time-travel through history.

'It's a special show. I thought you'd like it,' she told me.

It was an exhibition of women writers.

'They're not great lookers, are they?' said Sally as we peered at Jane Austen and Charlotte, Emily and Anne Brontë and George Eliot and Virginia Woolf and Beatrix Potter, but she was just teasing me because I was gazing at them reverently.

They didn't just have portraits in the exhibition. There were letters and notes and manuscripts. It was extraordinary peering at the first handwritten page of *Jane Eyre* and imagining Charlotte biting the end of her pen and then starting that amazing first paragraph in her neat sloping handwriting.

'Maybe your red notebook will be here in a hundred years' time,' said Sally.

'Well, it's just as well I'll be dead then, because I've just written all about you, and I'd be embarrassed to have strangers reading it,' I said.

'You've written about me?' Sally asked, looking pleased.

'Heaps. All about everything,' I said.

'You'd better hide it away somewhere very safe and secret. Imagine if your sister read it. Or your *mother*!'

'Well, it would be really embarrassing – but they do *know* how I feel. I've told them.'

'You haven't!'

'So you haven't told anyone about us?' I asked, a little disappointed.

'No, and I'm not going to either.'

'It's nothing to be ashamed of.'

'It's secret. I'd be crazy to tell my family. God, imagine what my brother would say! And my father!'

'What about your mother? Wouldn't she understand?'

'I don't tell *her* anything at all. I don't want anyone to know.'

'But they do. Marnie saw us,' I said.

'Oh, her,' said Sally dismissively. 'I've told her she got the wrong end of the stick. She'll believe anything.'

'You've seen her since the party?'

'She only lives up the road from me,' said Sally. 'I can't *help* seeing her. She's always around.'

'Sally . . . It's none of my business, and I know you two have been friends ever since nursery school, but now, you and Marnie – well, you've never been in love, have you? And kissed and—'

'No!' said Sally. 'With *Marnie*? Absolutely not.'

I knew it was horrible of me, I should feel sorry for poor Marnie, but I felt a stab of pure happiness that Sally seemed horrified by the very idea.

'So am I your first, you know, girlfriend?' I persisted.

'Of course you are,' said Sally, and she tucked her arm through mine.

She insisted on buying me postcards of all the main women writers as a little souvenir.

'You can stick them in your notebook if you run out of things to write about me,' she said.

'As if that's going to happen!' I told her.

I didn't even mind going to Topshop and Zara and All Saints, keeping guard over Sally's bag and clothes in the heaving fitting rooms while she tried on tops and jeans and dresses and jackets. I tried not to stare at her too obviously. I'd seen her undress heaps of times in the changing rooms at school. Sally was never the sort of girl to cower self-consciously in a corner and wrap herself in a towel. But then she'd just been Sally Mac, the most popular girl in our class, and later she became Hateful Sally, the girl who made my life a misery. But now she was *my* Sally, and it was so wonderful that the most striking girl in the fitting room was my girlfriend.

She wanted me to try on some clothes too, but I felt too self-conscious in front of her. I did try on her red coat over my Chinese jacket, wanting to see what it looked like. Without thinking I put my hands in the pockets, and felt something small and hard and familiar. It was the little carved bear Dad had bought me. I was so touched that she carried it around with her.

It was long past lunchtime when Sally had finally chosen her new outfits: a black satin top that made her skin look pearly white; trousers with a black-and-white dogstooth check; a purple calf-length dress with a swirly pattern, and a pair of black boots with pointy toes and Cuban heels. She looked marvellous in everything. She didn't seem to realize this, and kept asking my opinion, begging me to be honest, gazing doubtfully in the mirror. Zara would have snorted with laughter at the idea of anyone asking my advice about style and fashion, but it made me feel great.

I was amazed by how much money she had to spend. I think it embarrassed her too, because she kept begging me to choose something for myself. I eventually picked out a pair of black socks patterned with silver stars.

'You want *socks*?' said Sally. 'Oh come on, Frankie, socks are way too boring.'

'I'd love this pair, honestly,' I said. 'Maybe *I'm* boring.'

'You're the least boring girl in the whole world,' she said.

I found I *did* have just enough money to treat Sally to lunch, because Maison Bertaux turned out to be a lovely little café in Soho. It had wonderful cakes. We each chose a strawberry cream cake and then shared a coffee éclair. Then we wandered around Soho for a while, feeling very bold and sophisticated, and then went down the Charing Cross Road, where I had a little browse in the second-hand bookshops, though I was worried about Sally getting bored.

'Let's go to a park or somewhere – it's all so crowded,' she said.

We walked past Trafalgar Square and found our way to St James's Park. I hoped we'd find a shady private corner where we could hold hands, maybe kiss. But the park was full of day trippers and tourists too, so we just wandered up and down, while the ducks quacked loudly for food and the weird pelicans preened themselves on the rocks.

The light was fading and I knew Mum would be starting to wonder where on earth I was. I had a quick glance at my phone and saw she'd texted me twice already.

Sorry!!! Be home soon, Fxxx I fibbed, because it would take at least another hour and a half on the tube and train.

We had to stand most of the way back, even on the train. Sally wobbled rather, clutching her bags, and I reached out and steadied her. I carried on holding her for the rest of the journey.

We parted company at the station. I hoped we might be able to meet up the next day, but Sally said she had to get ready for school on Wednesday.

'But you'll text?'

'Of course! And then we'll be seeing each other every single day at school – *and* some weekends if you like,' said Sally.

'Every weekend!' I said.

We kissed goodbye – not properly of course, just a quick touch of lips on cheek – and then I hurried home, my heart thumping.

20

Mum was upset I was so late home.

'This is getting ridiculous, Frankie! Why can't you come home at a reasonable time? I seem to spend my life worried sick about you or Zara. Where on earth have you been?' she demanded.

'I was shopping. Look, Sally bought me some socks,' I said feebly.

'You can't have been going round Whitelands all day long! What do you think I am, stupid?' Mum stormed into the kitchen and banged the fridge door, fetching a bottle of white wine.

Coral was angry too, though I'd hoped she might stick up for me.

'For God's sake, Frankie, why couldn't you text at the very least?' she said, glaring at me.

'I did!'

'Not for hours. Your mum was so worried! It was so mean of you – especially when she's so anxious about meeting the consultant tomorrow.'

'I'm sorry, I didn't think.'

'Exactly! You don't think about anyone but yourself nowadays,' said Coral. But then she paused. 'Oh dear Lord, I sound like some ancient great-aunt! And I know you're not thinking about yourself at all, you're thinking about this wretched Sally!'

I knew I would go on thinking about Sally, but at least I could try to look after Mum better and show her that I really cared.

I wanted to go and see the consultant with her. I'd overheard her discussing the new treatment with Coral – apparently there could be severe side effects. Mum had to battle with so many horrible symptoms already. I went shaky at the thought of her having to cope with anything else. I just wanted her to be *better.*

'Please let me come with you to the hospital, Mum,' I begged early the next morning.

'I want to come too,' said Zara.

'And me,' added Rowena.

'No, darlings. I'm taking your mum,' said Coral. 'I'm going in with her when she talks to the consultant.

We've got a lot of questions. We can't all crowd in together.'

'We could wait outside,' I said. 'She's *our* mum.'

'I'll be fine, Frankie,' said Mum. 'I won't be having any actual treatment today. I just need to talk things over. You and Zara look after Rowena for me, OK? Go and see Lucy if there are any problems. I've told her I've got a hospital appointment, though I didn't say what it was for. Don't go wandering off anywhere either!'

'All right, Mum. Promise! I'm so sorry I worried you yesterday,' I said, giving her a hug.

'Good luck, Mum,' said Zara.

'I hope she's nice, Mum,' said Rowena. 'She won't hurt you, will she?'

'I'd like to see her try!' said Coral. 'I'll look after her, girls, don't you worry. I know how precious she is.' She put her arm round Mum.

They went off in the car and we were left behind. The house seemed very quiet.

'I don't like it without Mum,' said Rowena.

'I know, it's horrid, but if this consultant can help her feel better it will be wonderful,' I said, putting my arm round her.

'It isn't anywhere near lunchtime yet, is it?' she asked. 'I feel so *empty*.'

I knew exactly what she meant. We still had our Christmas tin of Quality Street, so we had three each. Then we humoured Rowena and turned all the shiny wrappers into bright glasses and gave a big party for her Sylvanians.

She cheered up enormously. She put all the mother Sylvanians on a special table together, and gave them the purple glasses, her favourite colour.

'There aren't enough glasses to go round,' she said. 'I think we need to eat some more chocolate toffees.'

'No, because then you'll be sick and Mum will be mad at me for not looking after you properly,' said Zara. 'The Sylvanians will have to share.'

'How about if we eat the chocolate toffees instead of lunch?' Rowena suggested. 'Is Mum going to be back by lunchtime?'

'I don't know. You have to wait ages when you go to hospital,' I said. 'But it's OK, Mum's left us a French loaf and some cheese and ham and there are lots of those little oranges you like.'

Sam came round to see if we were OK. He brought a book for Mum from Lucy. With it was a note that said:

Here's a little recipe book with all sorts of ideas for healthy eating. I think you might find it makes all the difference. I know I feel a totally new woman since I cleaned up my eating habits.

I glared at Sam. I suddenly realized that she *knew*, though he had promised faithfully he wouldn't tell.

'You told her about Mum! You totally swore you wouldn't!' I said, giving him a hard shove.

'She knew about the appointment anyway. I didn't tell – well, not till today. Before that she was going on about your mum, saying she'd got so much thinner and was she having a breakdown because your dad cleared off—'

'*What!*' I said furiously.

'I know, she was talking rubbish, and I got annoyed too, and so I just said she was ill, and then my mum wanted to know what kind of illness and it just sort of slipped out,' said Sam.

'Oh, Sammy!' I said. 'Now your mum will keep fussing and it's the last thing my mum wants.'

'But it was you who told Sammy,' Zara pointed out.

'Yes, I know, but Sammy's one of us.'

'Yes I am,' he said, looking pleased.

'When will Mum be back?' Rowena asked.

'Soon,' I said hopefully, but then, while Zara was distracting her with some dance moves, I turned to Sam. 'I can't help worrying,' I whispered. 'What if this consultant can't help Mum? She's pinning all her hopes on it. What if the treatment doesn't work for her? What if she gets sicker and sicker? I know it's daft, but I keep on sending her little messages in my head to try to comfort her. Like the people in *The Chrysalids*. Have you read it yet?'

'I read it on Boxing Day in one long gollop and loved it. It helped me get through the day. Dad and Grandad were out playing golf, so I was stuck with Mum and Granny. I really missed you guys.'

'Well, we were worse off, stuck with our granny and Dad and Helen.' I pulled a face. 'And goodness knows what it will be like when the baby's born!'

'*Do* you mind?'

'I suppose not.'

'And then yesterday you were out all day with Sally,' Sam continued. He paused. 'Without me.'

'She wanted to go shopping, Sammy! You'd have been so bored.'

'I go shopping with *you*. I quite *like* going shopping.'

'Yes, but this was a totally girly shop. You'd have spent hours hanging about outside the changing rooms. It would have done your head in,' I said.

'It would usually have done *your* head in, Frankie. What's up with you and Sally?' Sam asked.

'She's my *friend*,' I said, blushing.

'Shut your eyes,' he instructed. 'And I'll shut mine. Now, I'm trying to see inside your head, like *The Chrysalids*. Ah! I see it all now!'

I shivered. I knew perfectly well that Sam was bluffing, but it really *felt* as if he was reading my mind. I tried to blank out my thoughts but it was impossible.

'I'll read *your* mind,' I countered, keeping my eyes squeezed tight shut. Sam's fair head was so near I could touch it. I pictured his thoughts, concentrating so hard that there was a sudden shift inside my head and I felt I really could. I sensed his sadness and longing.

'Oh, Sam,' I said, feeling for his hand.

We still kept our eyes closed, hand in hand, head to head.

'Look at Frankie and Sammy! They've gone to sleep!' Rowena cried.

'Who do you think you are, Romeo and Juliet?' said Zara.

'Fat chance.' Sam lowered his voice. 'You're in a different play altogether, aren't you, Frankie? Juliet and Juliet.'

I squeezed his hand tighter. 'I'm so sorry, Sam,' I whispered.

'Well. So am I,' he said.

Then, much earlier than we'd expected, we heard the car draw up outside and we ran to the front door.

'What did she say, Mum? Will she put you on this infusion programme? Does it really work? Will it stop you having another relapse?' I gabbled.

'Frankie darling, let her get through the front door first!' said Coral. 'Let's put the kettle on. I'm exhausted, so God knows how your mum must feel.'

'Have you had an infusion already then, Mum?' Zara asked.

'Are you feeling better yet?' Rowena said hopefully.

'I *am* feeling a bit better, even though I haven't started the new treatment. I've just been having various tests and going through all my symptoms, telling this person and that before seeing the consultant herself. She's so kind and so positive. She's letting me take part in this trial treatment as I've had two relapses in one year. She's not promising any miracle cures, but many of her patients are much better, and coping well,' said Mum.

'Jen's having the first infusion on Friday,' said Coral. 'Then it will be once a month.'

'I think they'll be able to juggle my timetable at school to fit it in,' said Mum. 'I might feel a bit rough the day after an infusion, but I should be able to manage.

I spoke to one of the first patients to have the treatment – a lovely girl, so full of life – and she says the infusions have made such a difference. She still has some problems, but she can manage them, and she hasn't had any relapses.'

'And you're not going to have any more either!' said Coral. 'But if you *do*, I'm here now to help out. Let's drink to that! Let's have something fizzy to go with our bread and cheese!'

We still had a bottle of champagne Coral had brought us from the duty-free shop. We all toasted Mum, and Rowena was allowed two sips, though she said the bubbles went up her nose. The taste brought back such vivid memories of the New Year's Eve party. I wondered if Sam was going over it all in his head too.

'Let's go out somewhere this afternoon, just us two, Sam,' I suggested. I knew Mum would want a rest, so I didn't feel too bad about leaving her.

'Is Sally busy then?' he asked.

'No. Well, yes, but I'd want to see you anyway. Please, Sam. We can go anywhere. Skating? You choose.'

'Actually I'd better stay in and catch up with my holiday homework. I've got heaps and I haven't tackled any of it yet.'

'Then come round here to do it. I'll get on with mine. We'll cheer each other along.'

'I can't concentrate properly with you around.'

'Oh, Sam, don't be like this! We are still friends, aren't we? *Best* friends?'

'Of course we are. But I really *do* have to get this wretched homework done. Sorry.'

I could usually get Sam to change his mind, but he was adamant. I felt really miserable, and couldn't settle to my own homework.

Soon I was texting him.

2 much work! Bear restless. So am I. Come for walk??? F xxx

He kept me waiting for a while – but then texted back OK.

We took Bear to the park. He was happy racing along as always, but for Sam and me it seemed as if it had been a big mistake. For the first time ever we couldn't seem to think of anything to talk about, and trudged along in silence. But then Bear decided to chase after some other dog's ball, and we had to run like crazy to get it back. Bear thought it the best game in the world, and clenched the ball determinedly in his teeth, grinning – but eventually Sam managed to prise it away and give it back to the other dog.

'Well done, Sam!' I said.

'Yuck, I've got dog drool all over my hand,' he said, shaking it. He reached out, looking as if he was going to wipe it on my yeti coat.

'Don't you dare!' I said, outraged.

'Oh, come on, it's ages old!'

I swerved away from him and he started chasing me. Bear joined in, thinking this was a brand-new game. We all tripped over each other and tumbled in a heap, and somehow got bumped back to normal. I laughed, Sam laughed, and Bear barked his head off.

Sam wiped his wet hand on the grass. 'I was only joking,' he said.

'I know.'

'*I* know it was your mum's coat and special. I know everything about you, Frankie Bennet.'

'I know you do. We go *way* back, you and me.'

'Best mates,' said Sam.

'For ever,' I added, and we picked ourselves up and carried on with our walk, nattering away.

Later Sam went back to his house to tackle the rest of his homework. He really did have heaps. I was glad I didn't go to his school. But I did have my own homework – the fairy story for Mr White.

I spent the evening writing an elaborate version of *The Sleeping Beauty* in my school jotter. A king and queen of a distant land had an only child, a treasured little princess with golden curls who pricked herself on a spindle on her fourteenth birthday and fell into a deep sleep for a hundred years. Her palace became covered in ivy, with a tangled forest surrounding it. Her story was told far and wide, but most people thought it was just an old folk tale. The forest was so dense and dangerous that no one ventured in to find out.

My narrator, a peasant girl growing up near the hidden palace, was fascinated by this story of a sleeping princess, and decided to see if she could find a way through the forest. The brambles and nettles on the forest floor came up to her shoulders, but she found she could shin up one of the gnarled trees and swing from one branch to another like a creature in the jungle.

She reached the palace at last and discovered sleeping sentries by an open door. She crept inside, dodging round slumbering courtiers, and the king and queen snoring on their golden thrones. She found her way upstairs to the bedrooms – and discovered the princess, her golden hair tumbled across the pillows. She was still fast asleep – but the peasant girl bent over and very gently kissed her on the lips.

Then the princess opened her eyes and they fell in love, and when the king and queen died in the fullness of time, the princess and the peasant girl each sat on a golden throne and lived happily ever after.

I usually lost faith in my stories and let them peter out halfway through – I'd totally abandoned my dystopian novel – but this time I wrote steadily right to the finish, and then printed *THE END* in large capitals as if I was six again.

I texted Sally to tell her I'd written a story about us. Email it!!! she commanded, but I was too shy.

Can't! Handwritten. Show u at school. Can't wait 2 c u!!!

I really *couldn't* wait, so longing to get back to school that I'd had my bag packed and ready since the morning, my uniform neat and tidy, hung up outside my wardrobe.

I'd even sewed up my drooping hem and cleaned my scuffed old school shoes.

'I think the real Frankie's been abducted by aliens and a new weird robot girl got left in her place,' said Zara.

'I just want to stop looking such a scruff,' I said. 'I was wondering if you could help me put a little make-up on in the morning. I just look like a clown when I try, but you make it look natural.'

'No! It's enough of a rush as it is. *I* don't bother with make-up for school,' said Zara.

'Yes, but you've got lovely skin and rosy cheeks. I'm always ghost pale and— Aaargh!' I was peering in the mirror as I spoke. 'I've got a spot on my nose, right in the middle – oh my God, it looks disgusting!'

'Leave it alone! It's only weeny. It hardly shows at all. If you squeeze it you'll make it worse. Stop it! All this fuss fuss fuss, just because you're seeing Sally,' said Zara.

'Look, I can't help it if I want to look my best. I don't want her to take one look at me and change her mind.'

'You wouldn't care if she had a little spot, would you?'

'That's different. Anyway, Sally never gets spots, ever. And her hair never goes all lank. I washed mine this morning, but do you think it looks a bit greasy already?'

'No! You're driving me nuts, Frankie,' said Zara, but she wasn't really cross.

We all went to bed early, but I was much too het up to sleep. I wrote page after page about Sally in my scarlet notebook, and when Zara complained about my bedside light, I wrote on in the darkness – though when I looked

366

at what I'd written in the morning it was mostly gibberish, the lines criss-crossing drunkenly.

We were all out of the house by ten to eight. Coral waved us off in her silk pyjamas, Bear by her side.

'Are you going straight back to bed, Coral?' I asked.

'No, I'm going to get myself organized. Start job hunting. And I suppose I've got to start flat hunting too,' she said, sighing.

'Can't you stay with us?' I begged.

'Well, I'm not going anywhere just yet. It's been so great to spend time with you all.' Coral gave me a hug and whispered, 'Especially you, goddaughter. I hope it goes well at school.'

'It will, it will!' I said. 'I can't wait to see Sally!'

'Go, girl!' she said, grinning at me.

Mum was more cautious. 'Have a lovely day, girls,' she said when she drew up near school.

Zara jumped out of the car.

'Hang on a minute, Frankie,' Mum said as I started to follow her. 'Remember, school is school. Do behave sensibly!'

'What do you think I'm going to do, Mum?' I said. 'I'm not going to start snogging Sally in front of the whole class!'

'I wish you wouldn't use that horrible word! And I'm serious, love. Don't feel you've got to rush around making statements to everyone.'

'I'm not going to. Though why not? I'm not ashamed of the way I feel. If I was in love with a boy in my class, I'd tell all my friends.'

'You're thirteen years old, lovey.'

'Very nearly fourteen.'

'All right. Even so. I know people fall in and out of love in Year Nine, but it's not something teachers encourage,' said Mum.

'I'm not going to fall *out* of love. This is the real thing, Mum, truly,' I insisted.

'I know you think that. I just don't want you to get hurt, that's all. Or teased,' she said.

'Mum! Look, maybe teenagers got teased if they were gay back when you were a schoolgirl, but it's different now. It's not even an issue. We've had a special talk about it,' I said.

'We had a special talk about kindness last term,' Rowena said from the back of the car. 'And I vowed to do a kind thing every single day, but sometimes I forget. Say hi to Sally for me, Frankie. She's the kindest person in the world for giving me the Sylvanian treehouse.'

'I'll tell her you said that,' I said. 'Bye, Rowena. Bye, Mum. Don't look so worried!'

'Bye, Frankie,' said Mum. 'Take care, sweetheart.'

I ran off across the playground. I looked at the orchard in the distance, wondering if Sally and I might risk sneaking in again. I wished Sally got to school earlier. She wouldn't be here for at least half an hour.

I went up the stairs to the library, and there was dear old Mr White in a new blue jacket with red edging round the collar and cuffs. His feet were up on his desk, clad in red boots.

'Hello, Mr White! You look very colourful today!' I said.

'You should see my Christmas jumper!' he said. 'Good morning, Frankie. You look full of the joys of spring, even though it's January. Did you have a good Christmas?'

'Yes, lovely,' I said.

'Thank you very much for the fudge. It was delicious.' Mr White patted his front. 'Bad for my waistline but very good for me.'

Ivneet was sitting at her favourite table, writing away. George and Peter were at the computer. The little gang of Year Elevens were copying holiday homework. Nothing had changed – and yet everything had changed for me.

Ivneet looked up and waved at me. 'Hi, Frankie! Did you write a fairy story?'

'Hey, is that yours?' Ivneet was at least halfway through a notebook, page after page of neat handwriting. 'You've written heaps!'

'Well, I got started and then I couldn't stop. It's about this girl with ten old aunties, and she has to visit each and every one and complete a task. It's got magic in it, and a princess and an ogre and various other fairy-tale ingredients, but it's actually heavily autobiographical. We've been zipping up and down the motorway visiting relatives all holiday. Did you have to do something similar?' she asked.

'I haven't *got* many relatives to visit. Just my granny and my dad and his girlfriend, only I don't count her as a relative. Though she's going to have a baby, so I suppose it'll be a half relative, which is a weird thought,' I said.

'So did you get to stay home in peace?'

'Well, I went out several times. With Sally, actually.'

'Ah,' said Ivneet, nodding.

'Yes, we've become really close,' I said, unable to stop myself.

'That's good,' she said. 'So maybe you haven't had time to write your own fairy story . . .'

'No, I have actually. It's nowhere near as long as yours though. But I have finished it,' I said.

'What's it about?'

I hesitated. 'It's a sort of variation on *The Sleeping Beauty*.'

'That sounds interesting,' said Mr White, coming over. 'Perhaps you could read it out to us.'

'We don't want to hear a stupid baby fairy story!' said George, turning round from the computer.

'Lickle silly-willy fairies,' said Peter, and they both spluttered with laughter.

'Boys, your satirical wit overwhelms us,' said Mr White.

'We don't want any reading aloud either – we won't be able to concentrate, and we've got our mocks coming up soon,' said one of the older boys.

'Far be it from me to interrupt your earnest studies,' said Mr White. 'I'm left with only one option. Girls, would you like to join me in my inner sanctum?'

He stood up and beckoned us to the door behind his desk. Ivneet and I looked at each other with interest. We hadn't realized before that Mr White *had* an inner sanctum, whatever that was.

It turned out to be a very small room, not much bigger than a stationery cupboard, lined with very full bookshelves. There were hardback novels in faded dust wrappers, old orange and green and blue Penguins, collections of literary diaries and letters, filmstar biographies, large art books, and even a few children's books – Beatrix Potters and Just Williams, and an enormous red *Babar the Elephant*.

I squatted down to look at them.

'Careful now. Handle with care, Frankie. The children's books are first editions,' said Mr White.

'Goodness, they must be very valuable,' said Ivneet.

'They are. Cost a fortune, especially if you're only on a teacher's salary. That's why they're here. They're my guilty secret. I'd be in serious trouble if I took them home.'

'Would your partner tell you off for being extravagant?' Ivneet teased.

'Undoubtedly,' he said. 'Anyway, sit yourselves down on the rug, girls. As you can see, there's only one chair, and although it's not very gentlemanly *I'm* going to sit on it. If I sat down cross-legged I'd never be able to untangle myself and I'd have to be carried around like a yogi, only looking much less dignified.'

'I've got a chair in my bedroom but I always choose to sit on the rug,' I said. 'I think this is the loveliest little room, Mr White.'

'Don't you dare tell on me! It's supposed to be kept for reserve stock and catalogues and old filing cabinets – but

I trundled them all down to the boiler room one day after school. Right – off you go, Frankie.'

I cleared my throat. I'd never been shy of reading my work aloud before. I rather liked it, and usually spoke out clearly, with expression. But now, in this minute room, with just Mr White and Ivneet, I suddenly felt painfully shy.

I knew they'd listen attentively and be polite, even if they thought my story was a load of old rubbish. They were kind, and I counted both of them as friends. I'd been pleased with my story when I'd finished it, but now it seemed much too personal. It would be almost like reading out the secret thoughts in my scarlet notebook.

I could feel myself blushing. 'It's not very good,' I said awkwardly.

'Frankie! Read!' said Mr White.

So I cleared my throat again and got started. It wasn't so bad once I'd read the first paragraph. In fact, when I got properly into the story I sped along, liking the flow of the fairy tale, the sound of my words. But as I got near the end I slowed down, praying that the bell would ring for the start of school before I got to the part where the peasant girl kisses the sleeping princess.

But the bell didn't go, and I couldn't pretend that I hadn't finished the story because they could both see there was still another page to be read. I carried on, my voice softer now, so Ivneet and Mr White leaned forward to hear what I was saying.

I struggled on to the end and hardly dared raise my eyes. But they didn't look shocked. They didn't look exasperated. They didn't look bored. They were both smiling.

'Oh, that's beautiful!' said Ivneet. 'I just love it. It's so full of emotion. Mine is just silly and repetitive compared to yours. I'm going to have to start all over again!'

'Don't do that, Ivneet. Your story sounds very promising. But I do agree, Frankie's story is excellent. Well done!' said Mr White.

'You're both just being kind,' I said coyly, but I was utterly thrilled.

Then the bell *did* go, and Ivneet and I had to hurtle downstairs to our class. The first person I saw was Sally, lighting up the whole room. She was with Marnie and Georgia and Scarlett, and yet she came running over and gave me a hug in front of everyone.

'Frankie! I've missed you so!' she cried, and I glowed with pride and joy.

After registration we had English. Miss Allen came into the room and shook her head at us as we milled around chatting.

'Settle down, everyone. Dear goodness, you're acting as if you haven't seen each other for aeons!' she said dryly. 'You can catch up at break time, but in the classroom we're here to learn assiduously, so get out your textbooks please. Frankie, what does assiduous mean?'

'With great determination?' I suggested.

'Indeed. So let us apply ourselves,' she said.

I did my best, but I was so lit up inside the words on the page in front of me didn't make any sense whatsoever.

They juggled themselves into a scribbly heart saying, *SallySallySally.*

I didn't even hear when Miss Allen asked me a question. I was staring at the back of Sally's head, sending her little thought messages, concentrating so fiercely I was deaf to anything else.

'*Frankie!* Dear goodness, girl, what's the matter with you?' Miss Allen shouted.

I was so startled I jumped visibly, making everyone laugh.

'She's in love, miss,' someone said, and they laughed all over again.

I hoped Sally might turn round and smile at me sympathetically, but she just stared straight ahead. She was probably feeling embarrassed for me. I tried to concentrate, because Miss Allen kept picking on me now, but it was a terrible struggle. It was a double lesson too, but at long, long last the bell went for break time.

Miss Allen shook her head at me. 'I should run round the playground three times and get some fresh air into that woolly head,' she said, but she didn't say it crossly.

A few of the boys charged off to play a quick game of footie, but it was a grey, cold day and most of the class stayed where they were, sitting on the desks munching crisps and catching up on all the holiday news.

I ran over to Sally and sat down beside her before Marnie could get there.

'*I* sit next to Sally,' she said pathetically.

'For God's sake, there's room for all of us,' said Sally. 'Hey, have some Swiss chocs, they're gorgeous.' She brought out a blue-and-white box and generously shared them round – two each for me, for Marnie, for Georgia, for Scarlett, and for her too.

'Oh yum! Can I have one, Sally?' Josh asked, coming up to us.

'I can't give one to all you guys, there won't be any left,' said Sally, but she threw a chocolate high in the air and Josh caught it in his mouth like a performing dog.

'So what did you get up to in the holidays, Frankie?' he asked, his mouth unattractively full of chocolate. 'Did you get to go skating?'

'Yes, I went with Sally.' I was so proud to say it that I momentarily forgot he'd asked me first.

He looked crestfallen and I felt guilty.

'Sorry, Josh. I was just hanging out with Sally over the holidays.' I wanted to appease him, and I didn't care if I was hurting Marnie. She'd seen Sally and me together at the party. She must understand about us. I was simply being honest and straightforward. I wanted to be frank, like my name.

'I've been to Sally's house and she's been to mine, and we had a fantastic day up in London together, didn't we, Sally?' I said.

'Yes, we did,' she said, but she looked warily at Marnie and Georgia and Scarlett.

'Oh right, I see,' said Josh. 'So Sally's your best mate now, yeah?'

I took a deep breath – but Marnie blurted it out first.

'They're more than that,' she said. She looked very pale and she was clenching her fists.

'What do you mean?' Josh asked.

'Marnie!' Sally murmured. 'Shut up.'

'I *won't* shut up,' she said. 'I've told Georgia and Scarlett. I'm telling everyone.'

'Tell away, you poor sad girl,' I said. 'We don't care, do we, Sally?'

'What's going on?' said Josh.

'Sally and I are in love.' I meant it to come out clear and proud, but my voice went shaky and I stammered over the last word.

'Is that what you call it, you dirty cow?' said Marnie. 'Going to Sally's bedroom and *kissing*?'

The whole room went instantly silent. Everybody stared at us, stunned.

'You mean actual girl-on-girl action?' said Josh, and all the boys gave stupid whoops.

'Stop it!' I said. 'Stop being so horrible! What's the matter with you? It's totally cool for a girl to love another girl.'

'It's totally brilliant!' said one of the boys. 'Give us a show then, Frankie and Sally!'

'Stop being so disgusting!' I snapped furiously.

'*You're* the one who's disgusting,' said Marnie. 'Sally was just being kind because she felt sorry for you. Then you try and turn her gay! And she's not – she likes boys, everyone knows that.'

'Oh, Marnie,' said Sally, sighing.

'You're just jealous, Marnie, because you love Sally yourself,' I said.

'Not in *that* way.'

'It's nothing to be ashamed of. It's – it's wonderful, isn't it, Sally?'

The whole room went still, waiting for Sally's answer. I felt my blood beating in my temple, in my neck, thrumming through my veins, thumping in the chambers of my heart.

Sally shrugged. 'Yeah, wonderful,' she said, but with the wrong emphasis. 'So we kissed at my party, everyone. Why is that such a big deal? It was just a bit of fun.'

I stared at her. She looked me straight in the eye. 'Lighten up, Frankie,' she said.

My throat was so dry I couldn't respond. Then one boy made stupid kissing noises, and another asked if Sally would kiss him, and one of the girls said her parents had walked in on her when she was making out with someone at *her* party, and Sally joined in all the conversations, commenting, quipping, laughing.

The noise sounded distorted, not properly tuned in. I couldn't see that well either. The strip lighting on the ceiling seemed to be flashing. I couldn't make anyone out clearly. Their faces were distorted, like a Picasso painting, even Sally's.

My tummy suddenly lurched. I leaped off the desk and ran out of the classroom and down the corridor, bumping right into Mrs Hurst!

'Frankie! Stop running in the corridor!' she said crossly.

'I'm going to be sick,' I said urgently, and heaved. I clamped my hand over my mouth and rushed round the corner to the girls' loos.

I made it into a cubicle, knelt beside the toilet and threw up again and again. I'd been too het up to eat properly at breakfast, so I had nothing much to be sick with, but I kept on heaving. It was as if I was throwing up my inner self.

When I'd finished at last, I felt too weak to stand up. I flushed the toilet again and again, trying to get rid of the smell. Then I leaned against the cold wall of the cubicle, staring at the silly messages and crude drawings. They were so stark and ugly. I banged my fist against the wall, and then started crying.

The bell had rung while I was being sick, but I didn't think I could ever go back in again. I sat where I was until I heard footsteps coming into the toilets. I tried to stifle my sobs, listening.

I wondered if it was Sally. I so hoped it was Sally. It _had_ to be Sally.

'Frankie?' It was Ivneet.

I didn't answer, but I couldn't help sniffing.

'Are you all right?' She spoke softly, right outside my cubicle now.

'I've been sick,' I said. 'Ivneet, the bell's gone. Go back to class. You'll get into trouble.'

'As if I care,' she said. 'Are you crying?'

'No!'

'I think you are. Do you really love Sally so much?'

I put my head on my knees. 'Yes,' I mumbled.

'You poor thing,' said Ivneet.

'Are you shocked? I mean, does your religion disapprove of same-sex relationships?' I asked. It was somehow easier to say it without us being face to face.

'Well, my mum and dad would certainly be shocked if it was me. But they'd be shocked if I had any kind of relationship – they want me to marry a nice Sikh boy, preferably very bright and studious, bless them.'

'Is that what *you* want?'

'I think I'll keep my options open,' said Ivneet. She tutted. 'That's supposing anyone's ever interested in me. I'm not exactly a beauty – and most boys don't like ultra geeky, brainy girls. Girls don't like them either, come to that.'

'*I* like you,' I said. 'I don't mean I like you the way I like Sally, but as a friend. My godmother says friends are more important than lovers.'

'She could be right,' said Ivneet. 'Do you think you're going to be sick again or can you come out?'

'I suppose I can,' I said, mopping my eyes with toilet paper.

I opened the door and shuffled out, feeling a total fool.

Ivneet gave me a little smile. 'There you are,' she said.

I rinsed out my mouth with cold water and then stared at myself in the mirror. 'God, I look a mess,' I said.

'Just a bit wobbly.'

'Ivneet, what did Sally do when I rushed out of the

classroom? Can you tell me the honest truth?'

'Well, she went on larking around, chatting with the boys. I think she was a bit worried though. She laughed a lot, but she kept glancing at the door, maybe hoping you'd come back.'

'But *you* were the one who came after me, not Sally,' I said. 'Do you think she really cares about me deep down, or has she been pretending all along? When we're alone she says such special things, and she's been texting me and telling me she really loves me, truly. So *does* she love me?'

'How would I know? Maybe she does,' said Ivneet. 'Or maybe she just likes you loving her. Sally's the sort of girl who needs everyone to love her.'

'That's right. I think I've always known that. I used to hate her when she said all that stuff about my mum. I still don't always *like* her. But I love her even so. Does that make me some sort of masochist?'

'No, just a nutcase,' said Ivneet, but she gave my arm a squeeze.

'I can't go back into class now, with everyone staring at me and saying stuff,' I said.

'You don't have to straight away. I'll take you to the secretary's office and they'll let you lie down in the sickroom. Stay there till lunchtime. Then I'll come and find you,' said Ivneet. 'OK? Is that a plan?'

'It's a good plan,' I said. 'Thanks so much, Ivneet. You're a great friend.'

'Well, when I'm a world-famous psychiatrist I'll treat you for free,' she said, grinning.

'And when I'm a world-famous novelist I'll put you in a book as a great hero,' I said.

I managed to act almost normally until I was lying down on the hard little bed in the sickroom, one of those unpleasant grey cardboard bowls by my side. Mrs Mathews, the secretary, fussed around me for a while, taking my temperature and wondering if she should phone my mum. I begged her not to, and said I was sure I didn't have anything serious. In fact, I lied and said it was the first day of my period and I often felt sick then.

'You poor girl. I used to suffer terrible cramps when I was your age,' she said sympathetically, and pressed a couple of paracetamol on me.

Then, thank goodness, she left me alone. I cried again, burying my face in the thin pillow to muffle the sound. I must have fallen asleep, because the next thing I knew Ivneet was back, carrying a tray from the canteen.

'I didn't think you'd want very much, so I've just bought you some fish and a toffee yoghurt,' she said. 'And a little bunch of grapes my mother popped in my packed lunch today.'

I couldn't face the fish in its orange batter or the weird-flavoured yoghurt, but the grapes were very good.

'There now, what a kind friend,' said Mrs Mathews. 'Do you feel a bit better, Frankie?'

'Not really,' I said, because I dreaded going back to the classroom.

'Well, I should go out into the playground for the rest

of lunch break, see if a little walk around helps. Ivneet will keep an eye on you, won't you, dear?'

'Of course I will,' said Ivneet.

When we were out in the corridor, I said, 'I *can't* go out to the playground, Ivneet. Not with all the boys saying stuff. And Marnie being spiteful. And Sally probably just ignoring me, pretending none of it meant anything.' My voice wobbled when I said her name.

'We'll go to the library,' said Ivneet. 'Mr White's our friend.'

He greeted us warmly, though he was eating his own lunch. It was a very healthy lunch – a Tupperware bowl of salad, and an apple and a sparkling mineral water.

'I've put on a lot of weight over Christmas, so I have to do something about it,' he said, munching his way wearily through his salad. 'Dear goodness, how do sheep eat grass all day long? My jaw is practically dislocated already.' He was looking at me carefully. 'You were positively blooming this morning, Frankie, but now you look a little woebegone.'

'I'm fine, Mr White,' I said, but when he started talking about my *Sleeping Beauty* story I started crying again.

'Oh dear, oh dear,' he said.

Josh came bursting into the library at that moment, which made it worse.

'Oh no!' I said, shrinking.

'Perhaps you'd like to retreat to my inner sanctum for a moment, Frankie?' Mr White suggested. 'I'll put the kettle on and we'll have a cup of tea.'

I sat in his private room and breathed in the sweetish smell of old books. I opened *Babar* very carefully, and started reading the story, loving the soft watercolour pictures of Babar as a baby – but when I came to the part where Babar's mother gets shot I wept again.

What was the matter with me, getting so anguished about Sally when my own mother was seriously ill? What if the infusions didn't work? What if she had another relapse?

I curled up in Mr White's chair and sobbed. I'd thought I didn't have any tears left, but now they spurted down my cheeks uncontrollably, and I had to put my hands over my mouth to stop myself wailing.

'Oh, you poor girl,' said Mr White, coming in with two cups of tea. 'I've just made Ivneet my temporary library assistant. She's keeping control outside with her own cup of tea and a Mars bar. I know I'm on this wretched diet, but chocolate is such a comfort in an emotional emergency.'

He insisted I stay in the chair, and crouched on the rug in front of me, offering me tissue after tissue until I managed to stop howling.

'I'm so, so sorry,' I gasped, hiccuping.

'Sometimes it helps to have a good cry,' said Mr White. 'There now. Have a sip of tea and a big bite of Mars bar. They'll help even more.'

I wasn't sure I could do either without choking but I gave it a try. I had another sip, another bite.

Mr White waited, nodding encouragingly. 'Now, I've asked Ivneet what's troubling you, but she is the soul of discretion and simply says you're very upset, which is obvious. Would you like to confide in Mrs Hurst or Miss Eliot?'

'No! Absolutely not,' I said.

'Well, I know I'm only a silly old librarian, and a man to boot, but would it make you feel better if you told me what's happened?' he asked, looking at me with such kind concern that I started telling him about Mum.

That was easier, because anyone would be upset and worried if their mother was ill. Mr White was lovely, listening properly, sympathizing, but not fobbing me off with false promises about her getting better.

'It must be such a strain on you, Frankie. You obviously love your mum so much,' he said. 'Please don't feel embarrassed about needing a good weep. You're welcome to come here any time it overwhelms you. I shall keep a special cache of Mars bars at the ready.'

He was being so kind – and I felt such a hypocrite.

'I'm not just sad about Mum,' I blurted out. 'I've made a total fool of myself too. Over Sally.'

'Sally. Ah, she's the pretty one with the fair curls?'

'Yes, that's her.'

'There was a bit of teachers' gossip in the staff room that there was some sort of feud between the two of you earlier last term?'

'Do the teachers *gossip* about us?'

'Only in the most caring, concerned way. Well, hopefully. Anyway, what's happened now? Has the situation escalated?'

'Yes, but – well, I don't know how to say this. I know you'll think I'm stupid and far too young – everyone else does – but the thing is, I've fallen in love with her,' I said wretchedly.

'Oh, my dear,' said Mr White. 'Of course. I'm so slow to catch on, and yet you read your magnificent fairy story to me only this morning.'

'Well, that's all it is, a fairy story, because Sally and I aren't going to live happily ever after,' I said.

'She doesn't feel the same way about you?' Mr White asked, his head on one side.

'Well, I was sure she *did*. She said so. We had the most wonderful time together during the holidays. We even had a day in London, just us. I thought we were – well, like a couple. But this morning Sally's friend Marnie said something nasty about us, and everyone started saying horrible things, especially the boys. You know what they can be like.'

'I do indeed.'

'That wouldn't have mattered so much, but Sally acted like we *weren't* in love, and just turned everything into a joke. She told me to lighten up,' I said.

'Ouch,' said Mr White, as if he understood exactly. 'Ah well. All is not lost, you know. Sally might well feel exactly the same way about you, but she's not quite brave enough to tell the world just yet.'

'Ivneet says the only person Sally loves is herself,' I said.

'Oh, wise and wonderful Ivneet. She's clearly a forty-year-old woman in a fourteen-year-old's body. It's a privilege to know such a glorious girl,' said Mr White.

'Yes, I know that. But . . .'

'But you've still got strong feelings for Sally?'

'Yes, even now. And yet I know I'd be a fool if I let her play all these games with me, blowing hot and cold, and wanting to keep everything secret,' I said despairingly. 'How can I be so stupid?'

'Oh, Frankie, you're not alone,' said Mr White. 'This is what first love can be like. Agony! It's highly inappropriate for teachers to talk about their own love lives, but just between you and me I had a ludicrous passion for the captain of the rugby team when I was fourteen. He made it brutally plain that I was wasting my time, and behaved like a perfect boor, but I still went on loving him.'

'What was his name?'

'Robbie.'

'What did he look like?'

'Well, long ago he was big and broad and hunky, with fantastic brown hair. But now he's probably even fatter than me, with a grey comb-over, and I wouldn't even recognize him,' said Mr White. 'You see, that's the irony of first love. You think it's your one and only love at the time, and years later you'd walk right past each other in the street. When you're my age you'll see some ageing dyed-blonde woman and she won't mean a thing to you. You'll have probably forgotten all about her.'

'I don't think I'll ever forget Sally,' I said.

'Perhaps not. But you'll have lots of other loves, I'm sure of it. And if you're gay, be proud of yourself – and very pleased you're not living forty years ago, when life was very different.'

'Have you had lots of other loves, Mr White?'

'Well, not really. I've never been one for the gay scene – tubby librarians don't tend to shine on the dance floor. But I've been with *my* one and only for the last twenty-five years, and we might have the odd little tiff but we really *are* living happily ever after, I promise you.'

'Oh, Mr White, you're being so kind. I can't thank you enough,' I said.

'Well, perhaps you can make me another little package of that totally scrumptious fudge,' he joked.

I found that, with Ivneet by my side, I had the courage after all to go back to the classroom for afternoon school. There was quite a bit of staring, and some muttered remarks, but weirdly no one made a big deal of it. Sally seemed to have convinced them it was a silly drunken experiment that neither of us took seriously.

It didn't seem to have put Josh off.

'I'd still love to go out with you, Frankie,' he said. 'We could go skating together – the rink's open till next weekend.'

'I'm sorry, but I really don't want to, Josh,' I said, hoping I wouldn't hurt his feelings.

'Oh, go on. I could take you to a film instead. Or a meal. I don't mind a bit about you and Sally. You could still see her if you like. And maybe tell me exactly what you do,' he said eagerly.

'Oh shut up, creep!' I said, suddenly not caring about his feelings in the slightest.

Marnie kept looking back and glaring at me in class, but Sally didn't turn round once. I wondered if she'd try to talk to me after school – but she went off with her little gang of three. I watched her walk off, and told myself it was well and truly over.

It was a struggle having to tell Mum and Coral and Zara and Rowena a highly abbreviated account. They were all indignant and lovely to me, and Zara managed not to say I told you so. *Dad* even phoned up, wanting to know how I'd got on.

I tried to pretend I wasn't too hurt, but when I went to bed I wrote page after page in my diary long after Zara was asleep. I kept staring at my phone, terribly tempted to text Sally. I made up angry messages in my head. Sad and sorrowful messages. Desperate pleas. Loving declarations. But I didn't send anything until I got a text from Sally at midnight.

R u ok? I still love u, u know that, don't u? Your Sally xxxxx

I sat up in bed staring at the little message until my eyes blurred. I didn't know what to say. Well, I knew, but it was a good half-hour before I could make my fingers tap out a reply.

I still love u 2, but it's over.

It was awful going to school the next day. Mum gave me a special hug when she dropped Zara and me off outside the school gate.

'Chin up, chickie,' she murmured into my hair. 'Sally will probably want to make it up with you now. But you'll be fine, no matter what.'

'Yes, I will,' I said, trying hard to convince myself. 'And I don't care what Sally wants. It's all over now. I know she doesn't really care about me. She just wants to keep me dangling.'

'I think that's very brave and sensible of you, darling,' said Mum. 'But whatever happens, I'm there for you.'

'I'm there for you too, sis,' said Zara.

'And me,' Rowena piped up, hanging out of the car window.

'Stop it, all of you. You'll make me cry,' I said. 'I'm fine. Honestly.'

I went up to the library. I was worried that Ivneet and Mr White would be especially sweet to me too, and then I really *would* burst into tears, but they both seemed pretty much their usual selves. Ivneet had finished her own fairy story, and so we squeezed into the Inner Sanctum again while she read it aloud to us.

She seemed very hesitant at first, and her hands shook as she read. I was surprised. Ivneet always seemed so composed and sure of herself. I smiled at her encouragingly when she stopped and looked up.

She gave a little grimace. 'It's rubbish, isn't it?'

'No, it's really good. Funny. Different,' I told her.

'Absolutely,' said Mr White.

'But it's a bit silly and childish, when Frankie's was so beautiful,' said Ivneet.

'Well, we can't all be Frankie when it comes to writing,' said Mr White.

I argued at once, but I was truly thrilled. I'd been feeling so pathetic, a complete dumbo compared to Ivneet. And her story about all these different aunties crammed into one small kitchen, elbowing each other out of the way to get to the stove, each adding her own secret ingredients to a great vat of soup was truly funny. At first I giggled determinedly to reassure Ivneet, but as she read on and the aunties' behaviour became more and more outrageous, I started laughing properly, and Mr White joined in.

'Well done!' he declared when Ivneet finished. 'I feel honoured to be sitting with two such outstanding writers. Frankie might win our fairy-tale award, but you're our number-one folk-tale contender, Ivneet. I think you both deserve a prize.' He offered us the jar of Mars bars.

'But they're yours, Mr White,' I protested.

'Yes, but you're saving me from myself by eating them on my behalf.' He patted his tummy ruefully. 'I seem to be a scientific marvel. I've been eating rabbit food for days and I've actually put *on* a kilo. Well, I suppose I've been having the odd sneaky little snack. In fact, I might give in yet again.'

He quickly helped himself to a Mars bar and ate it in three bites. 'Dear goodness, I'm such a pig,' he groaned.

'Why not accept yourself, Mr White? If you're a pig, be proud of it,' I said, parodying his advice to me about being gay.

He laughed, and then the bell went and it was time to go to the classroom and see Sally. There she was, chatting to Marnie and Georgia and Scarlett.

'Here's your girlfriend, Sally,' one of the boys shouted.

Sally scarcely looked up. I put my hand up in a little half-wave but she didn't wave back. She didn't exactly cut me dead – it was just as if she seriously hadn't seen me. Didn't *want* to see me.

'Whoops. Looks as if they've had a tiff,' another boy said in a silly voice.

Sally rolled her eyes and then carried on talking. When it was break time she walked straight past me, as if I wasn't there. I wondered whether she'd come up to me at lunchtime, maybe suggest we go off together and talk. I didn't go up to the library with Ivneet. I hung around the playground, just in case. Sally didn't come near me. She didn't even look in my direction.

It was worse than when she'd teased me. At least then she'd been taking notice of me. This way it was as if I didn't even exist. Every time I looked at her my eyes stung. It was so humiliating.

I'd said it was over. I knew it was the right decision. But somehow I thought we could still be friends. She'd said she still loved me. I'd said I still loved her. I'd thought it would be sad and wistful, but we'd still be *talking* to each other.

Josh was playing football with the others but he came over. 'Hey, Frankie,' he said. 'Do you want to play?'

'No thanks.'

'What's going on then?'

'Nothing,' I said ridiculously.

'Have you and Sally split up already?'

'No. Yes. Oh, Josh, I don't want to be horrible, but could you just leave me alone?' I said.

He shrugged. 'OK. I was just feeling sorry for you, that's all.'

Oh God, this was awful. I didn't want people to feel *sorry* for me. I saw Zara at the other end of the playground. She was with Julie and some other friends, but she was peering over at me. She was sorry for me too, clearly wondering if I was all right.

I was such a fool. I'd vowed not to mope around like Marnie, desperate for Sally's attention. I marched back into school and went up to the library again.

'Aha, Frankie,' said Mr White.

Ivneet gave me a nod and a little smile. She was colouring her medical book again.

'I thought you'd decided to be a psychiatrist,' I said.

'I'm going to need one. My head needs examining.'

'You have to train as a doctor first.' She flipped to a page of an eerie transparent head. I stared at the brain, wondering how that weird cabbage-like organ contained so many dreams, so many delusions.

'You can colour it in if you want,' she said.

She was being so sweet. But maybe she was just feeling sorry for me too. No, I had to stop this. Ivneet was my friend. She liked me, I knew she did.

'I'd better not. I'd use all the wrong colours and put little cartoon thoughts in the brain. It used to really annoy my sister Zara. She loved colouring when she was little, but she used all the right shades and did it all so neatly and properly, just like you, but I couldn't seem to stop messing about,' I said.

'Zara's in Year Ten, isn't she? The girly one with the dimples?' said Ivneet.

'Yep, that's her. We're so different. We used to fight like cat and dog – still do, I suppose. But she's OK, Zara. And I've got another younger sister, Rowena – she's a hoot.

394

She's into Sylvanians. You have to watch your step if you come round to our place. Tiny rabbits trip you up on the stairs and little badgers line up on the edge of the bath, watching you.' I paused. 'You'll have to come round for tea some time and see for yourself. If you'd like to.'

'I'd love to,' said Ivneet. 'And you must come round to my house too. I haven't got any sisters and my brother's away, but I've got my mum and dad and my grandma, who doesn't speak much English, but I'll translate for you, and my auntie lives with us too.'

'Will she make us soup for our supper?'

'I hope not!' said Ivneet. 'But wait till you taste her rasgulla and gulab jamun and halwa!'

'What are they?' I asked cautiously.

'Sweets! And they're very yummy.'

Mr White looked up hopefully and we both laughed.

Afternoon school was a little easier, though I couldn't help glancing at Sally every now and then. She wriggled her shoulders as if she could actually feel my eyes boring into her. She didn't turn round once. Marnie did though. She looked triumphant. She kept passing Sally little notes. I was pretty sure they were about me. It seemed so childish. As if I cared. Well, I did care. I cared a lot. But I tried very hard not to take any notice.

I pretended to Mum and Coral and Zara and Rowena that school had been fine and I didn't really care about Sally any more. I don't think even Rowena believed me, but they acted like they did. Mum and Coral were really pleased that I was making friends with Ivneet.

Zara wasn't so keen. 'Is Ivneet the serious girl with the glasses and the plait who wears her skirt way down past her knees? The ultra geeky one who wins all the prizes?' she said, raising her eyebrows.

'Yes. So?' I said.

'Well, she's OK, I suppose, but couldn't you actually make friends with someone cool?' Zara asked.

'And your definition of cool is?'

'Someone fun, with good dress sense.'

'Oh, *Zara*! Then that counts me out as friend material too.'

'Well, yes, rubbish dress sense, though you look great in your Chinese jacket. But you *are* fun. When you're not moping around,' she said. Then she came up close and put her arm round my shoulders. 'Try not to mind so much, Frankie. You know Sally's not worth it.'

Sam was lovely to me too. He came round offering to help me with my maths homework. We went upstairs and he went over the sums twice, very slowly and gently, not once getting impatient when I made silly mistakes. When I was able to work out the next page of sums by myself we called it a day. Sam sat cross-legged on my bed, peering at all the books on my shelf. I lolled on the rug while Bear nuzzled up to me, happy that I was home from school at last.

Sam was looking down at the nursery end of the shelf. He leafed through a battered copy of *Milly-Molly-Mandy* that had once belonged to Mum, or maybe even *her* mum.

'Remember your mum used to read it to us when we were about four? And then she made us jacket potatoes and we ate them in our dressing gowns when I stayed over at your place? You were Milly-Molly-Mandy, and I pretended to be Little-Friend-Susan. It's weird that you turned out gay and not me!' he said.

'I wish we were still four. It was all so uncomplicated then,' I said, sighing.

'I gather things aren't quite so rosy with Sally after all?' Sam said delicately.

'It's all over,' I said.

'She broke it off with you?'

'No! I broke it off with her actually. Because she hated everyone knowing at school,' I said, rubbing my head against Bear's.

'Did you tell everyone then?' Sam asked.

'Well, Marnie was saying horrible stuff about us so I tried to make it plain that Sally and I were in love, but Sally made out we'd just been fooling around for a laugh. Maybe that was all it meant to her,' I said.

'Perhaps she just didn't want to be outed. You shouldn't really have said that,' said Sam.

'I wouldn't have said a word if Marnie hadn't said I was a dirty cow,' I protested.

'A dirty cow!' said Sam. 'Oh, poor Frankie!'

He got off the bed and came to sit beside me. He parted my hair at the back and very gently massaged my neck.

'That feels nice. I've got a splitting headache from trying to understand those awful maths problems,' I said.

'If this was a rom-com, then this would be the moment when you turned round and looked up at me and I kissed you and you realized that you loved the boy next door after all, and we walked off into the sunset together while the credits rolled.' Sam said it very lightly, like a joke, but I wasn't sure if he meant it or not.

'Maybe the moment isn't going to happen,' I said.

'I know.'

'But it *is* the moment when I realize that you're my best friend in all the world and you always will be.'

'And you'll be mine. All my future girlfriends are going to hate it that I always put you first.'

'And all *my* future girlfriends will hate it that I always put *you* first,' I said. Then I sighed. 'If I ever *get* a proper girlfriend.'

'Of course you will. A lovely girlfriend who won't mess you about,' he said.

'Sam, do you think Sally ever really loved me?'

He shrugged. 'I don't know.'

'Do you think she was after you all the time, not me?'

'No, I don't think she was ever seriously interested in me. Even though I'm considered quite a catch,' said Sam, grinning.

'Coral thinks you are!' I told him.

'Really?' He tried to sound casual, but he looked thrilled.

Coral came dashing up the stairs just then, and put her head round the door. 'Just finding out if you're staying for supper, Sammy,' she said.

He blushed. 'Yes please!'

'That's good. I make a great spag bol, or I have any number of Chinese specialities. I thought I'd be Chief Cook tonight – Jen's feeling a bit whacked,' she said.

Mum kept saying she was absolutely fine, but she was looking exhausted after just two full days at school. She went to bed straight after supper. Sam left too, so I slipped upstairs to see Mum. She was lying back on her pillow with notebooks balanced beside her.

'Hey, baby,' she said, doing her best to smile at me. She looked as if she might have been crying.

'Why don't you leave the marking for once and just snuggle down?' I said, sitting on the bed beside her. 'You could always do it in the morning.'

'It's certainly a very tempting idea,' said Mum. 'But it's such a rush in the mornings and I'm always so blessed tired now. Oh, Frankie, I do hope these infusions make a difference. I don't know what I'm going to do if they don't.'

She looked so small and vulnerable lying there that I wanted to cry too.

'I'm sure they'll make you feel heaps better,' I said, wishing it with all my heart.

'Well, I could hardly feel worse,' said Mum. 'I'm sorry, darling, I hate it when I go all self-pitying, I feel like giving myself a good slapping. It's just that I felt so great when Coral came, and I couldn't help hoping that I was somehow getting a bit better. Yet now I feel totally rubbish. I don't know how much longer I can go on working like this. Coral's being such a help, but she won't be here for ever.'

'We'll all do more about the house. Zara and I could take turns doing the cooking,' I said – though apart from fudge and the gingerbread men the only thing I'd ever cooked was cheese on toast. 'We'll do the shopping too. And the housework – even Rowena can do a bit of dusting. We should have started helping properly ages ago.'

'You do a lot already, sweetheart, you all do. And I feel so bad. I don't want you to have to be my carers. *I* want to be the carer. I'm your mum,' she said.

'The best mum in the world.'

'No I'm not, I'm the moaniest. Don't tell Zara or Rowena, will you? You just caught me at the wrong moment.'

'Oh, Mum.' I lay down on the bed beside her for a moment, and gave her a cuddle. 'You feel free to moan to me any time you want.'

'And you feel equally free to moan to me. So, how's the Sally situation?' Mum asked.

'She's not really speaking to me,' I said.

'Is it very upsetting?'

'Well, I'm trying not to care. And yet I do. If I'm absolutely honest I keep wishing I hadn't broken it off with her. It's so awful when she just ignores me.'

'I think you did the right thing, love,' said Mum. 'I can totally see why you fell for Sally. She's very beguiling. There's a little girl in my class this year, Ava Matthews, and she's totally a Sally – she's got the pretty hair, the smiles, the attitude. She manages to stay just this side of cheeky with me. I know I should tick her off severely, but she just makes me laugh. The whole class adore her. Even Danny Diddums runs around after her and fights to sit next to her at circle time. But she's already had three best friends and two boyfriends in just one term, and discarded the lot of them. I've never dealt with so many woebegone little kids before.'

'So why does she do it, this little Ava?' I asked.

'Goodness knows. Attention? Glory? Insecurity? Maybe she was just born like it, needing to be a little heart-breaker. I don't want *you* to have your heart broken, Frankie,' said Mum.

I put my hand on my chest. 'It's still banging away, Mum. Not broken, I promise.'

The next day Mum had her first infusion, while her lovely head teacher took over her class herself. Coral went with her. Zara and I had to collect Rowena from her school and walk her home. She was a bit tearful.

'You took such a long time! I was beginning to think you'd forgotten me,' she said, wiping her eyes with her coat sleeve.

'We ran all the way here!' said Zara breathlessly.

'As if we could ever forget you,' I said, giving Rowena a little poke. 'Come on, cheer up. Shall we make fudge again when we get home?'

'And I'm in charge of supper. You can help me roll out the pastry for the pie,' said Zara.

'Maybe you can make a little tiny pie for all the Sylvanians,' I suggested.

We were both trying hard to be good grown-up sisters, but when the fudge and the pies were made and Mum and Coral still weren't back, we started to feel tearful too.

Zara and I both tried texting Mum, but she didn't answer.

'Maybe she's attached to this machine and can't reach her phone,' said Zara.

I tried texting Coral, but she didn't answer either.

'Perhaps they're in the car and Coral's driving and Mum's asleep,' Zara suggested.

'What if they've had an accident in the car?' I whispered to Zara, not wanting Rowena to hear.

'Shut up!' she said.

'Or what if Mum's had some awful kind of reaction to the infusion and they've whisked her off to intensive care, or—'

'*Shut up!*' Zara repeated furiously.

Just then a text pinged into our phones simultaneously.

Sorry so late! Absolutely fine, just took longer than I thought. No reception in hospital. Home in half an hour. Love Mum xxx

She was home in twenty minutes – Coral was a determined driver. We all peered at Mum anxiously. She looked a bit pale and tired, but then she nearly always did nowadays. She smiled at us reassuringly.

'Don't look so worried! It was fine. *I'm* fine, truly,' she said.

The three of us flew at her, wanting a big hug.

'Careful! She's still a bit fragile, no matter what she says!' Coral warned. 'Look, all of you sit down on the sofa and hug there. OK, Jen?'

I had my share of the hug and then went into the kitchen, where Coral was dishing up supper.

'You girls have done a grand job,' she said. 'Hey, I like the teeny-weeny pie.'

'It was my idea. It's for Rowena's Sylvanians,' I explained.

'Ah, bless!'

'Coral? What was it like for Mum? Was it awful? Did it really hurt? Did they have to keep sticking needles into her?' I asked.

'No, I don't think it was painful for her, just a bit unnerving. They were a nice crowd, the other patients. She's made a couple of friends there already. The nurses were great too. She'll feel a bit tired now, and they say she'll maybe feel a bit rough tomorrow, but *then* she should start feeling much better,' said Coral. 'Hey, have you got any hugs left, Frankie? I get a bit anxious in hospitals. *I* feel a bit wobbly now.'

'Dear Coral!' I gave her an enormous hug. 'Mum couldn't have a better friend.'

She made Mum stay in bed on Saturday morning, even though she still insisted she felt fine, just a little achy. She got up in the afternoon but lay on the sofa with a blanket wrapped round her because she felt shivery.

I kept peering at Mum and consulting Coral.

'Are you *sure* she's all right? She doesn't look that great to me. Don't you think we should take her back to the hospital so they can check on her?' I whispered.

'They *said* she'd probably feel ropey today. It's just a reaction to the infusion. It won't last,' said Coral, but I could tell she was worried too.

She squashed up beside Mum on the sofa and they watched an ancient old film called *Beaches*, about two women who have been best friends since childhood. I thought it a terrible choice because one of the women dies at the end, but Mum and Coral seemed to be enjoying it, eating fudge.

'If you're sure you're OK, then do you mind if I meet up with Julie and the others and go to Whitelands, Mum?' Zara asked. 'I want to spend my Christmas money.'

'All right. Back by six though, OK?' said Mum.

'Promise promise promise,' she said.

Mum looked at me. 'Why don't you go shopping with Zara, Frankie?'

'I hate shopping, especially with Zara. And I'm certainly not tagging along when she's with all her mates!' I said.

Zara looked immensely relieved and cleared off quickly.

'Oh dear,' said Mum.

'It's OK,' I said. 'I'll just hang out with Sammy.'

I texted to see if he wanted to take Bear for a walk with me, but he texted back to say he was round at the sports centre with some of his school friends.

'You'll come for a walk then, won't you, Rowena?' I said. 'We could take a pocketful of Sylvanians and make them a real treehouse in the park.'

'No, I'm going to Sarah's party,' said Rowena. 'Mum, can I wear my blue dress even though it's winter?'

'Who's Sarah? Is she your new best friend now?' I asked.

'No, I don't think I like her much, but the whole class is going. It's in a church hall and there's going to be a real disco and pizza and birthday cake,' said Rowena. '*Please* may I wear my blue dress, Mum?'

She was allowed to wear it, but with her blue cardigan on top, because Mum said church halls were always draughty. I walked her round there with Bear, Rowena skipping along beside us, her hair brushed free of her plaits.

'Would you say I looked a little bit pretty?' she asked, peering in a shop window.

'I would say you looked very, very pretty,' I said. 'Come on, or we'll be late for your party.'

There was a whole crowd of excited six-year-olds filing into the hall.

'Rowena!' they shouted as she ran to join them. She was clearly everyone's favourite. I glowed with pride for my little sister – but I couldn't help feeling lonely as I tramped around the park with Bear.

I let him off the lead and he ran over to a little terrier and they played chase together, both of them barking like mad. Every now and then they changed direction, and then all of a sudden flopped on the grass, grinning at each other, already firm friends.

I seemed to be the only girl in the whole town who didn't have anyone to hang out with on a Saturday afternoon. I should have fixed a proper date with Ivneet. I didn't even know her phone number to text her. I'd fix up with her to come to tea next Saturday. I wasn't quite sure what she'd want to do. I hoped she wouldn't want to teach me how to play chess.

It had all been so different with Sally. I didn't plan in my head what we'd do together. I didn't think up topics for conversation. It was just like we'd been friends for ever. I didn't see how anyone could ever take her place.

I imagined what it would be like if she were with me now, and tried talking to her in my head like the characters in *The Chrysalids*. I knew her so well I could make her talk back, saying typical Sally things, passing comments on all the people passing by. She said something so funny about a very rotund man with a plump pug that I started laughing. He looked at me sharply, and I sobered instantly. He must think I was totally weird, spluttering to myself. I *was* totally weird, pathetically talking to someone who wasn't there, a girlfriend who ignored me, and pretended she didn't care tuppence about me in front of all the others.

I struggled not to burst into tears. I really *was* acting weirdly, laughing and crying randomly. I whistled to Bear.

'Come on, Bear! Time to go home!'

He'd never understood instant recall, and always ignored me if he was playing, but he left the terrier without a backward glance and came bounding up to me. Perhaps it was because I sounded so needy. I bent down and he licked my face, as if he was telling me that he still loved me more than anyone else in the world.

I gave him a hug and we hurried home together. Mum and Coral were now engrossed in *Thelma and Louise*. Mum beckoned to me, and so I squeezed onto the sofa between them and we all watched together, Bear sprawled beside us. Then Zara came home from Whitelands *twenty minutes early*. She said she hadn't bought anything, but I heard the rustle of a bag as she slipped upstairs.

We let Mum and Coral watch their movie to the end while we went to collect Rowena from her party. She came skipping out with chocolate buttercream all round her mouth, two balloons in one hand and a flat pink parcel in the other, her going-home present.

'It's felt tips, I've already had a peep,' she said happily. 'And see my sparkly ring – I won it for second-best disco dancer!'

It was faceted glass, and the metal on the shank was already turning her finger green, but we pretended to be very impressed.

'Do you think it's a diamond?' Rowena asked, and we nodded firmly. 'I bet you're dead envious, but I'll let you both borrow it if you really want. And I've got you a balloon each, see? They can be your prizes. You can both be first best sisters.'

I suddenly felt so much better. I really *did* have the best sisters ever. And when Zara and I went up to bed that night, I saw there was a Zara clothes shop bag on my bed.

'Hey, what's your namesake shopping bag doing on *my* bed?'

'It's on your bed because it's for you,' said Zara.

'For *me*?' I scrabbled in the bag and brought out a T-shirt. It had blurred stripes of red, orange, yellow, green, blue, indigo and violet. I held it up, my hands shaking. 'Oh, Zara! A rainbow T-shirt!' I whispered.

'It might stop you wearing that manky old jumper,' she said.

'Thank you so, so much! You bought it specially for me rather than buying something for yourself!'

'Well, there wasn't anything I really wanted, and anyway it was a total bargain, half price in the sale,' said Zara.

'You won't fuss about what people will think?' I asked, hugging her.

'You wear it with pride, little sis,' said Zara, hugging me back hard.

I wore it the next day, even though it was a bit chilly for a short-sleeved T-shirt. Still, the kitchen was warm with cooking. Mum made us blueberry pancakes, batch after batch. She was still in her pyjamas, with her hair tucked up in a ponytail, white splashes of pancake batter freckling her cheeks. She suddenly looked almost as young as Rowena, and she was larking around like a six-year-old too, singing old pop songs with Coral.

'Doesn't your mum look marvellous, girls?' she said joyfully. 'It looks as if that infusion has worked already!'

'Are you really better, Mum?' Rowena squealed, rushing to her and butting her head into her tummy.

'I can't get totally better, darling – but I certainly feel great!' said Mum.

'You certainly *look* great too, Mum,' Zara said.

I didn't say anything, because I'd actually started crying.

'Frankie?' said Mum anxiously.

'I'm crying because I'm so happy!' I sobbed.

It was so weird. I still had the deep unhappiness of everything going so wrong with Sally, and yet I was bubbling with joy too because Mum really was so much better. I kept an eye on her all morning, worried that the effect of the infusion might start wearing off in a few hours, but Mum stayed full of energy.

She put a big chicken in the oven and then we all went for a walk together, the five of us and Bear. Coral kept fussing over Mum, making her wear a woolly hat and tucking a scarf round her neck, while Mum laughed and protested.

'I'm fine, I'm fine, I'm fine,' she said, and for once she really meant it.

We didn't go as far as the park because Mum's legs still felt a bit funny, but we had a good half-hour walk even so, much further than she'd been for ages. Then we went back home for our Sunday roast. Mum and Coral opened a bottle of sparkling wine to celebrate. Zara and I were allowed a very small glass each, and Rowena had a sip and giggled because the bubbles went up her nose again.

I remembered the champagne on New Year's Eve and felt desperately sad for a few moments, but tried hard not to let it show.

It's over, I told myself fiercely. *It meant so much to you but it was just a lark for Sally. Stop minding so! Forget all about her.*

Then the doorbell rang.

'Oh no, who's that?' said Mum, taking another sip of wine.

'Lovely Sammy?' suggested Coral.

'He just rattles the letterbox,' I said.

'It's Dad!' cried Rowena.

'He didn't say he was coming,' said Mum, getting up reluctantly. 'Who comes calling at two o'clock on a Sunday?'

'I'll go, Mum,' said Zara.

She went out into the hall. We heard her open the door. We couldn't hear who she was talking to, but she didn't sound very welcoming. Then she slammed the door shut again and came back into the kitchen.

'Who was it?' Mum asked.

'Oh, no one,' said Zara.

'What do you mean?'

'Well, no one important.' Zara screwed up her face.

I stared at her, my heart thumping. 'It was Sally!'

'Well, yes. But I told her to get lost.'

'Oh my God,' I said, jumping up.

'Frankie! Don't go running after her! She's just playing games with you,' said Zara.

I knew she was right. She was only trying to protect me. But I couldn't stop myself.

'I won't be long,' I gabbled, and then I rushed out of the room, grabbed the black yeti coat and opened the front door. When I got to the garden gate I spotted Sally, halfway down the road already, running.

'Sally! Sally, wait!' I shouted, and started running after her.

She didn't slow down. She was a fast runner – but I was too. I thundered after her, and by the time she'd reached the corner I'd nearly caught her up.

'Please wait for me!' I yelled, and she stopped at last, and sat on a garden wall, trying to catch her breath.

'Sally?' I sat down beside her.

She covered her face with her hands. 'I feel such a fool. I shouldn't have come,' she muttered. 'Your sister hates me, doesn't she?'

'No. Well, she does a bit. She hates that I got hurt,' I said.

'Do all your family hate me now?' she asked.

'No!'

'Do you?'

'Don't be an idiot.'

Sally peeped sideways at me. 'So how do you feel about me now, Frankie?'

'Mixed up. Angry. Unhappy,' I said.

'I don't blame you,' she sighed. 'I've messed you about big time.'

'But *why?*' I burst out.

An old lady was walking past and looked round.

'Shh! She's staring,' Sally whispered.

'So what?' I said.

'She'll think we're having some kind of . . . I don't know, lover's tiff.'

'Well, we are, sort of.'

'Oh, Frankie. Look, can't we go somewhere more private?'

'I suppose there's the park.'

'Can't we go somewhere indoors? I'm freezing. I've walked all the way from my house – it's miles and miles. And I'm hungry. I couldn't face a family dinner. Let's go and eat,' Sally suggested.

'But I've just had *my* lunch. And I haven't got any money,' I said.

'Oh God, don't be so irritating. Come *on*. There must be somewhere round here. We could go to a pub, but I'm not dressed up enough to pass for eighteen.' She glanced at me too, in a disparaging way.

'Look, I'm not going anywhere with you if you're going to keep criticizing me,' I said. 'You've got an awful cheek. You were so lovely in the holidays, and then you totally ignore me at school, and then suddenly you come rushing round to my place and start telling me what to do. You haven't got the right any more. It's over, I told you.'

'No it's not,' said Sally. She lowered her voice. 'We still love each other.'

'I don't think you've ever loved me. And I'm not sure I love you any more anyway.' I peered at her carefully. She certainly didn't look that great just then. She was wearing an old beanie instead of her jaunty trilby, and her face was very pale without make-up, and pinched with cold. I didn't like the leather jacket she was wearing and her legs looked spindly because her jeans were so tight. If I hadn't known her, I wouldn't have given her a second glance. But actually it didn't matter in the slightest. I *did* still love her and we both knew it.

I took her to Sam's old-fashioned café near Whitelands.

'You've marched me for miles just to bring me *here*?' Sally said rudely. 'It's an all-day fry-up-and-mug-of-tea kind of place!'

'You shut up. Sammy and I come here and we love it,' I said.

'Oh, OK. Right. I'll try the all-day breakfast then,' said Sally. 'And you?'

'I'm full of Sunday roast.'

'Well, have something, for God's sake,' she snapped.

I had a cup of coffee and a doughnut. Sally had tea, and bacon, egg, sausage, black pudding, baked beans, hash browns, mushrooms and tomatoes. She ate the egg, and just stirred the rest around her plate.

'*Eat it!*' I said.

'I feel a bit sick now if you must know. This is all going wrong. I've been so miserable ever since I got your awful text. Last night I went out with Marnie and the others, and it was so boring – *they're* so boring – and all I wanted was to be with you. Then today was even worse, and I felt so lonely and wanted to be with you, and I went out for a walk just for something to do, and I kept on walking, and I realized I was coming all the way over to see you. I thought you'd be feeling the same way, and the minute you opened the door we'd just kind of fall into each other's arms,' Sally murmured, so quietly I could hardly hear her. 'But then your sister ruined it all, and she was so hateful to me.'

'What did she say?'

'That I was a spoiled little bitch and messing with your head playing games with you,' said Sally. 'She said she couldn't see what you saw in me, and you were fifty times better than me.'

'Really?' I said. 'Goodness.'

'I don't know what she means anyway. I mean, I don't want to sound like I'm boasting, but I'm the one who's always been popular and had heaps of people wanting to be friends with me.'

'Yes, she meant you exploit that, because you love it when people run after you. Come on, Sally. You're no fool. You always know exactly what you're doing.'

'I don't do anything,' she said.

'You go out of your way to charm people, and then you ignore them totally.'

'I don't. I've never ignored you. Well, except for this week – I was scared to say anything to you at school in case you made another scene. Here, help me out, I can't eat any more of it.'

'I'll take the bacon and sausage home for Bear,' I said, wrapping them in the paper napkin and putting them in my pocket. 'Eat some of the mushrooms.'

'They look disgusting, like little slugs,' said Sally. 'Is this *really* where you go with Sammy?'

'Sometimes. I like it. You should have had a doughnut like me. Try a bit,' I suggested, and held it out to her.

She took a big bite and nodded. 'Yeah, it's OK, I suppose,' she agreed.

'You deliberately took all the jammy bit!' I said.

'Well, how was I to know? For God's sake! We're bickering like an old married couple. Is this how you carry on with Sammy?'

'We bicker a bit, I suppose. But not much. You can't really pick a quarrel with Sammy, he's too lovely.'

'I don't get why you don't think he's fit.'

'I do. I just don't fancy him. Or any boy,' I said.

'But you fancy me?' Sally said softly.

'You know I do. But it's not *just* that. I fell in love with you.'

'Keep your voice down! It's like you're announcing it to everyone. It's so not cool,' said Sally, blushing.

'It's not cool to say you love someone?'

'Shh! Not like that. It's embarrassing.'

'So you can whisper it to me when we're alone or write it in a text, but keep it quiet in front of other people?' I said. 'What if I was a boy? Would you be the same then?'

'Probably. It's just not cool to be so mushy all the time,' said Sally, pushing her plate to one side.

'Why does it matter so much about being cool?' I asked.

'It just does.'

'Is that why you made out that our kiss was just a laugh when we were at school?'

'I'm sorry. I shouldn't have acted like that, I know. But if you'd just shut up about things, then we could still be together, *love* each other – and no one would tease or say stupid stuff. Why can't we be like that?' Sally asked.

'But it's not really a relationship then, is it?' I said.

'Well, what's so great about relationships? My mum and dad are both on their second marriages, and their own relationship now is pretty rubbish. *Your* mum and dad have split up. I don't think relationships ever work long term. It's an entirely old-fashioned concept. Why can't we have some secret fun together without taking it all so seriously?'

'I think you're the old-fashioned one. You're scared of admitting you're gay,' I said.

'But I'm not. Anyway, I'm not into labels. I just want to have a good time. You're the person I most want to be with. Isn't that enough?'

I looked down at the table. Sally's messy congealing plate was making me feel sick now.

'You're the person *I* most want to be with. But it isn't enough. Not for me,' I said. 'I can't be another Marnie.'

'You're not a Marnie!' said Sally.

'But you're doing your best to turn me into one,' I said.

'So what are you saying? You really, really, really want to stop seeing me?' Sally asked.

'Well, we have to see each other, don't we, at school?'

'That's not what I meant. We could see each other *out* of school.'

'But that's the difference between us, Sally. You don't want anyone to know about us, and I want to tell the whole world,' I said.

'You're just a hopelessly naive blabbermouth,' said Sally.

'And you're a manipulative coward,' I said.

We stared at each other, shocked – and then it all seemed so ridiculous having such an emotional argument over a congealed plate of food that my lips twitched, and Sally's did too, and we both burst out laughing.

'Let's get out of here,' she said. She left a note on the table that more than covered the bill, and then we went rushing out into the cold.

Sally grabbed my wrist. 'Come with me,' she said.

She hurried us towards Whitelands. I felt a pang of disappointment. Did she really think that buying me something would make me do what she wanted?

'What's the busiest spot in the whole shopping centre?' Sally asked.

'I don't know. Those performing bears, I suppose,' I suggested.

'Right! Come on then.'

Sally pushed her way through the crowds. Sunday was always really busy, especially when the winter sales were on. There were hordes of people milling around the mechanical bears as they performed their antics, still singing silly Christmas songs.

'Right,' said Sally. 'I'll show you who's a coward.'

Then she pulled me close and kissed me on the lips in front of everyone. The songs stopped and the crowd faded away and we were just two girls together, loving each other. Then at long last she took her lips away, and the noise and the jostling started up again. I blinked, trying to focus on her blue eyes. Sally was looking around. Only a few people were staring – a toddler pointing at us curiously, an old couple shaking their heads and tutting. No one else noticed or cared.

We walked out of Whitelands hand in hand. We were both trembling. We stood on the pavement, not knowing what to do or say next. Then my phone pinged with a text. There had been several since I went running after Sally, but I hadn't looked at any of them.

'That'll be Mum,' I said. 'Or Zara. I'd better get back.'

Sally nodded. 'So *is* this goodbye?' she asked.

'I don't know,' I said.

We squeezed hands – and then I walked off one way and she walked the other.

HAVE YOU READ THEM ALL?

LAUGH OUT LOUD
THE STORY OF TRACY BEAKER
I DARE YOU, TRACY BEAKER
STARRING TRACY BEAKER
MY MUM TRACY BEAKER
WE ARE THE BEAKER GIRLS
THE WORST THING ABOUT MY SISTER
DOUBLE ACT
FOUR CHILDREN AND IT
THE BED AND BREAKFAST STAR

HISTORICAL HEROES
HETTY FEATHER
HETTY FEATHER'S CHRISTMAS
SAPPHIRE BATTERSEA
EMERALD STAR
DIAMOND
LITTLE STARS
CLOVER MOON
ROSE RIVERS
WAVE ME GOODBYE
OPAL PLUMSTEAD
QUEENIE
DANCING THE CHARLESTON

LIFE LESSONS
THE BUTTERFLY CLUB
THE SUITCASE KID
KATY
BAD GIRLS
LITTLE DARLINGS
CLEAN BREAK
RENT A BRIDESMAID
CANDYFLOSS

THE LOTTIE PROJECT
THE LONGEST WHALE SONG
COOKIE
JACKY DAYDREAM
PAWS & WHISKERS

FAMILY DRAMAS
THE ILLUSTRATED MUM
MY SISTER JODIE
DIAMOND GIRLS
DUSTBIN BABY
VICKY ANGEL
SECRETS
MIDNIGHT
LOLA ROSE
LILY ALONE
MY SECRET DIARY

PLENTY OF MISCHIEF
SLEEPOVERS
THE WORRY WEBSITE
BEST FRIENDS
GLUBBSLYME
THE CAT MUMMY
LIZZIE ZIPMOUTH
THE MUM-MINDER
CLIFFHANGER
BURIED ALIVE!

FOR OLDER READERS
GIRLS IN LOVE
GIRLS UNDER PRESSURE
GIRLS OUT LATE
GIRLS IN TEARS
KISS
LOVE LESSONS

QUIZ

Which character are you from *Love Frankie*?

I would describe my style as . . .
A Bold – I love my bright jumper and Doc Martens
B Fashionable – I love to keep up with the latest trends
C Cool – I don't try too hard

My perfect Saturday is . . .
A Spending time with my best friend.
   Or going on a date . . .
B Going on a HUGE night out.
   What's the point of relaxing?
C Hanging out at the shopping centre with my friends

At Christmas, I like . . .
A Giving thoughtful gifts
B Getting loads of presents, with no expense spared
C Spending quality time with my friends and family

My family are . . .
A A handful. It's not always easy, but we are really close
B A bit distant. I don't really get on with them
C Full-on, but they really do want the best for me

At parties . . .

A I find everything a bit awkward –
especially when people aren't acting like themselves
B I'm always wild. That's what they're for, right?
C I really enjoy chatting to new people –
it's a great way to make friends

If you answered mostly **A** you are Frankie. You're thoughtful and clever, and even though sometimes you doubt yourself, you're actually very confident and mature.

If you answered mostly **B** you are Sally. You're popular and love to party, with lots of friends, although there is more to you than you let on.

If you answered mostly **C** you are Sam. You're well-liked by everyone and a brilliant friend to people close to you, especially when they really need you.

ABOUT THE AUTHOR

JACQUELINE WILSON wrote her first novel when she was nine years old, and she has been writing ever since. She is now one of Britain's bestselling and most beloved children's authors. She has written over 100 books and is the creator of characters such as Tracy Beaker and Hetty Feather. More than forty million copies of her books have been sold.

As well as winning many awards for her books, including the Children's Book of the Year, Jacqueline is a former Children's Laureate, and in 2008 she was appointed a Dame.

Jacqueline is also a great reader, and has amassed over twenty thousand books, along with her famous collection of silver rings.

Find out more about Jacqueline and her books at www.jacquelinewilson.co.uk

ABOUT THE ILLUSTRATOR

NICK SHARRATT has written and illustrated
many books for children and won numerous awards
for his picture books, including the Children's
Book Award and the Educational Writers' Award.
He has also enjoyed great success illustrating
Jacqueline Wilson's books. Nick lives in Hove.